THE SHADOW OF REICHENBACH FALLS

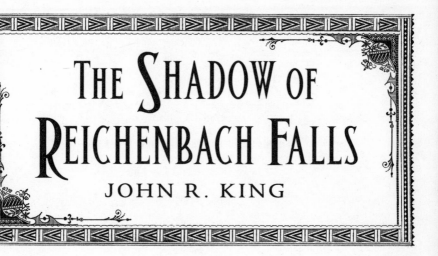

THE SHADOW OF
REICHENBACH FALLS

JOHN R. KING

A TOM DOHERTY ASSOCIATES BOOK
New York

THE SHADOW OF REICHENBACH FALLS

A Forge Book
Published by Tom Doherty Associates, LLC
175 Fifth Avenue
New York, NY 10010

Forge® is a registered trademark of Tom Doherty Associates, LLC.

ISBN-13: 978-0-7653-1801-5

Printed in the United States of America

FOR LESTER,
poet and friend
(Why not spell it *Leicester*?)

ACKNOWLEDGMENTS

Thank you, Frank Weimann, for coming up with the great idea.

Thank you, Brian Thomsen, for making sure it came to fruition.

Thank you, Tom Doherty, for filling the shelves of the world with great books.

Thank you, Aude Nyhlen, for the beautiful French you added to this book.

Thank you, Jennie, Eli, Aidan, and Gabe, for discussing homework assignments and possible trumpet lessons while I sat on the screened-in porch and worked on my novel.

Thank you, Alliterates, for listening to concepts and critiquing chapters and being my colleagues through thick and thin these past twelve years.

Thank you, William Hope Hodgson, for creating Thomas Carnacki.

And most of all, thank you, Sir Arthur Conan Doyle, for creating Sherlock Holmes!

3 December 1911

Dear Dr. Watson:

You may not remember me, but twenty years ago you saved my life. I suppose hundreds of people could make that claim, given your profession, but our encounter was singularly strange.

The scene was Paris in 1891.

I sense even now that you are nodding in remembrance and will nod the more deeply when I tell you that my name is Thomas Carnacki.

A month ago, I was recounting our adventure to my biographer, William Hope Hodgson, and he suggested that I write down the fantastical events and send the account to you. Of course, as my rescuer, you deserve to know the whole story, but I imagine the enclosed document may prove even more valuable as a missing part of the chronicles of our mutual friend.

Yours truly,
Thomas Carnacki

BOOK I

OF MEMORY
AND DEDUCTION

PLUMMETING

Y ou can't expect a day to end well when it begins in negotiations with a rat.

We stood there, the rat and I, beside a fragrant rubbish heap behind a cheese shop in Meiringen, Switzerland. Both of us eyed a large, moldy chunk of Gruyère that the cheese seller had recently tossed out. I was using a stick to argue that I deserved this breakfast, and the rat was using his front teeth in rebuttal. He was a lean, mangy critter, with one blind eye and a lame forepaw, and he argued that this cheese would be his only meal today.

But the same was true for me—the bit about the meal, not about being blind or lame. I was a bit mangy, though. I was twenty-one and skinny, with a few bits of hay clinging to my black hair from the loft where I had spent the night. When I'd quit Cambridge in 1890, I'd weighed two stone more, but my travels on the Continent had reduced me to skin and bone. My only resources now were a tattered Russian greatcoat and a rucksack with a change of clothes, a matchbox, a slingshot, and assorted tools. For a year, I had lived by my wits, my scientific prowess, and my genial nature—which meant that I was desperate for that cheese.

"What does a rat need with Gruyère?" I wanted to know. "I mean, you want to eat it, of course, but what are you going to do with it afterward? Just waddle back to your nest for some sleep, yes? I need that cheese to propel me up the Alps!"

The rat blinked its one good eye, unimpressed.

"Look, I'm young. I have my whole life ahead of me. How old are you? Four? Five? *Ancient*. Maybe it's time you gave up the mortal coil. I mean, what have you to live for, anyway?"

I had my answer a moment later when another rat waddled up—a creature that seemed fat enough already until I realized she was pregnant.

"Oh . . . right . . ." I dropped my stick, bowed to my new friends, and gestured them toward the Gruyère. "Far be it from me to stand in the way of romance." My stomach growled its protest, but when I straightened back up, my altruism was rewarded.

Beyond the rubbish heap, I glimpsed another sort of feast.

She was leaving the front of the cheese shop, a white bonnet on her head and a blue skirt rustling about her legs. . . . Surely that was a bustle under there, not her natural endowment. It was too perfect. I determined then and there to unravel this mystery.

She glanced my way.

I ducked behind the compost heap and waited there, breathless, before chancing a second look.

The girl wandered on down the cobbled road, swinging a small basket in which two wedges of Gruyère gleamed like bars of gold.

What luck! If I played this right, more than one appetite could be sated.

I brushed the hay from my hair and from my almost-beard (I called it a Vandyke, or at least that was what the fashionable set called it back at university), and followed her.

Though I was behind the young woman, I caught glimpses of her face and assembled them into a mental collage: She had blond hair that circled her head in long braids, wide blue eyes above freckled cheeks, a mouth just small enough to seem prim, and lips just round enough to seem luscious.

Could she really not have noticed the young man in the tattered greatcoat who followed her so worshipfully? Really?

The girl headed to a bakery and bought a baguette, and then to a vintner to buy a bottle of wine. A picnic, then! All she needed was company. . . .

Occasionally, she glanced behind her as if she knew I followed. If she did know, she proved unable or unwilling to escape . . . until she came to a bridge. It arched over the engorged Aare River at the edge of town. I could not follow her onto that span without being seen, but neither could I give up my quarry. My decision was made: Bridges are fine places for proposals.

As I approached from behind, the girl quickened her steps, but I caught her at the top of the arch and tapped her lightly on the shoulder. "Excuse me, miss."

She stopped and pivoted toward me, her cheeks flushing.

I gave a small bow and a large smile. "Do you speak English?"

Was that a tiny reflection of my smile on her lips? "English and French and German and Italian," she said, and her voice musically blended these languages.

She would be a one-woman tour of Europe. "Thank goodness. I'm a traveler, and I was wondering if you might know a place to stay."

"I'm sorry, monsieur," she demurred. "I'm a traveler, too."

"Then, surely you're staying . . . somewhere?" I pressed.

Her lips clamped together for a moment, and then she said, "Well, yes. The Englischer Hof, up the hill, at the foot of the mountain." She daintily lifted her nose, indicating the spot, and I saw a grand chalet tucked up beneath the rocky face of a cliff.

If I had had a pocketbook, it would have fallen out of my pants. I couldn't even afford to stay in the stables. I'd have to work fast. "Would you mind if I accompanied you there, Miss—?"

"Schmidt." She said the name precisely, like a pair of scissors snapping together. "Anna Schmidt."

I bowed again. "Pleased to meet you, Miss Anna Schmidt. I am Thomas Carnacki." I took her basket of food and extended an arm to her. She tentatively laid her fine fingers on the ragged coat I wore.

"Are you traveling with anyone, Miss Schmidt?"

"I appear to be traveling with you."

I blushed. "Not just now, but in general."

Her eyes wandered my figure, taking my measure. "No. I am traveling alone."

I nodded gravely. "Hmm . . . a quandary . . ."

Anna looked at me, her eyes so wide and guileless I felt like a cad. "What quandary?"

"Well, you see, I too am traveling alone," I replied. "But if we travel alone . . . together, well, we shall no longer be alone—"

"A quandary," she said.

"Yes. A quandary for the head," I said, daring to touch one of her braids, "but not for the heart."

She gazed at me, and for a moment her face was unmasked. More than that—it seemed made of glass so that I saw directly into her soul. Something was broken inside her.

"You're a learned man, aren't you?" she asked.

"Cambridge," I said, but added quickly, "and Paris and Rome. I'm really a student of the world. And you?"

"Student of the world," she echoed with a hint of sadness.

"Well, my collegial friend," I said, "what place around here holds lessons for folks like us?"

"Reichenbach," she murmured distractedly.

"Reichenbach?"

"The falls." She gestured up the mountainside. "A half-hour trek by carriage. Great black stones and ten thousand gallons of churning water in a thousand-foot drop." She nodded at the basket in my hand. "That's why the cheese and bread and wine."

"To think a girl like you would picnic alone beside the Reichenbach Falls," I said, lifting my hand in mock dismay.

Anna ignored my theatrics, even waiting for my hand to drop before she said, "I wouldn't have been alone."

"No?"

She leveled her eyes at me. "I'm going to the falls because . . . because that's where my father died. He was hiking above the falls, five years back, when I was just fourteen, and he . . . fell. They never found his body."

"Oh, Anna," I said. "I'm terribly sorry."

I couldn't press on now: Grief trumps seduction.

I decided to make a clean breast of everything. "You've been candid with me, Anna, and I'll be candid with you. You're the loveliest woman I've ever seen, and so, I had hopes of, well—"

"Seducing me?" she supplied.

"Um, well, *wooing* was the word I would have used, but yours is more to the point. Yes, I had hopes of seducing you."

"I know."

"The fact is that I have only a few francs, not really enough to stay at the inn. Not even enough for a carriage to take us to the falls. So—"

"So . . . I will pay for it," she said, taking my hand. "My father was a wealthy man, and . . . and I would like some company."

"Truly?"

"Yes, Thomas," she said. "You would make better company than a hansom driver—that is, if you can handle a horse."

"Handle a horse?" I echoed, hoping that I sounded affronted rather than affrighted. "I would be honored to drive you to the falls." I bowed before her, deeply and honestly, there on the river-stoned approach to the inn. As I rose from my bow and saw the genuine blush on her freckled cheeks, I sensed that I was falling for Miss Anna Schmidt.

Arm in arm, we walked up the curving carriageway before the inn. It was a truly grand chalet—a steep roof bedecked in gingerbread, wide windows with ornate shutters, and an arched red doorway—well beyond my means. However, with a few francs from Anna, I went into the stable to hire a hansom.

The hostler looked askance at me, but not at Anna's money. In a trice, we had a horse harnessed to a carriage that pointed up the road toward the falls. I escorted Anna into the compartment and climbed up to the driver's seat in back. Taking the reins, I clucked once or twice to the horse and waited for something to happen.

Nothing did.

Anna lifted the hatch in the roof and glanced up at me. "Try snapping the reins."

I gave the reins a shake, but the horse merely glanced back with a long-suffering look.

"Yah!" I suggested. "Get up! Off we go!"

With a snort, the horse turned its head away from me and started plodding forward. The hostler had been wise to point us in the right direction and to lend us a horse that knew the way. I experimented with guiding the beast a little left and a little right and found that it was willing enough to respond. Then I settled in for the ride.

The mountain air was cold and sweet, charged with sun on that fateful morning—the fourth of May, 1891. The road wended along the base of high cliffs and rose slowly until it broke out across a wide valley. Here and there, other tracks met ours, and at intervals I called out to Anna to make sure I was going the right way. She assured me I was.

We soon reached the Reichenbach River—a white serpent that hissed and foamed in its rush down the mountain. The cart path meandered along the unquiet stream. On either side of the river, meadows spread out to majestic forests of pine and spruce.

It was a fine morning, and I felt almost giddy, thinking of a picnic with Anna beside a magnificent waterfall. I was glad I had been honest with her and that I was no longer trying to seduce her. If anything, she was seducing me.

The wide pleasant fields soon gave way to boulders, and they to rocky rills, and they in turn to huge cliffs of coal-black stone. The cliff faces gradually closed around the river, funneling us inward. Ahead came a new sound: a deep thunder. It rumbled in my breastbone.

"Is that the falls?" I called out to Anna.

Anna leaned to glance through the hatch, and she gave a pensive nod.

Poor grieving girl. The sound of the falls made my heart tremble. For Anna, the sound must have been the drumbeat doom.

Soon, the road cut into the black cliff face. On one side, sheer slopes soared up to the sky, and on the other side, they plummeted to the river below. We came around a bend, and I spotted the falls.

What a sight! A long white cascade surged over the cliff face high above as if the water were pouring directly out of the sky. The falls were gossamer at the top, then fine and striated like a mare's tail, and then massive and columnar as they poured down the black throat of stone. Water blasted into a wide bowl that boiled white among jagged rocks. Mist rose from this cauldron, sometimes welling up to fill the valley, sometimes peeling away like ghosts. It was a beautiful and horrible place.

"You can turn the hansom around just up there," Anna called out, pointing to a wide spot in the road. "There's a ledge below where we can have our picnic."

Here was the test of my horse-handling skill. With my lip held firmly between my teeth, I drew on the reins, clucked and cajoled, tugged and taunted, and jolt by jolt brought the horse and cart around to face the way we had come. Sighing with relief, I pulled us to a halt and climbed down—to the left side. Our right wheel rested a scant foot from the precipice.

I gave a sheepish grin as I lifted a hand to help Anna down from the carriage.

She smiled knowingly. "I'm glad you know how to handle a horse."

She led me down a narrow path to a stony ledge surrounded by tough little wildflowers that grew out of cracks. There, we sat. I produced a small Scots dirk from the sheath in my stocking and sliced the baguette and cheese. I also dug through my rucksack to draw out my corkscrew. I'd bought it in Paris, and it had proved itself more valuable than any other tool I owned.

Soon, we feasted on Gruyère and bread and an 1885 Burgundy. . . . But our feast was a quiet one. Anna was looking everywhere but at me, her eyes tracing the rugged rocks, the pathways, the boiling pool. . . .

To sit in silence in the company of a beautiful woman was a skill I had never attained. "So much water," I said stupidly.

She did not respond.

"Judging from the dimensions of the cascade, I would guess you were right to put it at ten thousand gallons per second. Now, given that an inch of rain equals a foot of snow, roughly speaking, the mountaintop above must be melting one hundred twenty thousand gallons of snow a second. Impressive."

She showed no sign of being impressed.

"Science, you see," I said, lamely trying to coax her into the conversation. "I'm a scientist. I took a first in maths and physics at Cambridge."

"It must have been fascinating."

I nodded deeply. "Yes. Yes, it was. Everything bows to science."

"Not everything," she replied, looking into my eyes. "There are mysteries science cannot plumb."

I wagged a finger at her. "Cannot, or simply *has* not? Think of lightning. A century ago, it was the hammer of God. Now it's just electricity. And since science has harnessed lightning, well, we have the hammer of God, now, don't we?"

"Do we?"

"Do you know that once at Cambridge, I used a tesla tube to shock a plenary worm back to life? Dead one moment, shocked the next, and alive the third. How's that for science? It penetrates even the mystery of death!"

A ghost seemed to pass between us, and Anna looked away toward the falls and rubbed a tear from her eye.

I was such a fool. "It must be hard," I ventured, watching her.

Still, she did not look at me, but only said, "Yes." Then her back straightened, and she stared toward the head of the falls. "Looks like . . . Is something going on up there?"

I trained my eyes on the spot—great shoulders of black stone with the water pouring over them. "What is it?"

Anna pointed, her eyes narrowing. "Don't you see that motion, up there beside the falls? Something big."

I squinted and put a hand visorlike above my eyes, but still could make nothing out. "Probably a stag. They've got their winter velvet now and—"

"It's not a stag. It's . . . a man. No, two men—and they're . . . they're fighting!"

"Are you sure . . . ?" The mist in the cauldron was building, and it started to draw its veil across us.

Anna waved it irritably away, her eyes pinned to the top of the cliff. "What if . . . what if one of them fell?"

Still I looked, honestly looked, but I saw no one. "Anna, let's head back to the hansom."

"You think I'm seeing things," she accused, though she still did not turn her eyes away.

"I don't know what you're seeing . . . but even if they are up there, you can't—there's nothing we can—"

"Oh, no!" she said, grabbing my arm. "One of them is falling! A man is falling."

I turned in terror, looking to the falls, and it seemed indeed that something was plunging down the cascade— perhaps a log or a boulder broken loose . . . or a man. We watched the dark shape descend, wreathed in foam. Then it struck in the cauldron. Standing now, we peered into the boiling water, half expecting a head to pop up, or an arm or leg—something. There was only the whiteness.

"You saw, didn't you?" Anna asked.

I nodded slowly. "I saw something fall. Something large— but it may not have been a man."

"It *was* a man. I know it was." She looked to the top of the

cliff and shielded her eyes. "The other man is gone. He's—
he's a murderer. . . ."

"Only if . . ." I stopped. It was no good trying to speak reason. "I'll go down. I'll stand by the bank, maybe find a log or
something to extend out if . . . if the man comes to the surface . . . but . . ." I ambled away, down to the wild pool.

What if she was right and a man struggled in the water or,
perhaps, tumbled, dead, in the churning stuff? The thought
was horrible. But what if she was wrong and this was just a
ghost of her father, long gone?

I stood by the cauldron for perhaps ten minutes. Aside
from the roar and mist and foam, there was nothing. By the
time I returned to Anna, her eyes were wide and rimmed
with tears, and she seemed to be staring at something ten
thousand miles away.

"Let's go, Anna," I said gently, taking her hand. She followed me as if in a trance, up the narrow trail to the road, and
up again into the hansom cab. I climbed to the driver's seat
above, took a deep breath, and then snapped the reins. This
time, the horse did not quarrel, but only plodded away down
the road.

I felt numb and cold, as if a shadow had been cast over me
and Anna—not just darkness but evil. There had been something very wrong at those falls, some angry and undying presence. It was more than the blackness of the place, the
merciless pounding, the convulsing mist—more even than
the terrible suggestion of death or the terrible reality of it.
Something pernicious haunted that place. Its claws were still
in me.

We had gone half a mile down the road when Anna cried
out, "Stop the cart! Stop it!"

I pulled up on the reins, and the horse plodded to a halt.

Anna spilled from the compartment, dress and hair streaming back from her as she ran past the horse and clambered down the slope toward the water. She was screaming.

I leaped down from the seat and rushed after her. Was she going to drown herself? "Stop! Anna!"

With a last desperate wail, Anna flung herself into the whitewater.

"No! Anna!" I shouted, vaulting down the slope. I thought she was gone forever, but then I saw her head rise above the waves. There was something in her arms—something heavy— a body: bloodless skin drawn tight over bone. The man was stripped of overcoat and shirtsleeves, flesh scratched by stones. He had been boiled white in frozen waves.

Anna struggled to turn him over, then stared incredulously into the man's aquiline face. "It's not my father! It's not my father!"

Scrambling down the bank, I plunged into the river—so cold!—and grabbed under the man's arms. A groan escaped his lips, perhaps the sound of life or perhaps merely air forced from dead lungs. With my hands beneath his armpits and my feet wedged between stones, I hauled the body up out of the water and laid it on solid ground.

Anna staggered up behind me. "It's not my father!"

"No, of course not," I snapped, kneeling beside the man. "Wake up! Wake up, whoever you are." I slapped his cheeks—wretched cheeks scratched by stones and fish-belly white. "Wake up! Are you alive?"

The eyelids of the battered man quivered and then slid back, and I stared into eyes more brilliant than any I had ever seen. The man sputtered water from his mouth and gasped, "I'm alive!" He blinked. His wrinkled fingers patted my hand as if to comfort me. "I am alive."

I leaned toward him and studied his face. He was a man in

his fourth decade, with a serious expression and eyes that beamed blue beneath tangled brows. Perhaps I should have checked his vital signs—looked for bleeding or broken bones—but I could only blurt, "Who are you?"

"What?" he asked.

"Who are you?" I repeated. "What's your name?"

Those radiant eyes grew dim. "I don't know."

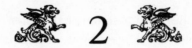

CALL ME SILENCE

I'm staring into a face—a young face with black hair and eyebrows and dripping whiskers that might someday amount to a beard. The face stares back at me. Is this a mirror?

The face asks, "Who are you?"

"What?"

"Who are you?"

A face in a mirror wouldn't ask *who are you?* but *who am I?*

"I don't know."

The face considers me in amusement or annoyance. "What do you mean, you don't know?"

I raise my hand between us. My fingers are slim but strong, the middle one marked with a deep callus above the final knuckle. My skin is white and mottled with scars, like stains from acid. "I'm old," I realize. It's not a pleasant thought.

"You're more than old," the young man says, "you're washed up—literally." He gaped at the left side of my head. "You've got a big knot just here. Concussed, I should think, and in shock, and likely half frozen." He unbuttons his woolen coat—a peculiar gray color, with a tag that includes an upside-down *h* as in Russian. Shrugging quickly, he shucks his coat and lays it over me. I only just realize that I'm lying down. "So—you don't remember anything about how you got in the river—?"

River? Yes, I hear it now, just to my left—chattering over stones. "No. I don't remember."

The young man gives a grim nod and clamps two fingers on my wrist. "Pulse seems slow—but at least you've got one. Yes, I'd say shock, most definitely. Let me see your pocketbook."

Without waiting for a response, he rifles through my pockets. Perhaps he's a thief—except that a thief wouldn't lend his coat.

"What does it say?" asks a new voice—a woman's. I shift my head, seeing now beyond the shoulder of the man a young, beautiful face, framed by dripping blond locks. Worry knits her brow. "What does the pocketbook say?"

The man holds up empty hands. "Says nothing. No pocketbook, no identification except . . ." He tugs at the collar of my shirt and turns it outward. "What's this? 'Harold Silence, clothier, London.'" A lopsided smile grows across his face. "Harold Silence?"

"That's his tailor. Not him," says the woman.

"Still, we've got to call him something. Mind if we call you Harold Silence?"

Harold Silence. It's a name, I suppose, as good as any other. "For now, no, I don't mind." Though it certainly doesn't seem like my name.

"Right, then, Harold. I should check the rest of you—for injuries, you know?"

"You should call him Mr. Silence," the young woman urges.

"Mr. Silence? No. What about Harry, or H.S., or just Silence?"

"Whatever you want," I say. "But, um—what are your names?"

The young man splays a hand on his chest and says, "I'm

Master Thomas Carnacki, scientist and student of the world. This"—he gestures over his shoulder—"is Miss Anna Schmidt."

The woman curtsies slightly and gives a blushing smile.

"Now for a diagnosis." Master Thomas Carnacki leans toward me, sets his fingertips on my skull, and probes through my hair. He seems surprised to find no damage except at the left temple—

"Ahh! Blast!" I cry, recoiling.

"It's this whole left side of your head," young Thomas says. "I'm surprised you're even conscious—"

"Or alive," Anna blurts.

I'm panting from pain, and there's a claxon in my skull. It isn't just my head that hurts, either: "There's . . . there's something wrong with my arm."

"In time, my friend," Thomas replies. He gingerly draws back the coat he has laid over me and gently probes the sides of my neck, my collarbone, my shoulders, my upper arms. More pain erupts.

"Broken left arm," Thomas says.

My eyes clamp shut, but they seep tears as Thomas continues his inspection. He finds bruises, abrasions, and a few weeping wounds, each of which he grimly itemizes.

At last he sighs. "Well, Harry—"

"Please, call me Silence."

"Well, Silence, you've got some nasty knocks—head and arm, here and there. We'll splint your arm—we can use my kerchief for ties—"

"And what about the napkins, from the picnic basket?" Anna volunteered.

"Those, too, and we'll find sticks for braces. Other than that, though, there's not much we can do for you out here.

We'll take you in our hansom to Meiringen, find a doctor . . .
maybe even somebody who knows you."

"Thank you," I say. "I owe you my life."

"Not that you remember any of it," the young man replies
with a smile and a shrug. "But—hey—it's like your first day
on earth. Clean slate. Happy birthday!"

He's a sardonic young man, this "scientist and student of
the world." As he gathers the cloths for my splint, I see a
shiny Christ College ring on the third finger of his right hand.
So, Thomas is a recent graduate of Cambridge. The adjacent
pinky also wears a school ring, but it is much more battered,
and it bears the crest of St. Petersburg Polytechnic—perhaps
his father's alma mater. The man must be dead, now, or he
would have worn the ring himself. The small diameter of the
Russian ring indicates that the older Carnacki was a small
man, perhaps due to deprivation. It might be the reason he
left Russia and came to England.

Yes, Thomas Carnacki puts on a brash face, but his glib
outside shields troubled things within. "Off to fetch some
sticks," he says.

And what of Anna Schmidt? She has a German name
and face, but her voice is inflected with London, Paris,
Rome. . . . She could as easily be Anna Banks or Anna
Chaillot or Anna Morenzi. Her outside, also, does not match
her inside. She defers to Thomas in outward ways, but as
he looks for splint sticks, she searches his rucksack, only
to neatly replace the contents before he returns. And now
that he is back, working on my splint, she frets about how
cold and wretched I look, so that Thomas volunteers his
own clothes, and Anna praises him for his insight and gen-
erosity.

She is playing him. Perhaps he even realizes it.

Thomas draws the last cloth napkin tight over the splint. "Is that too snug?"

"It's fine."

Anna comes up to hover behind him, her eyes shifting between us. "Do you think you can walk?"

"I don't know"—I'm so tired of saying that—"I'll try." Anna rewards me with a smile, and I see how easy it would be to be played by her.

"Then, up we go," Thomas says as he and Anna lift me to my feet. I stagger, but these young people are strong. They lead me to their carriage—a black hansom with room for two within and a driver's seat above and behind. A few jolting steps up bring me into the compartment.

"Do you need help?" Anna asks sweetly.

"I'll manage."

She hands me a neat stack of clothes that she has produced from Thomas's rucksack. "We'll give you a few moments' privacy." She and Thomas turn and step away from the carriage.

At first, I stare stupidly at the stack of clothes in my hands. Then, shaking off my torpor, I examine them: A shirt that had been tailored for the young man—five years back judging by its nap and the wear beneath the arms; ah, the label confirms it. Thomas's father must have lived then, to buy a shirt like this for a young man entering university. The shirt that Thomas currently wears is newer—perhaps a year old— but not tailored. So, there was not much money when this new shirt was bought, which places the death of the father from one to five years back. The trousers give an even graver comment—for the cuffs at the bottom have been let out, leaving the smallest possible hem. These had been the pants of Thomas's father, adjusted by an inexpert hand—perhaps his mother, or he himself. Judging by the fading of the pants, the cuffs, and the portion still tucked under, I would say these trousers had been altered in the last year.

"How's it coming?" Thomas calls from nearby.

"Fine," I reply, setting to work to strip off my ruined clothes and don these instead. "Just a bit awkward."

"Take your time," Anna says.

I don't, quickly pulling off my soaked rags and pulling on my comrade's clothes. The splint is tight in the sleeve, but I manage. There are even shoes, slightly large for me, but serviceable. A glance out the hansom window shows my comrades deep in conversation. I take a moment to check the basket they have left in the corner. It holds remnants of a baguette, a brick of Gruyère, a half-drunk bottle of Burgundy, a Scots dirk, and—something else. . . . Beneath the cloth in the basket, there is a map of Meiringen, Switzerland. A hotel is circled, and a route marked out, leading into the mountains to a place called Reichenbach Falls, also circled. The time of 2 P.M. is written there in a man's hand. Beside it is a notation in dark script, the ink smudging at each terminal of the letters as if the writer had perseverated on each one: THE FINAL PROBLEM.

"About finished?" Thomas calls.

I fold the page, slide it back under the cloth, and say, "Yes, all finished."

Thomas approaches the hansom. "Well, let's get back to town so a doctor can look to your arm and your head." He opens the carriage door, and I offer him his greatcoat, folded neatly. He takes it, unfurls it, and slips it on, all the while studying me with amused suspicion. Then Thomas steps back, and Anna piles in, pretty in her dripping white lace and blushing cheeks. She takes the seat beside me.

"Ah, you look better," she says. "Warm and presentable and alive."

"Better than cold and repulsive and dead." Outside the window, Thomas pats the mare with a fretful hand that shows he has no experience with horses. "I have big shoes to fill," I say, and lift one of my feet.

"Well, you know what they say about big shoes . . ." Anna remarks suggestively.

What *do* they say? That you must walk a mile in a man's shoes? That a man must get his foot in the door? That a man's shoe size correlates with . . . ? But surely not Anna—not this prim German, if indeed she is what she purports to be.

"We'll get you to Meiringen and to help."

"Medical," I ask wryly, "or psychological?"

"Yes."

The carriage dips as Thomas mounts to the driver's seat, snaps the reins, and cajoles a little motion out of the horse. The mare sets off at a walking pace down the trail, dragging the hansom behind.

"He's not the best horseman," Anna confides.

They're charming, these turtledoves, though I doubt Thomas and Anna have known each other long. They are still sizing each other up, from shoe size to skull size.

Oh, I don't even like to think of what my skull size currently is.

Who am I? The thought of finding out sends a chill through me. What sort of man must I be to end up in a river in Switzerland? I almost prefer not knowing. I glance out the windows at the rugged cliff on one side and the plunge to whitewater on the other.

Anna meanwhile appraises me. "You really have no idea who you are?"

I shake my head grimly.

"Well, you're a Londoner, for starters—"

"Ah, yes. The accent . . ."

"A man of letters, which your slender hands show."

"A right-handed man of letters," I add as I point to the pen callus on my middle finger.

Anna flashes a smile. "Who needs memory when there is deduction? Surely the whole of your life is written on you."

"Read on."

"What of these?" Anna asks, turning my hand over and finding a few irregular blotches on the skin. "Burns? But not from fire . . . from acid!"

She is right, of course. But why would I have acid-burned hands? I withdraw them uncomfortably and avert my eyes, but Anna is not done with her game.

"Your hair has only just begun to thin on top," Anna says, adding, "Baldness is becoming in an older man."

"As you say, I am *becoming* bald."

"A clever fellow, you are. Aware of the shape of things." Anna brightened, nodding decisively. "And in your midforties, I would guess."

"A medical person, are you?" I ask.

She shakes her head. "A keen observer is all. You are slightly taller than Thomas, who is slightly taller than I, and so you must be five foot eleven."

"And ten stone, soaking wet."

She proceeds as if I haven't spoken. "You are a man of importance."

"Now, how do you know that?"

She lifts her eyebrows. "How else would you have ended up in the river?"

"I don't see your meaning."

"Someone was stalking you. Only important men get stalked."

"Stalking me?"

Her mouth drops open. "Oh . . . we didn't tell you, did we . . . ?"

"Tell me what?"

Anna pauses, and her eyes flit as if seeking escape. "Apparently . . . someone threw you . . . or pushed you . . . from the top of the Reichenbach Falls."

A frisson of dread tingles up my spine. I don't even know who I am, but there is a man out there—an enemy—who does. "Who was it? Who threw me down?"

Anna glances at her feet. "I don't know. I only glimpsed you two, fighting each other atop the falls, and then . . . and then you were falling."

"What of the other man?"

A shout comes from beyond the carriage—a distant but angry sound. Anna leans toward the window and glances out. She cranes her neck to see the height of the cliff, and her hand tightens on the windowsill. "That's the man."

I drop to my knees beside Anna and look toward the cliff's edge. A man stands there—narrow and angry like a scarecrow. He holds a walking stick, and he is shouting something down at us.

"What's he saying?"

"I don't know," Anna responds. She reaches over our heads to a hatch in the ceiling and props it open. "Thomas, can you tell what he's saying?"

Thomas leans down, his face red and worried in the hatch. "He says stop or he'll shoot. What with, I can't tell—unless that walking stick isn't a walking stick." Thomas's face tightens as he draws on the reins. The horse slows.

"You can't stop. He wants to kill me."

"Right." Thomas whips the reins, and the mare picks up her pace. The carriage lurches down the road. "Another fifty feet, and we'll be behind a bend, out of the line of fire."

Thomas suddenly grimaces, and a second later I hear the profound boom of a rifle shot.

Thomas slumps forward onto the roof of the hansom, his eyes bulging and his cheeks swollen. The carriage veers toward the precipice.

"Look out!" I shout.

The sound rouses Thomas, and he looks up, tugging at the reins to bring the horse back in line. He grits his teeth, eyes riveted to the road. "I've been shot!" His left shoulder is mantled in blood.

I look up to the gunman, seeing him run atop the cliff. "He's following us!" The man has a tall, knifelike form. He plants his feet and levels his strange rifle, and a gray puff of smoke comes from it. I yank my head back from the window, and a bullet ricochets off the metal sill and careens past my ear to punch through the compartment and clip the horse's haunch.

The mare panics, rushing away at full gallop. Thomas grips the reins in both hands and struggles to stay upright. His eyes flutter with pain. He swoons.

I reach up through the hatch and grip Thomas's shirt, managing to hold him in the seat.

"The horse is loose!" Anna shouts, pointing to the reins that flap furiously beside the cab. "It'll run us into the river!"

"Reach up through here and hold Thomas. I'll try to get control."

Anna extends her arm through the hatch and grabs Thomas's shirt. As soon as she has a solid hold, I let go of him and lunge for the carriage door.

The hansom is rocking terribly, the wheels roaring over rough stone, and it is all I can do to keep my legs beneath me. Beyond the door, the reins whip in the wind, trailing from the horse's harness.

"Here I go." I press down on the door handle. The door swings wide, smashes into a boulder, and crashes back into me. I kick the door out again and slide through the frame. Half out of the compartment, I hang with the door battering my back. The reins are just out of reach, flipping against the cliff wall. "There's nothing for it."

I hook my splinted arm through the door, ignoring the screaming pain, and reach outward with my other hand. Rocks hurtle by, and the mare bolts erratically between the cliff wall and the precipice.

"Hurry!" Anna calls from within. "I'm losing hold!"

With a growl of agony, I lunge out on my tormented arm. My fingers claw at empty air. The reins are just out of reach. Suddenly, the carriage bounds up over a rock. I topple, hanging beside the door. The jolt, however, flips the reins into my hand. My fist tightens. Inch by inch, I slide myself back into the compartment until I am sitting on the floor, the reins in my fingers.

"You got it!" Anna exults.

"Can't steer from here," I reply breathlessly, "unless we want to head into the cliff wall."

"Well, then, get up there," Anna suggests.

"Yes, lass, yes." Taking a deep breath, I clamber to my feet and slide back out the carriage door. While the rugged cliff spins past, I inch my way along the side of the carriage, heading for the driver's seat. My good arm does the double duty of hanging on to the carriage and gripping the reins. It's now or never. I scramble up beside Thomas, brace my feet, and haul hard on the reins.

The horse fights me, bucking against the leather thongs. With steady pressure, however, I rein in its panic and my own agony. The beast slows from a gallop to a trot to a canter. Only then do I dare look up behind us.

On the cliff top, farther back but still distinct, stands the man who threw me from the top of the falls, the man who shot Thomas—the man who wants to kill us, still. He squeezes off another shot, and I cringe down as it sails by overhead. He's too far back for accuracy. He breaks into a run.

"Yah, there," I say to the mare, giving her some rein. The beast begins to trot, ears pricked high for the next gunshot.

Anna looks up through the hatch, her eyes wide. "What are you doing, Silence?"

"Fleeing," I say tightly.

The man above us still runs in pursuit.

"Simply fleeing."

3

Desperation

I'd been desperate plenty of times during my travels. In fact, the morning's negotiations with the rat had been one of those times. But I'd never been this desperate—never been shot.

My left shoulder was a mass of blood and muscle and bullet.

I clung to the rattling top of the rattling coach, clung with my good arm while my bad one seeped a red puddle out across the bonnet. Silence crouched beside me, alternately whipping the poor mad horse and reaching over to save me from tumbling off. Intermittently, Anna's terrified face appeared in the hatch of the carriage, and she advised us to "slow down!" or "watch that rock!" or "duck!"

Again a bullet whistled by. Again came the report of the rifle, rankling among the canyon walls.

"Damn," Silence growled. The reins leaped in his grip, and the horse's hooves leaped as well. We descended into a trough in the road and then climbed a hill on the other side. The carriage fairly vaulted over the ridge, and the road dropped out beneath us. My heart lodged in my throat. The wheels came down all aclatter.

Silence glanced back. "He's lost behind the ridge!"

"Look out!" Anna cried.

Silence turned to see a great boulder dead ahead: a fork in the road.

"Hold on!" he shouted, hauling the horse away from the rock. The beast screamed as it narrowly missed the stone, and the fenders of the carriage screamed as they narrowly hit it. Metal wrenched loose from the carriage and flew out into the air. It tumbled, wreckage in our wake.

"That's the wrong way!" Anna shouted. Her objection was punctuated by another bullet. The slug struck the carriage just two inches beyond my clutching fingers and pinged away into an alpine wood nearby. "You're taking us up to cross his path."

Silence nodded with grim frustration. "You want me to turn around?"

The horse galloped faster, even though the road rose steeply. The air grew colder and thinner, and overhead, daylight was abandoning us. I took a glance back at the man— half a mile away now but still running. At least he wouldn't be able to shoot us at that distance. Barring a disaster, we could outrun him. . . .

Then I glimpsed the disaster. Ahead of the gunman, farther along the ridge, another man sat astride a horse. This second man seemed to be watching us in our mad dash along the canyon. He didn't, therefore, see our pursuer top the rise, plant his feet, level his rifle, and fire.

The horseman clutched his chest and toppled from the saddle. He fell over the cliff and tumbled down its rocky face. His body vanished among the trees at the base of the cliff as the sound of the gun reached us.

The gunman ran to the rearing horse and grasped its reins. He calmed the beast, steadied it, and hauled himself up into the dead man's saddle.

"There'll be no outrunning him now," Silence said.

"Take the right fork," Anna called out, and I looked ahead to see another branching way. Yes. If we took that, the man

would have to ride a mile past us and double back to the fork.
Perhaps then we could at least lose him in these upper paths
through the mountains.

Silence complied, steering the carriage through a pine forest. After the first half mile, he eased his grip on the reins,
letting the frantic horse slow to a trot and catch its breath.
The road climbed amid encroaching trees and wound so that
all we could see were pines and the darkness between pines.

"Well, Silence," I said, struggling to sit up, "you've seen
him now—the man who threw you from the falls. Who is
he?"

Silence's eyes looked empty.

"Surely you remember something?" I panted.

He seemed to be looking through me into some deep well
of memory. "Surely . . . I do . . ."

"Tall? Thin? A gun? A great shot?" I prompted through
gritted teeth. "Does any of that strike a chord?"

"A chord . . ." In his reverie, his hands eased on the reins,
and the blown-out beast dropped immediately into a walk.
"Yes. A feeling."

"What feeling?"

"The feeling of a chess match," Silence murmured. He
blinked apologetically.

"A chess match with guns." Well, it was something. "You
have a feeling how long this match has been going on?"

"A long time. Maybe a lifetime. That contest at the head
of the falls—that was just one part of the match. This is another."

A sudden pang gripped my shoulder, and I grimaced as it
passed. "Do you have an idea how . . . how we're supposed
to . . . what we can do to . . ."

I woke up midfall, sliding down the side of the coach and
leaving a smear of blood in my wake. Silence lunged to catch

me, but his fingers closed on air. Anna screamed. I struck the
ground on my good shoulder, which exploded with pain, and
then I rolled, limp as a rag doll.

"Whoa, there," Silence called.

The horse stomped to stillness, and Silence leaped down
from the driver's seat. He circled round and crouched beside
me. A moment later, Anna arrived as well.

"Oh," she said as Silence rolled me onto my back. "Oh,"
she repeated as she brushed dead pine needles from my face
and then from the wound on my shoulder. "He's lost a lot of
blood."

Despite my pain, I smiled up at her. "I'm fine."

"You're delirious," she replied.

Silence meanwhile prodded my head and neck. "Seems to
be intact. Let's get him inside so you can tend him . . ." He
glanced behind us. "And so we can keep moving."

Silence stooped down, set his shoulder to my waist, and
hoisted me up over his back. I was surprised how strong he
was. Anna hurried in front of us, opening the carriage door,
and Silence stooped into it and levered me onto the bench.

"Sit tight, there, Thomas. You're in good hands."

Anna clambered up beside me and sat down, pulling the
door closed behind her. A moment later, the carriage lurched
into motion again. The weary horse snorted as it took up its
clip-clopping pace.

"Oh," Anna said again. The space was small for two
people—small especially with me slouching bonelessly in
one corner. Anna bit her lip and leaned forward to study the
bullet hole in my coat. "I should see what I can do. . . ."

"Please," I said.

Anna drew the coat sleeve back from the bloody shirt.

"Use my dirk," I said, nodding toward the basket that yet
lay in the corner. "Cut away the shirt."

Anna retrieved the knife from the basket and set to work,
slicing the fabric. She pulled the sleeve off my arm and
craned to see the back of my shoulder. I tried to slump forward to give a better view, but the motion made me dizzy. I
almost slid off the seat onto the floor.

"Maybe," Anna began quietly, "maybe . . . you should—
lie down . . . across my lap—so I can see this wound."

"I . . . couldn't. . . ."

"You'd better," she said, pulling me across her knees. I lay
with one arm draped over her and the other trailing down beside her feet. My chest pressed against her blue skirt, and I
was afraid of getting blood on the white lace. "Now, hold
still."

"Yes, ma'am," I replied.

Anna set to work with the knife, gently pressing back the
edges of the wound and peering within. "I see it—deep in
there."

I drew a breath. "It has to come out."

"Yes." Anna eased the blade into the bullet wound. The
tip probed down until it scraped against the butt of the bullet. I shuddered and clenched my eyes against the pain. Anna
stroked my hair. "Easy now."

"I'm sorry about all of this."

"You . . . sorry . . . ?"

"Yeah," I replied. "You . . . you came out to grieve. Just
wanted a quiet moment to remember . . . your father.
Then . . . all this . . ."

"It wasn't your doing," Anna said. With little nudges, she
eased the bullet up the oozy socket. "It's Silence's and . . .
and that other man's doing. This has nothing to do with you."

"Or you," I responded. "If I hadn't delayed you . . . you'd
have never seen those men fight. You'd have been back at
the chalet now, safe in some inglenook beside a bright fire."

The bullet popped from the wound, tumbled across my shoulder, and fell to bounce on the floor. That blood-crazed hunk of metal looked so small, so . . . inconsequential. Anna sighed. "I'd have been safe beside a fire, but Silence would've been facedown in the Reichenbach River."

"I guess that's true."

"I just wish that there was some way to sterilize this."

"Actually," I said, "there's a flask in my rucksack—"

"Thomas!" she blurted, sounding scandalized. "You should've said so before I started digging in your shoulder."

I snagged the rucksack and dragged it toward me. My fingers flipped back the familiar latches and slid expertly through the organized jumble to grab the flask. With a quick spin of my thumb, I unscrewed the cap and lifted it to my lips for two stinging swallows. Then I passed the liquor up to Anna.

"Gin?" she asked.

"Whisky."

She took a mouthful and then poured a bit more over the wound. Sudden pain tore through me. I gripped her knee, my knuckles going white.

"Easy!" she said.

"Sorry."

Anna cut my shirtsleeve into long linen strips and bound my shoulder, making sure not to cut off the circulation. Then she eased my arm back into my father's coat and said, "That'll have to do for now."

"Thank you," I said, wiping off my dirk and stowing it in my rucksack.

Knuckles rapped the top of the carriage. "Hold tight!" Silence shouted. "Here he comes. Yah!" The horse whickered and broke into a run.

I slumped back into the corner of the carriage as Anna

leaned to peer out the side window. Her face grew pale. "I see him, Thomas. He's riding at full gallop, three bends back. A lantern high . . . a look on his face . . ."

"What kind of look?"

"Hatred," she said.

What a miserable ride! Anna and I clung to the coach handles; the horse's head pitched against the reins; the carriage reeled among pines; Silence shouted and cursed; and behind us, the man with the gun closed in. Worst of all, the night had grown so thick that Silence could not tell where the trail was.

The carriage veered suddenly, the wheels thumping. "What was that?" I hissed.

"We're off the path, in a field," Anna said from beside the door. "Maybe we can lose him."

Beyond the carriage came the thrash of the horse's legs against the tall grass, the squeak of the springs, and the growing fear that we were about to run out of meadow.

"Whoa," Silence called quietly, pulling on the rein. "Whoa."

The winded horse gratefully slowed. Its hooves pounded ground a few more times, but then it pulled to a stop and stood, wheezing. I had never heard so loud a horse . . . or so silent an evening.

Silent but for the distant approach of hooves.

I turned to peer out the window, to see our pursuer.

He galloped from the woodlands, and his lantern shone across a sour face with glaring eyes. Next moment, the man stood in the stirrups and reined hard. The horse beneath him planted its hooves, skidded to a halt, and reared. Expertly, the man kept the saddle, his lantern trained on the road.

"Let's go," Anna said even as she slid out the door. The carriage jolted as Silence, too, leaped down. I went to the door but froze as I looked back at our pursuer.

He peered down above the telltale tracks of our wheels. A slow, satisfied smile crossed his face. Lazily flipping the reins, he guided the horse off the road and headed directly toward us. The man's smile solidified into a mask of steely determination. The light of his lantern laid its glow dimly across the rear fenders of the coach.

I pulled my rucksack over my good shoulder, eased open the carriage door, and slid slowly, silently, out onto the grass.

"Hold it—" the man said, halting his horse and leveling his rifle at me, "unless you'd like a second bullet to match the first."

Last time, he had shot me from two hundred feet with the carriage at a gallop. This time, he was twenty paces away, and we stood stock-still. I had no delusions he might miss.

"Who are you?" I asked.

"You seem to have misapprehended your situation, young man. I have the gun. I ask the questions." He grinned humorlessly. "Where are the others?"

I glanced over my shoulder—I couldn't help it—but there was no sign of Silence or Anna. "I don't know."

The gunman clucked softly to his horse, which edged closer. "For a young man, you're not a very good liar."

"I don't know," I repeated angrily. "It's the truth. I don't even know who the man is that you are hunting."

The gunman seemed surprised. "And yet you rescued him from the water, bound his wounds, helped him escape . . ."

"It's what anyone would do."

"Not what I would do."

"Anyone decent."

He was getting very near—only a dozen feet or so—and his

eyes were locked on my face. The gunman would recognize me now on any street in any town. "And that's all you are, I suppose: a decent man. Or, perhaps, a henchman."

I laughed. "You already said I wasn't much of a liar."

The man lifted the rifle, and his index finger tightened on the trigger. "Yes. And soon you won't be anything at all." He fired.

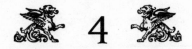

4

THAT MARVELOUS GIRL

I crouch in the darkness behind a boulder and watch in terror as our pursuer closes in on poor, wounded Thomas. I study the gunman's face, hatchetlike and cruel, and my stomach turns.

Why can't I remember that face?

The man lifts his cane-rifle and levels it at Thomas. "Yes, and soon you won't be anything at all."

Thomas is doomed . . .

Except for that marvelous girl.

FLIGHT BY SNOW

The slug ripped through my collar, grazed my neck, and punched a hole in my rucksack. It should have killed me, that shot . . . but the gunman's horse had spooked. As I fell from the coach, I saw with strange clarity the muddy stone that had smacked the neck of the rearing horse. The gunman dropped his lantern in a vain attempt to catch himself, but he fell all the same, along with that plunging light. The gunman, the lantern, and I struck the earth simultaneously. The lamp went black.

I sat panting in the darkness as my foe shouted and cursed.

Then came a whispered voice some distance behind me. "Thomas! Come on!" It was Anna.

The gunman hushed, listening.

I held my breath and climbed to my feet.

"I can hear you," he warned. A click told of another shell settling into the chamber.

Turning, I ran, arms outstretched. Ten paces carried me away from the gunman, but then the ground dropped out from under me, and I sprawled in a ditch. Breath burst from my lungs, and the noise was answered by the rifle's report. The bullet struck a nearby rock and ricocheted into the night. I breathed more easily after that. It would take him a few moments to fit another shell, and by then, I'd be away in the dark. I scrambled up the far bank and staggered on, even hazarding a call, "Anna? Anna, where are you?"

"Here," came the reply, up and to the right.

I followed the sound, stumbling over loose stones to reach her. "That was a nice throw."

"Father taught me to throw like a boy," she whispered.

"Marvelous," came Silence's voice, nearby.

I blinked, trying to clear the afterimage of the lantern from my eyes. "What now?"

Anna sighed tightly. "We climb. There's a path away to the left, rocky steps upward. I saw it before the lantern broke. If only there was a moon tonight."

I craned to see a sky cluttered with stars. Arcturus hung within a U-shaped mountain pass overhead. "The moon is rising now in the east—beyond that ridgeline. The higher we climb, the sooner we'll be in the light."

Anna tapped a stick on the ground. "I'll lead the way." She headed up the slope, and her blue skirt showed gray in the starlight. She would be our beacon. I levered Silence up from the ground and braced him as we both found our balance.

We were in this now and no mistake—Silence and Anna and I hunted by a gunman. Surely he could hear our struggling steps. Surely he was following, wanting to get as close as possible before squeezing off his next shot.

We climbed, we crawled, we scrambled through stands of pine and then through a whole forest of them. For minutes at a time, we lost sight of the mountain pass above, and we had no way to know where our pursuer was below. I wished he would make a sound so we could know whether he was half a mile behind or half a yard.

We had just cleared the forest and staggered out onto a

snowy slope when Silence whispered breathlessly, "I have to rest." He slumped to the ground and wheezed.

"Just a little farther," I said. The snowy pass was a quarter mile above us, glowing white under the sickle-shaped moon. "We have to keep moving. The gunman—"

"There hasn't been sight or sound of him for an hour," Silence whispered. Then he called out in a clear voice, "Anna, dear—we're taking a rest."

Above us, Anna wailed, "It's just a little farther!"

Silence reached to me. His hand was gray in the moonlight. "Thank you, Thomas. You and Anna—you could've left me in the river. You could've abandoned me miles ago. But you didn't."

I sat down beside him. Immediately, the snow began to melt into my trousers. "We're simply doing the right thing."

As the words trailed away, I heard a new sound—the furtive crackle of a stick beneath a gently laid boot. I clutched Silence's arm and held my breath. The hush around us was intense. Another boot shifted in the darkness below. The gunman was stalking through the wood. He couldn't be more than sixty feet back.

I rolled to my side and pushed against the ground, trying to get up, but my left arm rebelled. In the wan light of the moon, I saw dark drops fall from my neck and soak into the snow. Beside me, Silence struggled to his feet and began to climb the slope. Gritting my teeth, I shoved myself upward and followed.

"Anna!" I whispered. "Get moving!"

Ahead of us, she climbed, nearly invisible against the snow and pulling away rapidly.

The footsteps behind us grew loud and quick. The gunman knew we were on the move.

Silence and I strove upward side by side, like oxen yoked together.

The gunman gave an indistinct curse and fired.

The air around us shook, and a bullet screamed past our tucked heads. I looked toward Anna, fearing I would see her fall, but she climbed on soundlessly.

Another bullet roared out, this one grazing Silence's splinted arm. He growled and went down.

"Get up!" I snarled, grabbing his collar and trying to hoist him. "Get up!"

Silence only stared at me, stunned.

The gunman clambered toward us. We'd never escape him now.

Except for the snow—tons of snow lay in fragile layers across the mountainside. The chemistry of the situation was perfect—a chain reaction waiting for the right catalyst.

While Silence lay clutching his arm, I turned and cut a path across the slope. I dug my feet in and dragged them, making as deep a trench as I could.

Above me, Anna stood in the pass, her eyes wide with terror.

Below me, the gunman planted his feet and raised his rifle.

Anna screamed, "Thomas!"

Her shout triggered the avalanche. I stood, amazed, as the shelf of snow below me broke free of the mountainside and began to slide. At first, it moved as one great raft, gray beneath the winking moon. As it picked up speed, though, the slope broke into huge slabs of snow and ice, and then into tumbling boulders and then a roaring cascade. I felt like a god hurling down vengeance on my adversary.

The gunman stood stunned, rifle firing uselessly into the white rush and eyes goggling. Then the avalanche engulfed

him. He was swallowed up, though I fancied to see his feet
tumble in the churning stuff. There was no more sight of him
as the avalanche slammed into the forest and plowed down
trees.

He's probably dead now, I thought, *dead or as good as dead*.

I was suddenly sitting, my legs too weak to hold me up.
Exhaustion had done it to me: exhaustion and relief at having escaped . . . and guilt at having caused another man's
death.

Silence sidled up to me and collapsed likewise. He lay on
his back and laughed at that sickle moon. "You did it, Thomas.
Brilliant!"

"I suppose it was," I replied as the last of the avalanche
rumbled itself out a few miles below.

"Ingenuity and morality—a rare pairing." Silence's eyes
were wide beneath the murk of the moon, and the smile he
wore was genuine.

"Is everything all right?" Anna called down from the pass
above.

"Everything except the gunman," Silence replied. His
voice was filled with relief that sounded almost like gloating.

"Dead?" Anna called out in a strangled voice.

"By all the laws of physics and metaphysics," Silence
replied grandly, "dead."

A sick feeling rose in my throat, but I swallowed it. Anna,
too, was silent for a time. Then she called out, "There's a cave
up here."

"A what?" Silence asked.

"Shelter. A place to rest. Come on."

6

THE SHEPHERD'S BARROW

As we enter the cave, Thomas digs a matchbox from his rucksack, strikes a match on the cave mouth, and uses it to ignite a pinch of wattle. A tiny flame illumines the shelter.

It is more than a cave—carved first by nature but later by humans. The floor is worn smooth by the feet of men and the hooves of sheep.

"This must be a shepherd's barrow," Anna says, "where they shelter when crossing from summer to winter pastures."

The center of the cave boasts an ashy fire pit where a few charred logs remain. "Aha!" I gather straw from the ground and dump it into the pit. "Quickly, Thomas. We can't waste matches."

He brings the wattle forward, and in moments, he's woken a neat little blaze, which casts a glow around the whole chamber.

"Much improved," Anna says. She approaches the fire to warm herself. Meanwhile, I stalk about, surveying the area.

The flame illuminates straw pallets that lie on ledges of stone: apparent beds for shepherds. Away from the fire, rushes cover the floor, providing bedding and fodder for sheep. "Crude as they are," I tell my young friends, "the accommodations seem heavenly to me. I could collapse and sleep a week."

"You're bleeding," Anna says.

I grip my wounded arm, where a second bullet had ripped a shallow trough. The wound burns. "A trifle."

"A trifle that needs tending." Anna crouches down, takes hold of a lower hem of her skirt, and tears it. "It may be a little snow soaked, a little dirty. . . ."

"No more than I am, my dear," I reply gently.

"We should get Thomas's flask for this—for the infection. Thomas, how's your flask holding out?"

He turns toward us, eyes looking haunted in the glow of the fire. "Enough for each of us." He slides the rucksack from his back, fishes a flask from it, takes a draught, and then slaps a little whisky on the wound on his neck. Wincing from the pain, he hands the flask to Anna.

"You two are pretty shot up," she observes as she dabs a few drops of whisky on my arm.

"Yes," I reply through clenched teeth. The stinging is done in a moment. "The gunman was kind enough to spare you."

Anna's eyes flare, and her brows arch inward. She studies my face, seeking a hidden meaning in my words. She has a secret, this one, and she fears that I have stumbled on it. What secret, though? A moment later, her eyes go opaque, and tears gather in the corners.

"What is it?" I ask

Anna busies herself with the bandage. "It's nothing. . . ."

I catch her hand. "Save some of the bandage for Thomas."

"Of course. Thomas." She rips the rest of the fabric free and ties off my bandage. Her eyes are flooded with tears.

Comforting her is not the province of an old man. I am that—yes. I know precious little else, but I do know that. "Thomas needs you, Anna. Go to him."

She nods, rises, and crosses past the fire, where her ragged dress gleams like raiment. Reaching Thomas, she sits him down on one of the straw mattresses and begins tending his neck wound.

"What now?" Thomas asks.

I reply, "Now, we sleep the sleep of the just—"

Anna laughs bleakly. "Or at least of the exhausted."

"—and tomorrow, we hike back down the mountain into whatever village you two came from. . . ."

"Meiringen," the two young people say together. Their eyes meet.

I look away. Let the young have their entanglements. What I need is time—time to sort out my head. "Yes, Meiringen. We'll get the medical attention we need, and . . . and we'll go our separate ways, as if none of this had ever happened." The irony of those words strikes me. My whole life never happened. I've lived only these last hours, all of it at the verge of death.

Such thoughts should keep me awake, but the weary body has its own weight, and it drags me down. In moments, lying on a mean mat of shepherd's straw, I plunge into sleep.

OF COURSE you haunt my dreams, Gunman. I see you entombed in snow like a cadaver in earth, ice packing your joints and turning skin to porcelain and turning meat to stone. But there is a heart still beating in you, and a will to kill. You are still alive, Gunman.

But that is not your name. That is only what you do, what you plan to do to me. What is your name?

Something that starts with *m*. Murdock? Mordred? Something with death in it—Morbid? Murder? Something with betrayal and hatred. . . . Your name is but a room away, and I can hear it like a faint sob through the wall: Morpheus? Monstrous?

You are not dead. You will not die—cannot. Your heart is

stoked with a preternatural flame, and it melts your stony muscles and your porcelain skin.

You are breaking free!

Frozen hands claw at the ice sheath around you. Frozen arms scull through the snow. They break open a space for breath. Time to climb out. Punching handholds, kicking footholds, you bull your way to the surface. Your head breaks through, and you cry out. Your hands pull you up. Slick and hot and furious, you are born out of the white slope and into the air. Snow-crusted eyes rise toward the starry sky. The stars show you this saddle pass where I lie asleep.

Oh, if only the avalanche had taken your memory as the river took mine—but no. You remember who you are. You remember who I am, and what you plan to do to me, don't you, Gunman?

Maybe that is the best name for you, for even now you lift the rifle and smack the ice out of it and fill the chamber with another shell.

And then you toss your head back and laugh, a shriek that freezes the stars.

7

Thomas's Dream

I slept fitfully that night. I dreamed of Anna and Silence, of horses and gunshots, of a madman's laugh. . . .

I saw him, standing atop the snowpack left by the avalanche—standing and staring toward the mountain pass and loading his rifle.

No man could have survived that avalanche; no man could have clawed his way up out of the sarcophagus of ice. But he did.

He was Noman.

Then I saw *into* him, past his flesh and into the alien spirit that dwelt within him. It was vengeful, like an angel sent from heaven or a demon escaped from hell. It was greedy, like a creature from another world taking human form. . . .

But whatever it was, it was decidedly not human. . . .

8

Dawning Realization

Thomas and Silence tossed fitfully in their sleep, murmuring questions into the air. Anna lay and listened as long as she could, but when dawn began to slide its bloody fingers into the cave mouth, she rose to see the morning.

Walking on tiptoe, Anna sneaked past the sleepers. The smooth floor of the cave gave way to hoarfrost and then to trammeled snow. Easing her way past it, she emerged into the gloaming light.

The mountain pass spread out before her, black peaks standing sentinel over a wide saddle. The spot was pristine except for the ragged footprints she and Thomas and Silence had left the night before. Anna retraced her steps, wishing she could retrace every last one, back to Reichenbach, back to Meiringen—could undo all the terrors that had been done. . . .

At the edge of the pass, she looked down the avalanche field, the skinned belly of the mountain, the fallen trees lying far below like ruffled plumage.

Someone moved down there.

Someone climbed the slope, his eyes intent on her.

For a moment, Anna could only stare in shock and dread. Then, turning, she ran back to the cave. "Thomas! Silence! Wake up! He's coming!"

9

TRAPPED

W hat?" I started awake and sat up. The dream of demon spirits and possessed men faded away, and the reality of cave walls and sheep shit solidified. "What?"

Anna was a black silhouette in the cave mouth. "The gun-man is coming."

Dreams and reality collided: The demon was coming to the cave. I rolled from the straw mattress and stuffed my flask and clothes and matchbox back into my rucksack and pulled it over my shoulder and stood. "Let's go."

"No," Silence said. He sat on his straw mat and stared bleakly at the two of us. "I've had enough of running."

Anna and I were speechless. Then we both spoke at once: "He still has his gun—" "Are you out of your mind—?" "We have no weapons—" "He's bent on killing you—"

"All of which is reason not to run," Silence said calmly.

"You're going to fight him?" I asked.

He shook his head. "I'm going to trap him."

"How?"

Silence blinked thoughtfully. "Let's list our assets."

"Legs—" I pointed out, "for running!"

"Yes," Silence allowed. "What else?"

"A slingshot and a dagger," Anna offered.

"What else?"

I lifted my hands in exasperation. "The clothes on our backs. *My* clothes on *your back*."

"Precisely," Silence said, rising from his mattress and crossing to me. He grabbed my shoulder, spun me around, and dug into my rucksack, pulling out my last shirt, my last pair of pants, and a beret that a French farmer's daughter had given me. "Clothes make the man," he said, taking the items to the back of the cave and stuffing them with straw.

"He won't fall for that."

"He will—snow-blind," Silence replied. "It's just a lure—bait to get him inside—"

"Inside so he can shoot us!"

"We could hide," Anna blurted. "There's a niche just inside the cave mouth. We all three could fit in, out of sight."

I glared at her.

"Good girl," Silence said.

"Then what?" I asked in exasperation. "A slingshot against a gun? We'll be slaughtered."

Anna peered beyond the cave into the pass. "It's that or a flat-out run with him fifty feet behind. How good are you with that slingshot?"

"Good enough," I groaned, pulling the thing out while Anna scooped up scree from the ground to use as shot. At the back of the cave, Silence propped my clothes in a niche. The straw man had the awkward attitude of a man relieving himself.

"This isn't going to work," I said.

Silence looked near exasperation. "It'll work—as long as you can shoot straight."

"Time's up!" Anna hissed from the front of the cave.

Silence and I rushed to her, and all three of us slipped sideways into the niche inside the cave mouth.

And only just in time. The gunman's breath ghosted in the

air above the horizon line, and next moment his head crested the rise, too.

We held our breath as he approached, fearing any sound would be our last. Anna offered hands full of rocks. I selected a round, walnut-sized stone—big enough to make a pigeon explode—placed it in the much-used sling, and drew back. Then I peered out around the edge of the niche.

The man approached warily. His strange rifle jutted before him as he stalked up to the cave mouth. He was so close I could have grabbed him. In the silence, his teeth skirled on each other. I caught a whiff of him: sweat and anger and something else—something like excitement. My fingers twitched on the sling, but I didn't release. His eyes raked blindly past us, and he stalked into the cave.

"There you are!" he growled at the dummy, and Silence gave me a little smile of triumph. "Don't move, or I'll shoot. Where are the others?"

"Now," Anna whispered, nudging my elbow.

I let fly the stone, though I shouldn't have—should have realigned after that nudge from Anna. The shot whistled into the cave, clipped the man's ear, and flew past to strike Silence's dummy. It fell as if lunging, and the gunman fired into it. The boom was deafening in the cave, and the bullet ricocheted among the stone walls.

"Run!" Anna said, shoving Silence and me from the niche. "I'll cover."

"What?" I said.

"He won't shoot me," she growled. "Run!"

Silence grabbed my shoulder and hauled me after him, and both of us darted from the roaring cave mouth and out over pristine snow. My heart pounded faster than my feet, and the rubber tubing of the slingshot thrashed my legs.

"What are we doing?" I yelled.

"Escaping."

"No. I mean Anna." I skidded to a halt and pivoted back toward the cave. "We can't leave her with that madman."

Silence grabbed my arm and swung me around. "Don't you understand? She *knows* that madman." His eyes fixed on mine. "Come on!"

I lumbered after him, my head and back and legs stiff with disbelief. "She knows him?"

"Of course!" Silence snapped. "Couldn't you tell? The way she wept when she thought he was dead? The way her words caught whenever she spoke of him—her eyes averted, her voice falling to murmurs and whispers? The way he never shot at her?"

"He wouldn't have shot a lady."

"He's a madman! He would've shot a baby if given the chance! But not Anna. She means too much to him. . . . Get a move on, man!"

I was running in earnest now. The dread of it, the certainty of it, was catching up to me. Anna was on the gunman's side. She'd had my knife in her hand, had been probing my wound with it. She could have slit my throat. I'd been such a fool. Of course, from the very start, I'd known she was playing me—that was simply part of any seduction. But none of the other women had been playing at murder.

I looked back. There was no sign of Anna or the gunman. Silence and I were two hundred yards from the cave now and running still. We topped the spine of the pass and began to descend the opposite slope.

Before us lay a wide valley with a great glacier sliding slowly down the belly of it. The snow beneath our feet crunched more loudly, no longer a thin skin over rock but now a thin skin over ice. The footing grew treacherous.

"Look out!" Silence shouted even as his feet shot out

from under him. He sprawled to his backside and slid away down the sloping glacier.

"Damn!" I shouted as my own feet were stolen from beneath me. I thumped down on my buttocks and back. I tried to dig in my heels, but they just skated atop the ice. My skid turned into a slide and then into a luge. Thrashing, I flipped to my belly and tried to grab this knob of ice or that rill, tried to kick my toes into the cracks in the ice sheet.

"Help!" I called out stupidly.

Silence would be no help. He was a hundred yards ahead of me, shooting down the mountainside like a human toboggan. Worse yet, a hundred yards ahead of *him*, the glacier split open into a wide, deep crevasse.

"Silence! Look out!" I cried.

"What do you think?" he responded in exasperation. He flailed with his one good arm, fingertips dragging scratch marks down the ice sheet. Still, his strategy was working. He was slowing, or I was speeding up. The distance between us closed, but he'd be over the edge of the crevasse in two more seconds.

Silence slid onto the final shelf of ice and gave a great roar of desperation as he rammed his hands into a crack. He jerked to a halt, and ice popped and crackled with the strain. Even so, he was stopped. Hanging with hands wedged in a crack, belly lying on ice, and feet dangling above a thousand-foot plunge, Silence was safe—for the moment.

I hurtled down directly at him. I fought for purchase, nails clawing the ice. Incrementally, I slowed, but it wouldn't be enough.

"Sorry!" I called out just before smashing into him.

My feet rammed his shoulders; my backside struck his head. I flipped over him but snagged his shirt—my shirt!—and went over the edge. Fingers clenched to fists. The white linen in my grip yanked tight across his back as I jerked to a halt. My legs pitched back and forth over the abyss while threads popped at the seam along his shoulders.

"Don't let go!" I shouted.

"Let go!" he cried.

"No, *don't* let go!"

"No! You! Let! Go!"

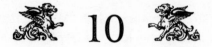

10

REUNION

The bullet still cracked and pinged off the cave walls as Anna shoved her friends out of the niche and out of her life. It was a horrible moment. She never expected to see Thomas or Silence again and felt she didn't deserve to. They had been her heroic dream. Now, she was confronting her villainous reality.

"Don't shoot, Father," Anna said.

He whirled around to face her. A moment before, her father had been crouching while the bullet ricocheted about him, while the roar of the rifle reverberated. Now steel and sound had spent themselves, and he rose to stare at her. He seemed all darkness, the grimy color of the cave itself.

"Anna," he sighed heavily. Four simple letters, two syllables, one word, and yet in the last five years, her name always carried a freight of meaning when her father spoke it. The name meant simply *I am so disappointed*. Her father used it as an all-purpose curse: "Anna."

"What?" she snapped.

He lowered his rifle—the gun that he himself had built, disguised as a walking stick so that he could take it with him wherever he went. He was a clever man, clever enough not to shoot his own daughter—though his words could be as lethal as bullets. "Always, this is the way with you."

"What?"

"Let's review," he said. It was his way of signaling a litany of complaint stored up against her. "My empire in London is destroyed by a man—no, let's not give him that credit—by a termite, a sleepless worm that wriggles through the foundations of my house and gnaws and gnaws away in darkness and silence until my empire crashes into dust. The work of my life—*my life*—becomes food for this worm. I have nothing left—nothing except vengeance."

"Nothing, Father?" Anna interrupted in their age-old pattern: He would rage a while about his injured self, and then Anna would interrupt to remind him of his injured girl. "You have more than vengeance left. You have me."

"Yes, you! You! Napoleon flees his Waterloo, not a man beside him, not a moment to snatch up a treasure chest, a masterpiece—some remnant of his empire—because he must needs snatch up a little girl. You escaped alive *because of me*. You are my only spoil of war, and how spoiled indeed!"

"I did everything you asked!"

"Oh, yes. Everything I asked."

"I did! I was your spy at the Englischer Hof, this innocent girl in white lace, planning a picnic at the falls. I watched your foe, reported every movement to you, goaded the men to hike to the falls that afternoon, made a fuss at the front desk to get a messenger boy to take your message to the good doctor, made sure you could have your 'final confrontation.' I was the spring in your trap—just as you asked—but you said it wouldn't be murder."

"Stupid girl!" he growled. "It wasn't murder!"

"Throwing a man from the top of the falls isn't murder? Shooting at him? Shooting at him and at the man who saved him from the river—that's not murder?"

"You cannot begin to understand."

"You didn't used to be this way, Father," Anna said. "I thought if I helped you resolve this, perhaps—perhaps you'd be done with this mania, be once again my father. I did everything you asked. And even though you didn't ask, I went out to witness your moment of triumph. I wanted to be there when this whole nightmare would end, and I would have you back, so I went . . . and I saw . . ."

All through Anna's tirade, her father had been edging nearer to her. Now, they stood toe to toe, eyes locked, breathing the same air. There was grime in the anger lines of his face. "You did everything I asked, yes. But then you did this last thing that I did not ask. You read me wrong, Anna." He spoke each word that followed in a dead, calm voice. "I . . . did . . . not . . . want . . . you . . . there." He stoked his voice with heat and hate. "I did not ask you to bring a young man with you. I did not ask you to pull my enemy from the river. I did not ask you to splint his arm, to lead me on a wild chase across the mountains. I did not ask you to bury me alive in an avalanche and spend your night sporting with your new young lover!"

Anna smacked his face. She had never done that before. She had received slaps but never given one, and this first one showed how much she had changed.

Her father took a step back, his eyes blazing, as if they would light his brows on fire. It was a terrifying look from a man who specialized in them. Anna was ready to feel the slug in her belly, to crumple to the floor of the cave and bleed out for having raised a hand against her father. At least then it would have been over.

In his inimitable way, though, her father exceeded her fears: "Well done, Anna."

She stiffened.

"All your life, you have simply been the failure. There is nothing admirable or even interesting about a failure. Now, your failures have become so deep and systemic that they have evolved into outright betrayal. A traitor, at least, is interesting."

"Father, shut up," Anna said, but it was too late. She dragged her hand across her eyes, but he had seen them pregnant with tears. "Oh, shut up!"

"Interesting . . ." he continued as if she had not said a word, "but not trustworthy." With that, the cane-rifle flew up in his fist, and the handle hit her head, and everything went black.

11

RESONATION

Why would I let go?" Silence raged at me.

"Why would *I* let go?" I shot back.

"Because you're going to drag us both down into the pit!"

"You want me to sacrifice myself?" I demanded.

"You want *me* to sacrifice *myself*?" he spat back.

My shirt—on Silence's back—gave its own complaint. The seam along one shoulder popped open, and thread by thread it started to tick itself wider.

My weak arm slipped from the shirttail but clenched onto the trousers' waistband.

Silence groaned. "You're going to cut me in half!"

"Now, just hold tight—"

"Good advice!"

I took a deep breath, willed strength into my wounded arm, and gathered my legs for a midair leap. I lunged up and caught a handhold higher on the ripping shirt. "This would be easier if I didn't have a wounded arm."

"You're telling me."

My good hand clawed higher, dragging my body up over the icy edge of the crevasse. Scrabbling, scraping, swearing— I scrambled up beside Silence and wedged my hands in the crack beside his.

We lay there on our stomachs and stared at our bloodied hands jammed into the crack. Between panting breaths, we could hear a tinkling sound, like a thousand tiny, brittle chimes—splitting and cracking.

"Is that what I think it is?" I asked.

"Yes."

"So—we've got to get off this slab?"

"Yes."

"Even though moving could send it plummeting into the crevasse?"

"Yes."

The race was on: Two exhausted, freezing men with only two good arms between them shimmied side by side on a frictionless surface above a thousand-foot plunge.

"The crack is widening!" Silence said.

As we watched in horror, the two-inch crack became a four-inch crack—then one foot wide, then a yard. . . .

Then we were falling.

The great wedge of ice beneath us lurched downward. For a second, I thought we'd plunge right into the abyss, riding on the head of that gigantic spike. Instead, the tip of the spike snagged the wall of the crevasse. Silence and I stared into each other's terrified eyes as the ice wedge slowly teetered away from the cliff face and out over the thousand-foot plunge.

"Pull yourself up!" Silence shouted beside me. He dragged his body up the edge of the ice wedge, struggling to get on top and kicking me in the process. "Pull yourself up!"

Clinging with frozen fingers, I scrambled up beside Silence.

A moment later, the head of the ice wedge struck the far wall of the crevasse. *Boom!* If we hadn't moved, we would've been spattered across the face of the cliff. Instead, Harold Silence and I shuddered atop a great bridge of ice that spanned the chasm. As the boom reverberated away into the depths, little splitting sounds filled the air. A fine network of cracks spread through the ice beneath us.

"We need to get off this bridge," Silence advised.

"Yeah." We scooted backward, sliding on our bellies toward the wall of the chasm behind us.

The cracks widened into actual gaps in the ice. The central span of the ice bridge slumped, on the verge of giving way.

"Well," I said, "I hate to die beside a stranger. If you know your name, you'd better tell me now."

Silence locked eyes with me, gritted his teeth, and shoved himself upward. I did likewise, and we stood with our backs to the cliff face.

With a tinkling roar, the ice bridge bowed downward and lost all cohesion. The span disintegrated, each block launching itself into clear air. I gave a strangled yelp as the solid mass cascaded away into a cloud of clods and then into blue oblivion.

Even the ice beneath our feet shifted and slid down.

Roaring, Silence swung around and gripped a crack in the ice cliff. I grabbed a narrow ledge just as our footing gave way entirely. Once again, we hung side by side above the crevasse—though this time we were on the other side.

"Now what?" I asked.

Silence laughed, and the sound echoed below us as if the great glacier were deeply amused at our plight. "Not having any memory gives me a very clear head, you know."

"Clear, yes," I said, feeling my grip begin to fail. "Empty. Echoing even."

Silence stopped laughing and started singing. His voice was loud and somewhat grating, wandering up and down the scales.

"Really, Silence—do you think now's the time for singing?"

"Yes," he said, his blue eyes fixing mine. "The thing about ice is, it's crystals."

"So?"

"The thing about crystals is, they have resonance points."

"So?"

"Oh, memory must be such a blight. Think, Thomas! Think!"

I blinked, staring at the icy cliff before me, the vertical fissures in it, the possibility for a crack to open and let us climb. "You're singing to find the resonance frequency of the ice?"

Instead of answering, Silence began to sing again. His voice echoed down the throat of the chasm and back up, and the ice before us began to hum.

"That's it! That pitch there!" I said.

"Well, help me out, then."

I joined my voice to his, trying to match his pitch, trying to find that singular note. The striated sheet of ice before us began to crackle and groan. We centered in on one high tone. The ice between us shivered. We sang louder, holding the note, and soon little crystals shook free of the wall.

Suddenly, a whole chute of ice shattered and plummeted away like a chandelier dropping from a ceiling. It sluiced down between us and plunged into the icy rift, opening up a crevice that we both lunged for.

In the next moments, we were climbing, frozen hands and feet scrabbling on ice, bent backs bashing against each other. Inch by inch, we shimmied higher until at last we clawed our way to the top of the glacier and lay on our backs, panting.

"You know, Silence," I said hoarsely, "ever since I met you, it's been one insane predicament after another."

"I could say the same," he responded.

"Yes, but *my* life was different before this. Your life—who knows?"

We breathed a while more and then sat up, staring soberly over the cliff.

"Well, for the time being, we're safe," Silence said. "Safe from the gunman. Safe from Anna."

I glared at him. "You're a cold one."

"They can't get at us in a straight line. They'll have to go twenty miles in either direction, or straight back—"

"That's not what I'm talking about. She saved you. She saved me."

"She's plotting with the gunman."

I was incredulous. "She stayed behind to stall him!"

"Or to join him."

I shook my head angrily. "You're too old to understand."

"I understand perfectly. You've fallen for her."

"She's fallen for me."

Silence stood and slapped snow off his backside. "You see, that's where you and I differ. You think love explains everything about Miss Anna Schmidt. I think loyalty does—her loyalty to the gunman. That key unlocks all she has done—and all she will do."

"None of it matters. It's all over now. Past and future. Done," I said bitterly, getting up and stepping away from the precipice. One step turned into two and four and a dozen, and Silence fell in stride beside me.

"It's not over, Thomas," Silence said. "We've bought

ourselves time. That's all. The gunman and Anna will be back."

"They're after you, not me."

"Anna's been after you from the beginning."

"You don't know. You weren't there. I went after her. She had a picnic for one, and I practically invited myself along."

"When did she buy the cheese?"

"What?"

"There was a bottle of wine in the carriage and the remains of a baguette—fair enough. You can't buy half a bottle of wine or half a baguette. But there were also the wrapping papers of *two* hunks of cheese."

"Maybe she likes cheese!"

"A girl with a twenty-four-inch waist does not eat two hunks of cheese. Did she buy the cheese before you approached her or after?"

"You twist everything around."

"It's a simple question. Before or after?"

"Before, all right?"

Silence nodded. "She was planning to reel you in."

"She was walking away! All I saw was her backside."

"Proves my point."

"Oh, you're insufferable," I said. "I wish you'd get your memory back so you could give up your little guessing games."

"Guessing games!" Silence spat.

"You're just a palm reader."

Silence planted his feet in the snow and grabbed my right hand. "I do read palms, my boy, but none of that mumbo jumbo about lifelines and heart lines. It's not the future that's written on your palm, but the past. Look here." He pointed to my fingertips. "See how these are blunt on the ends—and yet your nails are quite long. You've been a nail-biter from childhood, which gives your fingers this shape—and it tells that your life has been a fretful one until lately. The fine condition of your nails now shows a year of relative bliss, but look here—look at these fresh tooth marks. You've begun biting again—in the last two days!"

"Mumbo jumbo."

"What of these little pinch points between your index and middle finger—little burn scars that healed up perhaps a year ago. A cigarette would be too thin to admit this many sparks this far down. It was cigars, then, that you'd taken up smoking. Eh? A year of cigar smoking—in a kind of ferocious way—starting two years ago. Why, then? Why does a young man take up cigar smoking? Because he wants to be an old man, a big man. Because he's nervous—or full of sudden grief. Answer me this, Thomas. Was it two years ago that your father died?"

"Hey!" I yelped, pulling my hand back.

"Don't be so surprised. I knew of that already from the rings." He lifted my left hand and pointed to the thick callus under my father's ring and the thin callus under my own ring. "You've had two years to build this callus, two years back to your father's death, but only one year since you graduated from Christ College, Cambridge."

I pulled my left hand away and began walking, a tingle of dread moving up my spine. "I know who I am. Who are you, Silence? Read your own palm."

Silence matched me stride for stride. "I have been. Of course I have. There are many scars there for so thin a hand. The palm has tobacco burns, the sort that would come from embers falling from a pipe, and acid burns as from mixing caustic chemicals. The back of the hand has black powder scars from firing a gun, and here—do you see these?" He rolled back his sleeve and showed me the purple depressions of veins leading from his inner elbow.

"Opium."

"More likely, cocaine. These are recent scars. If I were an opium addict, I would not be able to think clearly now that I have been without the stuff for two days. No, I must be addicted to a less-invasive poison."

"But a poison, all the same."

"True enough."

"So, then, who is Harold Silence?" I pressed. "A cocaine addict—perhaps a drug dealer, whose hands are burned with whatever caustic chemicals he uses to prepare his wares, whose hands are burned from the guns he has shot to defend his criminal empire?"

"Perhaps," Silence said quietly.

"Perhaps? What other explanation could there be for these scars?"

Silence took a while to respond. "The evidence tells what I have done, but not why I have done it. I've shot cocaine in my veins—but why? An addict? A drug lord? I've shot guns—but why? To oppose the law, or to uphold it?"

I laughed grimly. "The cocaine-addicted crime fighter—yes. A very plausible explanation. And I suppose this madman trying to kill you is a criminal you have brought to justice rather than a rival drug lord—or even a police officer trying to bring you in."

"He's not that. No police officer would shoot an innocent man and steal his horse."

"Right," I said. "Still, we know more about the gunman than we do about you."

"That fact will soon be remedied," Silence said, gesturing out ahead of us. We had reached the base of the glacier and gazed out past the tailings, across a broad valley, to a green land. At the other side of the green land lay a large city, gleaming in the sun. "There will be a sanatorium there. There will be food—"

"Yes, food . . ."

"And bandages, and nurses, and perhaps a doctor—who can help me regain my mind."

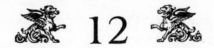

Admissions

The receiving nurse sat in the arched foyer of the Prefargier Sanatorium and made jagged little notations in tiny columns and rows. Number by number, abbreviation by abbreviation, she itemized the insanities and treatments of her inmates. For the old man with whooping cough, a dram of heroin. For the young man with sexual perversions, thirty minutes in the electric bath. For the young woman with violent episodes, an ice-pick leukotomy. The nurse etched notations like a mason chiseling gravestones.

Few folk sick enough to walk through the doors of Prefargier Sanatorium ever became well enough to walk out again.

The great walnut door swung wide, and in stepped a man leaning on a spike-tipped cane. He gripped the brass handle of his walking stick in a slender but strong hand. The man and his cane crept toward the nurse's desk, and her eyes traveled up his long arm to his shoulder, his neck, his face.

She winced. The man's flesh was lank, a mere veil over the skeleton beneath. His lips snarled perpetually, and above them hooked a great nose that must have been broken at least once. On either side of the nose were two dark eyes that gave back no light whatever, like the eyes of a shark.

"Dr. Gottlieb Burckhardt."

The nurse stared, uncomprehending. *"Was ist?"*

"Dr. Gottlieb Burckhardt."

Blinking, the nurse said in German. "You are not Dr. Burckhardt."

The man also spoke German, but with a strong English accent. "I want to see Dr. Burckhardt."

"Do you have an appointment?"

The man lifted his walking stick horizontally, catching the spiked end of it in his left hand, and leaned his scarred knuckles on the desktop. "I do not need an appointment. Tell Dr. Burckhardt that Herr Schmidt has come to collect on an old, important debt."

The nurse stared a moment longer at this gaunt apparition. "Debt collector," she snorted, and then rose to stride to Dr. Burckhardt's office. She tapped on the beveled-glass door and eased it open.

"Dr. Burckhardt, there's a bill collector here."

"Bill collector?" came the testy reply from within.

"A Herr Schmidt. An old bill. Very serious."

At first, no answer came from the other side of the door except a deafening silence—answer enough. Then chair legs scraped on hardwood, leather-soled shoes scuffled across the floor, and a wheezing doctor trundled through the door. "Why didn't you say so? I hope you've not left him waiting long." Dr. Burckhardt's jowls quirked in a smile. "Herr Schmidt, my friend—how good it is to see you!" He extended his hand, but the visitor did not take it.

Herr Schmidt instead lowered his cane to the floor and leaned on it, scratching the tiles. "I would like a word, in private."

"Of course! Of course!" Dr. Burckhardt said, ushering the skeletal man through the doorway. Burckhardt pulled the door shut behind them, but not before the nurse glimpsed a fearful flash of his wide eyes.

Within the office, Burckhardt turned and spread his arms. "Make yourself at home."

His guest already had, slouching in the chair, one boot lolling idly atop the paper-strewn desk. "I have no love of you, Burckhardt, as you know."

"I know."

"And so I will get right to the point. Two men will be arriving here today or tomorrow—a young man with a wispy goatee and a man a little younger than myself and about my build who will complain of amnesia."

"Yes?" Burckhardt prompted as he circled around his desk and sat down. He templed his fingers before his face. "Go on."

"You are to admit the older man," Schmidt replied. "Do not fuss about money. He likely has none. Say that Switzerland provides charitable treatment for the elderly—whatever it takes to allay their suspicions and admit him."

"Whatever it takes, I shall admit him," Dr. Burckhardt replied dutifully.

"You are to do everything you can to heal your new patient, to return his mind to him and his health to him. But do not release him. I will call for him and dispose of him as I will."

"What about the younger man?"

"Toss him out. Or if he insists on remaining with his friend—well, you have had accidents before, and there's always the incinerator."

"Herr Schmidt," Burckhardt replied, affronted, "how could you ask me to—"

"You seem to forget our mutual friend, the one whom you killed, the one whom I have not spoken of but would, and the five others you treated and killed the same way. You seem to forget—"

"But they all were deeply psychotic. There was no other hope for them. Only the new procedure—experimental."

"You murdered them, Doctor. Murdered them for science as other men murder for money. The courts will not see much difference. And now, if the young man insists upon staying, you will murder him, too."

"But I . . . what if the police—?"

"Follow my directions to the letter, or I will expose you." Suddenly, Herr Schmidt stood, eyes blazing. "No—worse than that. I will kill you myself."

Lowering his gaze, the good doctor said, "I will do it, then. I will heal the old man and—if necessary—kill the young one."

13

CIVILIZATION

We don't present a very noble picture, Thomas and I, loping into town like a pair of starving hyenas. It's been two full days since either of us has eaten, since Thomas dragged me from the Reichenbach River. I've not eaten for even longer: I doubt the gunman and I were sharing cheese and baguettes at the top of the falls.

Needless to say, as we stagger into Bern, everything looks appetizing—the roasted almonds at a street vendor's stall, the great sausages hanging trophylike in the butcher's window, the Swiss chocolates that rise in a pyramid in the candy store, the little hunks of Edam in the fromagerie—even the red apples and orange carrots and shaggy cabbages at the greengrocer's.

I pluck an apple from a bin and lift it to my nose. It smells luscious, but I feign distaste and lower the fruit again. Instead of returning it to the bin, I slide the thing into my shirt-sleeve. The greengrocer is none the wiser.

When at last Thomas and I step beyond the marketplace, I guide him to a dark alley and produce the apple from my sleeve. I take a bite and offer him some.

"Astonishing!" He snatches up the fruit and bites. Around chunks of half-chewed apple, he says, "Where'd you get the money?"

I swallow before replying. "Money is a crutch for crippled fingers." To demonstrate, I lift a carrot from my vest pocket.

Thomas has munched halfway through the apple, but now he hands the sloppy thing back in favor of the carrot. We eat. It's a quiet moment, a small feast in a dark alley in a foreign town. Still, it cheers us both.

"Maybe we don't need the sanatorium," Thomas says.

"Huh?"

"Your arm's splinted; my wounds are dressed. We've got as much produce as you can shove up your shirt. Maybe we're fine, then. . . . Fresh slate. New beginning. All that. You don't know how many times I've landed just this way in a new city. Start again."

There's something hopeful and infectious in his voice, but I can't give in to it. "I have a past whether I want one or not. The man with the gun is my past. Until I know who I am, I can't be safe."

Thomas's young face clouds. "Then, my friend," he says, dropping the carrot nub to the cobbles and flicking the apple core from my grip, "it's off to hospital."

14

SANATORIUM

By the time we marched up the steps of the sanatorium, I'd hatched a plan. "I know what our story should be."

"Better fill me in," Silence replied.

"It's simple enough," I said. "We're obviously British—"

"The moment we open our mouths."

"So, let's be father and son—tourists who were beaten, shot, and robbed."

"You? My son?" Silence said, studying my goatee and the greatcoat on my shoulders.

"I'm the black sheep."

"I don't know, Thomas. It's not the best plan." Silence opened the door before me, gesturing me in.

"Maybe not, but it's the only one we've got." I walked through the huge oak double doors into a high-vaulted space with walls of sterile white. A few patients sat slumped in a semicircle of chairs around the outer walls, and in the center of the room stood a great walnut desk with papers spread out across it. An elderly nurse sat there.

"Mademoiselle?" I began.

The woman looked up, her wrinkled face unfolded, and she coughed. "Frau."

"Do you speak English, Frau?" I asked.

"Yes."

"Oh, thank goodness. You must help us. My father and I are on tour from Britain, and we have been beaten, shot, and robbed."

"Robbed?"

"*Beaten, shot*, and robbed," I repeated. Silence nodded gravely as I went on. "We'd been hiking the Alps above the Reichenbach Falls and a man with a rifle held us up. Father surrendered his pocketbook, but I tried to be the hero and lunged for the man, which earned me this bullet in the shoulder."

The nurse peered dubiously at my bandage. "The blood's all in back. How did he shoot you in the back when you were lunging at him?"

I felt my face flush. "Well, all right, you caught me." I approached the desk, leaning confidentially toward her. "I was running when he shot me. Shoulder and neck. That's when Father jumped the man and got shoved off a cliff and broke his arm and hit his head. You see? Amnesia."

The word *amnesia* made the nurse's eyes jump to Silence, who was affecting a very convincing idiot stare. "All right. I'll need your names."

"My name is Thomas—" I broke off, amazed that I had almost blurted out my true name. "Er, James Thomas."

"All right, and your father?"

"Harold Thomas."

She noted both names. "And how do you plan to pay?"

"Pay?" I said, suddenly recognizing the limits of my plan. "Well, our pocketbooks have been stolen, and—"

"Switzerland provides charitable treatment for the elderly. Your father is covered, but you will have to pay for yourself."

"Well, I, er—I'll be fine. Just a bullet wound. Got the bullet out—Father did, I mean. And my neck—bandaged. I'll be fine."

"I'll repack your bandages for you, out here, but that's the best I can do. Please ask your father to sit there with the other new patients. Then seat yourself here so I can quickly tend your wounds."

As I helped Silence to his seat, the nurse turned with chart in hand and headed for the surgical theater. I leaned over to Silence and whispered, "We're in!"

"We'll see."

Not a moment later, the door to the surgical theater burst open, and out rushed a jowly doctor with eyes ablaze and fingers riling. "Where's the amnesiac?"

The nurse strode out behind him and gestured to Silence. "Right here."

"Excellent! Excellent!" The doctor gripped Silence's good arm and levered him up from the chair. "Mr. Thomas, my name is Gottlieb Burckhardt."

"Gottlieb . . ." Silence muttered. "That's German for 'God's love.'"

"Come this way, Mr. Thomas. I have just what you need. Just the thing to restore your mind."

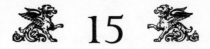

15

ELECTROCUTION

My misgivings only deepen as I clap eyes on Dr. Gottlieb Burckhardt. The man's wide eyes, florid cheeks, and slack mouth show that he believes he has just found his salvation. But why would I be this man's salvation? What doctor ever greets a patient this way? "Gottlieb," I say wonderingly. "That's German for 'God's love.'"

He practically hauls me out of my seat and across the floor to the surgical theater. I glance back at Thomas, but he only nods, proud of the little deceit he has pulled off.

But who is deceiving whom?

Dr. Burckhardt ushers me into the surgical theater. The room hosts two examination tables surrounded by tiers of benches. Dr. Burckhardt guides me to one of the tables, arranged in a star shape with separate sections for head and body and legs and feet. *"Guten Morgen. Sprechen Sie Deutsch?"*

"Ah—English, actually."

"Sit here, sir," he says, patting the middle of the table.

I do sit.

The doctor goes to a closet, where he plucks out a strange contraption—a machine about the size of a breadbox, with a crank jutting out one end and thick black wires emerging from both sides. The wires are woven copper with a coating of black rubber over them, and each wire ends in a metal alligator clip.

"What's that?" I ask.

The doctor crooks a look my way and says, "You're an am-nesiac, yes?"

"Yes."

"Then I imagine you do not know of the Austrian inventor named Nikola Tesla."

"I imagine I do not," I respond.

"Nikola Tesla and scientists on both sides of the Atlantic," begins Dr. Burckhardt with a professorial air, "have developed the therapeutic form of electricity—'alternating current.' Unlike the dangerously powerful 'direct current'—which can slay an elephant—alternating current is as safe and therapeutic as bath water. This contraption—called an AC generator—has proved the most powerful device imaginable for restoring memory."

I nod nervously, seeing the six black wires reach out spiderlike, each tipped in a steel pincer. "How does it work?"

"Well." He lifts one of the clips and lets the jagged metal jaws slap shut again. "It's very simple. I dip each of these clamps in a solution of lamp oil—yes, the same harmless spermaceti that lights your home—and clamp it to your flesh."

"Where?" I ask.

He shrugs. "Ears, fingertips, and toes—the outer extremities. Your body completes the circuit."

"You're going to electrocute me?"

The doctor's hands spread defensively before him. "Not electrocute. *Electrify.* This isn't a lightning bolt, but alternating current—the very kind your brain uses day in and out. The alternating current will help sort out your own confused brain patterns, will help align them."

It all seems to make sense—the science of it. I still have to wonder about that eager face, though, those smiling jowls. "All right. I'm ready."

"Excellent," says the doctor, pushing me to lie down on the segmented table and slipping my shoes off. The doctor seems to relish the preparations. He lifts one alligator clip, dips it into a jar of spermaceti, and fastens the thing to my right ear. He does the same with more clips—for the left ear, and the fingertips, and the toes. Then he retreats to the box and positions one hand on top and the other on the crank.

"What should I expect?" I ask.

"Health," the doctor responds, and he begins to furiously crank the crank.

Electricity surges into my ears, my hands, my feet. At first, the energy feels like bees swarming me and stinging my skin. Then the voltage sinks deeper. It stands nerves on end and makes every muscle turn to metal. It delves deeper still, past muscle and into mind, into soul.

I see visions. It is like that twilight place between waking and sleeping, when your conscious mind gazes on the panoply of the unconscious. . . .

I see an upstairs study with books lining the walls and a cabinet filled with little cross-referenced cards: a murder, a theft, a rape, a betrayal. Names of the perpetrators and names of the crimes, lists of evidence, of tools used, of ways of using them.

And then, there are more visions—of a pipe at my lips, a bowl filled with fragrant tobacco and spewing blue smoke and smoldering with red embers. A breath moves through those embers, and one leaps free to fall on my palm and burn it—one of many little freckle scars on my right hand.

But something else is in my left hand now—the finely wrought, finely curved neck of a violin caught between thumb and forefinger, nestled in the soft couch of the palm, with fingers ambling languidly over the strings. There is a long song in the air, a long, low, melancholy song, a melody

by Beethoven, pulsing slowly through the air, a sonata for piano that I have learned for violin—*Moonlight*.

And there is a listener beside me. He is a stocky man with
an intelligent face and sensitive eyes. His skin is sallow, as if
he had spent years beneath the Middle Eastern sun only to
return for years beneath an English fog. He has a reddish
mustache, this man, and a square jaw, and trained hands. I
look upon this slumping figure, who takes in my violin playing as a drunkard takes in gin, and I see greatness in him.
Greatness and friendship.

But then, the pain is too powerful.

I feel my body transfixed, like a Sioux brave pinioned to
the prairie earth and waiting for the warriors to ride past and
hurl their spears down into me. I feel stretched out, like the
man on the cross to demonstrate the power of Roman rule
over Jewish mysticism. I feel like the wicker man, deformed
or demented or perverse, wrapped in a cage of reeds and entombed in fire by the Celts.

My every cell is on fire. They burst and burst and burst,
giving up the water in them and turning the rest to fire—to
burn and burn and burn.

16

In Defense of Silence

Here's the conundrum about nurses: the young ones are beautiful but incompetent, and the old ones are competent but ugly. When my complaint is mild, I seek out a young, beautiful nurse. She will take twice as long to dress my wound (and do half as good a job) as an old nurse, but her wide eyes, smooth skin, and rose-red lips—these have a healing power that well-applied bandages do not. When I'm in grave shape, though, I look for the oldest, ugliest nurse around. She will work with grim dispatch, doing exactly the right thing and not relying on weeping eyes or pouting lips to heal me.

The charge nurse at the Prefargier Sanatorium was ancient and hideous—and thus brilliant. She unwrapped my shoulder wound and picked two more bits of bullet from it and debrided it of dead flesh and sanitized it and stitched up the gulf, all while wondering why a young man would run for his life when his father was in mortal danger. She also redressed the wound on my neck and taught me why Scotch—in any proof—is not equal to wood alcohol administered by an expert.

"All right. You're fine," she said, "better than you could've hoped—and for free. Now, you've got to get out of here. We've got no beds for folks that don't pay."

I was about to agree—the streets of Bern are not inhospitable to the man who knows how to purloin an apple or a carrot—but then Silence screamed.

"What's that?" I asked.

"Treatment," the nurse said solemnly.

"What sort of . . ." I stood up, trailing a final bandage from my arm and heading toward the beveled-glass window. Gazing through it, I saw a sight I couldn't believe.

Silence lay there on some kind of segmented examination table, his neck and hands and legs tied down, and alligator clips clinging to ears and fingers and toes. Electricity vaulted through him—arms flexing against his bonds, abdomen clenching above the main table, legs arcing as energy moved through them. His electrified figure formed the shape of a pentacle—a five-pointed star—but there was something more. Silence's spirit seemed to be driven up from his body, an ectoplasmic presence that roiled in the air. It was as if this electric therapy had exorcised his soul from his body.

I thought of my plenary worm . . . dead one moment, electrified the next, and alive the third. But that had been science. This was—exorcism.

I looked to Dr. Burckhardt, who crouched beside Silence and cranked the demonic box that sent charges through him.

"No!" I shouted, and pushed open the door and rushed forward to grab the box that the doctor cranked. "No!" I cried again, and pulled the wires loose from Silence and hurled the box away. It slid, sparking, across the tiles of the operating theater.

"You!" shouted Dr. Burckhardt. "Out! Out, I say!" He grabbed my newly bandaged shoulder and hauled me out of the operating theater and dragged me across the floor of the waiting room. Ahead of us, a semicircle of insane people seated around the perimeter of the room pulled their feet up from the floor as we passed, as if we were floodwaters. Reaching the double doors of the sanatorium, Dr. Burckhardt barked a few words in German and hurled me out onto the stone steps.

I tumbled to a halt, shaken, bruised, and not a little bit annoyed. You haven't been thrown out of a place until you have been thrown out by someone barking at you in German.

My plan had failed.

For a scamp, there's nothing worse than a failed plan. It is as if a carpenter built a shed that fell down, or a priest baptized someone, accidentally, into the worship of the devil. A failed plan for a scamp—or for a scientist, and I was both—meant that I was perhaps too inept at my chosen profession to survive.

I sat on the steps that Silence and I had scaled and took stock of my situation. "I wonder if I'll ever see him again."

All right, Thomas, I thought, *you're in a spot now—kicked out of an asylum with Silence kicked in. What's your next brilliant plan?*

I had a heavy feeling in my gut. What was it: responsibility? No. It was stronger than that. Guilt? Honestly? I'd already saved Silence five times over, and I didn't owe him a sixth. . . . But I couldn't just leave him in the hands of that mad scientist and his brutal breadbox.

Think, Thomas! Think! I stood up and walked down the steps. Something about the rhythm of feet on pavement—it always untangled my thoughts. How could I get in? I couldn't return as a patient. Nurse Cragface would recognize me right away. I couldn't disguise myself as a doctor—not young as I was, dressed as I was, with a British accent. If only they had a maintenance crew, or a carpentry crew, or an exterminator. . . .

I imagined myself in a pair of overalls, a metal cylinder at my waist and a spray nozzle in my grip. "I haff come to spritz zee rats!" Laughing, I stepped into the street . . .

And was nearly run down by a four-wheeled phaeton. The horse whickered at me, and the driver knocked me back with the butt of his whip. He growled something in German: *"Ver-dammter Tourist!"*

I staggered back. Well, that would've been one way into the hospital—or the morgue.

A lamplighter passed by, carrying a wick stick in one hand and a slender ladder in the other. He leaned the ladder against a lamppost, climbed, reached up with his lighting stick, and flicked the glass open. The wick darted in to ignite the lamp, and then he flipped the glass closed again. I looked to the light, only then realizing how dark the sky was becoming. A black ribbon of soot rolled up from the lantern and twisted into the night sky.

There was something in that smoke—the key to my predicament.

I turned toward the sanatorium and saw a similar line of smoke drifting from the top of a cigar-shaped smokestack. The smoke waved to me and then swept down in a gray ribbon across the street before dissipating on the wind. There was a faint stench in it, the stench of burned flesh.

"Crematorium!" I said in glee. I was, perhaps, the first person in the history of the world to say that word that way. Trying to clamp down on my enthusiasm, I strode excitedly toward the smokestack. A wooden fence shielded it from the road, sheltering an alley just wide enough for the ash man to wheel his cart up and shovel out the bones and ash.

Ah-ha! The ash clean-out. I reached down to grab the large metal handle and pulled. A six-foot-long drawer slid out on hidden rollers, revealing a wide pan filled with ashes and bones. Heat rose from the remains—not killing heat, but the spanking radiance of spent coals. With a final glance behind me, I brushed back the waste, curled up in the drawer, and gingerly rolled myself into the incinerator.

As the drawer slid closed, darkness enveloped me. Darkness and heat. I reached up, feeling the warm edges of a brick chute, and above it, wide-spaced bars that were crusted with grease. I shoved on the bars, and the whole grillwork lifted loose. Then I scampered up through it, pushed open the incinerator door, and climbed out onto the tiled floor of the crematorium.

"I'm in!" I said to myself excitedly.

"*Qu'est-ce que c'était?*" someone else said in the nearby hallway. Footsteps approached.

I had to hide, but the room was small and bare. Fighting every instinct, I opened the incinerator door and climbed back in, closing it behind me.

I heard the men step into the room. They whispered suspiciously to each other, and their voices grew nearer. One of the men barked something that made me lurch, my foot striking the incinerator door with a bang. I stilled myself, held my breath, even kept my eyeballs from moving. I lay there in that stiff terror for three long seconds before hearing the creak of the incinerator door lifting.

"*Merde!*" one of the men said as he clapped eyes on me.

I held still, legs and arms and body and lungs and all and tried to play dead. Out of my peripheral vision, I could sense that they were blinking in disbelief, their mouths hanging wide. In time, movement came to those slack jaws. They spoke to each other in brusque whispers, nodded once in unison, and eased the door of the incinerator closed.

I breathed again at last.

Then the blue flames burst out below me.

I smashed against the incinerator door, bashing back the two faces that had been just outside, and dropped to the floor. Little flames clung to my clothes, but I rolled over to extinguish them. The men danced back and shouted in consternation—giving me room to roll until the fires were out. Wide-eyed and terrified, I stopped on hands and buttocks and heels and stared up at the two men.

"I'm alive!" I said. "I'm alive!"

They returned my amazed look. *"Pas encore une fois."*

One man shut off the gas, and both swept forward, hoisted me, and carried me toward the door of the crematorium. With their free hands, they brushed off the ash that clung to my clothes. When I tried to explain, one man clamped his hand over my mouth, and the other man shushed me.

They conveyed me out of the crematorium and up a long white stairway. At its top, we passed through another hall and into a ward that was lined on both sides with beds. Anguished souls lay in them in various states of consciousness. With another shush, the men carried me to an empty bed, dragged back the covers, shoved me in, covered me up, and stalked nervously away.

I struggled to hold still, but laughter jiggled up in my throat. I couldn't hold the sound and let loose. My giggles turned to chortles to guffaws that rang from the vault above. Luckily, insane laughter was commonplace in the Prefargier Sanatorium.

After the jag was done, I lay still and felt the sweetness of the silence, the softness of the pillow, the sense that nothing could harm me. I felt invulnerable.

It was time to find Harold Silence.

Sliding my legs out from under the covers, I stepped out across the ward. The first bed held an ancient fellow. His leathery face was surrounded by a shock of white hair and a beard that shuddered with each voluminous snore. Obviously not Silence. The second bed held a young man who watched me with cloudy eyes and moaned, "Clarice . . . Clarice . . . Clarice . . ." I stalked past another blasted soul, and another, but none was the blasted soul of my friend. I checked every bed in the ward, but no Silence.

Creeping to the doorway of the ward, I looked out. Beyond was the circular receiving room with another ward opening on the other side. Smack in the middle, however, sat Nurse Cragface. She continued her grim itemizations, her eyes as keen as they had been two hours before.

I'd never get past her, unless . . .

Retreating to the nearest bed, I stooped down in hopes of finding—yes, a metal bedpan. As I gingerly lifted it from the floor, I discovered it was full. "All the better."

I judged the distance between me and the poor sod who was muttering "Clarice," cocked the bedpan in my arm, and hurled it. The missile flew with a wobbly motion over three sleepers, its contents sloshing ominously, before it descended. The metal pan struck the foot board of the young lunatic's bed, clanging monstrously, and then plunged to hit the tiles with a wet, tumbling racket.

The young lunatic shouted, "CLARICE!"

Hard-soled shoes clacked beyond the door, approaching, and I ducked down into a shadow beside one bed.

Next moment, Nurse Cragface arrived, feet planted wide like a rugby player's and hands angrily jammed on hips. "Meister Boniface!" she roared, striding now between the rows of beds.

"CLARICE!" he responded in desperate apology.

Though some inmates had slept through the clanging

chamber pot, none remained asleep after this exchange. Patients sat up and yelped to see the formidable nurse marching toward the patient.

In the general tumult, I scuttled from my hiding place and stole out of the ward.

The receiving room beyond was deserted and silent. I rushed past the nurse's desk and into the opposite ward, skidding to a halt between two long rows of beds.

This ward was different—utterly silent, utterly still. Each bed had an occupant, but the patients were not free. Straitjackets fastened hands to shoulders and tied ankles together. Bed straps bound bodies in place. Gags filled mouths, propped jaws open, kept tongues from being bitten off—or from forming words. I stared in pity at the patients and heard the quiet panic of breath in eighty straining nostrils.

I stalked among the beds and studied the fugitive faces in their sterile white wrappings. Some could be ruled out by sight—that redheaded berserker, that black-headed boy, that man with the double eye patches. Others required a check of the chart that dangled from the foot of the bed: "Johannes T. Godiva—melancholic" . . . "Michael Hartwick—megalomaniac" . . . "Jean Paul Rouel—opium addict . . ." Such perfectly sane names beside such damning diagnoses. "Fritz G. Heimsen—sodomite" . . . "Casimir Thoris Storaski—deviant" . . . "James Thomas—violent addlepate."

"Addlepate, perhaps—but violent?"

I stopped and stared. I would hardly have recognized him—his eyes closed, his skin sunken, the gag across his mouth biting into sallow cheeks, hair spiking on the pillow. Silence looked like a corpse, wrapped in straitjacket and straps. . . .

I pulled the Scots dirk from the sheath in my stocking. It

was a small knife, but exceedingly keen, and its tooth quickly chewed through the straps on the bed. As each popped, Silence breathed more easily. "Now, just the strait-jacket," I said, cutting away first the buckles on wrists and then the straps on feet. I canted the blade in those canvas sleeves and sliced them free of Silence's arms. The staff had set a cast on his broken arm, a plaster tube between his shoulder and his elbow. It was well done. I slid my dirk through the torso of the straitjacket and the legs as well and, last of all, cut that damned gag. Sheathing my dirk, I whispered, "All finished. You're free."

Only then did Silence's silvery eyes open, fixing on me. He sat up, and the straitjacket and bindings fell away as if they were paper. Only his bedclothes remained.

"Come on, then. Let's go," I said, grabbing his hand.

Silence clenched my fingers and rose in a flash. His eyes darkened with malice. "You threw me down once, but not again. This time, you're the one who'll die." He lunged, his hands wrapping my throat.

"Silence . . . it's . . . it's . . . me."

A dire smile spread across his teeth. "The Great Man—terror of London, lord of crime from Glasgow to Paris. But snip his lines—snip! snip! snip!—and his web folds and strands the spider—scurvy and scared."

"No . . . it's . . . Thomas. . . ." My throat closed as his hands tightened.

Enough. I buried my fist in his gut.

Silence whoofed and bent forward, though his viselike hold on my neck didn't release. Desperate, I kicked his knee sideways. Silence growled and fell beside his bed but pulled me down on top of him. We rolled once, getting tangled in the cut-up straitjacket. We rolled a second time, and I smashed my elbow into his chest. That blow sent air exploding out of his lips. I wrenched my neck free of his grip and scuttled back, panting.

"What's . . . happened to you?" I gasped.

Silence rose from the ground and hurled down the cut-up straitjacket. He gave me a wicked smile. "Watch out."

"What?"

A burly arm wrapped my neck, and its owner grunted as he tackled me. The orderly growled something in German.

"Wait! I'm not the patient!"

Silence strode past us and out of the ward, into the receiving room.

"He's the one!" I yelled, but the orderly only growled louder.

From the receiving room, there came a great crash.

The orderly lifted his head to look toward the noise, and for a moment his grip loosened. I bit his arm and rammed my elbow into his side and ducked my head and scampered away. The man was down for only a moment before he clambered up and lunged for me. I kicked a chair into his path and watched with satisfaction as he tumbled over it and sprawled to the tiles again.

Another crash came from the receiving room. I ran to the door and saw Silence clutching the white lapels of a different orderly. Silence hoisted the man into the air. "So, the trap closes!" he raved, hurling the orderly backward to smash against the door of the surgical theater. The door split in half, and beveled glass shattered.

Silence stood in the hailstorm of glass and wood. "Ha-ha! I know baritsu!"

He's mad, I thought. *Even more than before.*

Rapid footsteps approached behind me, and I remembered

the other orderly. I lunged aside and tumbled into a roll. The orderly charged, roaring, into the room, and he and Silence clapped eyes on each other.

"Was ist?"

Silence triumphantly crowed, *"Das ist!"* and vaulted toward his new foe. The two men grappled each other like bears. Beyond them, I glimpsed motion. The other orderly was clambering up from the wreckage of the door. He paused a moment to catch his breath and then threw himself also into the scrum.

I cringed, unsure what to do. Silence was out of his mind and violent. I couldn't take him with me. But if the orderlies *did* subdue him, there would only be more torture from the box with the wires. . . .

And, too, the scientist in me was intrigued by this strange device. . . .

I crept around the edge of the fight until I reached the doorway to the surgical theater. There, on one of the examination tables, sat the box with the wires and the crank. I tiptoed across the glass-strewn threshold and reached the device. It was heavy in my hands.

Silence's electrified figure formed the shape of a pentacle—a five-pointed star—but there was something more. His spirit seemed to be driven up from his body, an ectoplasmic presence that roiled in the air. It was as if this electric contraption had exorcised his soul from his body.

I studied the box. This machine held the secret to Silence's insanity. I swung it under my arm and stalked to the door to see how the fight progressed.

The two orderlies and Nurse Cragface were dog-piling Silence, calling for assistance and more straps. Soon, he would be back in his bed, and tomorrow, Dr. Burckhardt would work him over again.

I'd bought us a little time, though—time to learn what had caused this new madness, and time to correct it.

Stepping gingerly over the shattered glass, I picked my way to the front door, threw back the lock, and strode out into the nighttime streets of Bern.

17

WRAPPED VERY TIGHTLY

They have me. They won't let me get away. That's because I'm not supposed to get away. I'm supposed to be bound down and lie and wait.

I am a pupa. I am wrapped very tightly, and I am transforming. I can't remember what sort of worm I was before . . . can't guess what sort of bug I'm soon to be. Is this a cocoon or a chrysalis? Will I be a moth or butterfly?

18

UNDERSTANDING THE CONTRAPTION

It felt wonderful to march out the front doors of the Prefargier Sanatorium—especially given that only an hour before I'd been crawling into the ash trap in back. In fact, I felt downright rakish for the first time in days. *This* was my specialty: breaking, entering, taking, leaving. . . . I derived extra satisfaction from the generator under my arm. It felt like a grisly trophy—the heart of Cerberus ripped out by my own hand and borne away from the shattered gates of hell. . . .

Delusions of grandeur, however, cannot stand up to cold and wet. I spent that night holed up under a train bridge. Ah, yes—*this* was my true specialty: skulking, shivering, starving, snarling . . . A tramp. It took me a solid hour to fall asleep, at which point the Bern Express shrieked overhead, rolled to a stop in the station, and then rumbled back out again.

Another hour of boredom ensued. The exorcism machine proved too tempting to leave alone. Idly, I clamped it to the metal girders above my head and cranked. A shower of sparks rained down over me and burned little holes in my coat. That experiment should have convinced me to quit, but bored as I was, I decided to hook the machine to a dead rat near the riverbank. After all, I had once used electricity to bring a plenary worm back to life. The rat was not as cooperative. He merely sparked and shuddered, eventually emitting a thick gray smoke.

Scorched rat fur has a distinctly unpleasant odor.

By the time the sun rose, I wondered who had fared worse that night: me under my wet bridge or Silence in his nice warm straitjacket. Getting up and brushing myself off, I walked to the open-air market that had fed us the previous day. There, I snatched one small leek and was trying for a radish when someone grabbed my shoulder and spun me about.

I was poised to run, but the grinning, bewhiskered man greeted me avidly in German and pointed to the contraption I carried. I think he was an inventor—or mad. He held out a grubby fist with a few silver coins, and I felt tempted to sell the device—what with leeks and potatoes to look forward to. But I was not done experimenting with my exorcism machine.

I escaped the German, found a suitably dark alley, and gobbled my meager breakfast. Silence would have done much better. Though my belly was far from full, it was time to fill my mind. I wended my way to the Stadt- und Universitätsbibliothek. It was a grand old building: white limestone columns, windows with deep casements, a proliferation of porticoes. . . . Such architecture made sense in Rome, where windows could be flung wide for Mediterranean breezes, but not here on the roof of the world.

With the exorcism machine at my side, I climbed a set of broad stairs, entered a pair of double doors, and strode to the main desk. A young woman stood there, and I told her that I was a repairman there to check the gas lines. *"Bonjour, mademoiselle. Il y a un problème avec le gaz."* I hoisted the electrical contraption, clicked two of the alligator clips together, and gave the machine a crank. Sparks dutifully leaped between the metal ends.

Her eyes grew wide, and she smiled at me. *"Oui."*

I told her that the trouble was apparently in the science library and asked if she could point me to it. With heels clicking and skirts swaying, the librarian escorted me through the cavernous central hall and into a large wing behind it. The young woman gestured grandly to the maze of tight-packed stacks. *"Voilà, c'est là, la bibliothèque de sciences."*

I thanked her, kissed the back of her hand (I couldn't resist), and was rewarded with a blush as she pivoted and clicked away. It was a pleasant sight, watching her go: I was tempted to ditch the machine and this whole adventure and pick up where I had left off, but the last time I'd followed a skirt, I'd ended up hanging from a glacier. Even Anna hadn't been worth that much trouble. The librarian's swishing bustle was long gone before I roused myself from my reverie: "Silence in a straitjacket."

I attacked the stacks with a vengeance, first searching through books on electrical science—volts, amperes, frequency, direct current, alternating current—which led me at last to explanations of circuits and diagrams of generators. Aha! The very contraption beneath my arm was built on the specifications of the Gramme dynamo, with three sets of outputs for three separate circuits.

At last I understood the machine, but I still wondered what it had done to Silence. I shifted to books on medicine. The trail led me first to the "torpedo fish," an electric sea creature prized from the time of Christ for healing through electric shock. For fifteen hundred years, those poor fish were dragged from the Mediterranean and applied to one forehead or another. Then Ewald Georg von Kleist developed his Leyden jar—a device that could generate and store large quantities of electricity. By discharging his jar into patients, he claimed to cure paralysis, epilepsy, hysterics, and memory loss.

Memory loss! So Burckhardt wasn't a solitary quack: He came from a long line of them. But the generator hadn't restored Silence's memory. It'd left him raving mad. Why?

My hunt followed a new lead—men who had been struck by lightning. In *Galvanic Phenomena*, I read the following account:

A Lord Colin McComb of the Moffat McCombs has the unlucky distinction of being struck by lightning five successive times. Each strike temporarily rendered him savage and feral, like a man turned animal. On the occasion of the first strike, locals did not even recognize Lord McComb, so wild was his hair and demeanor. On the second occasion, he attacked a Scottish longhorn bull and wrestled the creature to the ground and gutted it and ate its spleen. On the third occasion, he pillaged a town and was driven off only by local lads who pelted him with rocks. When lightning had struck Lord McComb a fourth time, locals chased him to a lonely tor, intent on vigilante justice. Their job was done for them, however, by the fifth—fatal—lightning bolt.

Another account read as follows:

Among the Finns, one Iron Age cult of Thor used their native metal to fashion *skvias*, or twelve-foot-long lightning rods. With these implements, they made sacrifices to the thunder bearer. Priests conducted a prisoner to a mountain peak, required him to lie supine with legs and hands spread, and then chained his ankles, wrists, and neck to the *skvias*, which were pounded into the ground in the shape of a five-pointed star. If the prisoner could escape before a storm came, he was considered pardoned by Thor. If, instead, a storm came and struck him dead, he was considered a sacrifice. If the prisoner

was struck and lived, the priests considered him a wizard—
his mortal soul driven out of his body, and a divine soul driven
in. A few such wizards became priests in the service of Thor,
though most became necromancers in the service of Loki.

I was on the verge of discovery. The electric pentacle had
some arcane power to drive out one's spirit or to drive in the
spirit of another. Seeking the final piece of the puzzle, I con-
sulted a book of Celtic mysticism, which described the major
arcana of the tarot cards:

The pentacle, or five-pointed star, is a symbol of earth in its
perfect form, either the lost earth of Eden or the restored
earth of the end of times. The five points of the pentacle represent the five powers of good: Lugh's spear of living fire,
Mannon's magic ship, Conory Mor's singing sword, Cuchu-
lain's speaking sword, and the stone of destiny, Lia Fail. Human beings may claim any or all of these symbols of hope and
light in order to justly rule the world. When the star card is
laid in its dignified position, it symbolizes protection from
evil, divine help, and new birth.

And then, later:

The inverted pentacle, or the devil, is a reversal of the natural
power and beauty of the earth. It is an inversion, a perversion,
bringing an end to hope and life. Instead of claiming the divine power of good, the querent receives the destructive
power of evil. Instead of protection, this card offers plunder.
Instead of new birth, it offers demonic possession.

A chill crept up my neck. I remembered Silence's soul
driven up from his body, his demon-charged fingers gripping

my throat . . . I stared at the pentacle of protection and the inverted pentacle of destruction, and glimpsed another world. It overlaid the world of science; it churned up the phenomenological world like invisible winds churning up the sea. My body tingled. Every hair stood on end. I felt a queer, uncanny urge to flee.

Then a hand touched my shoulder. I leaped and spun around.

"Anna!" There she was: the same doe eyes and rosebud lips, the same blond braids arrayed in a heart shape around her head—and yet, she was different. In place of the white blouse and blue skirt, she wore a black dress with a high neckline—even a white bonnet. She looked like an old woman. I laughed harshly. "You've changed."

She glanced down at herself and blushed. "These aren't mine."

"Stole them from a line, did we? Not a very good thief—"

"I didn't steal them. I'm not a thief."

"No, you're worse. You're working with the gunman. He's your . . . your father." It was sheer speculation, but the sad steadiness of her eyes confirmed it. "You were planning a double murder, weren't you? While Daddy flings a man from the waterfall above, Daughter drowns another in the cauldron below!"

Anna's face grew red. "I don't know why I even came here." She strode off down the dark row of stacks.

"I know why," I said, picking up the generator and following her. "You came to play me. That's what you've been doing all along—all that helpless act, all that mourning for a father who didn't die five years ago, who's been hunting us for the past week. 'Let me stay,' she says. 'Let me buy you time,' she says, when really she's plotting with the killer. From the beginning—from *before* the beginning—you've been playing me . . ." I grabbed her arm and turned her about to face me, but her eyes were so hurt, I blurted the only thing I could think of: "I know about the cheese!"

"What?" she demanded, stepping forward.

We bumped together, and I stumbled—had to drop the generator and grab her waist to keep from falling. "A girl with a twenty-four-inch waist doesn't eat two blocks of cheese!"

She stared into my face. "You're insane."

"Am I? Is the gunman your father?"

"Yes."

"Have you traveled with him to Bern?"

"Yes."

"Did you rope me into all this?"

"Yes."

"Then I'm right about everything."

"About everything that's happened," she admitted, "but not about why it's happened. I *did* 'rope you in' but not because I wanted to kill you. Because I . . . I'd seen you—been watching you for days—wanted to find out who you were—"

"Part of your father's plan."

"Part of *my* plan. Father was tracking down his own quarry, and I'd helped him, yes—not knowing it would be murder. He promised it wouldn't be. He said when it was all over, we could start again, he and I. I wanted to see it. I wanted it all to be over, so Father's mania would be done, so I could have him back."

"Your father's a killer."

Her eyes glistened. "I know. I know that now. Maybe I knew it then. Maybe it's why I latched on to you. Father'd always taken care of me, always kept me alive, and if the worst happened—I don't know. Maybe I thought you could take care of me."

I shook my head bitterly. "You can take care of yourself."

"It wasn't just that. I have feelings for you, Thomas."

"You're *still* playing me!"

"No," she said quietly, "at first, it was a game, yes—for both of us."

"Yeah, at first."

"But now it's more than that. I stalled for you. I gave you a chance to escape."

"While you plotted with your father."

She drew her bonnet back from her face, revealing a purple bruise that ran from her jaw across her eye. "While I got beaten by him."

The sight of that bruise made my heart quail. I gently cupped her jaw. "I'm . . . sorry."

Anna seemed to be looking right through me. "He clubbed me and carried me down the mountain, held me hostage until we got to Bern, bought me these old woman clothes and took me to a flat and chained me to the radiator while he went to the sanatorium—"

"The Prefargier Sanatorium?"

"—to see his old friend Dr. Burckhardt."

"Burckhardt!"

"He's there, now, again," she said angrily. "He headed out before dawn, leaving me chained. But I could reach the rug, and I rolled it up and swung it to knock the pitcher and soap from the basin table and used the water and soap to grease up my hand and dragged it through the shackle"—she pulled back her sleeve to show her hand, the skin peeled by rough iron—"and I escaped. I came to warn you."

I stared at her wounded hand and took a step back. "But—how did you know I was here?"

"Father. He anticipates everything. He knew you would go to the sanatorium, knew you would run afoul of Burckhardt, watched as you came, watched as you left, when you

tried to rescue Silence, when you hid under the bridge. . . .
He told me your every move. Taunted me with it all. Loved
to report how my 'lover lad' was so inferior to him. So, when
he left, I escaped and went to the bridge and spotted you
leaving and followed, waiting for a chance to talk to you—"

"You expect me to believe all this? Whenever you need an
excuse, it's father-this and father-that. You're his puppet."

"She is," said a new voice: a man's voice. I spun to see a
living nightmare—the gunman leaning on his rifle-cane not
five paces from me.

I cringed back, keeping my eyes on the man while I
growled to Anna—"You led him to me."

"No . . ."

"It was all a trap."

"No . . ."

Her father advanced, his cane scraping the hardwood floor
beneath the stacks. "Yes, Thomas Carnacki. It all was a trap,
down to this very moment. But Anna didn't know. She was
simply the bait."

"So—you're going to shoot me?" I said, laughing. "You're
going to bring every person in this library running?"

Anna's father shook his head slowly. "I build better traps
than that."

He lunged atop me, and something glinted in his fist. I felt
a burning agony in my neck.

I staggered back, the man clinging to me, his weight riding
on the thing in my neck. Anna tried to catch me, but her father landed on top of us both. He laughed bleakly. "This ice
pick has poison on it, Thomas—a tree-frog neurotoxin from
Brazil, given to me by Burckhardt."

"No!" Anna screamed. She grabbed her father's fist and
tried to wrench the ice pick from my neck, but his fold was
implacable.

My nerves jangled, but even as my body began to slump, I felt the generator wedged under my leg. With one hand, I grabbed the alligator clips, and with the other, I cranked the generator. Sparks snapped. I rammed the clips into my attacker's mouth and cranked again. He lurched off me and staggered back, lips smoldering.

Anna yanked the ice pick from my neck and hurled it away. She stared in amazement and horror at her father. "I'm not your daughter anymore," she yelled through her tears. "If I ever see you again, I'll kill you."

The man stumbled backward. His hand clumsily swept a pile of books from a shelf. Then, wordlessly, he stumped around the corner and out of sight.

Anna bent down over me and kissed my face. "Oh, Thomas."

"You . . . you aren't . . . on his side."

She smiled sadly. "No . . . I'm with you." A tear fell from her eye onto my cheek.

Something creaked. Anna looked up. Dust streamed from the top of the bookshelf as it tipped ominously toward us. Then thousands of books and the shelves that bore them came crashing down on top of Anna and me.

19

BURIED ALIVE

They were buried alive in books, Thomas and Anna. Or at least Anna was. For all she could tell, Thomas was dead.

Under an avalanche of books and shelves, Anna couldn't move, couldn't see anything, but she could hear nearby voices muttering in consternation. The library staff must have come running when they heard the crash, and there must have been patrons out there, too. It sounded as if they were simply standing and looking at the mess, not digging into it.

"Help! Help us!" she cried. Her voice was weak in the airless space, but she drew a long, ragged breath and shouted in French: *"A l'aide! Aidez-nous!"*

The voices ceased.

"A l'aide! Aidez-nous!"

A half-dozen people all began speaking at once. Footsteps approached. Men growled instructions to each other and then chanted, *"Un, deux, trois!"* and groaned. Wood creaked, and an incredible weight lifted off the pile. A low boom sounded as they righted the bookshelf again.

"Nous sommes là, en dessous!" Anna called out, pushing weakly at the black mound of dusty volumes. Books cascaded down the outside of the pile and thumped on the floor, and hands began snatching them, lifting them, stacking them.

Someone grasped Anna's shoulder and let out a shout. Others worked rapidly to dig her out. A pair of gendarmes arrived with a canvas stretcher slung between two long poles. *"Rien de cassé?"*

Anna replied in French that she did not know if anything was broken. The gendarmes gently dragged her from the pile and slid her onto the stretcher. As they checked her head, neck, and arms, another pair of gendarmes arrived with another stretcher.

"Il est là. Aidez-le!" Anna pointed to the spot where Thomas lay, and the library staff and police set to work digging him out.

As they worked, one of them shouted, *"Qu'est-ce que c'est que ça?"* and lifted a walking stick—her father's gun. Anna nearly fainted to see it—but at least he no longer had it.

It was as much as she could bear. She laid her head down and nearly fell asleep. In time, rescuers dragged Thomas out of the book pile and conveyed him to the other stretcher.

"Est-il en vie?" Anna asked, trying to see his chest rise and fall.

They told her that he was alive, but his pulse and breathing were weak. *"Il s'accroche!"* Only then did she notice that Thomas still clutched the strange contraption that he had used to shock her father. The gendarmes tried to wrest it away from him, but Thomas held the thing in a death grip. They gave up, grimly discussing where to take the two injured people.

"Au Sanatorium Prefargier," Anna told them, *"vite!"*

20

VISIT FROM AN OLD FRIEND

I'm buried alive, can't move—can hardly breathe. But I'm not buried in earth. If this were earth, it might have been an accident, some cave-in. I'm buried alive in cloth—a straitjacket.

I'm a captive.

"Hello, Harold Thomas—or is it Harold Silence?"

I hear the words but can't see who speaks them. I see only the white-painted rafters above me, occasional gables poking through to show a sky cluttered in clouds.

Is this a hospital?

"You look miserable, my friend." A dark figure enters my line of sight—a tall man with an expression that combines snarl and smile. He stands over me. "Do you know who I am?"

His face makes fear skitter across my back. It's a face I've fixated on, one I should know. "I don't . . ."

His smile only widens. "Do you know who you are?"

This is a brutal question. I can't see myself, can I? How could I know who I am? Unfair. "No."

The man stoops over the bed and sets his hand gently on my forehead. He pats me as if I were a dog. "My dear, dear boy. Your head isn't what it once was. That great bump. Not so much here, but"—he shifts his hand to the side of my head, to a swollen mass beneath bandages—"here."

Pain stabs through my skull. I recoil in the straitjacket and shiver away from him beneath the straps of the bed. "Don't touch it! Don't!"

Again the smile, that brutal smile. The man pulls his hand back from my head and sits slowly in a nearby chair. "Yes. That is the problem. This brain of yours. Empty. It's not what I paid for. It's the attic without the treasure. . . ."

"Who are you?"

"How awful. You really don't know, do you? Tragedy! It's as if the library of Alexandria had burned!" The playfulness drains from his eyes, and rank resentment takes its place. "It *did* burn, my friend. That library, with all the wisdom of the ancient world—that goddamned library is gone. Gone! And your goddamned mind is gone, too. All that you knew, all that you were—gone, except this pathetic, festering hunk of meat. . . .

"I wanted you whole. It was part of my grand calculation. You destroyed me at the height of my powers, and revenge demands that I destroy you at the height of yours. Equations must equate, my friend . . . my pupil. But truthfully, you were never my equal, ergo any expression that equated us was an a priori falsehood. So if Burckhardt can't fix you, I shall have to settle for finishing what little remains. . . ."

"Nurse! Nurse!" I cry. This must be a hospital, and there must be a nurse.

"Don't bother. Burckhardt is a friend of mine—well, he's a man I'm blackmailing. And the difference between a friend and a man who is blackmailed is that you can control a man who is blackmailed." He pats my shoulder. "The nurse won't come, either. It's just you and me now. And in an hour, it'll be just you and the incinerator."

I don't want to die, but how can I save myself, strapped down as I am? I stall. "My mind is not entirely blank. There are many things I know about you."

His eyebrow twitches. "Truly? Do tell." He is unsettled. The eyebrow tells it. Let's see what else I can make twitch.

"You are a brilliant mathematician . . . a professor—the greatest teacher I ever had."

"Flattery can't save you," he says, but his eyelids are straight lines, and I know that he believes everything I've said so far.

"But the fawning, cloying admiration of your colleagues was an annoyance. They kept you from achieving what you could. They grasped the hem of your robe, begging you to pour your knowledge out into them, but in truth, they were holding you down."

His eyes drift from me, seeing things elsewhere. I look to his right hand, with its callus where the stylus would rest, with its shivering as if it had written a million words, all ignored.

"Your research had gone beyond them; you discovered equations that would save every one of us, every last mother's son—but some people misunderstood. They thought your calculations were immoral."

His jaw moves, and I see the word *yes* on his lips.

"And so, at last, you were forced out from among them. You'd gone as far as they would let you go, as far as mortal creatures would allow. Their laws were made for their own kind. Their morality was fashioned to control the rabble, not a man like you—not an immortal man. And so you experimented in ways that other men would abhor. You made advances that they could never recognize."

A faint sweat dapples the professor's brow.

"And you would have continued on this path, this trajectory that would carry you out of the world and among the stars—except that there was someone who wouldn't let you."

The professor shakes himself like a dog flinging away ditch water. His eyes focus on me, and his lips purse in satisfaction. "This isn't memory, is it? You don't know any of these things. You're fishing. It's deduction—your famous capacity for deduction." He laughs again. "You don't *know* me. You simply *read* me." He leans forward. "Well, I don't have to read you because I know you. And let me tell you about yourself."

"Please," I said.

"You are a strange little man. You have not completed a degree, though you pretend to have extensive knowledge in your fields of study. You are not an officer of Scotland Yard, though you plague them incessantly with your crime-fighting theories. You are not a musician, though you scrape at a violin at every chance. You are not a lothario, though you have saved many women and keep the intimate company of one man." His face is very near my own now, very large and threatening. "I could spend all day listing what you are not, but I would have a very hard time telling you what you are."

"I am your enemy."

The man withdraws his face from mine and nods deeply. He pauses to take a breath, an indulgence that tells me I have struck on a core truth. "You are my enemy," he repeats, and his hand rises above me, holding an ice pick. The shaft is stained red with a purplish liquid that glistens on the point of the tool. "You are my enemy. Nothing else matters—my name, your name. . . . It matters only that we hate each other, that we fought valiantly one against the other—and that I won."

He lifts the ice pick high above his head and then brings it down furiously to skewer my neck.

21

Admitted Again

The gendarmes lifted the stretchers from the wagon and carried Anna and Thomas up the steps of the Prefargier Sanatorium. They entered a receiving room that smelled of camphor and rubbing alcohol, and Anna coughed into her hand. At the center of the room sat an elderly nurse at a desk. She looked up in alarm, set down the charts she had been completing, and bustled toward the new arrivals.

"Tell Dr. Burckhart that Anna Schmidt has arrived," Anna said, but the nurse simply held out a warning hand before her.

In German, the nurse greeted the gendarmes and asked them rapid-fire questions about the patients, how their injuries had been caused, who was in worse shape. . . . The gendarmes gabbled out answers, and the nurse guided them to the surgical theater.

As the door barked open, Dr. Burckhardt started out of sleep in his wingback chair. He lurched up and crossed toward the patients. His eyes leaped between the stretchers, and his hands twitched excitedly. He directed the gendarmes to drape Anna's stretcher across one examination table and Thomas's across the other.

"*Was ist das?*" Dr. Burckhardt murmured, lifting the generator. "*Mein Generator?*"

"Es ist der Mann," the nurse said, tapping the bandages on Thomas's shoulder. She glanced at the other stretcher.

Burckhardt toddled up to Anna and looked down avidly, naked desire in his eyes. He began probing her head, neck, and shoulders for injuries. *"Guten Tag."* His hands moved downward.

"English, please," Anna said.

"Good afternoon, Miss—"

"Schmidt," she replied sharply. "Anna Schmidt."

He drew his hands off her hips, where they had lingered a moment too long, and he took a step back. "I—I . . . you've grown so much in the last two years, Anna. You're a woman."

She sat up and slipped her feet over the edge of the table. "My father sent me."

"Your father." Dr. Burckhardt blanched, but a weak smile squirmed on his lips. "Interesting . . ."

Anna slowly dragged one of the straps loose from the examination table. "He wants the antidote to the tree-frog neurotoxin."

Dr. Burckhardt took another step back. "Antidote?"

"Give it to me."

Burckhardt glanced at the nurse, who nodded once grimly. "Well—er—your father is, actually, here right now, and we'll need to clear it with him first."

Anna lunged, whipping the table strap around Burckhardt's neck and drawing it tight. He shrieked. She twisted the strap and cut off the sound. "You can breathe again after Thomas has been given the antidote." Anna glared at the nurse. "Get it!"

She looked a question at Burckhardt, and he nodded in red-faced exasperation. The woman crossed toward a large pharmaceutical cabinet with many drawers. Her finger wandered the cards on the front of the drawers until she found the right one. Then she drew it open and pulled out a small vial. "It may be too late."

"For the doctor's sake, it better not be. Give it to my friend. And if Thomas dies, Burckhardt dies."

The nurse shot a piercing look at the doctor, who struggled, purple-faced, in Anna's grip. He held out imploring hands. Giving a great sigh, the nurse replaced the first vial and pulled out a different one. Then, going to Thomas, she poured the liquid into his mouth.

Anna loosened her hold on the strap, letting Burckhardt gulp a bit of air. He tried to scramble away, but she pulled him back. "Grab another one of those vials, nurse—no tricks—and then show me where my other friend is."

"Your other friend . . . ?"

"The patient who arrived with Thomas here—the man my father is so interested in."

The nurse returned to the pharmaceutical cabinet and lifted another vial from the same drawer as the last. "Good girl. Now, I'll follow you. And if either of my friends dies, Burckhardt dies."

The nurse gave a perfunctory nod, palmed the antidote, and stalked from the surgical theater. Anna followed, keeping Burckhardt in front of her like a dog on a leash. She couldn't walk him through the hospital that way, so she snatched up a scalpel and slid the knife into the small of Burckhardt's back. Dragging the strap off his throat, she said, "Try anything, and I'll carve out your kidney."

Burckhardt nodded, the motion making beads of sweat cascade down his forehead. With a shambling step, he followed the nurse out of the surgical theater and into the receiving room. Patients waiting for admittance looked up hopefully as Burckhardt entered. He gave them a corpulent smile and waved as the scalpel drove him after the nurse into the violent ward.

Silence wasn't the only one bound down in that place. Beds lined either wall, and in each bed lay a patient in straitjacket and straps. They were belted down as if they were cargo instead of people. The nurse walked with a metronome gait between the beds until she reached the fifth one on the right. There lay a tall, thin man in a cloth cocoon. It was Silence, with his long face and hawklike nose, his narrow eyebrows and great lantern eyes. But those eyes were empty. Dead. Anna glanced down from his face, seeing a little red spot on his neck—a wound just like the one Thomas had.

"It's too late," the nurse said sourly.

"It can't be." Switching the knife to Burckhardt's throat, Anna reached down to Silence. His skin was still warm, and faint breath ghosted through his cracked lips. "Give it to him! Give him the antidote!"

"For God's sake, give it!" Burckhardt growled tightly.

Grimacing, the nurse popped the cork from the top of the vial and dumped the antidote into Silence's mouth.

Anna watched, fearful, wishing the blue cast of Silence's face would fade to pink, but there was no sign of life returning.

"It's too late," the nurse repeated.

"Shut up!" Anna commanded. The scalpel trembled in her hand, nicking Burckhardt's neck. *It can't be. It can't be.* All her thought had been bent on this moment, on undoing the things that she had helped her father do. But if Silence died after all . . .

"Damn you!" Anna thrust Burckhardt away across the floor and stooped to cut loose the straps that held Silence.

They popped one after another, and she flung them aside. "Get up, Silence! Get up!" The scalpel made swift work of the straitjacket as well. She dragged back the last bindings, but the man lay in his bedclothes as if he were a corpse wrapped in cerements. "Damn you."

"Vermin!" the nurse growled as she yanked a strap tight around Anna's throat. "Here's your medicine!"

"Good! Good!" Burckhardt declared, rubbing his own neck. "Finish her, if you wish. Her father has given her over. The orderlies can carry all three of them down to the incinerator." He flashed her a furious smile, turned, and ran for the door.

The moment he reached it, though, Burckhardt stiffened like a board and fell back, toppling slowly. He crashed to the ground, and out stepped Thomas Carnacki, shaking his hand as if his knuckles hurt.

"I've wanted to do that for two days." He stepped over the unconscious Burckhardt.

"Not a step closer, or I'll kill your girlfriend," the nurse shouted. She wrenched the strap tighter around Anna's neck.

Thomas halted, hands in the air and eyes wide with dread.

A sudden clang came from behind Anna, as if a cowbell had struck the nurse's head. She teetered for a moment, lost hold of the strap, and crumpled to the ground. Anna turned to see Silence standing there, smiling, a bedpan lifted high in one hand.

She returned his smile. "I'm glad to see you're back."

He shook his head bleakly. "I don't know who I am."

"As I said . . ."

Thomas hurried through the ward to reach his companions.

He still carried that ridiculous contraption beneath his arm. "Well, let's get him dressed and get him out of here," Thomas said. "I know a place where we can catch a train—for cheap."

COMPATRIOTS

We marched out of the sanatorium arm in arm: compatriots. We marched like those American revolutionaries in that painting *The Spirit of '76*—the old man with the fixed and somewhat insane gaze, the young man with the bandage around his head and the fife (or in my case, the generator) in his grip, and the drummer who glanced nervously at the other two.

"You know of a train out of here?" Silence asked, his eyes riveted to the road.

"Hey, Harry, you remembered something! Good for you. Short-term memory is better than no memory," I said, slapping him on the back. "And, yeah, I can get us on the Bern Express, no questions, no tickets."

Silence nodded as we marched toward the outdoor market. A breeze moved among the particolored tents and brought the aroma of roasted chestnuts to our noses.

Anna took a deep breath. "I'm hungry. I wish we had some money."

Silence growled, "I wish we'd eaten at the sanatorium—wish we'd hijacked a food trolley."

"No need for trolley or money," I replied. "We've got Silence."

He ended his staring contest with the road and looked at me querulously. "What have I got to do with it?"

"Don't you remember, Silence? You're a master pilferer. You can walk into that market with nothing and walk out with two bushels of potatoes in your back pocket."

"You're daft."

"Pot calling the kettle . . ."

Silence halted there in the cobbled lane. "Even if I am a master at . . . pilfering . . . I don't remember how to do it. And if I can't remember how to do it, I can't do it."

"I beg to differ. In Cambridge, I studied the brain. It's not just a big blob like the liver. Different parts do different things. This part, here—" I said, touching the swollen side of his head.

Silence howled, caught his hands between his knees, and doubled over.

I cringed and shot an apologetic look at Anna. "Sorry, Silence. Still sensitive . . . eh?"

He heaved a few breaths. "I—I—that spot . . . that spot . . ."

"That spot holds your identity—the memories of your life. Everything else is working fine. And one of the things that works fine is your talent for thievery."

Silence gave me a baleful glare.

"You fed us yesterday—an apple here, a carrot there, no one the wiser. I tried my hand this morning and nicked a leek and nearly got collared by a mad German."

Silence set his long, thin face toward the marketplace. He blinked in consideration. "You want me to go in there and . . . pilfer a lunch for us?"

"Yes."

Silence nodded and strode into battle.

Anna grabbed my arm. "What are you doing? The man's been poisoned, and you send him to steal food?"

"I've been poisoned *and shot*," I reminded her, "and just watch what he does."

Silence meandered into the market and paused for a moment beside a rugmaker's stall. He struck up a polite conversation with the gray-haired woman seated there, smiled and garnered a smile from her, examined her tassels with peculiar attention. . . . Bidding her good day, Silence moved to the next stall, where some sort of meat—I think it was pigeon—was skewered on thin sticks of bamboo and jutted from a rotating stand. Silence spoke to the swarthy man who sold the stuff, seemed to ask him about his cooking methods, and then, with hands folded behind his back, moved on.

"He doesn't know what to do," Anna said.

"I wouldn't bet on that."

As Silence walked farther into the market, the two of us followed. He chatted up a greengrocer, spent a good five minutes admiring the work of a blacksmith, tried a comb at the haberdashers, inspected eels at the fresh fish market, and ended his spree at the shop of a photographer who specialized in pictures of topless women.

Anna and I followed Silence out of the market and into a narrow alleyway. Anna approached him. "Sorry about that."

I said, "I'm not apologizing until I see how you made out."

Silence looked sidelong at me. "I couldn't bring myself to do it. They were such friendly people."

"Then what is that in your pocket?" I asked.

Silence patted the bulging spot, and confusion wrote itself across his brow. He reached in to drag out a picture of a woman in pantaloons and nothing else.

I snatched the photograph from him and took a long look. "Well done, my friend! I'll be keeping this."

"No you won't," said Anna, snatching the picture away, folding it once, and flinging it to land in the slop channel at the center of the street.

I laughed and pointed at Silence's shirt. "You're still bulging."

Silence dipped his hand in between buttons and pulled out a long, slim dagger.

"Brilliant!" I said. "You got the best one from the shop."

Before I had finished speaking, Silence reached into another pocket and produced a yam, two pears, and a stalk of celery. "I don't know how this got here."

"I do," I said, gathering the loot into the belly of my shirt. "But there's something else."

With a look of chagrin, Silence reached into his trousers and dragged out not one but three bamboo stakes with meat on them.

"This is scandalous!" Anna said.

I grabbed a stake and a pear and started in on my meal. Speaking around a mouthful of food, I said, "What else've you got?"

Silence shook his head in confusion, reached into his collar, winced, and pulled out a rose. His finger was bleeding where a thorn had pricked him. Ignoring the injury, Silence bowed his head and handed the rose to Anna.

Her annoyance melted away, and she accepted the flower. Then, with unseemly speed, she snatched up one of the meat sticks and started eating. I laughed, and Silence did as well, and soon all of us were giggling and eating and marching away down the alley.

Our walking feast was nearly done when we rounded a half-timbered cheese shop and spotted our destination: the train bridge where I had spent my sleepless night. My whole body shivered to see that merciless trestle, to think of the smoldering rat that remained beneath. Still, I put on a brave face.

"Here's our salvation!" I gestured grandly toward the train trestle. "The Bern Express stops there, the paying passengers lug their luggage to the porters and bustle about with tickets and all that nonsense—"

"While the unpaying scamps scramble up the ironwork of that bridge and clamber on between cars," Anna supplied, her brow furrowed.

I smiled sheepishly. "Great minds think alike?"

Silence meanwhile stared with starry eyes at the train bridge. "This seems an excellent plan—"

"Compared with being straitjacketed and poisoned," Anna observed, "it would."

"I'm glad we're in agreement," I said, extending an arm around each of them and propelling them onward.

We descended to the riverbank and walked along it until we reached the underside of the bridge. Night was full upon Bern, lending us its anonymity. I was about to brag about how I had spent the night here when Anna and Silence let loose a torrent of complaint against the place.

"Is that a fried rat?" Anna wondered, pointing.

I laughed nervously. "Must have fallen into the firebox—"

"The moss beneath the girders is worn away," Silence broke in. "Probably the bed of some opium addict with syphilis."

"Very perceptive," I allowed.

"What's that smell?" Anna asked. "They're not supposed to use the toilet while the train's in the station."

"Aha! Here comes the train now!" I lifted myself on tiptoes and listened intently. Yes, the train was on its way, some mere mile off, but still, my comrades could see through the ruse.

"*You* stayed here last night, didn't you?" Silence asked.

"I what?"

"You slept here last night," he repeated.

"Well . . . I . . . um . . ."

"Someone did," Silence elaborated, "as evidenced by that spot up there beneath the girders." He lifted the green-stained edge of my coat. "Moss." He sniffed. "Then, there's the smell. I'd first noticed it in the sanatorium. I thought it was fish, or rat, or some combination."

"It was fish and fried rat," Anna announced.

"Yes, but what about the burn holes in his coat? There's no sign of a fire built here—only . . . charred fabric, as if from sparks."

"Thomas!" Anna said with mock outrage. "You electrocuted a rat!"

"It was dead already. I was trying to . . . bring it back."

They laughed at me. When you are laughed at by a man who has spent two days in a straitjacket and a woman who wears clothes two sizes too large and three decades too old, you have been laughed at indeed.

"Here it is! The express!" I proclaimed above the sudden roar and rush and hiss of the arriving machine. It clanged and clattered across the bridge over our heads and pulled to a stop in the station.

"The express to what?" Anna asked.

I shrugged. "Does it matter?"

Silence gave a desultory shake of his head. "No." He scrambled up the slope before us, and Anna and I traded glances before we followed quickly after.

In moments, we had reached the level of the bridge. The train loomed large on the tracks, steam hissed from the engine, and dark figures moved around it. A metal arm swung out to pour fuel into the coal car and an elephantine tube poured water into the engine. I glanced toward the front of the train and saw the driver lean against the engine rail and light a pipe. Beside the passenger cars, conductors helped passengers. Directly ahead of us, a man stepped from one car, crossed the coupling, and entered the car behind.

"Here's our chance," I said. I vaulted toward the coupling and climbed up. Anna and Silence scurried after. I grasped Anna's hand, pulled her up beside me, and gave her an impetuous kiss. "For luck." Then I wrenched open the door of the rearward car. We stumbled through, Anna and I and Silence behind, into the packed passenger car. Folk still settled luggage into the overhead racks or beneath the benches.

"I think I'd better visit the powder room," Anna said, opening the door beside us.

"An excellent idea," I replied.

Silence piled in after us, closed the door, and turned the handle that said OCCUPIED.

Anna stared at us with a shocked expression. "Don't you think it's unseemly for two gentlemen and a lady to use the same lavatory simultaneously?"

"No one saw," I said.

"And it would be even more unseemly," Silence said, "for three people to be on a train without a single ticket among them."

Anna studied us both and then cast a glance at the metal toilet that emptied onto the ties below. "So, we have to stay here until the train is in motion?"

"Well, until the conductor passes by," I clarified.

Any tight space—a cloakroom, a closet, a boudoir—would have been uncomfortable for the three of us, but the tight-packed, stale-smelling lavatory on a transcontinental train was perhaps the most uncomfortable of all. Our feet crowded the tiny floor, our hips swayed outward to try to avoid intimate contact, our shoulders pressed the wooden walls of our enclosure, and our faces rose not only to avoid eye contact but to lift our noses out of the rising odor from the toilet. We listened.

Beyond the door came the clamor of a packed car, with passengers jostling for space, the occasional cry of a paperboy on the platform, and the hiss of pistons firing. Then—jolt and heave—the train lurched, car by car, into motion.

"Billets!" cried the conductor in the back of the car. *"Billets!"* Amid the chatter of passengers and the flutter of proffered papers, we could hear the man's patient punch, marking each ticket.

"Once he passes, we'll slip out and find seats," I said.

A sharp rap came at the door. *"Billets!"*

We traded fearful stares.

"Monsieur, je dois composter votre billet."

"Pas monsieur, mais mademoiselle," chimed in Anna, *"et pas maintenant!"*

"Toutes mes excuses, mademoiselle," came the man's reply, and he moved on. We heard the swish of the carriage door opening, the cacophony of the world outside, and then the quiet murmur of other passengers.

"He's in the next car. Let's sneak out," I said.

"One at a time," replied Anna.

"Right. One at a time." I opened the door and stepped out, closing it behind me.

The car was tight-packed, with every seat filled. I knocked on the lavatory and whispered, "I'm moving farther down, into the next car." Then I went to the end of the coach, opened the door, stepped out across the rushing gangplank, and looked through the window into the next coach. It was a sleeper, with a long aisle that luffed with thick curtains. At the far end, the conductor punched a pair of tickets, positioned them in a clip beside the bed, and then exited the car.

I opened the door, stole past berths with tickets, chose one lower berth that was empty, and climbed in. Turning, I peered out to watch for Anna. She appeared a moment later, and I stuck out my hand to motion her toward the berth. She clambered in beside me. Silence came staggering through the door shortly afterward, and Anna motioned him in.

"Here we are," I whispered. "Three peas in a pod."

"Three bugs in a rug," Anna said, sounding pleased at last.

"Three men in a tub," Silence volunteered faintly.

"*Billets!*" cried the conductor, and he ripped back the curtain.

As the gaslight of the aisle broke over me, I ducked my head beneath the covers and wished that Anna would do the same. Instead, she sat there rigidly beside Silence, a man more than twice her age.

"*Mon Dieu! Qu'est-ce qui se passe ici?*" asked the conductor.

"Ah, we are traveling companions," Anna said.

The conductor began to switch to English: "*Tous les deux* of you in the lavatory at once?"

"I'm incontinent!" Silence proclaimed. I could not see the reaction from Anna or the conductor, but I had to exercise a great deal of restraint to keep from laughing. "This is my nurse, and she helps me in the lavatory."

"He makes a terrible mess otherwise," Anna volunteered. "And he stops breathing at night, which is why I must tend him even as he sleeps."

"Well," the conductor said, "it all makes sense now. I feared somehow this geezer had robbed the cradle."

"Oh, no," said Silence.

"I have a much younger beau," Anna piped in.

"And I suppose I was looking just at your face before," the conductor said. "But judging by your dress, well—you're nearly thirty, aren't you, mademoiselle?"

"Nearly," she said.

The conductor laughed. "All right then. Still, I need to see your tickets."

"Well, ah," Anna said nervously, "where did you put the tickets, Mr. Thomas?"

"I, well," Silence answered, hands rustling though his shirt. "I . . . thought I . . ." He stopped, and I heard the sound of paper in his fingers. "I don't seem to have tickets, but will this do?"

What have you done, Silence—pulled out more erotica?

"That will do nicely, sir. Twenty Swiss francs for a sleeping berth to Paris."

"Paris!" Anna exclaimed before she could help herself.

As the conductor punched a pair of tickets for them, he said in a rueful voice, "Yes, I'm sorry. It was just fifteen francs to Paris until last month, but—such is the price of progress."

"A high price, indeed!" blustered Silence.

"Don't get worked up," Anna said. "You know how that affects you."

"Thank you both. And enjoy your time in the City of Lights."

I heard the curtain draw closed again. Silence nudged me: "He's gone."

I came up for air. "That was a close shave. Where did you get the cash, Silence?"

"Apparently, I pilfered more than celery back there."

The three of us allowed ourselves a little laugh, which subsided soon into quiet. We lay side by side, staring at the ceiling and counting our fortunes. We had a berth to Paris on an all-night train, a pair of tickets in the clip outside to keep anyone from disturbing us, and the certainty that we had left Anna's father far behind.

"Hey." I looked at Anna. "All this time—in all this craziness, you've never even told us who your father is."

She breathed deeply, steeling herself. "My father's name is . . . Professor James Moriarty."

I let that name sink in before asking, "Who?"

Anna laughed. "We have a long trip. Why don't I tell you the story of me and my father?"

BOOK II

A PROBLEM
FINALLY SOLVED

23

THE THIRD TONE

FROM THE MEMOIRS OF PROFESSOR JAMES MORIARTY:

A man does not become great: He is born as he is—great or petty. Men do not get to choose the magnitude of their lives, but only the direction, whether they will be good or evil.

From birth, I, James Moriarty, have been great. For the majority of my life, I had chosen to be a great good man. Three years ago, though, my choices began to change, a change that the mild reader will come to understand.

Let me begin at the beginning—or what I remember as the beginning. My first memory comes from 1849, when I was four. My father, Matthias Moriarty, took me to a vespers service in Jesus College, Cambridge. Father was not a religious man, but he sought solace after the loss of my mother to whooping cough. During that vespers service, the organist performed a Bach fugue in C. While Father sat in the pew, steeped in grief, I slipped off, sneaked along the nave, and took up a post behind the organist. There, I stood—mesmerized.

"C," I murmured.

Father had shown me the note on the clavier in our apartments and had told me it was the key to unlocking all of music. From that day forward, I could find any C on any keyboard—even on the six stacked keyboards of the organ console and the foot pedals beneath. I tried to make out the movements of the organist's hands, climbing the keys like a pair of demon-possessed spiders, but I could not. The movements of his feet, however, were clear:

When his foot rested on C, the music was grand, broad—stable.

When his foot leaped *down* five notes from C, the music was new and hopeful.

When his foot leaped *up* five notes from C, the music sounded like it was on the verge of changing—pregnant with possibility.

I stood rapt, listening to the same fugue that everyone else heard but finding in it the sweet mathematics of music itself. Those three notes—C and what I later learned to be F and G—were stability, movement, and transformation . . . or earth, water, and fire . . . or body, mind, and soul . . . or Brahma, Vishnu, and Shiva. . . . It was no wonder that music could fashion landscapes in the air.

"There you are!" Father growled, clutching my collar. "Disrespectful, disobedient, disastrous!" He hauled me down the nave and out of the sanctuary. I tried to gabble out an explanation, to outline the forces in music, but no explanation could prevent the beating.

I've held on to that moment for the rest of my life—my first memory. I've clutched it to my chest like a memento, and it has defined me. I was doomed to hear the same music that everyone else heard, but to be changed by it, to have the mathematics of it imprint on me. And it would not be simply music that plagued me, but every human endeavor: sculpture, architecture, statecraft, history, phrenology. . . . I was defenseless against the exquisite mathematics of the world, and whenever I tried to tell others about it, they turned a deaf ear or a sharp hand.

As time went by, my four-year-old self grew into a precocious and irrepressible young man. My father meanwhile grew into an intractable alcoholic. In his sober moments, he made arrangements for me to board at Barswidge public school, and I went gladly, eager to escape my horrible home.

By the time I reached boarding school, I had learned to keep silent about my theories. I confided only in a tattered notebook locked at the bottom of my trunk. In it, I continued my study of the mathematics of music. I discovered other sounds that moved the mind: moods of melancholy or love, ferocity or bliss. I also discovered that there was a devil in music, a note three whole steps above or below C. *Diablos de musicale*, the composers called it. It lurked between the perfect fourth and the perfect fifth—a half step into destruction.

I soon learned there were devils in the world, too. An upperclassman named Gerald Johnstone had begun pounding my shoulder whenever I passed. Gradually, the abuse escalated. One day, Gerald waited until I was in class and then broke into my locked trunk. He paraded my clothes around the dormitory, ate the crackers that I had stored to quiet my stomach at night, and then found my notebook. Gerald gathered a jeering mob around my bunk and staged a dramatic reading. As he finished each page, he tore it out, crumpled it, and tossed it into the fire.

By the time I returned, my tormentors had fled, leaving my shirts, breeches, and knickers tossed all through the dorm room. I ran to the trunk, but my notebook was gone. Snickers came from the hallway as I gathered my belongings.

In the days that followed, my classmates wouldn't identify the vandal, but Gerald Johnstone's smug smile made the culprit clear.

Then I would defend myself in my own way. I turned my mathematical mind to a new endeavor: building traps. I wired my trunk so that if a certain switch were not triggered, a small catapult within the trunk would launch a brick at the intruder. I returned the next day to find my clothes thrown in the fire, but also to follow a trail of blood drops to the infirmary, where Gerald Johnstone was recovering from a broken nose and a knocked-out tooth. It was a victory of sorts: I could eventually save up for more clothes, but Gerald would nevermore have that tooth.

When he returned to the dorm, he was full of bluster and threats. I met these with my own quiet warning: that anyone who tried to open my trunk again would regret it deeply. I had already secretly rigged the box, fastening a cleaver within the upper lid and bolting a powerful set of springs on the hinge. I also included a timing device so that the trunk would stand open for ten seconds. At that point, if the trigger was not set, the trunk would slam shut—cleaver and all.

Next day, when I returned to the dorm room, my trunk was closed tight, and the rest of the boys looked at me with a sense of horror. I went to my trunk, pressed the trigger, and opened it. The box was empty except for Gerald Johnstone's right thumb and forefinger.

I had no more trouble with Gerald Johnstone or anyone else at Barswidge. My traps had earned me something that I had never had before: a reputation. Its power was uncanny. Though no lock could have stopped the likes of Gerald Johnstone, a ferocious reputation could. That devilish demeanor soon became a prized possession of mine, a defense against the bullies of the world. I have maintained and further cultivated that reputation throughout my life.

At sixteen, I had outgrown Barswidge and won a fellowship to Jesus College, Cambridge—the place where I had first discovered the mathematics of music. In the intervening time, I had applied my calculus to a thousand other things—the flight of birds, the intricacies of snowflakes, the branching of arteries, the formation of thunderheads. Out of the ashes of my first notebook rose tome after tome of calculations. My notes were so extensive that one student anonymously reported that I had stolen the sketches of Leonardo da Vinci. A minor tribunal resulted, in which my notebooks were compared to those of the master. The differences were obvious: though we both wrote in Latin, I wrote only in the *forward* direction; for that matter, Leonardo occasionally failed to carry a 1.

All of these doings were only trifles for me, simply ways of passing time. I had not had a truly profound revelation since that night in Jesus College when I was four.

But then I took a Christmas break in London. In a cheap walkup flat in Whitechapel, I sat at the window and stared down at a slushy street called George Yard. Carts clogged it and people tromped along the pavements and filth sluiced down the slop channel—and I suddenly heard the fugue again.

Those primal forces of stability, movement, and transformation weren't just in music. They were in the world. They *moved* the world.

I began sketching the trajectories of the cabs as they raced along, the policemen as they walked their beats, the nannies as they led their gosling broods, the whores as they staggered from gin to John. I plotted the motions of all the people who happened along George Yard and graphed them against the three great tones.

First was the pedal tone of stability. Everyone followed that sound: the need for food and clothing and shelter, the desire for safety and love. This was the foundation of civilization. Leaders played that tone to fill mines and pews and trenches.

The second tone was that of newness and movement. It extended the wish of self-preservation to sons and daughters, to those who would carry on. The bosses of men played this tone also to move the masses, and the mothers and the teachers followed its path.

The third tone was the pitch of transformation—of transfiguration. It promised escape from the world and the flesh and the limits of life, escape into something altogether new. No ruler had learned that tone, no boss of men; they themselves were deaf to it.

But I heard it. I had been hearing it all my life. It was the sort of tone that makes a young man sit at a window for a week and map the trajectories of passersby. But who else could hear that tone?

On my fourth day of charting, I found someone—a baker who led his wife and seven children on an afternoon stroll to the closed bakery. They would feast on day-old pastries. For that reason, I had ascribed the man's actions to the second tone and would not have given him a second thought except that a scamp decided to pick his pocket.

The baker swung about and clamped his fist down on the boy's wrist and stared at him furiously. "What're you up to then, eh?" the baker growled, the words rising through my open window. "Takin' hard-earned keep out of the hands what bled to make it? Me rising before dawn and workin' a full day before you even roll over in that gutter you're in? See them, there? Eight mouths plus mine. You snatch the bread out of 'em? Since when've you been adopted? Since when're you my son?" The scamp cringed back and twisted to get his arm free but couldn't. The baker grabbed the coins out of the boy's hand, struck him a blistering slap across the cheek, and sent him sprawling to the pavement. He leaped up, bawling, and bolted into the street.

Then, the third tone struck—for this baker who had just lectured the scamp about his hard work and about his wife and children forsook them all. He dropped the coins and charged out into traffic and hurled the scamp away just as the four-horse carriage thundered up. Sixteen steel-shod hooves punched through the baker, and four steel-rimmed wheels mashed him. In an instant, he had left the world, had made his wife a widow and his seven children orphans. The scamp, meanwhile, scampered away.

That man had heard the third tone. At least for the briefest second, he heard its call to transcend, and he answered. He was mortal no more.

Two days later, there was another such man—a young man with an easel under one arm and a box of paints and a folded-up stool under the other. He positioned himself beside a street lamp with a view down George Yard and began soliciting passersby to have their portraits painted. A dozen solicitations, a dozen rejections, and then at last a black-suited businessman lingered. He reached into his waistcoat pocket, handed over a crown, and sat down on the stool, as stiff as a tailor's dummy.

The artist took the measure of the man and set to work.

Strangely, though, the young artist did not paint the man, but instead a portrait of the sun—a brilliant white disk emanating rays through a swollen red sky. The sense of vitality in the canvas was overwhelming, a furious outpouring of life like that in Blake's *Ancient of Days*. This was not a portrait of the man's outside, but of his inside—the blazing soul buttoned up in the business suit. It was as if by painting this portrait, the artist was transforming the man himself.

At last, the painter finished his work. Pitching brushes into a pot of kerosene, he rubbed his hands on a rag, lifted the painting from the easel, and turned it with slow savor to show to his subject.

The businessman snatched the canvas out of the painter's grip and began to shout. His hand jabbed into the artist's pocket and wrenched out the crown. Then the businessman lifted the portrait—the eternal image of himself—and broke the frame over his knee. Some of that white-golden paint smeared his trousers. He stalked away.

I sat, cold sweat dappling me, and watched the artist grieve his work. For a long while, the young man did nothing but crouch beside that broken canvas, trying to straighten the frame, trying to dab out the knee print. At last, he sorrowfully set the painting in the gutter.

Then he did something remarkable: He pulled out another canvas, set it up, and began to ask passersby if they wanted a portrait. Twenty solicitations and twenty rejections—and then a dowager with a magnificent oval hat and a minuscule lapdog sat on the stool. The drama played out just as it had before. Again the painter painted a radiant portrait, again the woman cried her outrage. . . . Another crown lost, another painting defiled, another time to mourn. . . .

And the painter set up a new canvas and began again.

By the time the lamplighter had come, there were five ruined canvases in the gutter, and the painter's easel and paints were smashed beside them. The painter was gone, clapped in irons by the police and led away to jail—or perhaps to an asylum.

Gone was another soul who heard the third tone.

"Next time I see such a soul," I pledged to myself, "I'll go to the gentleman and meet him before he can be killed or jailed."

But next time, it was not a gentleman at all, or even a lady. It was a whore.

24

A Lady Found

FROM THE MEMOIRS OF PROFESSOR JAMES MORIARTY:

Out of the darkness, she appeared: Susanna was her name. I did not know that then, of course, though she is now emblazoned on my mind, and I cannot think of her as anything but Susanna.

She arrived on George Yard with the slatternly tread of a streetwalker—a saunter that began at her high heels and propagated itself to the peak of her head. And Susanna not only walked like a woman of ill repute: She looked like one. She was dressed in a red-tiered skirt trimmed in black lace and a low bodice that displayed her bosoms like a pair of apples. Her face was painted as thickly as an actor's. And she smoked.

How could this be any kind of transcendent creature?

But she didn't solicit. She paid no heed to the men who shouldered past her down the pavement, nor to the women who hissed as they went by. Instead, Susanna stood with her head tilted back and stared up into the sooty heavens. I followed her gaze.

The night was starless, moonless, black beyond the reach of the street lamps. The sky was as dark as the descending boot of God. But staring up into that abyss, Susanna smiled.

What could she be seeing?

Hope tingled through me. This was my last chance. I could not forgive myself if I let a hansom roll up and the door swing wide and the girl glide in and vanish forever. Turning from the window, I grabbed my coat and raced out the door and down the stairs and onto George Yard and dodged among hurtling cabs. The other folk on the sidewalk parted before me, and I ran to her and skidded to a halt. I didn't know what to say, but it didn't matter: She took no notice of me.

My eyes flashed from her painted face—dramatic like a Kabuki mask—to the black sky overhead. "What . . . what are you looking at?"

She didn't move, as if she were unaware of my presence—or were very aware. "The snow."

The sky was pure black. "What snow?"

Instead of answering, Susanna sent a thin jet of breath purling up from her lips. It floated into the air, formed a small cloud, and then began to sparkle. Next moment, tiny snowflakes cascaded down to settle on her face. They shimmered there for the briefest instant before melting and sinking into her skin.

There it was: transfiguration. Her breath became snowflakes. Some man had tarted her up in this costume and had troweled makeup onto her face and had booted her into the street where her lips were meant to pucker for men, and yet she saved them to kiss the black sky.

I doffed my coat and whirled it out like a cape and wrapped Susanna in it. She breathed deeply, drawing my scent into her lungs, then sent the essence of me into the air to freeze and sparkle. Her shoulders spread within my coat. Still, she had not looked at me.

"Come back with me," I urged her, "to my room."

Before she could answer, a man and wife, buttoned up against the cold, waltzed past, arm in arm. The man sneered at us: "The fellow and the slut."

I stared defiantly after them. "Announcing yourself, guvnor?"

The man—a foot taller than I and twice my weight—stopped in his tracks and pivoted smartly about, his brass-headed cane hoisted in one hand.

I flashed him a fearless smile: "Let's go, then."

His fat face twitched, and he tried to affect an imperious air: "Yes, young man. Do—go!"

My feet were planted on the pavement, and my smile only grew.

He and his wife pivoted again and strode rapidly away. At intervals, the man glanced back at me until he and his wife had disappeared beyond Bucks Row.

I turned to the young woman and saw that her face was still lifted to the sky, still wet with melted snowflakes. "Come back with me, to my room."

Only then did I realize she wasn't looking at the sky. She was looking at me. And it wasn't snowflakes that wet her cheeks. "It's like you fell from heaven."

"I did." I raised my elbow toward her. She lifted her hand from within my coat and set her slender fingers on my forearm. With the lady at my side, I turned and set off down the pavement. "And where did *you* fall from?"

She blinked, drawing a deep breath. "No great distance."

We said little else, she and I, as we strolled along the shopfronts and wended our way past parked cabs and dashed among rolling ones. On the other side of George Yard, I opened the door of the boardinghouse and gestured her within. She climbed the narrow stairs past the flickering gaslight, and I guided her to the wide-open door of my rooms. Glancing within, I suddenly noticed how dismal the place looked.

"Forgive the squalor," I said.

"It's nice," she answered, entering. Then, in a different voice, she said, "I'm supposed to ask to see the money."

I laughed, closed the door behind us, and slid the coat off her shoulders. "Why? Are you a burglar?"

"The money's supposed to be on the dresser before anything happens."

"Who says?"

"My fath—my . . . manager."

I drew her to a settee and compelled her to sit down. Then I knelt before her and held her hands. "Your father sends you out?"

Her face trembled behind the cracked paint. "I'm supposed to see the money."

"All right." I dug into my pocket, dragged out my last five sovereigns, and smacked them into her palm. "There. Will that be enough?" She tried to slide three sovereigns back to me, but I wouldn't take them. "Your father sends you out?"

"I got eight sisters to support—"

"Isn't that your father's job?"

She shrugged. "This is what he does—"

"What about your mother?"

"Mother?"

I blinked impatiently at her. "You have eight sisters."

"None of us have a mother."

"Well, where did you come from?"

"The orphanage," she said, prying her hands out of mine.

I sat back on my heels, understanding at last. "You're all orphans?"

"A family, now. Some are older. They're kind of like our mothers. But you don't get too attached to any of them. They don't last long. Just Father does."

"Just Father does . . ." I echoed, thinking this through. My heart felt small and cold. "Listen—do you love this man?"

"What?"

"Do you love your father?"

"No," she said, her eyebrows furrowing. "But he's . . . *Father*."

I gently reached to her, taking her hand again in mine. "I don't have much money—just those five sovereigns until I return to Cambridge—"

"Cambridge!"

"Yes, and there, I have a monthly stipend from *my* father—enough for both of us to live and eat."

"What are you saying?"

"Come with me."

"What?"

"Come live with me."

"For sex?"

"No. Not for sex. For life. For learning."

She shook her head miserably. "I can't read."

"I'll teach you."

She was beginning to weep. "You don't even know my name."

I smiled fearlessly. "What's your name?"

"Susanna," she said in surrender. "Susanna Peshwick."

"Pleased to meet you, Susanna Peshwick." I kissed the back of her hand. "My name is James Moriarty."

She was crying. "Why? Why would you do this?"

I reached up to catch her tear on the tip of my thumb. "Because . . . because . . ." What was I to say? I was doing this because of the third tone, that strange, transformative tone? For a moment, I feared she wouldn't understand, but then I remembered the snowflakes on her face. "It's because of the snowflakes," I said at last, tilting my head back and pursing my lips and letting breath roll into the air.

Susanna watched me, and the tears stopped coming, and a slow smile cracked the makeup she wore.

THAT NIGHT, I washed Susanna's face and shared with her the last of the cheese and bread I had. She slept in the bed, and I slept on the settee. Next morning, we went together to the train station, and we bought two tickets to Cambridge and arrived to set up house together in my apartments.

I sold a few books from my freshman studies and bought Susanna some new clothes. Otherwise we lived off the money from Father—and the few extra sovereigns I could earn per month by tutoring. Susanna was my main student, though—and my best. She had never learned to read or write, but within a month, she had grasped the basics of letters and words. In two, she could follow along as I read from Milton and Newton. More than letters, though, she had a natural genius for numbers and chemistry.

In one of our first projects together, we worked out the geometry of snowflakes. Beginning with two hydrogen atoms and one oxygen atom, we mapped the possible molecular combinations and settled on the most stable structure. Then, we modeled that structure in clay and quills and played with the little forms until we discovered the manifold ways that these tiny pieces could fit together. All were hexametric—six sided.

I wrote up our results in a monograph, and Susanna provided illustrations. We published *The Molecular Basis of Snowflake Formation*, by James Moriarty and Susanna Peshwick—and it remains the authoritative document on the subject.

How prophetic those first snowflakes had been.

And so it went with us. I taught her what I was learning,

and Susanna joined me in research and experimentation. We published our findings together, and I soon came to be known as the heir apparent to the seat of Newton. Susanna came to be known as my brilliant and mysterious and beautiful mistress. It was, of course, unfair that she should be eclipsed by me, though I hoped she would be content enough until I could secure a position and pay for her own schooling.

I had just begun my final year, though, when I realized Susanna was not content. The sweet serenity had drained from her face, and she always wore a look of severe focus. I did what I could—placed her name first on our next monograph, encouraged her to conduct her own research, but nothing could bring back her joy.

At last, I guided her to a chair beside our apartment window, knelt before her as I had on that first night, and begged to know: "Susanna, what have I done?"

She looked quizzically at me. "What do you mean?"

"I've tried to be true to my pledge—food and clothing and shelter, learning, life—"

She nodded. "You have been true."

"I've never required anything of you except that."

Her eyes began to tear. "Yes. You have never required anything of me—"

"What is it, then? What have I done?"

Susanna blinked. "I *want* you to require something more." She stood, still holding my hand, and led me to the bed. I had, of course, wished for this moment from the start, but my oath as a gentleman had bound me. Susanna unbound me.

I found a new course of study that year. While I earned a first in maths and physics, I learned even more about the body and heart of a woman. And just after I had accepted a fellowship at Jesus College, Susanna educated me in a new mathematics—that of trimesters.

"You're pregnant?" I asked.

"Yes," she said gently.

I looked about at that apartment we had shared for a year and a half, and I tried to imagine where we would put a crib. "We'll need a bigger place."

Susanna smiled at me. "We'll need a bigger life."

She was right. No longer would it be just the two of us against the world, but now three. No longer could we stroll hand in hand across Jesus Green, but now would have a pram bumping along between us. I felt grieved. Our new life together would come to an end, and an altogether different life would begin.

"I suppose I'll have to marry you," I murmured, thinking aloud.

The smile melted from her face, and she said, "For a mathematical genius, you certainly are an idiot."

I stared at her. "I won't have to marry you?"

"No," she replied, taking my hand. "You will, but—but what sort of man proposes by saying 'I suppose I'll have to marry you'?"

Of course, she was right. I was a fool—and I nearly compounded the problem by apologizing. Instead, I knelt before her, looked her in the eye, and said, "Susanna Peshwick, will you marry me?"

"I suppose I'll have to."

WE WERE married on the Bridge of Sighs in St. John's College, a small ceremony with the rector and two colleagues as witnesses. There, in the sight of God, we were joined in holy matrimony till death us do part.

Despite her pregnancy, Susanna began her formal studies that very term. Her classmates were appalled that a woman— that a *pregnant* woman—should be among them. They became even more appalled as they discovered how very much she knew and how rapid her thought processes were. Jabbering tongues were silenced in the first few weeks of her time among them, replaced by gaping mouths and then by smiles. Soon, a number of the fellows were asking for her help with assignments, and a few even had designs that went beyond that—until I disabused them of their youthful ambitions.

And in time, as slight as Susanna was, her pregnancy was apparent to all. By then it did not matter. Her power as a scholar was matched only by the severe reputation of her husband.

She began to bring home her own theories and ideas: More monographs lay in our future. She turned her mathematical genius on social issues, creating models of human behavior that were powerfully predictive in large populations. Susanna studied the effect of education on reproductive age, the effect of career choice on life span, the effect of subsistence style on political affiliation, the effect of opiates and alcohol on cognition and performance. . . .

Though she began her work with large populations, she refined her models to be increasingly specific. Eventually, she claimed to be able to prognosticate the actions of five strangers to a specific stimulus.

"I'll have to see it to believe it," I said.

"Come along, then."

"I was afraid you'd say that."

Susanna led me to the banks of the Cam, where we met two of her professors—Drs. Applewight and Green. She asked us all to sit down on the grass. It was a fine September day, the dew just gone from the ground and a gentle mist meandering atop the river. Nearby, a young man sat beside a tree and worked feverishly on a manuscript he was writing. Behind him, two old gentlemen were engaged in a lawn-bowling match. In the distance, a young man poled his punt up the Cam, a young woman sitting within the boat and holding a picnic basket on her lap.

"If a pregnant woman were to fall into those waters," Susanna asked us, "which of those five people would leap in to save her?"

I laughed, fishing a sovereign from my waistcoat and pressing it into Susanna's hand. "None, I would wager."

She glared at me, both affronted and intrigued. "You think no one would save me?"

"No one," I replied flatly, "because your husband would not let his wife get near enough to the water for such a thing to happen."

Susanna smiled, wrapping her fingers around the coin and lowering it into a pouch at her waist. "One wager lost," she said. "After all, no good husband would stand in the way of his wife's work. This is your wife's work, and you are a good husband, ergo—"

"Oh, Sue, be serious! *I* will rescue you."

She replied archly. "You cannot swim."

"It makes no difference!"

"And you're wearing your best suit."

I nodded grimly. "Now *that* does matter."

Dr. Applewight let out a roar of laughter and smacked my shoulder, and Dr. Green gave me a sympathetic shrug.

"I want that coin back when I'm proved right," I said.

Susanna turned to the other two. "Well, gentlemen. Place your bets."

Dr. Applewight, a rosy-cheeked fellow with muttonchops, looked dubiously at the old men bowling, the young man writing poetry, and the other young man in the boat with his ladylove. He reached into his own purse and clapped a sovereign in Susanna's hand. "The young woman."

I barked, "You must be joking! She's got twelve petticoats if she's got one. She's a walking sponge. She'd soak up the Cam."

Though all of us laughed, Applewight said, "Ah, but the physics of sponges do not occur to young ladies, who have especial empathy for their own kind when great with child."

Susanna flashed the coin in her hand, smiled, and secreted the thing again in the pouch at her waist. "I can tell you, you are wrong, sir."

"What?"

"I have been a young, single woman recently and can attest that they see pregnant women as creatures altogether different. The one is trying to find a man, and the other trying to keep one."

"And both are doomed to failure," said Applewight cheerily.

"And what do you say, Dr. Green?" asked Susanna.

Dr. Green was a round, bald-headed man with a congenital squint that might have been confused with a smile. "Clearly, it will be the brown-haired lawn bowler."

"Clearly?" Susanna repeated, holding out her hand for the coin.

"Well, yes. The poet would like to believe he would save a girl, but he is a poet—all dreams and no action. He is sitting alone for a reason. And he is poor—a poet with perhaps two sets of clothes. He'll think twice before wetting them."

Susanna laughed, a scintillating sound that always scoured away the gloom. "You are right on every count about the poet—just as I would have said it—but what of the punter and the two bowlers?"

"The punter wouldn't abandon a girl he himself is hoping to impregnate—if you pardon my candor—"

"Nothing to pardon—"

"—to save a girl that"—he gave me a sheepish grin and blurted—"that someone else has impregnated."

"True."

"So that leaves the two bowlers. Now, the astute observer will see the lurching step of the gray-haired one and will glimpse beneath the fold of the pant knee a rounded hinge, and will know that the man has a wooden leg."

"Excellent!"

"Which, coupled with his age, makes him incapable of saving a pregnant woman—whereas the brown-haired man is hale and whole and younger, too. If anyone saves her, it would be he."

Susanna took his coin, spun it between finger and thumb, and tucked it into the pouch at her belt. "I'm sorry to say that you, too, are wrong. The man who will save me is the man with the wooden leg."

The professors and I all spoke at once: "Bosh!" "Preposterous!" "What nonsense!"

"I'll show you." Susanna undid the purse and tossed it to me. "For safekeeping." Then she rose and strode away from us, her black skirts swaying back and forth. She walked along the path until she had come to a point equidistant between the subjects—the poet at the tree, the lawn bowlers, and the punter and his date. Then, with theatrical flare, she slipped on a stone and went tumbling down to crash into the Cam.

The punter stood tall, staring into the brackish water and prodding with his pole. The young woman with him wailed quietly and pushed the water gently aside as if she was clearing sand from the lid of a treasure chest. She apparently could not catch a glimpse of the drowning woman.

Meanwhile, the poet leaped up and screamed, and a rogue breeze riffled the pages of his epic poem and bore them away. The poet gave chase.

Last of all, the two lawn bowlers stared at the spot where the young girl had fallen. The brown-haired one ran to the riverbank and stood with hands wringing as he said, "I can't swim." The gray-haired one ambled down beside him, paused a moment to unscrew his wooden leg, and handed it to his friend. Then, grabbing the wooden toe, the one-legged man hopped into the river. He extended the leg out across the water, and in moments, caught hold of Susanna's shoulder. He hoisted her up from the water.

Only now did I run for the bank (I had not wanted to destroy her experiment) and clambered down beside the one-legged man, who towed my wife to the side. I grasped her shoulders and pulled her farther up from the muddy water and said, "How'd you know?"

She pointed at the Royal Navy medic pin on the man's lapel, and the wooden leg that had been his lifeline to the side. With a simple smile, she said, "Reach, throw, row, and go."

"What?"

"A Navy medic knows how to save lives from the water, so I knew when I saw his pin that he had the training. And when I saw his wooden leg, I knew he had a way to reach before throwing, rowing, or going. These observations led me to believe he would intervene first."

The one-legged man had heard this discussion and stood there beaming, his gray hair matted with river water.

"And," Susanna said, suddenly gritting her teeth, "it is my sincere hope that this Navy medic knows another thing—"

"What?"

"How to deliver babies," she gasped, sinking onto the grassy bank and clutching her belly.

I don't know if it was the shock of the cold Cam or the glad warmth of being so definitively right or the trauma of men clutching her every limb, but my wife went into labor then and there. Gladly, the one-legged Navy medic did know what he was doing. He took a moment to screw his leg back on and then positioned himself on the bank below my wife. He lifted her heels to rest on his shoulders and coached her gently.

"Ah, you're a natural, you are. The babe is crowning." The gray-haired medic smiled, eyes wide with amazement.

Susanna clutched my arm, gritted her teeth and pushed.

For a long while, this unpleasant process continued. Slowly the little dark head protruded. Then, with a great gush of fluid, the baby came rushing into the world. The old sailor caught her in his hands and laughed and held her up for Susanna and me to see.

The little girl squalled, covered in blood and smelling of river water.

"What should we call her?" Susanna asked.

"Let's name her after you," I said.

"Name her Susanna? Won't that be confusing?"

"Then, how about Anna?"

"Anna," she said, drawing the bloody baby toward her and kissing her on the forehead. "That's who you are, then. Anna Moriarty."

25

A LADY LOST

FROM THE MEMOIRS OF PROFESSOR JAMES MORIARTY:

And so, Anna entered my life just as her mother had, catching me all unawares. I had never had much contact with children, let alone newborns, and this naked, bloody, mewling thing seemed to me to be hardly human—perhaps a pupa.

I crouched beside Susanna, breathing raggedly as the Cam rolled lazily along below us. The Navy medic handed Anna to the other lawn bowler, who swaddled her in his overcoat. (I had already given my coat to my shivering wife.) The medic then drew a river-soaked handkerchief from his pocket and wiped the blood off the infant. (I would have proffered my own except that I was already using it to clean up Susanna.)

I could see the baby's features now: the squished face, the bruise under her jaw where the man had pulled, the tiny hands and toes. She almost became human, but then I saw the umbilicus. That strange, quirked cord ran from the belly to the placental sac, which even now dangled bloodily above the ground.

I know fathers say that they love their daughters at first sight—that it is an obligation if not a compulsion. But I did not. I already had an all-encompassing love. Was I suddenly supposed to divide my love in half, giving a portion to my soul mate and the rest to this stranger? Or was I suddenly supposed to become twice the man I had been?

I distinctly remember looking at that child, that half-drowned thing, and wondering who she was and what she meant.

"Isn't she perfect?" Susanna asked me.

"Isn't she?" I echoed.

We returned to our apartments, and Susanna gave the baby a proper bath, and I sliced the umbilicus with a pair of scissors and crimped it off with a bit of wire. Susanna showed me how to pin a diaper, and I watched with bemusement, trying to imagine myself doing any work on that end of the baby. But Susanna honestly expected me to, and soon I was to discover that I had no choice in the matter.

That should have been my first clue that everything had changed. I had always been the authority, had drawn Susanna up from the literal gutter and taught her to read and write, and opened a new world to her. I had been almost a father, but now she spoke to me in slow words with lots of deep nods as if I were a daft uncle. She was the parent now, and I was—what?—an assistant?

And the baby had done this to us.

Little Anna had stolen our lives. Once, I could lecture while Susanna learned—whether in my class or in another—but now one of us had to be home, or the baby had to go along. We even attempted it a few times, wheeling a pram in and hoping for a long nap. Little Anna would sleep until class began and then would break into ferocious wailing. I could not well change a diaper while lecturing on logarithmic functions, and I didn't have the mammary equipment to placate her other needs. It came down to this: either my wife or I had to quit.

I told Susanna that I could not imagine ending my career to spend all day, every day, tending a baby. She said she would quit school. I was relieved at first, but our decision worked doubly against me.

Spending all day together, mother and daughter developed a powerful bond. Anna gradually edged me out of Susanna's heart. At the same time, the baby drove all thought of theories and monographs and discoveries out of her mother's mind. For four years, Susanna bent all her will on this little life. The two of them grew inseparable, a female syndicate that plotted against the Fatherland. I had to put a stop to it.

"I have a surprise for you, my dear," I said one August, sweeping into our too-crowded apartments. Susanna and four-year-old Anna were working together to fold the washing. I raised my hand from behind my back and presented a bunch of roses I had clipped from a wild bush near the Cam.

"For me?" Anna asked shrilly, running forward.

I swept the flowers out of reach. "For your mother." When I saw the pouting look on her face, I said, "They have thorns, dear. I didn't want you to get pricked."

"I, on the other hand—" Susanna said sarcastically, and both of them laughed. "What's the occasion?"

"It's threefold," I said. "First, I have become Dean of Maths and Physics."

"No!" Susanna cried, standing and wrapping her arms around me. "Congratulations!"

I returned the embrace, careful not to snag her dress with the thorns and not to let Anna get hold of them. "And there's more."

"What?"

"As dean, my first act is to readmit you into the program, picking up where you left off."

Susanna stared at me, her face betraying shock and a little annoyance. "But I can't—not until Anna is in school. We spoke of this."

"You cannot wait any longer, my dear. Your faculties have been slowly declining—"

Her eyes flared. Anna saw the look and mirrored it a moment later. Susanna said, "I am, if anything, sharper for my work raising a child."

"And though I may be dean, I cannot stretch your credits indefinitely. You must return to your studies."

Susanna wrapped Anna in her arms and stared at me. "And what happens to our daughter?"

"We'll hire a nanny."

"A nanny?" they chorused.

"As dean, I have a substantial pay increase. We can afford it."

"But can Anna afford it?"

"What are you talking about?"

"Nannies are embittered spinsters or closeted Sapphites—"

"You're being too harsh."

"They're paid to love—mercenaries, prostitutes."

I looked at her in frustration, my lips holding back the words so *were you*.

"How dare you!"

"What?"

"I know you, James Moriarty. I know your every thought," Susanna said angrily. "This is not for me, not for Anna. This is all for you. You want to divide and conquer, to put your wife in her place and put your daughter in her place. You want to make her an orphan in her own home!"

The blood fled my face. At last, I understood. Susanna, who had never had a mother, was trying to be a mother not just for Anna, but for herself.

"I'm sorry," I said, spreading my hands, letting the roses fall to the floor. "I just want you back, Susanna."

Something in her broke. She peeled her arm away from Anna and crossed to me and nestled against my chest. I raised my hands to embrace her, but she said, "Don't."

"What?"

"Your hand is covered in blood," she said.

Only then did I notice the four deep punctures where I had clutched the rose stems too hard. The broken flowers lay on the floor between us.

"I will do it," she said in resignation. "I'll go back to school—*if* we can find a suitable nanny for Anna."

"No, Mother!" Anna wailed, clinging to her.

I clenched my hand, trying to keep the blood from falling on Anna's blond head. I whispered to Susanna, "You won't be sorry."

"You might be."

We both turned out to be right.

THE SEARCH for a suitable nanny dragged on for weeks. Partly, mother and daughter had decided to be extremely picky. Partly, Susanna had been right in her dire predictions. The old applicants turned out to be sour old Tories or dissolute drunks. The young ones often had cold sores on their lips, telltale signs of their true professions. Virtuous women were unwilling to sell themselves into domestic slavery.

In the fourth week, though, we found an old nanny with sterling references, a kindly face, and a will of iron. She spoke with the Queen's English, knew Latin and Greek, and voted straight-ticket Tory. Her only downfall had been a ne'er-do-well husband who had spent her fortune and died. Mrs. Mulroney was, therefore, a refined lady at a streetwalker price. Best of all, Susanna liked her, and Anna spontaneously referred to her as "Grandmum."

With that one utterance, Susanna was set free! I had at last won my wife back from our daughter. As Mrs. Mulroney settled into her domestic duties, Susanna dived back into her studies.

Her first class was a calculus tutorial, for which the professor was routinely late. When Susanna arrived, the four young

men sitting there laughed to see her: "You must be the sub-
stitute!"

Susanna smiled rakishly, strode to the slate, and scrawled
out a dizzying formula that crossed both boards. The giggles
slowly quieted, and one by one, the young scholars began to
copy down the equation. At last, Susanna turned around and
said: "Do any of you know what this equation describes?"

Dead silence answered. Finally, a student named Edward
Drake said, "A complex system of interactions."

"Yes. But what exactly does it describe?"

Drake shrugged. "Some sort of chemical reaction?"

Susanna tilted her head, her smile only widening. "In a
way." She reached into her waistcoat pocket and drew out a
peppermint—the type she and Anna always shared—and
popped it into her mouth.

Another young scholar named John Nelson said, "It doesn't
look like a chemical reaction, but one of physics—the tracing
of particles. But I can't make out what sort of particles these
are. There are four principals—D, N, A, and H, and they seem
to bounce off each other in numerous ways. A chain reaction."

"True."

A third classmate, Rupert Higgins, scowled. "You said 'in a
way' it was a chemical reaction, but also that it was a physical
reaction. Which is it? It can't be both, can it?"

"Can it?" Susanna replied.

The last, a student named Clive Andrews, said, "I don't
think it describes anything. There are too many other variables: $fm(D)$, $fs(A)$, $fh(H)$, $fp(A)$—I mean, $fh(H)$? What kind
of nonsense is that?"

"Just my question," Susanna pressed. "What kind of nonsense is this?"

"Oh, she's just playing with us," said Higgins.

"Precisely," Susanna replied. "Here are the variables: The

function of *m* represents mind, on a ten-point scale from dull to genius. The function of *p* represents personality, on a scale from depressive to manic. The function of *s* represents sexism, from chauvinist to feminist. . . ."

As they scribbled, Higgins said, "But what the blazes is the function of *h* times H?"

"The function of *h* stands for hangover," Susanna said. "So clearly f*h*(H) represents how your current hangover affects you, Mr. Higgins."

"What?" he blustered.

Susanna smiled sweetly. "There you are, gentlemen—D for Drake, N for Nelson, A for Andrews, and H for Higgins. I've calculated the effects of your minds, your personalities, your sexism, and your hangovers to determine your actions."

"What actions?" Drake and Andrews both blurted.

"This elaborate chain provides a probability of proper action." She began to work through the equation, rubbing out variables and replacing them with numbers and running them through—at first two and then three and then four calculations ahead of the class.

Susanna was nearing the final calculation when she drew a quick breath, and the peppermint on her tongue rushed back and lodged in her throat. She hitched, trying to cough it out but couldn't, and by the time she pivoted round, her face was blue. She collapsed onto the floor, passing out.

WHEN SHE awoke, Drake and Higgins knelt above her. Drake's face was racked with dread, but Higgins was patiently picking chunks of shattered peppermint off his fingers.

Susanna smiled up at them, a smile that had always melted me: "What happened?"

Drake said, "Well, um. You choked—on that candy there. I was the first one to see it, and I ran up, trying to knock it out of you. Then Higgins told me to stop, said I was just lodging it down deeper. He grabbed you, miss—and, well, I'm ashamed to say—"

Higgins broke in, "I lifted you up with your back to my chest and wrapped my arms around your breasts and—"

"And that's when Andrews shouted rape and ran from the room."

"Yeah, but it wasn't rape, see, miss, because when I squeezed your chest, the candy came popping out, and I caught it in my hand and crushed it."

"You saved my life."

He blushed deeply. "I guess I did, miss."

She nodded. "Thank you. But what about Nelson? What did he do?"

Both men looked at each other and shrugged.

"I'll tell you what he did. He finished the calculation, realized what it meant, and skulked out of the room." The two young men traded looks of shock. Susanna extended her hands to them. "Help me up, and let's go see."

They lifted her to her feet, and the three of them went to Nelson's desk to see the completed equation.

"Here it is, in black-and-white," Susanna said. "You, Drake, have a high intelligence and a moderate personality—are even an egalitarian, with deep compassion—but you're feeling quite dulled by a raging hangover from last night's revels."

Drake laughed in a self-effacing way. "Right there in black-and-white."

"Your attributes put you in the eighty-fifth percentile for correct action. Your score was second only to Higgins, in the ninety-eighth percentile." She turned to her rescuer. "Though your intellect is not as keen as Drake's, and though you tend toward depression and are a staunch chauvinist, you've no hangover at all—due to your alcoholism."

Higgins only stared in amazement.

"The combination of these less-than-stellar attributes, though, actually gave you an advantage in this crisis."

"How could that be?"

"Look at Lord Salisbury," Drake said, clapping his classmate on the back. "He's got all the same demons as you, and he's brilliant in Parliament."

Higgins allowed himself a small smile. "What of the other two?"

"Well, here's Andrews—a genius who tends toward mania, a feminist of the highest order, and moderately hungover. He ranks in the tenth percentile."

"Rape!" Drake shouted mockingly, lifting his hands and pantomiming running from the room.

"While Nelson has a brain of no particular brilliance, a depressive nature, deep chauvinism, and a terrible hangover. He scored in the fifth percentile—and skulked away."

MY WIFE had returned, and I couldn't have been more delighted. In fact, I had helped her plan this whole experiment: I am the professor who was late. I'd given her the names of the four other students and had profiled them for her, and all the while that this drama played out, I was waiting beyond the door. Susanna had made me promise not to rush in, though I had no notion she planned to actually inhale that mint.

"One of these days, my dear," I chided her after that class, "your sociological experiments will get you killed."

"WOULD YOU like to see my master's thesis?" Susanna asked me one March morning, just prior to receiving a *summa cum laude* in maths and sociology from Jesus College. It was a provocative question. Of course I wanted to see it. After all, her history of publication had begun with me, though for the past three years, she had kept her master's thesis a secret. She had dropped only occasional titillating clues. To ask if I wanted to see her master's thesis was only slightly less provocative than asking if I wanted to see her naked.

My eyes strolled over the hundred fifty pages of schematics and formulae, and I tried desperately to parse out the meaning of it. Had she mathematically mapped every tissue in a human body? Had she captured the lineage of every royal personage in Europe? As my puzzlement grew, Susanna's delight grew likewise. At last, I had to admit my ignorance. "What is all this?"

"This, my dear Dr. Moriarty," she said, "is a map of the criminal underworld of London."

I gasped involuntarily. "Indeed?"

"Indeed. You see that this map began with my so-called father. He had worked out a very advantageous trade. His prostitutes would occasionally become pregnant. They could work in that condition, of course—some men preferring it— but once they delivered, he donated the babies to the orphanage: little wicker baskets and little desperate Cockney notes, just what the beadle fell for. Well, the orphanage fed and clothed these children until they, too, became ripe, at which point Father appeared and adopted the pubescent girls. He magnanimously took them away, a philanthropist who alleviated the orphanage's terrible burden while simultaneously sating London's terrible desires. See? That's how Father's scam works."

"Remarkable," I said miserably.

"Well, I'd mapped out that whole scam and realized it was connected into a hundred others. I realized that the commonality was human desire. Prostitution satisfied one human desire. What criminal enterprises satisfied others?

"Well, first off, there were the gambling dens. The less

imaginative used craps and poker, cockfights and bear-baiting to draw in their clientele. The more imaginative bet on the prostitutes themselves as if they were horses carrying im-pounds, striving to deliver a winning time. The fact that gam-bling hooked so naturally into prostitution intrigued me."

"Contemplating a career change, are we?" I teased.

"Yes, though not for me. I plan to bring down Father and his prostitution ring, and the gambling that is connected with it, and the illicit usage of opium that forms a third part of this unholy triumvirate."

I shook my head in disbelief. "Honestly, Susanna, what are you going to do? One woman cannot bring down a city-wide crime syndicate."

"But I can. Archimedes said that, given the right pivot point and the right fulcrum, he could move the world. Well, James Moriarty. I am the pivot point. I am the fulcrum."

26

An Empire Crumbles

FROM THE MEMOIRS OF PROFESSOR JAMES MORIARTY:

Wearing her inimitable smile, Susanna drew a piece of common stationery from the rolltop desk. On it, in a brusque hand, she wrote five words: "Take It and Never Return." She blotted the ink, blew on the page, folded it once unevenly, stuffed it into a plain brown envelope, dribbled candle wax on it, and pressed the wax flat with a potato.

"Now you have gone quite round the bend," I remarked. "A potato?"

"Not just any potato." Susanna lifted it to show that she had carved an intricate design into its end—a grinning skull with an *RB* superimposed over the brow. "The signet seal of Regis Bachman, boss of the largest crime syndicate in London."

This was incredible. "How did you get his signet ring?"

"I didn't get the ring itself, but its clear impression in black and blue. I copied it off the face of a man that Bachman had punched."

My mouth dropped open. "But—this man could identify you!"

"Unlikely, since he is lying even now in the morgue on Buck's Road. This was the final piece of the puzzle. With it, I can set into motion a chain of events that will bring down the whole syndicate."

A knock came at the door, and Susanna leaped up from her seat to answer it. There stood none other than Rupert Higgins, the young scholar who had saved Susanna from choking on a mint. He was graduating this year, as well. Rupert held out his hand, and Susanna placed the letter in it.

"You understand what to do?"

" 'Course."

"You understand that your life and mine depend on your discretion—get in and get out without being seen."

"No problem. I know my way around Whitechapel—not that anyone knows me, mind you."

"I know. That's why I chose you."

"Under the door, one knock, and off I go." Rupert pocketed the note, pivoted, and stepped away.

Baffled, I closed the door. "What was all that, then?"

Susanna crossed the sitting room and luxuriously laid herself out across the settee. "I would have thought it all would be painfully obvious."

"Painfully obtuse, you mean."

"It's an experiment, like all my others, only much grander in scale. And I'm not going to be hurling myself into a river or choking on a mint this time."

"At last you've learned a little sense. But would you take a moment to explain just what the devil you are up to?"

"As you know, I've mapped out this sprawling empire of crime in London and profiled each man and woman—yes, there are women—at the key points in the hierarchy. I know their minds, their personalities, their skills, their desires, their histories—all. Thousands of variables have figured into my equation, and I have run calculations hundreds of times in order to discover the lynchpin that will make it all fall apart."

"All right, so what is the lynchpin?"

"Not *what*, but *who*. You see, Regis Bachman, the czar of

this empire of crime, has a son he has been bringing up in the trade—Jeremy. Young Jeremy does not have the hard-bitten temperament needed for a life of extortion and murder, though. He's a painter. On many occasions, he has asked his father to send him to Paris to study art, but Regis is determined to make a crime boss of the boy. Regis has named Jeremy his second and requires all his lieutenants—who collect revenues from the brothels and opium dens and union gangs—to submit their weekly takes to Jeremy, who counts it, takes ten percent for himself, and passes the rest on to his father."

"And Jeremy is about to receive a message from his father telling him to take the money and never return."

"Precisely."

"But how will this unravel the whole syndicate?"

Susanna drew a deep, satisfied breath. "Jeremy will run off with the money—the largest take of the year as a new crop of highly addictive opium has just landed at the docks—leaving no trace and changing his name and disappearing onto the Continent. Jeremy has dreamed of just such a day as this, and he will be content to have escaped his life of crime and be bankrolled for the rest of his existence. Tomorrow morning, however, Regis will discover that his payment is gone and his son is missing—"

"And will hunt him down."

"No. Betrayal will not occur to him."

"But surely the lieutenants will suggest it."

"Yes, but the lieutenants all hate Jeremy—always have—and Regis will determine that one of them, or all of them, have killed his son and stolen the money themselves. Regis will take them out, one by one, until the middle level of the organization is gutted and filled anew from below. These new lieutenants, though, will fear Regis. Some will fall in line, and others will go after the man himself. In the resulting cascade of gangland slayings, even Scotland Yard will take notice and step in—armed with an anonymous list of all the perpetrators and their crimes—and will sweep them all into prison."

I smiled, shaking my head in amazement and wonder. "You truly are a genius."

IN THE London *Times* a week later, we received the first evidence that Susanna's plan was playing out. The operator of a series of dockside opium dens was found murdered in his bed. When police arrived to investigate, they found the place ransacked, the man's throat cut, and no apparent motive for the crime.

"They haven't a clue, as usual," Susanna lamented. She wrote another pithy note, "Speak to Josiahs Kellerman," and sent it anonymously to Scotland Yard.

The following week, the *Times* reported that police had questioned the cousin of the murdered opium lord—a man named Josiahs Kellerman, who had assiduously kept the books of the drug trade. He had noted everything, from locations of dens to names of suppliers and names of users and even dates, prices, dosages, and deaths. Kellerman was arrested as an accessory to drug trafficking, but his ledgers were carefully carried in to Scotland Yard like some lost gospel.

"Phase One," Susanna said—though without the triumph that I had expected in her voice.

"What is it?" I asked.

She shook her head. "Never before has any of my experiments endangered another life. This time, though, a man was killed."

"An opium king," I pointed out. "Killed by his crime boss, not by you. And how many poor souls have you saved by shutting down those iniquitous dens? How many wives will have their husbands? You did not kill this man. You simply wrote a few words."

"A small act," she replied, her voice sounding haunted. "As small as pulling a trigger."

Over the course of the next few months, the *Times* broke story after story of opium-den raids and shutdowns, of proprietors and traffickers and users all going before the bench.

THE SECOND phase of Susanna's plan made the paper shortly afterward, and this time she seemed to feel no regret. The headline read "Prostitution Prince Pleads for Protection." Beneath the headline, beside a front-page story, was a picture of a gaunt, distraught man, his manacled hands clasped before him.

"Father," Susanna said.

Though I had never seen the man, Susanna testified that he had grown only the more wasted in the ten years since I had rescued her from the street. "His syphilis is ravaging him," she said, "but at least he got out of the grips of Bachman and into the hands of the police."

"As you knew he would."

"As I knew he would," she responded grimly. She went on to read the article:

> William Petit, self-proclaimed "Duke of Doxies" surrendered himself to Scotland Yard and promised a full confession of his crimes in return for protection.
>
> Investigators took the confession three weeks ago but little believed its lurid details. Subsequent investigations, however, have corroborated the facts of the case and have resulted in hundreds of arrests—and a total collapse of the vile industry throughout Whitechapel and much of London.

Petit's tearful confession can be summarized as follows: He
controlled a network of thirteen houses of ill repute, concen-
trated in Whitechapel with other operations spread throughout London. In total, these houses employed nearly three
hundred prostitutes, with an estimated total clientele of over a
thousand elicit acts per night.

Worse yet, Petit used local orphanages as breeding grounds
for his ladies of the evening. He assumed various names to
adopt nubile girls, but he anonymously dropped off any children born within his brothels. He boasted to have had a yearly
income equal to Carnegie himself, but said he had to give it
all up due to a threat on his life.

Petit indicated that he had become the target of "the Big
Boss," or "Mr. B."—the overlord not simply of Petit's flesh
trade but also of opium dens, robbery rings, and guilds of
thugs and assassins throughout the city. Six months before Petit's arrest, Mr. B.'s son and the heir to his empire of crime disappeared, and the Big Boss believes that Petit had a hand in
the matter.

"I didn't, though! I didn't, Mr. B.," Petit testified adamantly,
asking reporters to print at least this one detail. "I'd never turn
on you—won't give you up, even, but only just myself and my
life of crime."

Despite their disgust at this man's actions, the police have
been true to their pledge to Mr. Petit, providing him a cell and
armed guard within the fortresslike confines of Scotland Yard.

Susanna let the *Times* droop in her grip, and she stared out
bleakly beyond the valley of the paper. "It is a death sen-
tence."

"Nonsense," I said, coming to her and sliding my arm
around her. "Scotland Yard is the finest crime-fighting organization on the planet."

She looked askance at me. "You haven't read my full dissertation."

"*I have,*" I replied defensively. "I've checked and rechecked your calculations."

"Mathematically, perhaps, but you have not paid attention to the variables, to the names of the men. Appendix J is the algorithm that factors in the chief of Scotland Yard and every detective and inspector in it. Simply by introducing Mr. Petit in that equation, I end up with calculations that predict a sudden and not-so-accidental death."

I tried to laugh this off. "Even you, my dear—genius though you are—cannot prognosticate the inner workings of Scotland Yard."

Though she did not respond, I knew her thoughts. Often of late, Susanna had called herself a modern Cassandra—empowered to predict the future but powerless to change it.

Next morning, a peek at the front page of the *Times* proved her correct. The headline screamed: "Prince of Prostitution Dead in Police Custody." As soon as I read the headline, I folded the paper and shoved it under my chair.

"Don't bother," Susanna said from the other room. "I don't need to read it. I wrote that headline six months ago. And now, my dear, comes the downfall of the Big Boss himself."

THE FINAL part of Susanna's plan did not play itself out on the front page. Unlike the murder of an opium lord or the dramatic confession of a prostitution king, the disintegration of the cabal of thugs was indistinguishable from its daily operations. As always, bodies bumped along the nighttime Thames, and police fished them out at the accustomed pace. However, for each murdered man who floated at the top, ten murdered thugs sank to the bottom, their ankles bound to lead weights. This was Bachman's Inquisition. According to

Susanna's calculations, the man had become paranoid and saw enemies everywhere. He was purging his ranks of infidels, and every day, his definition of fidelity grew more stringent. Over the months of that summer, the always-fetid river grew downright rank—a stew of death. One morning, a fisherman caught a half-decomposed ear. One afternoon, a dredging crew pumped up a bargeful of mud and bones.

When she read this last account, Susanna told me, "They're reaching the point of collapse."

"Are they?" I asked in distraction, grading the papers of my first-term students.

"Now it's just a matter of watching the obituaries."

All through the execution of her plan, Susanna had monitored the death notices in the *Times*. Whenever a known criminal had died, she would cross his variables from the grand equation and run her calculations again. The formula now bore so many *X*s Susanna had to recast it.

A month later, Susanna crossed two more variables off the list and stared at the final one. "Bachman."

I approached from behind and embraced her. "Too bad. I'd hoped someone else would finish him off. I suppose you'll have to let the police round him up, instead."

"They'll never take him," Susanna said wearily. I had at last learned not to question her assumptions, but only to check her calculations. It was undeniable. My eyes traced through the equation, and I saw that Bachman's end was inescapable: suicide.

Two days later, the *Times* confirmed it. In an unassuming corner of the paper ran the narrow obituary:

> Regis Bachman of Whitechapel died August 25, hanged in his apartment, an apparent suicide. He had no known family or occupation.

So, it was done. Susanna's little five-word experiment had played itself out. Five words that brought down an empire of crime that had terrorized London. With the stroke of a pen, she had turned the murderers on each other and wiped away an entire underworld of extortion, drug trafficking, and flesh peddling. What Scotland Yard could not do with thousands of police, my wife had accomplished with five words.

"I've been thinking, darling," I said to Susanna one chilly night in May of 1881, as we reclined by the fire, "that your five words should go down in history among the most potent pronouncements of all time. You're overmatched only by Marie Antoinette, who destroyed a whole nation with four words—'Let them eat cake'—and Frederich Nietzsche, who brought down heaven with three words—'God is dead'—and God himself, who started the whole business with two words—'I AM.'"

Susanna sighed. "I will not spend any time congratulating myself. In the vast annals of crime in London, I've only ended one chapter. The next has already begun. The networks I destroyed were all founded on human desire, and I have done nothing to remove that. The world cries out for whores and opium, and new criminals will rise to provide them like weeds rising from fallow ground."

Footsteps came in the hall beyond, and a frantic knocking. I leaped up to answer, but before I could even reach the door, it flew inward, admitting none other than Edward Drake. His eyes were wide and black, his face the hue of a dinner plate. He gripped the doorknob as if to let it go would send him pitching over.

"What is it, man!" I said.

"It's Rupert. It's terrible!"

"What about Rupert?"

"He's dead! Murdered!"

"What?"

"I'm the one who found him," Drake said, staggering into the room.

I caught him and directed him to a chair. Then I splashed some brandy in a snifter and handed it to him.

He took it, swirled it in his jittering fingers, and dashed it back. "Throat cut ear to ear."

As I crouched down beside the man's seat, Susanna rushed to the rolltop desk to drag out her thesis. She flipped madly through the pages until she found the one she wanted. "Higgins," she murmured. Her eyes moved feverishly over the numbers, her fingers tracing out the complex equations. "Are you sure it wasn't . . . suicide?"

"I, well . . ." Drake began, panting, "well . . . it was such a deep cut—a vicious one. And . . . there was something else. In blood on the floor—there was a message written."

"Was Higgins's finger bloody?" Susanna asked.

"Everything was bloody." Drake trembled and looked at me imploringly.

I clamped my hand on his shoulder. "Steady, man. Susanna—put away those dreadful equations. They have nothing to do with it."

"It has everything to do with it."

"Please!" I said to her, and then said to Drake, "What did the message say?"

He blinked, looking past me. "Just—just four words. 'He points the way.'"

I sat back on my heels. "A message in blood. 'He points the way.'"

Just then, nine-year-old Anna came stumbling out of her bedroom, fists twisting in her eyes. "What's going on?"

"Nothing," chorused the rest of us.

Drake pried himself up from the chair and staggered

toward the door. "I'd better be getting back. The police've already grilled me about it all, and they released me, but they said not to go far, or for very long." Even as he said it, he swooned a little.

I grabbed his arm. "I'll take you back. Susanna, get Anna back into bed."

Susanna glared at me, her arm wrapped around Anna's shoulders. "There's something not right with all this."

"Of course there's something not right," I snapped. "A man has been murdered!" With that, I guided Drake out the door. Susanna closed it and locked it behind us.

How MANY times I have played that moment over in my head and wished I had not charged out that door. What a fool I was! My pride cost me everything. Susanna had proven her powers to me. Why did I dismiss her fears in that most critical moment?

Drake and I walked down from the apartments and crossed the road and set out across Jesus Green, heading toward the college. We walked along in choked silence, but all the while my head was spinning. What could it mean—"He points the way." Who points the way? Higgins or the killer? And points the way to what?

As we passed through the Jesus College gates and into the inner courtyard, we saw the police milling about beneath the dormitory door. One officer carried bedsheets stained in blood.

Points the way to whom?

"Susanna," I said, suddenly breathless.

I turned from Drake and, without another word, dashed back the way we had come. I tore across Jesus Green and reached the street beyond and angled down it to our walkup and vaulted up the stairs and saw the door bashed in and saw

Susanna lying in a pool of blood on the floor and saw the killer with straight razor in hand and shoulder bashing against the locked bedroom door. He did not see or hear my approach, so intent was he on breaking down Anna's door and so deafened was he by her terrified screams. I hurled myself at the assassin, snatched the razor from his dangling hand, and wrenched the blade up to the man's throat.

"Goddamn you, Jeremy Bachman! You were supposed to be an artist!"

I ripped the razor deep through his scrawny neck and sent him sprawling to the floorboards. He kicked for a moment, trying to right himself, but his throat was a fountain, and he soon slumped facefirst in the gore.

I meanwhile crossed to Susanna and knelt beside her and rolled her over. Her whole face was painted in blood, but her skin otherwise was yellow. I clamped my hand on the slit on her throat, but it was too late. Already the blood had stopped flowing.

"No! No! Susanna!" I clutched her still-warm body to me, but she was gone.

Only then did I see that one of her fingertips was red. I cast a bleary gaze out across the floorboards and saw these words:

"Take care of Anna."

At last, I could hear my daughter behind the door, screaming.

27

CALCULATIONS

FROM THE MEMOIRS OF PROFESSOR JAMES MORIARTY:

I gently laid Susanna on the floor and bent to kiss her bloody lips. "Good-bye, my darling," I said, glancing again at the message she had written on the boards. "I will take care of Anna."

I rose from my wife's dead body and went to Anna's door. She still screamed. I tried the door, but it was locked. "Anna. It's Father. Please stop screaming." She did not. "It's Father! Father!"

She fell silent, listening. Then, in a tremulous voice, she said, "What about the man?"

I glanced over my shoulder. "He's dead. I killed him. Now, please, unlock the door."

"What about Mum?"

I drew a long breath. "Your mother . . . she . . . she asked me to take care of you. Unlock the door, now, Anna, please. It's all right."

I heard the bolt grate slowly from its bracket, and I stepped back as the knob turned. The hinges keened open.

Anna stood there, face white and streaked with tears. She stared at me.

I was soaked in blood from fingertip to fingertip. Cringing, I turned away, nearly falling over the body of Jeremy Bachman. The dark pool beneath him had merged with the dark pool beneath Susanna.

Anna screamed.

I reached for her, dragged her into my arms, and held her tight. "Stop screaming. I'll take care of you. Stop screaming!"

"Mum! Mum!"

Footsteps came at the door. A man bolted to a stop, gripping the frame, and stared in horror at me. He stumbled away, shouting, "Murder! Murder!"

Anna continued to scream. It was deafening to hold her, but I held her. I had promised Susanna. I held her and didn't let go until the police came.

THE POLICE read it all wrong. They saw a girl screaming in terror and a man clutching her in a bloody embrace and two corpses with throats slit just like Rupert Higgins's had been. With a shout, they rushed us and ripped Anna out of my arms and clubbed me to the ground. A big black boot planted itself on my spine. My arms were wrenched up behind me, and iron shackles bit down on my wrists.

"In the name of Her Royal Majesty, Queen Victoria, you are under arrest for three murders," barked the man with the boot.

Meanwhile, another officer—beefy and smiling—knelt beside Anna and wrapped her in his arms. She quieted. In the sudden silence, I could hear the officer say, "You'll need to be rounding up your clothes, my dear."

"Why?" she asked tearfully.

"Well, you can't stay here. We'll take you to a nice place— the Brooks Street Home for Wayward Children."

"An orphanage?" I shouted. "No! You can't! She's mine. My responsibility. My daughter."

The man glared at me. "With all that you've done here, sir, you've orphaned her, and no mistake."

"Not the orphanage," Anna pleaded. "Please. Let me go to my grandmum."

"Your grandmum?" the officer asked.

"Yes. Please," I said. "Her Grandmother Mulroney lives at the Red Gables Boardinghouse on Charles Street."

When Anna began to wail again, the man relented. He took her in hand and escorted her two blocks to the boardinghouse. Meanwhile, the three other officers hoisted me to my feet, hustled me into a paddy wagon, and drove me to the Cambridge police station. There, a brutal interrogation began. A parade of different officers asked me the same questions for hours. At the end of the ordeal, my captors flung me into a holding cell—without even letting me wash away my wife's blood.

There I sat for four days.

It was Anna who finally saved me—Anna and Edward Drake. They told the police that I had been at home during the murder of Higgins and had been out during the murder of my wife. Anna described the man who had kicked in the door. She told how she ran for the bedroom, how her mother slammed the door and shouted for her to lock it, how the next sound she heard was a thud, like a body hitting the floor. Anna screamed, of course, and then the killer tried to break the door down. She kept on screaming until I came and killed the man and saved her.

It was a horrifying account, tearfully delivered. At last it convinced the police. They released me from my shackles and cell. I went straightaway to the undertaker, only to discover that Susanna had already been cremated.

"She wouldn't keep," he said in explanation, "not in May."

"I want her ashes."

He stared stupidly at me.

"I demand that you bring me the ashes of my wife!"

The man grabbed an urn from a nearby shelf, went to the

incinerator, and scraped ashes from the trap. He returned
with the jar brimming.

"These are my wife's ashes?" I asked. He shrugged. They
might be the remains of my wife or those of Jeremy Bachman. I took the urn and smashed it to the floor and stormed
out.

I spent most of that night walking the streets of Cambridge, terrorized by all that had happened. At last, my legs
and my grief were exhausted, and I staggered up the stairs to
my apartments near Jesus College.

It was a dreary homecoming. The door to our flat hung
loose, the latch broken out of it. I swung the door inward, and
the cupric tang of blood hit the back of my throat. A few
more steps brought me to the twin black pools where my
wife and her killer had died.

I filled a bucket with water, got a rag, and knelt to scrub
away the last remnant of Susanna. The blood would not
come up. Bucket after bucket turned red, but still the stains
remained.

At last, I surrendered. I drew up a bath, stripped to my
skin, tossed my clothes into the stove, and cremated them.
Then I bathed until every last smear of blood was gone.

That was her funeral: a shattered urn with someone else's
ashes in it, buckets made red with her blood and the blood of
her killer, and the noisome smell of burning wool.

I was a broken man. After my bath, I lay naked upon our
bed and let the tears stream down. How could she be gone?
How could these horrible things be true? She had calculated
every contingency except one—that Jeremy Bachman had a
heart of murder after all. His father's suicide had brought Jeremy back from the Continent, had set him on the trail of the
messenger who had delivered the note, had driven him to
Susanna. . . .

Eventually, no tears remained. I dressed and went out, picking my way down the dark streets until I reached the Red Gables Boardinghouse where Mrs. Mulroney and Anna lived. The windows were black, and I glanced up at the gloaming sky to determine what time it must be. Perhaps four A.M. Surely the scullery staff would be awake. I knocked on the door and waited. No answer. I knocked more loudly.

To the door came an old woman with squinting eyes and hair like a white rag on her head. She spoke in a querulous voice: "Who is it?"

"Professor Moriarty. I've come for my daughter."

"Do you know what time it is?"

"I suppose it is around four in the morning."

"Three-thirty, in actual fact."

I dipped my head and lifted my hat in apology. "Sorry, mum, but I'd lost track of time—what with having just been released from jail and having found my wife cremated without my permission and having spent the last hours scrubbing her from the floor of my flat. . . . One does lose track of time."

"I'll wake her." The woman vanished within the dark doorway, making sure to shut the door behind her. She left me standing on the stoop. Nothing moved in the street except for a tumbling newspaper, sketching out the invisible path of the wind.

The door opened again, and Mrs. Mulroney stood there. Her pruny face was pinched tight, but fear sparkled in her eyes. "Professor . . . you've been released."

"I've been cleared. I've come for Anna."

"Please, Professor. Let the child sleep."

"I'll pay you, of course—three times your usual rate for the past four days—"

"Thank you, sir, but I would have done it for free—the poor girl."

"And I want you to continue on with your daytime duties. Anna will need a female presence all the more now."

"She needs more than that," Mrs. Mulroney said, but then dipped her eyes. "She needs you to be a true father."

"I am her true father."

"A loving father. One who cherishes her, who dotes on her."

"I do not dote, Mrs. Mulroney."

"You doted on Susanna."

I stiffened, and my hand half rose to strike the woman.

She went on fearlessly, "You did, master, in the most beautiful ways. You watched her, smiled when she came by, sought out her counsel, called her 'darling' and 'genius.'"

"She was my one true love. I had no room for another."

"You have room now."

I did not dare to speak for fear I would break down entirely.

"Your daughter cannot replace your wife, Professor, but half of her *is* your wife. It's even in her name—Anna is half of Susanna."

"Half is not enough."

"The other half of Anna is you."

I relented. "Let her sleep. That's what a loving father would do." I stepped down off that stoop.

"I'll bring her by after breakfast," Mrs. Mulroney called after me.

She was right, of course, this nanny that Susanna and I had selected—this nanny turned governess by the stroke of a razor. When she and Anna arrived at the flat at nine-thirty, I was waiting with a bouquet of wild roses I had plucked from the banks of the Cam.

"Red roses are the flowers of love. I gave them once to your mother, and now I pass them along to you. It is your inheritance."

THE SHADOW OF REICHENBACH FALLS

Anna took the blooms, yelped a little, and set them on the table. Her hands were pricked and bleeding, but she stared with dawning hope at those vicious flowers. "For me?"

"Always and forever, now, they are for you."

I DID what Susanna asked: I took care of Anna. I also did what Mrs. Mulroney asked: I became a real father. Anna would not be orphaned as her mother had been, nor would Anna have to say the word *father* with sarcasm and disdain. I would make sure of it.

But how can a father repair nine years of neglect?

I began by doting. The day after the wild roses, I brought Anna a box of truffles. A little girl's heart can remain resolute against roses, but chocolates make it dissolute. Anna actually thanked me and bit into a cherry cordial, experimenting.

Next morning, I brought her a kitten. The animal was, of course, another calculated bribe, but he was also a living thing—warm and loving. He was a fuzzy ambassador from the once-cold Fatherland. Anna named the cat Merlin after the wizard of old, and I quietly lured Merlin and Anna into my oaken heart.

It took a full year before Anna began treating me like a real father, before I was feeling like one. She began to wait by the windowsill to see me march up the street below. She ran to meet me on the stairs and wrapped her arms around my waist and told me that she loved me.

The first time I heard those words, they shocked me. The second time, though, I was ready with a reply: "I love you, too."

I had never spoken those words to anyone but Susanna, and they passed my lips now with the power of a prayer. I was repenting all the wrongs I had done to this poor child. I was adopting Anna into my heart.

No more bribes. Now, I determined to give Anna the greatest gift I could give—an education. I bent my mind to teaching her Greek, Latin, French, and Italian; maths, physics, geometry, philosophy; biology, botany, astronomy, geology; art, literature, history, and . . . music. I was especially keen to discover whether she could hear the note of transfiguration. It had been my awakening, and Susanna's, too. In time, Anna also heard that note, and she tuned her mind to it.

How like this was to teaching her mother! Both young women had been abandoned, both had lived in a nightmare of brutal men, and for each of them, a Prince Charming had appeared to whisk her away into the palace of knowledge.

Soon Anna had become my new favorite student, pacing the floors and reciting Shelley and Keats or naming the constellations or describing the Peloponnesian War. All the while that she paced, her young heels wore away those twin bloodstains on our floor, and every night after she went to bed, I swept up little piles of rust-colored dust.

When Anna was fourteen, I began to bring her to my classes. Just like her mother before her, Anna was at first disparaged for her gender, and then was envied for her mind, and at last was prized for her help with assignments. And as before, I chased off any boys who tried to hatch other plans for her.

It was a blissful time for us, those seven years as father and daughter, before the horrors of the world intruded again. But intrude they did.

It all began as I walked down Newmarket Road on Valentine's Day in 1888. I had just bought a box of chocolates for Anna when I chanced upon a paperboy crying out the headline: " 'Extortion Ring Foiled!' Read all about it!"

I had ignored the papers since Susanna's death, hearing only occasionally of petty crimes or routine murders. Nothing, though, had amounted to a crime ring. It was an affront to the memory of Susanna.

I bought the edition and read the article as I carried it home. Once there, I set down Anna's chocolates and drew out a piece of paper and wrote down the names of the men nabbed. Then I scoured the rest of the *Times*, looking for other such articles—and found them in plenty: "Prostitution Rampant on East Side," "Bodies Found in Thames," "Opium Ship Impounded." By the end of that hour, I had gleaned two dozen names—and these were only the criminals that had been caught.

Taking my list of infamy, I crossed to Susanna's rolltop desk, untouched these seven years, and opened it. Her quill lay just where she had left it on the night of her murder, and her thesis lay open to the precise page she had been staring at. There, the name Jeremy Bachman was underlined in red ink.

"It begins again."

That night, after giving Anna her chocolates and sending her to bed, I started to transcribe Susanna's thesis. Doing so was like copying the work of an artist. Every variable, every function, all the idiosyncratic twists and turns—these were her brushstrokes. By copying them, I trained my mind until they became second nature to me. Through Susanna's grand thesis, she was indwelling my brain and living again.

In a month, the work of transcription was complete, and I began inserting the new names of the criminals who had taken the place of the old. Susanna whispered how. I outlined the structures as I understood them, and over the next few months, constructed from the papers a high-level view of the criminal underworld of London. All the old rackets had resumed. I glimpsed them first in the papers and then in police blotters and then in court documents and then in the city registrar's office. The trail led from illegal activities to legal ones, from blood money to laundered cash. I profiled the crime lords just as Susanna had, learning their minds, their personalities, their drives, their weaknesses. My data were reaching a critical mass. Now I needed only to find the lynchpin that would bring the whole mass crashing down.

On August 7, 1888, another headline stopped me: "Brutal Murder in Whitechapel." I read the article, expecting to recognize the work of one of the thugs I'd profiled, but the murder was like nothing I had seen before:

> Martha Tabram, a woman of ill repute, was found murdered this morning in the George Yard Building, Whitechapel. She had been stabbed thirty-nine times. According to police reports, Martha and another prostitute, Mary Ann Connolly, met a soldier and his companion last night and arranged to service them. Whilst Miss Connolly and the soldier walked up Angel Alley, Martha and her companion walked up George Yard. That was the last anyone saw of Martha's companion, and Miss Connolly was unable to describe him.

Three features of this account terrified me. First, the incident occurred in Whitechapel, on the very street and among the very buildings where I had stayed for my time in London. Secondly, Martha Tabram worked for a madam who had been one of Petit's own girls—one of Susanna's housemates. This woman who had been murdered could have just as easily been my Susanna eighteen years back. But worst of all was the way she had been murdered—stabbed thirty-nine times. No one that I had ever profiled killed like that. Here was a new kind of murderer—who did what he did not for profit or for business but for erotic joy.

I let the newspaper slump from my jangled fingers and stared at the wall. A monster like this could not live in a

world with my Anna in it. Before I brought down the whole
house of cards that had built up since Susanna's death, I was
going to track down this one killer.

I drew out a clean piece of paper and began listing what I
knew: Whitechapel, Angel Alley, George Yard, soldier,
Martha, Ann, thirty-nine stab wounds, soldier friend. . . .
This would be a new calculus. Susanna's work began with
the person and ended with the crime, but I must go in the reverse. I must begin with the crime and find the killer.

When the second and third murders hit the papers, I at
least had a name for my quarry: Jack the Ripper.

28

JACK THE RIPPER

FROM THE MEMOIRS OF PROFESSOR JAMES MORIARTY:

Martha Tabram haunted me. I imagined her murder—
a woman on the street, desperate for money; a man
with hidden motives engaging her; an empty apartment on George Yard; the squalor and his apology for it; her
request that he place three crowns on the dresser. . . . It was a
terrible fancy, but I could not banish it from my mind, could
not imagine Martha as anyone but Susanna.

And always, in the end, she lay on the landing in a pool of
blood.

"Father, what is it?" Anna asked one night.

I was sitting across from her in our parlor, the *Times* on my
lap and my hands draped across the embroidered arms of the
chair. She had caught me in the throes of another terrible vision. "Huh?"

"You look as if you've seen a ghost."

I folded the *Times*. "Um, yes, I—I'm not feeling well."

She rose and came to me. "It's as if you're back seven
years ago, on that horrible day."

I blinked in shock at her. "Yes, Anna. It's like that. It's very
much like that."

She sat down on the arm of the chair and placed her hand
on my shoulder. "What is it, Father?"

I shook my head.

"I'm not a child anymore. You don't need to protect me."

"Oh yes, you are. You're sixteen. And, oh yes, I do need to protect you." She scowled at me, and I tried to explain: "Anna—men are monsters."

"Not all men—"

"Many are. Too many."

Her hand flitted to the paper and flicked it open. "What's this? 'Dear Boss'?"

I sighed deeply. She had found it, the trigger of my latest bout of terror. "A letter. The police hope someone will recognize the handwriting."

I couldn't stop her from reading—Anna was too headstrong, too smart—and some small part of me wanted her help. She leaned over me and began to read:

Dear Boss,

I keep on hearing the police have caught me but they wont fix me just yet. I have laughed when they look so clever and talk about being on the right track. That joke about Leather Apron gave me real fits. I am down on whores and I shant quit ripping them til I do get buckled. Grand work the last job was. I gave the lady no time to squeal. How can they catch me now. I love my work and want to start again. You will soon hear of me with my funny little games. I saved some of the proper red stuff in a ginger beer bottle over the last job to write with but it went thick like glue and I cant use it. Red ink is fit enough I hope ha ha. The next job I do I shall clip the ladys ears off and send to the police officers just for jolly wouldn't you. Keep this letter back till I do a bit more work, then give it out straight. My knife's so nice and sharp I want to get to work right away if I get a chance. Good Luck.

Yours truly,
Jack the Ripper

Don't mind me giving the trade name.

PS Wasnt good enough to post this before I got all the red ink off my hands curse it. No luck yet. They say I'm a doctor now. ha ha

"Jack the Ripper," Anna murmured.

"There have been three murders, Anna—women in Whitechapel, where your mother came from: Martha Tabram, Mary Ann Nichols, Annie Chapman. Stabbed, throats slit, bodies mutilated, organs removed. . . . And this letter is either from the killer or from someone as sick as he."

Anna breathed quietly. Her eyes studied the handwriting: the kinked *J*, the arrogant *R*, the smooth strokes of fingers as clever with ink as with blood. "Sent to the Central News Agency?"

"Yes," I said, "which means he wants publicity. He talks of a 'trade name,' as if he is trying to sell something, Maybe it's just a newspaperman trying to make a fortune. On the other hand, maybe it's just a hoaxer—"

"Or maybe it's real. This letter feels real. That bit about trade names just shows we're dealing with a new type of killer. He's in it for fame. Immortality." Already Anna's mind had found the same groove mine had been following. "What about the police?"

"Useless," I snarled.

Anna turned from the paper and looked at me. "What about you, Father? I know you've been working this out."

How much did she know? "Equally useless," I said evasively. Anna frowned, and I felt the need to justify myself. "Oh, I've profiled each victim: they're about forty, poor, with common-law marriages, supported with prostitution. The killings have happened in secluded corners of Whitechapel, places accessible to the public. The crimes are stabbings and throat slashings and mutilations. So, I've profiled them . . . but what does any of that tell about the killer?" The question was rhetorical.

The answer was not. "It tells us quite a bit, I'd say." Anna got up to pace the floor. "The letter writer's sane, for one—though he'd like to be perceived as insane. An insane man wouldn't hide his crimes this way. An insane man wouldn't clean himself of blood or cover the blood up so well. He'd be noticed stalking away. This man isn't noticed. He is even careful not to mail the letter when he is still . . . so to speak . . . red-handed."

A chill went through me. Anna sounded just like her mother. She had parsed out in moments what had taken me days to deduce, and she was taking a rare delight in it.

"He's intelligent, well educated," Anna continued. "The handwriting is refined, and the spelling is, for the most part, correct. This isn't a thug's letter."

"Anything else?"

"The man clearly has trouble with authority. He mocks the cleverness of the police but indicates that he expects someday to be caught by them, with words like 'they wont fix me just yet' and 'shant quit ripping them til I do get buck-led.' He can't control women who are his equals, so he's 'down on whores'—preying on the most destitute, helpless, and hopeless women. He controls them first with money and then with a knife, making sure to 'rip' them before they have time to 'squeal.' He wants to be a grand man—to have a trade name—but he's really a skulker, afraid of police and prosti-tutes, both."

"Yes, you've parsed it out," I admitted.

Anna turned a triumphant smile on me. "We can catch this man!"

I shook my head. "No. No, not we, my girl. I couldn't risk you."

Wagging her finger at me, Anna came to sit again on the arm of the chair. "You *are* planning something, aren't you?"

"I can't let this man kill again."

"You're planning something right away."

"I have to stop him—for the sake of your mother's memory."

"Yes. *My* mother. Which gives me the right to help."

"Out of the question."

"Last time, you left Mother behind because you thought she'd be safer." Anna gripped my arm. "You can't leave me behind."

I shivered, thinking, *I damn well can*, but Anna had my number. For seven years, I'd regretted my actions that fateful night. I couldn't leave Anna now.

"What are you planning?" she asked.

"He kills on the weekends—as one month ends and another begins. Tomorrow begins one such weekend. He kills in Whitechapel, and I have already booked passage for myself on a train that will arrive there at six tomorrow evening."

"Book me as well."

I held up my hand. "Given the killer's monthly schedule, I deduce that he has work that keeps him away from Whitechapel for three weeks at a time. According to one account, the killer arrived in Whitechapel with a soldier friend. I'd guess the soldier to be a seaman—and our killer to be one of his comrades. Sailors are notorious for landing in port and seeking easy women. I've checked the manifests of all the Royal Navy ships that dock on the Thames along Wapping, and the steam cutter *Union Jack* has kept a schedule that perfectly matches the dates of the killings."

Anna's mouth dropped open. "The cutter *Jack*? Jack the Ripper?"

"Precisely," I said. "And on the ship's manifest, there are three men who answer to the description that you have given—well educated, intelligent, sane, socially awkward, trouble with authority and women: Bo's'n Drew Beckworth, Ship's Mate Greer Haines, and Master of the Tops John Harder."

"And so, it's merely a matter of arriving at Wapping before the ship docks, identifying these three men as they debark, and following them to see which will seek out a prostitute in Whitechapel."

"All of them will seek out a prostitute in Whitechapel," I replied, though it nettled me to think that I was speaking to my sixteen-year-old daughter this way. "We'll have to follow these men to see which one of them attempts murder."

"But there are only two of us, and there are three of them."

"Luckily, Beckworth and Haines are best friends and constant companions. I'm betting that they were the two men seen together the night Martha Tabram was murdered."

"So, you follow them, and I follow Harder."

Here it was, the fateful decision. "Harder is the least likely suspect. He is master of tops—an authority with a problem with authority? But you cannot follow him, Anna—only watch from a safe distance."

"Won't we be conspicuous?" Anna asked. "A Cambridge don and his frilly daughter in Whitechapel?"

"We'll be in disguise."

ON THE thirtieth of September, 1888, Anna and I crouched in the lee of a little alleyway in Wapping. We wore clothes from a ragpicker's stall—tattered gray jerkins and trousers, boots yanked to midcalf, and misshapen felt berets. Even our faces were disguised, rubbed with ash and coal. We looked like any other desperate blokes in the shouldering mass of humanity. No one would recognize us; we could hardly recognize ourselves.

The alley gave us a clear view of the docks, where the *Union Jack* even now settled in its berth. While deckhands hurled lines over the mooring blocks, other crew hoisted a section of rail from its posts and slid a gangplank through the gap. The great ramp boomed down onto the dock.

"They're ready to debark," I whispered. I'd brought a bottle of gin as a prop, though now I lifted it in my fist and took a little swig for courage.

Anna grabbed the bottle, took a mouthful herself, and sprayed gin across the alley. Coughing like a woman with consumption, she choked out, "You have your sap?"

I fished in my breast pocket and pulled out a little leather bag full of lead shot. "Yes. You have your nightstick?"

She opened the flap of her rucksack, showing ten copies of the *Times* folded over a small club.

"Follow at a distance. Don't approach. Don't make eye contact. Get out your papers and start to sell them. Notice every woman he approaches, and when he snares one, track them to whatever spot he chooses—"

"And blow the whistle," Anna replied.

"Right. And keep blowing it until I or the police arrive."

"I understand the plan."

"You need to understand, also"—I reached up to touch the side of her face—"that I cannot lose you."

Her voice was sullen in the alley. "I know."

"Be careful."

"You, too." She flashed a smile. Then she looked up beyond the alley. "There's my mark."

I glanced out to see the crew of the *Union Jack* rambling down the gangplank. There, in the mass of them, was John

Harder. We recognized him from a photograph in the Royal Navy archives. A short man in blue bell-bottoms, Harder walked jauntily down the gangplank. Though it was a cool night and fog was beginning to rise from the fetid Thames, most of the sailors wore no coat. John Harder, master of the tops, however, wore a greatcoat—sufficient in length to hide a long blade and the gore that it brought out.

"Be careful," I repeated.

Anna reached back to me, squeezed my hand, and said, "I'll be all right." She hoisted the rucksack on her back and ambled out onto the pavement.

I watched her go, strong and gawky like an adolescent boy. She was a born actress, just as her mother had been. "I love you," I said to her back as she marched out into the street and vanished.

I did not have time to fear for her, though. My own marks descended the gangplank now. Ship's Mate Greer Haines was easy to spot. He was a head taller than his mates, his hair was the color of straw, and his unclean teeth flashed in a perpetual smile. But the greatest evidence of his identity was the bosom friend at his side, Drew Beckworth, boatswain of the *Union Jack*. The man was squat, with long black hair in braids, a gold ring in his nose, and a silver tooth in his smile. One of these two men—the blond blade of grass or the black truffle—was my killer. I was sure of it.

They strode down the gangplank side by side, laughing, and I shambled up from my spot in the alleyway and went to lean on a wall of crumbling brick. Ahead of me, the tide of sailors moved like a river toward Whitechapel Road—the avenue that sluiced into the heart of the dissolute East Side. Haines and Beckworth simply rode the tide. With bottle in hand, so did I.

I followed Haines and Beckworth down a canyon of Tudor

shops, their upper stories leaning out above the pavements. The seamen stopped at a vintner's shop for a bottle of wine and had the cork out and the first swigs down before they had even emerged. With bottle in hand, they sauntered up to a mustachioed fellow with an apron across his broad belly and a little iron oven at his feet. He was baking great doughy pretzels in the oven, skewering them on bamboo, and selling them for a halfpenny each. Money changed hands, and the sailors snacked.

I began to grow nervous. What murderer buys pretzels?

As Haines and Beckworth reached the heart of Whitechapel—the throbbing center of prostitution, drug trafficking, and gambling, the game changed utterly.

Beckworth's hand sneaked into the hand of Haines.

I stopped, heart pounding. These two had come to Whitechapel not for prostitutes but for each other. They weren't interested in women at all—dead or alive—but only in the rites of Sodom.

It was a fatal error. Neither of these men could be the murderer, which meant. . . .

A whistle sounded—long and shrill and desperate. "Anna."

The bottle of gin fell from my nerveless grip, and I pelted down the street, trying desperately to track the sound of that whistle. Beyond the garrulous laughter, beyond the snort and humph of ill-used horses and the melody of an oblivious piano, there came that shrill tone. I rounded a corner and heard it the more: strident, terrified. As I dodged past the bleary walkers, I saw her: Anna. Alive. Blowing that damned whistle. She stood by a lamppost, her newspapers spilled out across the ground but the nightstick in her grip.

I rushed up to her and slid to a stop. "Where? Where!"

She was white-faced and horrified, her arm jutting toward a stairway across the street.

"Stay here, and stop blowing that thing!" I snarled, and then ran, dodging traffic to reach the stairway.

It was ancient and decayed, descending between two buildings into a dark emptiness. I wished I'd brought a lantern but grabbed the sap, the next best thing. My feet struck the stairs, and I bounded down them, three at a time, to the landing, and down again.

At the bottom, I bolted out into an abandoned square bathed in the blue light of a gibbous moon. Hip-high weeds jutted up through the paving stones, but some had been trammeled down into a narrow path ahead. Stalking along that trail, I heard a gurgling sound. I lifted the sap high, ready for Jack the Ripper. Instead, moonlight revealed a woman lying in the weeds—the dying form of Elizabeth Stride.

Of course, I didn't know her name then, but it lives with me now, forever. Long Liz lay in a wreck of weeds, eyes wide in terror as her slit throat bled onto the ground. I knelt beside her and lifted her head in my lap. I pressed my hand on the slit, but there was no way to stop the blood flow.

"Too late, my darling," I said even as her eyes fluttered. "Too late to save you." She shivered once and was still. I kissed her and embraced her. The tall Swede, the sad lady, lay dead in my arms.

But Jack the Ripper was still alive.

Anna's whistle sounded again—two short bursts, and then silence.

"Anna!" I laid Elizabeth among the weeds and ran back toward the stairs. My heart thundered as I vaulted to the top.

Anna caught me and dragged me to a stop. She had crossed the road to peer down into the darkness, and she was terrified. "He was here," she gasped.

"What?"

"He came bolting up this way, just a minute after you'd

gone down. John Harder. Jack the Ripper." Her hand went to her throat.

I dragged her fingers away, checking her neck. It had not been cut, but there were red welts rising on either side. "What happened?"

"He took my whistle," she said. "He knew I was the one who called you. He said, 'You squealed.'"

I stared in terror at her. "That's it? That's all he said?"

"That's all he could say. You came running up the stairs the next moment."

"He must have been in the weeds the whole time—must have skulked away even as I found her."

"Wait—he—he did say one other thing: 'Not done to-night.' Then he bolted across the street."

"Where did he go?"

"I don't know." She turned, pointing east along White-chapel Road. Men and women, horses and carriages, the great roiling serpent of desire coiled down that road, but there was no sign of John Harder.

"He's going to kill again," I said, taking her hand. It was all unraveling now, and I was not going to let go of her. "Damn it, and God damn it," I murmured. "He's seen you. It's just like Jeremy Bachman all over again. He can trace you." I dragged her with me down the busy street.

"What are we going to do?" Anna asked, dodging past a crowd that watched Punch beat Judy.

"We're going to catch him—tonight."

29

HUNTING THE RIPPER

FROM THE MEMOIRS OF PROFESSOR JAMES MORIARTY:

Anna and I jostled down the Whitechapel Road amid the welter of humanity. "Stay sharp! Watch everyone! Look for that greatcoat."

We passed a five-year-old urchin begging for food, a dozen men watching a pair of mongrels fight in an alley, a hurdy-gurdy man whose monkey shivered more than danced, a pair of teamsters groaning as they rolled a cask up a street, a fifty-year-old woman troweled with makeup to hide her pox. . . .

I grabbed the woman's arm. "Did a man proposition you, moments ago?"

"Yor a man, ain't ya? Yor positioning me, yeah?"

"I mean another man. We're on his trail. Jack the Ripper."

"Ho! Ho!" the woman cried. "Like I ain't heard that one a million times. You ain't hustling ole Bette off lest'n I see the money first."

I shook my head grimly. "Beware, ole Bette. Jack's killed once already tonight. He's prowling for another kill."

"A double job, then, is it, guv—? 'Cause I got another double job in mind for you an' yor boyfriend."

"Achh!" I growled, stepping away and pulling Anna along with me. As we dodged along the pavement, I craned to see past all the top hats and bowlers. "I just wish I could get a clear view."

Ahead, a lamplighter made his way along the road. He

paused at a pole, leaned his slender ladder against it, mounted up, and reached with a tall wand to ignite the gas. The lamp flared, casting a lurid glow over the downturned heads below.

"That's it!" I charged to the lamplighter, fished a crown from my breast pocket, and slapped it into his sweaty palm.

"Whoa, now, guvnor. What's this?"

"I'm renting your ladder," I said, pushing him aside and climbing up to gaze out over the crowd. "Just for a moment."

"A crown says you can stay up there all night."

"I haven't got all night."

There, two blocks away—where Whitechapel Road crossed Thomas Street—a veiled woman spoke to a man in a blue greatcoat.

I leaped down from the ladder and, holding tight to Anna's hand, ran forward through the throng.

"You saw him?" Anna asked.

"Two blocks up. We're lucky he didn't turn off."

"He's just going where the prostitutes are."

"Yes—but he's also taunting us. He knows we're on to him, and he's got a new victim—right under our noses!"

We reached the first street and crossed it, leaping the slops channel in its center. On the block beyond, the mob so packed the pavement that we had to thread our way between a line of parked cabs and the rumbling stream of traffic.

At last we could see the street corner where Jack had spoken to the woman in the veil—but both of them were gone. Anna and I ran up to the spot and turned in circles, searching the crowd in vain. "Do you see them?"

"No," Anna said, her voice tremulous.

"Damn," I growled, only then noticing another prostitute across the street—a different woman. Her lips were as red and curved as a heart. "Let's find out what she saw."

We bolted across the road, almost getting run down by a black coach. Seeing our desperate dash, the prostitute smiled with drunken amusement.

"Excuse me, ma'am," I said breathlessly as we approached.

"Such manners!" she replied, her teeth splaying in a smile. "Nothing to excuse. Name's Mary."

"Mary, did you see the woman across the street—the other woman?"

"Kate, you mean? You're too late for her. Somebody else got her."

"That someone was Jack the Ripper," I said gravely.

Mary's eyes clouded. "Now that ain't nothing to kid about."

"I'm deadly serious. Did you see which way they went?"

"Up Thomas Street," she said, and beneath the makeup on her face, her cheeks trembled. "You don't think—?"

"Are there any secluded spots up that way, somewhere out of the public eye?"

Mary's eyes shifted in thought. "There's alleys aplenty that way, and little nooks behind the wool warehouse and the rendering house."

"Take us there," I said, gripping her arm.

Just then, a faint shout came echoing down Thomas Street. "It's him, Mary! It's the Ripper!"

Mary flung my hand off her. Her eyes flared. "You're him, ain't you? You're trying to lure me away. Help! Help! The Ripper!"

I stood rooted to the ground, astonished. "No. No! We're trying to catch him."

"Jack the Ripper!" she shouted, pointing at me.

I glanced around, seeing angry men turn their faces my way. The bloodstains on my trousers didn't help my case. I growled to Anna, "Run!"

Anna and I darted up Thomas Street in the direction that Mary had indicated. I harbored some vain hope we might find him, might stop him, but running was perhaps our greatest mistake. It triggered the predatory instincts of that predatory mob. They ditched their smoldering hunks of meat and their dancing monkeys and their dogfights and gave chase.

This was disaster. We'd never catch him now. We'd never outrun—

A foot hooked my ankle, and I tripped, sprawling out on the pavement. I let go of Anna's hand. "Run!" Then the air was blasted from my chest as man after man piled on me. I tried to squirm free, but they were too many, their hot breath blasting my neck.

"That's right, boys. Hold him down till the coppers nab him. Saucy Jack!" said a craggy voice—a voice I was sure belonged to the Ripper himself.

Before I could call him out, though, the men on my back lunged in as one, and the crushing weight of them made me go black.

I AWOKE to a hot lantern shining into my eyes. I was tied to a chair, and in the stuffy darkness beyond the lamp, figures shifted listlessly.

"So, the Ripper awakes."

I gave a little laugh, which resulted in a slap across the face. The blow stung, and, if nothing else, woke me fully.

The man who had struck me paced slowly, just beyond reach of the lantern. "My name is Inspector Lestrade. What is your name?"

"It's bloody well not Jack the Ripper," I said. "I'm Professor James Moriarty, chair of Maths and Physics at Jesus College, Cambridge."

"A long way from Jesus, aren't we?"

"I know you won't believe me, but I will tell you anyway: I came to London to track down Jack the Ripper, and I have discovered his identity."

"Truly?"

"His name is John Harder, master of the tops of the steam cutter *Union Jack*, even now docked at Wapping."

"You talk a pretty story, Jack," said Lestrade.

And so began another night of monstrous inquisitions. They asked about the blood on my hands and all down my front, and I told them of the first woman that Harder had attacked, told them how I was only a few seconds too late. Rueful smiles flashed in the darkness. I indicated where they would find her body—that she was not mutilated like the others because I had interrupted the Ripper. I had been that close behind.

"So close, you might be one and the same man."

"The woman died in my arms."

"I bet she did."

"There was nothing else I could do for her, and I was determined to capture the Ripper, and he attacked my daughter so that—"

"Your daughter?"

I explained Anna's presence, disguised as a paper seller. The hyena grins all around me only grew. Lestrade snarled question after question at me, wondering why a professor would be so stupid as to bring his daughter to the hunting grounds of the Ripper, why he would disguise her as a paperboy, why he thought a whistle would keep her safe. I tried to dismiss all these issues, driving instead to the Ripper's words to Anna: "I ain't done yet." I told how Anna and I had given chase, had seen him at the corner of Whitechapel and Thomas with a prostitute named Kate.

"Oh, good guess! Every whore's named Kate!"

They jeered, certain they had gotten their man. As the horrible night wore on, I grew quiet, not only because I had testified to everything five times over, but also because I knew that Jack was still out there, carving up Kate. And once he was finished with Kate, Jack would make his way to Scotland Yard, would somehow find out the name of the man that the police were questioning, and would come after me—and Anna.

So, it was with both relief and terror that I greeted Anna as they brought her into the room. Her very appearance at Scotland Yard—a sixteen-year-old girl disguised as a paper seller—did much to quiet those laughing mouths. Her story then did even more. She corroborated my account in every particular. She also had her own adventures to tell about:

"The mob brought my father down, sure enough, just where you found him. They thought he was the Ripper, but that's only because Jack himself had stirred them up. I saw him—Jack in his blue greatcoat standing in an alley, calling my father out and taunting the mob. But when a few of those brutes looked up to see who was shouting, well, then old Jack turned and vanished into the shadows."

"Oh, simple enough to claim," Lestrade said. "So the real Jack got away up an alley?"

"No. He didn't get away."

"Then where is he? If he didn't get away, then you must have captured him. Where are you hiding him?" Lestrade mocked.

"I didn't capture him—but I did follow him."

I said, "Foolish!"

"I was careful," Anna said. "I didn't see Kate with him, so I was afraid it was all a trap to ambush me. I hung back—until I heard the scream."

Lestrade's expression grew intent. "His next victim."

"Yes. One quick scream, and then nothing more. It sounded . . . cut off."

Grim chuckles rumbled around us.

"Well, I went slowly, looking in every dark place. Without the sound of a scream to follow, it was blind man's bluff. At last, I came to Mitre Square, and in the corner opposite me, I saw a man hunched over in the dark, and I knew that great-coat on his back, and I screamed. He looked back at me. It was John Harder, all right, but his face was striped in blood. He turned, and something small and white flew off the knife in his hand. I think it was the woman's ear. It went in a bush, and he went to get it, but I screamed again, and he stalked toward me. 'Triple job!' That's what he said. 'Triple job!' "

"You should have run," I said.

"I started to, but then a crowd of people came charging up behind me. Some were from the same mob that had grabbed Father. They'd heard me scream and they came running and they saw John Harder, too. They saw that he was the real Ripper. He turned and dashed away."

"Didn't anyone chase him?" Lestrade asked.

"They started to, but then they saw . . . they saw . . . poor Kate."

Lestrade asked, "What did she look like?"

"Mutilated. Throat cut. Belly cut. Guts pulled out . . ."

"All right, all right," Lestrade said, waving away the testimony. "This has all been very interesting and dramatic, but all these intimate details—the names of the victims, the locations of the killings, the types of wounds inflicted, the fact that you and your father tell exactly the same story—they all might simply mean that you two planned and carried out these killings as a team."

"Except that," said Anna with a fierce look in her eyes, "when the police came, they brought ten of us back to testify.

There are nine others waiting to describe Jack the Ripper to you."

"You've got all the evidence, now!" I said. "Sweep down to Wapping and snatch this monster from the *Union Jack*!"

At last, we'd gotten through to Inspector Lestrade. He sent one of his men to the docks, though he retained Anna and me while he interrogated the other witnesses. Every last one corroborated our story.

An hour later, the officer returned, panting and covered in cold sweat. "It's as he said. Wapping, the *Union Jack*—even this John Harder fellow, master of the tops—"

"And? And?" Lestrade prompted.

"And the ship sailed again before dawn."

"Where's she bound?"

"Paris."

"Paris?"

"She's a steam cutter. Fast ship. No one'll catch her."

Lestrade leaned his knuckles on his desk, jaw working, eyes fiery as if they could burn through the wall. "We'll send another ship to intercept. We'll send a man to the Continent to wire the French. God damn it—the French! They're not going to nab Jack the Ripper. I'll go myself, will wire ahead from Normandy and then beat him there on the train and be ready to nab him at the dock at Paris."

"Inspector," broke in a new voice—a young officer who entered the interrogation room and waved a postcard in the air. "He sent it to the Central News Agency—and they sent it on to us."

Lestrade snatched the postcard, held it up, and read silently. His hand trembled.

"What is it?" asked several of the other detectives.

"It's from Jack, I'd wager," I said, "another taunt, yes?"

Giving me an imperious glare, Lestrade drew a deep breath and read:

I was not codding dear old Boss when I gave you the tip, you'll hear about Saucy Jacky's work tomorrow double event this time number one squealed a bit couldn't finish straight off. Ha not the time to get ears for police. thanks for keeping Mr. M. back so I got to work again.

"One of you morons gave him my name!" I raged.

Anna glared at me, a look that combined frustration and fear. Then she asked Lestrade, "Are we free to go now?"

Lestrade snorted and gestured to his comrades to un-shackle me.

I stood, rubbing my chafed wrists, and said, "I hope you buckle him—Boss."

30

REVENGE

FROM THE MEMOIRS OF PROFESSOR JAMES MORIARTY:

Anna and I cleaned ourselves up, purchased new clothes, and headed to Victoria Station. There, I bought two tickets to Cambridge.

"Cambridge?" Anna objected. "We can't go home. We almost got him. We could catch him in Paris. Do you think Lestrade will catch him?"

I laughed aloud. "We tracked him, we found him, we got his name, we would have captured him this very night if not for the police. No, they know less than the papers, and the papers know nothing."

"Then we have to go to Paris!" Anna pressed.

I stepped from the platform onto the train. "Do you honestly believe that John Harder will be on that boat when it docks in France?"

Anna shook her head sullenly. "Of course not." She took my hand.

I lifted her up beside me. "Of course not."

She was trembling; my darling Anna was trembling. All through that insane night, she had been a rock, even when Jack the Ripper was spewing his rancor into her face, but now she trembled.

Anna clutched my coat sleeve. "What will we do?"

"Mrs. Mulroney," I said heavily, leading her into an empty coach compartment. "We'll stay at the boardinghouse tonight. Jack's canny, but not so canny that he will have traced us out that far. We need a night's rest, need to be able to think clearly to outsmart him." I sat down.

Anna melted against me, all the trembling terror pouring out of her. "Oh, Father, I'm glad of it. A night's sleep—Mrs. Mulroney—a warm, safe bed tonight."

"Yes."

Evening was drawing down over the Cambridge platform when we arrived. I held Anna back, kept our train compartment dark, and watched out the windows to see if Jack lurked there. Every last passenger debarked. The conductor called, "All aboard to Ely!" Porters and passengers made their way onto the train, but still we waited. The first blasts of steam came as the brakes disengaged and the pistons surged—and Jack was nowhere to be seen.

"Let's go!" Grabbing Anna's hand, I hurried her from the compartment, through the aisle, and down the steps. Already the train was rolling, and the platform scrolled away below our feet. "Hit the ground running," I advised and leaped, barely able to stay upright. Anna followed—good girl—and landed with more grace than I.

The moment we had caught our balance, we ran together to the station house, passed through it, reached the street, and hailed a hansom. A cab pulled up with a rumpled man sitting on the board, his cap dragged down over his brow. Before letting Anna climb in, I stood up on the fender and knocked the hat off the man's head.

"What's this?" he asked, scrabbling to grab his cap even as I tugged his goatee. "Ow!" It was real.

"No offense, good man," I said, slipping a crown into his hand. That hunk of silver covered a multitude of sins. Then, as Anna clambered into the coach, I cupped the cabby's fuzzy ear and whispered, "The Red Gables on Charles."

We had a quiet ride, Anna and I. The steady clop of the horse's hooves sounded mournful on the cobbles. I kept Anna back from the windows, kept the curtains drawn except for a narrow slit of light out of which I peered. There was no sign of Jack or of pursuit of any kind.

At last, we reached the Red Gables. I paid the cabby well to keep mum about us, and then Anna and I dashed to the door. We knocked. When the doddering old proprietress answered the door, we forced our way inside.

She wailed, trying to drive us out.

"It is a matter most urgent, madam," I told her. "We're not safe on the street. This is Anna—don't you remember her?"

The gray suspicion on the old woman's face flushed to a pink smile, and she said, "Oh, the girl with Mrs. Mulroney."

"Mrs. Mulroney, yes."

The proprietress said, "Go ahead then, Anna, dear. I suppose Mrs. Mulroney is expecting you."

"You can suppose," I replied.

Up the stairs we went, and down the hall we came to our nanny's room and knocked. She opened the door in nightshirt and cap and stared at us in shock.

"We're in desperate need of your aid, Mrs. Mulroney," I said. "You must let Anna stay here with you tonight."

The governess, always a steady woman, gestured behind her to the small room. It held only a bed, a washbasin, and a folded cot. "Anna is always welcome, of course. . . . But what desperate business is this?"

"You'll be safer not to know," I said.

"I'll tell you," Anna said, stepping into Mrs. Mulroney's arms and hugging her tightly. After a moment, Anna pulled back and cast a glance my way. "But you must also let Father stay."

Mrs. Mulroney's mouth dropped open. "Anna. It would not be proper—"

"Quite right," I replied. "Not my intention: I spied a comfortable settee downstairs in the parlor. It'll allow me to keep watch over the whole place. I wouldn't wish to bring danger down on this house."

"But you need sleep," Anna protested.

"I'll have sleep," I told her flatly. Then stepping into Mrs. Mulroney's room, I embraced both women. "Now, it's time for you two to get some rest."

Anna clung to me as if she knew what mischief I had in mind. At last, I pulled away from her and bowed my thanks to Mrs. Mulroney. "Lock your door, Mrs. Mulroney, and don't open it for anything until dawn."

The door closed on my words, and the bolt snicked into position.

Turning, I stalked away down the hall. I had no intention of sleeping on a settee that night. I would occupy my own bed, but only after I had made it—and all the world—safe from Jack the Ripper.

Descending the stairs, I went to the kitchen of the Red Gables and found a long knife. Secreting it in the sleeve of my coat, I left the Gables out its back door and listened with satisfaction as the flustered proprietress locked it behind me.

There was no fear left. I was on the hunt. Perhaps this was how the Ripper felt night after night—knife in hand and murder in heart.

Jack was, of course, in our apartments, waiting in ambush. He would watch out the bay window to see my approach, would listen for my key in the keyhole and would slide into position to take me unawares. A marvelous plan, except that he had failed to factor in my own thirst to kill.

I did not approach up the front walk, but came through the
back alley. Also, I did not enter through the back door, but instead climbed a trellis two houses down and made my way
over slick slates, rooftop to rooftop, until I stood just beside
my bedroom window. It was a simple thing to slide the tip of
the knife beneath the sash and pry it slowly, soundlessly up.
Then I extended my leg in over the sill and drew myself
within.

The air inside was stifling. The apartments had a closed-
up feeling. My hope began to fade. I stepped lightly across
the floor, avoiding the boards that creaked, and made my way
to the bedroom door.

Beyond, the parlor looked empty. The curtains were undis-
turbed.

With knife out before me, I crept through the parlor. The
curtains revealed no one. I opened the cloakroom door and
stabbed through the coats, but the knife found only fabric
and air. Next, I checked Anna's room—in the wardrobe, beneath the bed. Then the kitchen, the larder, the dining
room. . . .

I'd been a fool. I'd overestimated the man. Jack may have
had my initial—Mr. M.—but he didn't know my name,
didn't know I was *Professor Moriarty*. He couldn't have found
out where I lived.

A breeze from the bedroom gusted into the hall, rolling
tiny motes of dust across the floor and against the toes of my
shoes. *I should shut the window*. Going into the bedroom, I
stepped past the bed, along the open wardrobe—

I saw him out of the corner of my eye, leaping from the
wardrobe.

Jack the Ripper smashed down on my back, legs around
my hips, arms grappling my shoulders, knife at my throat.
Ugh, the weight of the man—not a big man, but bony, wiry.

Bent on killing me. As I collapsed to the floor, I managed to shove my left hand up over my throat.

He drew his blade. It slashed the back of my hand. I hardly felt the cut, the knife was so sharp, but only pressure and the warm gush of blood.

Jack felt the blood, too, and he laughed, sitting up on my back. "So easy. Like a whore, you are. Go down hard and stay down with throat gushing."

He couldn't see my bleeding hand—laid open along the tendon from wrist to ring finger. He thought it was a neck wound. I gurgled and shuddered to keep him thinking it. Best of all, though, he couldn't see the knife from the Red Gables lying just under the bed, just within reach of my right hand.

Jack's tone changed to mock regret. "Sorry, Boss. I'd have left you alone if you'd have left me alone. I'm not down on professors like I'm down on whores—but you hunted me. You and your girl did. And you found out who I was. Couldn't let you go telling everyone who Jack is."

I let the gurgling sounds subside and released a long, sputtering groan. Then I lay still, hoping he would get off me before I had to gasp another breath.

"Too bad you got wise about my little trap. Climbing in the way you did. Leaving your daughter somewheres. I'll find her, I will. Not hard to get information from people. Just smile and seem a little daft and a little in trouble, and they tell you whatever you want. That's how I got your name, by the bye. Just showed up at Scotland Yard, pretending to be an idiot, asking them to let my brother go, crying, getting hysterical, saying he wasn't no Jack the Ripper—making them tell me it wasn't my brother they'd caught, but some fellow from Cambridge. 'My brother's from Cambridge!' I said to them, and they barked out, 'Is your brother named Moriarty?'

Ha-ha, that's when I had you. Mr. M., I called you—not knowing you were a professor and all."

My stamina was running out, but so was his story.

Jack gave a sigh and patted my back gently. "Well, there it is. I won't be cutting you any more. You're not my type." He pulled his knees up and stood, still straddling me.

I chanced a slow, silent breath, filling my lungs for an attack.

Jack lifted his right leg to step away. " 'Course, that daughter of yours—"

I grabbed the Red Gables knife, flipped over, and slashed across the back of Jack's left thigh—just above the knee. His leg was planted, his knee locked, and I bore down with all the fury in me. The knife severed fabric and folded back skin like warm butter and laid open tendons and made them snap. Jack's hamstrings leaped up in pain, bunching beneath his buttocks.

He jolted on that uncertain leg, staggered, could not bend his knee to catch himself, and crashed down on the floor beside me.

I scrambled to my feet. My left hand ached, blood falling hot from it, but the rest of me felt magnificent. I was standing, knife in hand, over the convulsing figure of Jack the Ripper. He looked small now, with a pale, pinched face and a weak jaw. "Is this how it feels, Jack, to stand above a person and hold life and death in your hand?"

He tried to scrabble away from me, crab-walking on his hands and his one good leg. He'd lost his razor, and now it lay on the floor beside a wide trail of blood from his sliced knee.

I kicked the razor away and stepped up to him and drew my knife across the back of his other knee. Now he was truly hamstrung. "There'll be no escape, Jack."

He twisted in pain, teeth gritting. How like a frightened

child he seemed—caught—shifting from belligerence to bargaining. "So, it's the police for old Jack, after all."

I laughed. "No. They're on your side. They held me while you did your last job. No. There'll be no police."

Jack smiled broadly. His rumpled face smoothed so that his head seemed a jack-o'-lantern. "You can't rip me, Doctor. You can't rip the Ripper."

I growled low, "My wife was killed by a man like you, murdered in this very apartment. It was because of her that I came after you. And now you've threatened my daughter. I very much can rip you."

His grin faded away, and his mercurial face now resembled only a wadded-up gunnysack. "I'll squeal."

"Then squeal. I'll still cut your throat. And when the police arrive, I'll tell them what happened, that you ambushed me in my own bedroom and tried to kill me—that you said you'd kill my daughter. They won't care about the hamstringing. You're Jack the Goddamned Ripper. I've got all the testimony I need to prove it. It'll be an inconvenience for me, of course, with all the interrogations, all the news stories, but in the end, I'll be the man who killed Jack the Ripper, and you'll be just a cut-up little corpse."

He looked sullen. Resigned. "And if I don't squeal?"

"If you don't squeal, I'll slit your throat and dispose of your body, and your legend will live on." A light entered his eyes, and I knew I had him. Here was a man concerned about his trade name, a man who wanted to live forever in infamy. Demonic. "And whenever another hacked-up body is found, folk will whisper that perhaps it was Jack the Ripper."

The light in his eyes intensified, becoming an actual glow. In those dark apartments, Jack's eyes shone red like the eyes of a cat in moonlight. So uncanny was that aspect, so preternatural the effect, that I paused for a moment, the knife hanging loose in my hand.

And then Jack said, "I'll not squeal. I'll be a lamb."

"Yes. You will." I gripped the knife tight and leaned in and set it on Jack's neck and drew it so fiercely across his throat that the blade grated on his spine.

Jack's neck boiled, and he slumped. I stepped back to watch him die, stepped back as blood pooled across the planks.

But there was something strange about that blood. It glimmered. Something energetic scintillated through it. It was teeming like a puddle full of pollywogs, like a pond with mosquito larvae twisting and transforming and taking wing. And suddenly, those points of light boiled up out of the blood and rose into the air, forming a red mist. It danced between us, a luminous vapor—a soul.

I stared. Never before had I seen such a thing. My own wife had died in my arms, and I'd seen no soul ascending. I'd held Long Liz as she died, and not even a gray shade came from her. But here, when this son of hell died, some eternal spirit rose from his wretched blood!

And then I knew. I was not seeing a soul. I was seeing a demon.

BECOMING THE RIPPER

FROM THE MEMOIRS OF PROFESSOR JAMES MORIARTY:

John Harder lay dying on the parlor floor, but above him, the demon soul of Jack the Ripper boiled and seethed, very much alive. It seemed a red mist, rising in tendrils from his blood and gathering above his body. There was intelligence in that cloud. It watched me . . . and it lunged.

I staggered back and gasped, and the mist rushed into my nose and throat. It burned like whisky. I snorted to blow the red stuff out, but then I had to breathe again, and more came in. I collapsed on the bed. The red cloud engulfed me. Thrashing, I rolled to my feet and ran for the door, unable to shake the stuff. It clung to me like oil, and my lungs screamed for air.

I breathed.

The red mist filled me, suffused me. It stung, but it also intoxicated.

Ah, what sweet relief, to surrender, to fight no longer, to give myself in to the possession of my enemy.

Another breath. I understood all that I had once despised. Let him in. Let him take over.

Another breath.

I became him.

For years I had feared death. Now, I was death.

I had killed twice now, without consequence—killed

Susanna's killer and killed Jack the Ripper, and the only consequence was this new, fearless life: this power.

At last I knew how it felt to stand above a still-warm body, to hold absolute power over it. My knife was sharp. Why not find out what the Ripper was made of? Why not draw the blade thus across his belly and see the great sac that was his stomach? Why not slide the knife between the pink snake of gut and this great gray pudding of pancreas, to feel the ducts sever one by one—*thup! thup! thup!* And, where is that thunder coming from, that panicked rumble that runs through his viscera? Ah, of course, a heart pumping itself dry, dying all the while! And by cutting thus and twisting the knife between the ribs so and reaching my hand in and yanking. Oh! Yes! This was how it felt to stand victorious above a foe and hold high the still-flailing heart!

The human body is endlessly entertaining. So many crannies, so many glands. How long I was at it, I do not know. By the time I was finished, though, the Ripper could fit into three small trunks. I know because I put him in them and set them by the door. The blood was all out of them, so they wouldn't seep. Then I set about to mopping. It was somehow not the chore it had been when I cleaned up the last time—almost a pleasure, as if I were waxing the wood with Jack. Bucket after red bucket, I worked, toting them two at a time to the sewer in the alley and then drawing more water at the well where the whole neighborhood drank. I worked in shirtsleeves, head held high in the biting night air. I worked with the cheerful demeanor of a man who has nothing to fear.

By morning, the work was done. The blood was up, and dawn winds sluiced through the apartments from bay window to bedroom sash, drying the floor. I changed my clothes and threw the blood-soaked ones into the fire. Meanwhile,

Jack waited by the door, packed for a picnic in the country—someplace nice and secluded. I'd have to buy a shovel.

A furtive knock came at the door. I threw back the bolt and flung the door wide, startling poor Mrs. Mulroney and Anna, who trembled on the landing outside. Mrs. Mulroney held a protective arm before my daughter and frowned. "You didn't sleep at the boardinghouse."

"I got restless." I flashed her a smile. "Business to attend to."

Anna entered the parlor and looked around. Our curtains billowed like ghosts, and the floor was still puddled in places with pinkish water. "What've you been up to?"

"Business."

She cradled her hand to her mouth. "Not—Jack?"

I pointed to the three trunks by the door. "We're taking him on holiday."

IT WAS a whole new life for me, life on a new scale. No longer was I mired in the everyday struggles of everyman. I had transcended them. Fear, worry, dread, grief, remorse—these poisons were gone from my being. In their place, I had a new, voracious appetite for knowledge—and power.

Anna refused to accompany me and Jack on our picnic. It was just as well. She would have simply fussed the whole while—might even have had a crisis of conscience and run to the police.

The porters complained about the weight of my trunks, but a few crowns shut them up. At Ely, I rented a farmer's wagon, complete with fork, flail, and shovel. As chance would have it, I did not need any of them, but only a peat bog and the rope I had brought and a few large stones. Jack would have liked the spot. Peat water works like formaldehyde, so Jack's flesh, as well as his legend, would be immortalized.

I committed one other act to ensure Jack's immortality. I
brought half of one of his kidneys back to Cambridge with
me, placed it in a jar filled with wine, boxed it up, and sent it
to George Lusk, president of the Whitechapel Vigilance
Committee. With it, I attached the following letter.

From hell.
Mr. Lusk,
Sor
   *I send you half the Kidne I took from one woman and
prasarved it for you tother piece I fried and ate it was very
nise. I may send you the bloody knif that took it out if you
only watse a whil longer*

                              signed
                              Catch me when you can Mishtr Lusk

Sending that letter was my final act on behalf of Jack. I did
not need to do more. The police and the press and the public
together kept him alive. So did other killers—men who
needed a scapegoat for their crimes. For example, on the ninth
of November, five weeks after Jack's own death, a Mary Jane
Kelly was found slain in her small apartment in Spitalfields.
The murder was entirely different from the others, though.
The victim was about twenty years younger than Jack's targets, she was far more mutilated than the others, and she was
killed indoors. Despite these discrepancies, all of London
credited the killing to Jack the Ripper.

But I knew who Mary Jane's real killer was. I'd already in-
corporated him into my grand algorithm of crime in London.
He was Joseph Barnett—an extortionist and opium addict,
and also the victim's lover. He would get his. My algorithm
would make sure of it.

And so, I returned to the mathematics of crime. After a few weeks, I'd filled in the last of the modern personalities that ruled London's criminal underworld. Then, a handful of calculations revealed the lynchpin—a pet cat owned by a gang lord named Jacob Ferny, a cat he was convinced was the reincarnation of his beloved mother. Skin the cat, and the whole organization would self-destruct.

But in my calculations, I couldn't help noticing other possibilities. There was Susan Graham, the aspiring opera star who was also the pampered mistress of another mob boss. If I got at her, I could get at him. I arranged the untimely illness of a diva in *Aïda*, and Susan stepped up from understudy to star. Then I made sure the mob boss understood that this had been no accidental illness. By careful and anonymous insinuation, I gained influence over a third of the East End rackets.

There was also Harold Jenkins, a drug lord who used opium to allay his own natural paranoia. Simply by adding a few other choice compounds to his daily hit, I put strings on the man. I controlled his every move and slowly took over his whole enterprise.

Then there was Bill Stewart, a minor but promising blackmailer who had a weekly appointment at a brothel. I sent him an anonymous tip that he should delay his weekly visit by half an hour—and thus he witnessed a Member of the House of Lords in flagrante delicto. Bill had struck gold. In the course of a month, he became king of the extortion racket—a king who religiously read every note that came to him from his anonymous benefactor.

A hit man named Emil Sykes received a similar note—indicating that his boss had taken out a contract on him. At first unbelieving, the hit man soon discovered the truth of the message—for I myself had taken out the contract in the boss's name. Sykes was desperate for a plan, and I provided him one, note by note. He followed my advice and soon chewed his way through the boss's other killers until at last he slew the boss himself. A new lord of murder was crowned, one completely loyal to me.

And so it went. With the right note sent to the right eyes at the right time, I could destroy a whole branch of crime and build it up again in my own image, under my own control. In six months, I had gained influence over every major branch of crime in London. By the end of a year, I controlled every operation. In two years' time, I had become the unchallenged and unchallengeable emperor of crime throughout southeastern England.

Susanna would have been proud.

But Anna wasn't. She had turned on me the very morning after I'd killed the Ripper. She wanted to involve the police, argued about what was "right," told me that I hadn't killed the Ripper—that he had killed me.

I laughed it off. It was just the sort of nonsense a young woman would say. Anna hadn't ever done an honest day's work. She was a china doll who did not cook or clean or raise children but only sat and stewed about "injustice." A whole generation of Victorian women did the same. They protested that they couldn't vote, they protested that their men ran out to prostitutes, they protested that their men got drunk, they protested that their men were opium addicts. And why were these men driven from their homes to the streets and the sins there? Because of the insufferable protests of the insufferable women in their lives. Anna's "concern" had the same effect on me. The more she complained, the more time I devoted to my criminal empire.

What a grave disappointment she had become.

And then even Jesus turned against me—Jesus College, that is. Here is the letter I received from the president.

> *Dear Dean Moriarty:*
> *Your genius is needed, now more than ever, at the head of the Department of Physics. However, your activities beyond the campus have been stealing you away with increasing regularity. Some of your students have reported that you attended only two of the twelve physics tutorials you were assigned to provide. This sort of disregard for your duties, if left unchecked, will result in your eventual dismissal.*
>
> *President MacWilliams*

Absurdity. Jesus College had the greatest mathematical mind of a generation, and they would let him go because of tardiness?

I decided to dismiss myself before MacWilliams could dismiss me. That very night, I packed up Anna and me, and we moved to London. The next morning, MacWilliams was found stabbed in his bed.

AND SO, mathematics herself delivered dominance into my hands. Other men rose through bribes and threats and murder. I rose through logarithmic functions. Like a tireless spider, I spun out my equations and sent forth my notes and wove a vast web of calculation and crime, a web that soon reached to York in the north and Cardiff in the east and Copenhagen in the west and Paris in the south.

But some men are immune to the Mother of Sciences. Mathematics has no hold on them. They are irrational figures: 3 divided by 0 or 5 divided by infinity or the square root of negative 9. When such a figure enters an equation, he brings it crashing down.

I met my irrational figure. I met a man who, like a plague, infected the smallest tissue of my leviathan and thereby destroyed the whole organism.

With no love of mathematics, he brought me down. And I will bring him down, in turn.

BOOK III

OF LEGENDS
AND MEN

32

HER STORY

As the Bern Express rolled toward Paris, Anna lay between Thomas Carnacki and Harold Silence and told them all she knew about her father's life: that James Moriarty was a genius, that he once had been a good man, that her mother was also a genius but had unwittingly set into his hands the keys to control a vast criminal empire. Anna told them that after slaying Jack the Ripper, her father had ceased to be the man who had loved her and whom she had loved, and had become a monster.

"Of course, I don't know all the details. Father's been writing his memoirs, and maybe someday I'll get to read them. But I do know this much: Whatever madness grips him now comes from outside. Deep within, my father is a good man."

Silence, who had been lying with his hands templed above his face, at last spoke: "So, you knew of your father's activities all the while that he was taking control of this . . . empire of crime?"

"Well, I knew what he let me know—or what I could discover on my own. At first, I pleaded with him to stop, but it only drove him into a rage. Then, I simply watched him, monitored, tried to understand his machinations. One day he caught me studying his algorithm, and he struck me across the face. From then on . . . I ceased trying.

"And when we moved to London, all that was bad became worse. I had no friends in the city, and Father spent no time with me anymore. His manias became terrifying—with ruined furniture and words that turned the air blue. At least he didn't kill anyone by his own hands anymore. He had others to do that. He even found this Dr. Gottlieb—a ghoul of a man whom Father had met at Cambridge—and enlisted his talents. Whenever Father had a particularly horrible man to kill, he would take the man to Gottlieb, who performed a lobotomy. Father always assisted. It was as if he wanted to see what was happening in their minds, wanted to harvest the evil in them."

Thomas, who lay next to the wall, took Anna's hand. "It must have been terrifying."

"It was. I only hoped I could somehow win him back. And then, one day, he appeared at the door with a storm cloud about his shoulders and his eyes flashing lightning. He stomped into the room and sat in his accustomed seat, and when I brought him his tea, he gently laid hold of my wrist and said, 'You may get your wish, Anna.'

" 'What wish, Father?' I asked.

"He laughed bleakly and squeezed my arm so that his fingernails left circular welts. 'Your wish to destroy me.'

"I protested: 'I don't want to destroy you. I want to save you. I want you to give up this life of crime.'

" 'Well,' he replied more quietly, 'you may get your wish. There's another man out there—another genius. He's figured out the algorithm. He's found the lynchpin.'

" 'Then let's escape, Father. Let's take the money and escape to the Continent—before the killing begins.' "

" 'There won't be any killing. This man has set everything up through the police. My whole empire will go before the docket and go to jail. There's nothing I can do.'

"I knelt before him and stared into his eyes. 'Yes, there is. Let's go to the Continent. Let's be someone else—James and Anna Schmidt.'

"His face brightened for a moment as if he saw the hope of a new life. 'Yes. The Continent. Why not travel there? It would be pleasant to have a diversion. I'd like to go hunting on the Continent.'

"I took his words the wrong way, of course. I took them as a sign that he would be giving up his life of crime." She looked to Silence. "I had no idea, until too late, that he had come to the Continent to hunt you."

The conductor's voice came, distant and muffled, through the compartment door, *"Paris! Saint-Lazare! Une demi-heure! Paris! Saint-Lazare! Une demi-heure!"*

Silence gave a sigh. "And your long story tells us everything except who I am."

Anna shook her head. "I'm sorry, but Father never told me your name."

"It's no matter. I'll know in half an hour."

33

THE MAN HIMSELF

After Anna's long and tragic tale and after Silence's bold pronouncement, I was ready for a little quiet. Only the train spoke as we approached Paris. Silence seemed to be dozing, though I had thought the same any number of times this past night and had always been surprised when he asked some probing question. Anna, for her part, was wrung out. She drew the blanket up and fell soundly asleep.

Let them sleep; I felt strangely wakeful. Anna's story had filled me with a terrible melancholy, and I wanted nothing more than to roll over, raise the window shade, and watch the dark night give way to gloaming.

The train moved through hilly country beneath a wine-red sky. Farmland undulated in wave upon black wave from our wheels out to the horizon. It was a dark and dreamy landscape, the chaos before creation. The rolling horizon was broken only by the occasional farmhouse, boxy and black.

In time, the sun roused itself and climbed into the sky. Morning light moved across the monochromatic land, and it bloomed with color: green and gold, brown and red—it was as if a watercolor brush were dragging across the charcoal hills and bringing them to life. I felt as if I were sitting beside the easel of God.

Gradually, the works of God were overtaken by the works of man. Farmlands gave way to Dark Age hamlets, and they to medieval towns, and they to the imperial capital of Louis the Sun King. Beyond the train window, Paris was taking shape. Limestone facades with thousands of gables, spoke-like avenues laid out by Napoleon III, gray cathedrals aspiring to the sky . . .

The tracks bore us on toward another cathedral, one built for machines. Our rail line delved in among a dozen others, converging from all points across Europe. Roaring engines of iron passed through viaducts and underground ways to emerge within the glass-topped station at Gare Saint-Lazare. Smoke belched from stacks and spread across glass awnings. Incrementally, we slowed, and at last the air brakes hissed, and the conductor called: *"Paris! Paris!"*

I heard it, but my comrades still slept. I did not want to wake them. Anna lay like a child, so fragile and weary and beautiful. I had loved her selfishly before hearing her terrible story, but now I loved her selflessly. I would defend her to the death. How could I wake her?

And Silence, if his pledge was true, would wake to somehow discover his identity. While he drowsed, he was still my friend, my comrade, but who would the man be in five minutes?

Let the other passengers bustle and stand in the aisles and curse as they yanked their trunks down the passage. I would allow my companions a few more minutes of sleep. To this day, I look back at those stolen moments as precious. They were over all too soon.

The tread of the porter came through the aisle, and his fist pounded the frame of the sleeper. *"Paris! Gare Saint-Lazare! Tout le monde descend!"*

"Indeed," said Silence, rousing suddenly, his eyes keen and clear. "I was merely waiting for the rabble to pass."

"A moment, please," I said to him.

Between us, Anna stirred. Disoriented, she glanced between the two of us and said, "Paris?"

"Yes," I replied, smiling. "Beautiful Paris. The City of Love."

"The city of identity," Silence corrected, and he drew back the curtain from the sleeping berth and stepped into the aisle.

Anna stared after him a moment. "Feeling energetic, isn't he?"

"We'd better catch him up, or we'll never find him. He's planning to have a new name in five minutes." I helped Anna to her feet. Turning, I remembered to hoist the damned electrical contraption I'd been carting since the sanatorium. I followed Anna into the aisle, empty now of any other passengers, including Silence. Hurrying to the end of the car, we climbed down the steps and onto a crowded platform. "Where is he?"

"There!" Anna cried, pointing to a newsboy who was handing a paper to Silence.

We ran up to join him as he shook the paper out before him. It was *Le Temps*, and the masthead indicated it was the eighth of May, 1891. When Silence scanned the first headline, he practically crowed.

"What is it?" Anna asked.

Silence flipped the back of his hand against the article and translated the headline: " 'Scotland Yard Arrests Five Hundred.' Here, my dear, is the fall of your father's empire. Surely this story will credit me with destroying his syndicate. Anna, my French is not as good as yours. Would you mind?"

Trembling slightly, she took the paper in hand and began to translate:

In a series of lightning raids last week, the London police rounded up hundreds of crime lords: opium dealers, proprietors of brothels, extortionists, racketeers, and all manner of other thugs. The detective who masterminded the crackdown was Inspector Lestrade of Scotland Yard.

I looked at Silence and let out a giggle. "You're Lestrade?"
Anna shook her head. "Of course not!"
Silence shot me a querulous look as Anna continued:

This is by far the largest criminal dragnet ever conducted by Scotland Yard. Previous cleanup attempts have been hampered by an inability to gather sufficient evidence to provide a case for trial. According to Inspector Lestrade, "This time we had an encyclopedia of evidence before beginning any arrests—letters, ledgers, physical evidence, a host of eyewitnesses, and the results of a few ingenious sting operations, which I oversaw. Over one hundred operatives made these arrests happen, and I would like to thank them. We were assisted, also, by Mr. Holmes."

Anna stopped reading and let the paper crumple. We looked at each other in blank astonishment, and then turned toward our amnesiac friend. "Mr. Holmes?" we chorused. "You're Sherlock Holmes!"
He drew a deep breath, nodding. "I'm Sherlock Holmes. Ha-ha! I'm Sherlock Holmes!" Then he blinked and looked at us. "Who's Sherlock Holmes?"
Anna's mouth dropped open. "No."
"You're joking," I said.
Our friend returned our incredulous expressions. "Honestly. Who is he?"

"Only the greatest detective who ever— You're joking! Everyone in England knows of Sherlock Holmes. Of course you're Holmes! Who else could bring down a criminal empire?"

Anna looked a little hurt, "My mother could . . ."

"Who else would be a match for your father?"

"My mother . . ." Anna repeated sullenly. Then she gasped, and her hand flew to her mouth. "My father threw *Sherlock Holmes* over the Reichenbach Falls!"

"Yes," mused Silence.

I felt stupid for not having seen it before—the knifelike features, the piercing eyes, the hawk nose. . . . He'd once said he didn't need memory as long as he had deduction. "How stupid we've been!" I said. "You're Sherlock Holmes!"

Silence—or Holmes—took the paper back, his eyes darting through the lines of French text. He set a finger on one part of the article and said, "My dear, can you please render this paragraph?"

Anna reached over to pull the paper close. She translated:

> The jubilant mood at Scotland Yard was dimmed, however, when police failed to apprehend the head of the criminal enterprise—a Professor James Moriarty, late of Jesus College, Cambridge. Disappointment deepened to remorse when word came from Switzerland that Professor Moriarty, in an apparent bid at retribution, had followed Mr. Sherlock Holmes and his longtime companion, Dr. Watson, to the Continent. According to the good doctor, Professor Moriarty caught up to them at the Reichenbach Falls, high in the Swiss Alps. There, the emperor of crime and the master of deduction battled to their deaths. Dr. Watson has testified that both men went over the falls and were killed.

"Dr. Watson . . . ?" Holmes mumbled.

"Yes! Of course," I said, "Watson—he's your dearest friend—the chronicler of your exploits."

"Not much of a doctor, declaring two men dead who are very much alive."

"The article says no bodies were ever recovered," Anna pointed out.

Holmes took a disappointed breath. "Funny. I don't feel like the greatest detective who ever lived. Especially since I'm purportedly dead."

"Rumors," I said dismissively. "But we know the truth— Anna and I."

"And Father," she added.

Silence nodded. "And Professor Moriarty."

"Yeah," I said, "and him." I was a bit annoyed at Silence's attitude. If I had found out I was Sherlock Holmes, I would have felt . . . well, honored. Or at least amused. "Look, there's nothing for it. We'll have to get our hands on Dr. Watson's chronicles of your adventures."

Anna chimed in, "The Bibliothèque Nationale is walking distance from the Gare Saint-Lazare."

"Well, then," Holmes said dubiously, "if my identity lies in books, let's go read me a life."

34

FINGERS IN THE ASHES

How strange it is to sit here in the Bibliothèque Nationale at a table piled high with stories of my life: *A Study in Scarlet, The Sign of Four,* and countless stories in the *Strand Magazine*. . . . The whole world knows more about me than I do.

I look to my two young companions, but they drowse on a couch, their chins resting on their chests. I am left to these books, these faded memories.

I start at the beginning, reading Dr. James Watson's none-too-complimentary assessment of my knowledge base. He seems to think it a character flaw not to know whether the earth revolves around the sun but to care deeply about the different varieties of tobacco ash.

Does the earth truly revolve around the sun? What difference does it make?

Of course . . . what difference does tobacco ash make? In a world with Mozart, with Tesla, with Kilamanjaro, what sort of fool would spend his time poking about in ash?

My sort of fool, apparently.

Even as the thought is forming, I am up from my seat, wandering among the reading tables, following the smoke signals. I gather the three nearest ashtrays, bring them back to my spot, and set them before me. The gentlemen who were using them seem put out, but when one of the men approaches my station and sees me rubbing ash between my thumb and forefinger, he retreats to find a different tray.

I inspect the ashes, noting the colors, the flakiness, the lingering scents of oil and tar. "Yes—this is India black—a cigarette tobacco, and this is Cuban maduro, and, unless I miss my guess, from a somewhat stale Upmann." A quick glance at two of the men demonstrates that I am right. "And this—it is not tobacco at all, but a burned paper note." I find one small, fragile remnant that bears the tops of the letters *l, o, v,* and *e,* written by a woman's hand—a distraught hand, judging by the tremulous marks and the jag atop the *o.* Again, it takes but a glance at the weepy-eyed man who had surrendered the tray to confirm my suspicions.

"How strange!" I exclaim, evincing scowls from patrons nearby. Yes, how strange. How strange I am, to care about such things. Ashes and the composition of soil and the variations in bootblack ... While other men filled their minds with planetary declinations and the properties of comets, I do idiot auguries in ash. It seems I have not lost my knack—though what good is such a knack? It's just a parlor trick, just deduction, when what I really need is memory.

I read on, learning of my considerable abilities on the violin; my left hand twitches, awakening to the notes that reside in these long fingers of mine. And then I read of my mastery of disguises; I can almost feel the thousand false beards and mustaches and fake noses and brows and improvised moles and boils that I have affixed to my face. And then I read of my addiction to cocaine, that white devil that comes in through the veins and pervades heart and soul and all; I need only roll back my sleeve to see its mark on me.

How strange a man I am! Oh, to remember ... I'm getting glimpses, but my memory is shot through with holes.

"Thomas?" I say, glancing over to where he and Anna slouch. "Thomas!"

He startles awake and stares blearily at me. "What? What is it? Moriarty?"

"No," I reply, lifting the volumes in my arms. "Let's find a flat somewhere, some garret we can rent for cheap, where Anna can sleep and you and I can work through something."

He sits forward and rubs his hands on his face. "Work through what?"

"I need that electrical contraption of yours."

Thomas shakes his head slowly. "Are you insane? Last time it drove the soul right out of your body."

"But you said it had been used to aid in restoring memory. The brain is, after all, an electric system. Perhaps my brain simply needs a shock to get it primed and firing again."

"At best, it's quackery, Sile—I mean, Holmes." Thomas groans. "At worst, it's a form of execution." Anna stirs beside him, and he looks at her. "But one thing's sure—we could use a place to rest—"

"Come along then. Pick up that lady fair of yours and your electric box and let's find a corner to operate in."

35

Being the Great Man

If there is any city that welcomes a weary young man with a weary young woman clinging to his shoulders and a weary old man ruminating about "not being the man I once was" as they walk down the street, that city is Paris.

It was almost pleasant, to be a walking divan for Anna. She was half asleep, languidly leaning on me. From the other side, Holmes was leaning on me, too—but in a different way.

"Do you honestly believe I could be the great man Sherlock Holmes?"

Hand catching Anna's waist as she stumbled in exhaustion, I looked him in the eye and said, "I know you're Sherlock Holmes."

My friend nodded vacantly and said, "He was a great man."

"He is a great man," I replied.

"We shall see."

36

CHASING THE THUNDERBOLT

We've found the perfect flat—one room with two gables and a tattered Indian screen that will allow Anna to sleep in privacy while Thomas and I pursue our experiments. I take a moment to analyze the contraption—a box with a crank on one end and black wires extending from the sides, each ending in a large alligator clip.

"Peculiar gadget," I say as I set the thing on a small table beside the chair in which I sit. "Part science and part magic."

"That's the whole issue. Bad science and black magic," Thomas replies dubiously. He is wetting a rag with a bit of red wine—which I'd purchased in part as anesthetic and in part to aid the conductivity of the skin. Thomas wipes the rag on each clip and on my fingertips, toes, and earlobes. "The current turns you into a five-pointed star, like the five points of the Celtic pentacle. The Finns used to create a similar pattern with lightning rods. It was a sort of shaman-generator—or an exorcism device."

I take a swig of the wine—ah, good French wine—and set it aside for the experiment. Holding two of the clips in one hand, I idly turn the crank. A stinging jolt leaps from clip to clip. Then, I reverse the motion of the crank, and the electrical sensation is altogether different—smooth and soothing. "Perhaps it's not a matter of voltage, but of polarity."

"What?"

"Which way did you turn that crank, my boy?"

"What do you mean? Clockwise, I suppose, being right-handed."

"Try it counterclockwise this time, and let's see if we gain a different effect."

Thomas's face is a study in annoyance, but he dutifully sets the clips on my toes and hands and ears. The metal bites into my skin, and red wine weeps down as if from wounds. "Counterclockwise," he says heavily.

"Yes, and slowly."

Thomas takes hold of the crank, mentally traces a clock's path, and then gently begins to turn the device. A warm buzz begins in my every extremity, propagating itself out across my skin. The sensation tingles, like ants marching up my legs and arms and down my neck. I feel as if I am faintly glowing. Still, though, my mind remains dark. "A little faster."

Thomas increases the speed of the revolutions.

The energy feels hot now, arcing out of the electrodes and into my muscles. Legs and arms flex, neck and jaw clench, and some of the stray bolts jag through my mind. Still, it is not enough. "More!"

Thomas spins the crank vigorously.

My skin snaps tight across my skeleton, and my hair sizzles. I shudder.

Next moment, I cannot feel a thing. I only see:

A MAN sits alone in a train compartment—a large man, though he is curled in on himself and seems small. His brow is graven with grief. He stares down at a blank sheet of paper that lies on a board on his lap. Opening a jar of India ink, the man pokes a pen within, lifts it, and begins to write:

> *It is with a heavy heart that I take up my pen to write these the last words in which I shall ever record the singular gifts by which my friend Mr. Sherlock Holmes was distinguished.*

This is not a hallucination. Nor is it a memory. It is an out-of-body vision. This train compartment truly exists somewhere, and this man truly sits within it, writing just those words.

I move toward him—though I have no body. I am only a location in space, a consciousness. I reach out to touch the man's shoulder.

He starts, looking toward me. A bead of sweat creeps its way down his temple. "Holmes?"

"Watson," I say.

Somehow, he hears me, and he stands. His eyes dart about the compartment, but then he blinks, flustered, and sits back down. "Only a phantasm . . . a dream."

"Watson."

His mustaches bristle, but he shakes his head. "Some stray memory from Baker Street."

Suddenly, the portals of memory open in my mind.

I remember the book-lined drawing room with the wing-back chairs by the grate and the pipe and the violin.

I remember Irene Adler, the opera star who bested me at my own game—the only person ever to see through one of my disguises.

I remember the speckled adder used to murder the rightful owners of a mansion in Stoke Moran.

I remember the beryl coronet and the young man accused

of breaking off a portion of it, though in truth he wished only to save the honor of a lady without any.

I remember the great black hound that haunted the family Baskerville in their lonely house on the moor.

But most of all, I remember Moriarty, that Napoleon of crime. I remember how I drew my web tight around him, and how I escaped his henchmen only to be cornered by the man himself at the Reichenbach Falls.

I remember writing the letter that Watson even now draws from his breast pocket and unfolds in trembling hands and reads yet again:

> *My Dear Watson:*
>
> *I write these few lines through the courtesy of Mr. Moriarty, who awaits my convenience for the final discussion of those questions which lie between us. He has been giving me a sketch of the methods by which he avoided the English police and kept himself informed of our movements. They certainly confirm the very high opinion which I had formed of his abilities. I am pleased to think that I shall be able to free society from any further effects of his presence, though I fear that it is at a cost which will give pain to my friends, and especially, my dear Watson, to you. . . .*

He draws a shuddering breath, and lifts bloodshot eyes toward the ceiling. "Holmes."

"I'm still alive, Watson. I'm still alive."

SUDDENLY, I am once again slumping in a chair in a garret apartment in Paris. Little acrid coils of smoke rise from my hair.

Thomas lets out a yelp, releases the crank, yanks a tablecloth from an end table, and pats down my smoking head. "Sorry, Silence—I mean, Holmes. I mean . . . What happened . . . ? I couldn't tell if . . . it seemed almost as if . . ."

"I went wandering, Thomas."

"Wandering?" he asks as he drags the singed cloth away.

"I saw my old friend Dr. Watson. I saw his grief, and I spoke some small comforts to him."

He shakes his head. "I knew it. Driven mad!"

"No. I am not mad," I say. "For the first time in days, I am myself. I remember, Thomas. Many things. Piece by piece, I'm becoming Sherlock Holmes."

37

Trap

When Anna awoke on their second morning in Paris, everything had changed. Beyond the Indian screen, the boys had made the garret into a war room. They had laid a large map of London across the floorboards and dotted the map with scraps of paper pierced by pushpins. Each scrap held some scrawled epithet such as *orange pips* or *engineer's thumb*. Beside this cluttered schematic lay another map: the streets of Paris with similar scraps—articles clipped from a newspaper.

The sound of slicing newsprint directed Anna's attention to Holmes—who reclined in a ragged divan and used Thomas's dirk to cut another article from *Le Temps*. The moment the article fell from the page, he caught it in dexterous fingers and sent it spinning through the air like a snowflake.

With an air of bleary annoyance, Thomas snatched the article from the wind and said, "Where does this one go?"

"Montmartre," Holmes said without looking up.

Anna stepped from behind the screen and stretched. "Where'd you get the maps?"

Thomas shot her a weary look as he pinned the latest article to Montmartre. "Mr. Holmes awoke me at three this morning so that we could be at the paper seller's when the first edition of *Le Temps* arrived."

"And the paper seller happened to have maps for lost travelers," Holmes interjected offhandedly.

"He wanted to plot his cases on the map of London, and now, on the other map, he's plotting the last forty-eight hours of crime in Paris."

"Patterns," Holmes said loftily from behind *Le Temps*. "Water follows the lowest course and so erodes canyons. Crime does the same. Thomas and I"—he flung another snowflake of villainy across the room, causing Thomas to dance to snatch it—"have simply been mapping those waterways of crime. When your father—Professor Moriarty—arrives in Paris, we may need this map to track him down."

"May?" Thomas exclaimed. He had just spiked the newest article to the map and now looked up with the watchfulness of a meerkat. "You said this was vital—absolutely essential to catching him."

"Absolutely essential if our first plan fails," Holmes said smoothly. He glanced to the window. "But we'll have to put Plan B aside for the nonce. We have only seventy-one minutes left."

Both Thomas and Anna stared blankly at Holmes, but Thomas was the first to speak. "Seventy-one minutes until what?"

"Seventy-one minutes until the next express from Bern arrives, the train that, no doubt, Professor Moriarty will be aboard." Cupping a hand to his mouth, Holmes leaned confidentially toward Anna and said, "*Le Temps* also has the train schedules."

"We haven't a clock or pocket watch," Thomas said. "How do you know the time?"

"Our window faces due south."

"So?"

"When we arrived last evening, I received the precise time from the proprietor, counted the number of seconds we took to climb the stairs, and scratched a single line on the windowsill to mark the sun's shadow at 8:42 P.M. I marked the shadow also at sunset, which *Le Temps* indicated would be at 9:14 P.M. Well, from there it is a simple bit of math to calculate minutes of arc. Then, I needed merely wait for sunrise—according to *Le Temps* at 6:18 A.M.—to mark the shadow and calculate the arc that would represent 7:38 A.M.—when we must enact our Plan A."

Thomas laughed aloud. "And yet you just wasted three of your seventy-one minutes describing your cleverness."

"I allowed four extra minutes—three for me to describe my cleverness and one for you two to stand in awe." Holmes let the eviscerated *Le Temps* fall from his fingers to the floor and levered himself up. "But enough awe. We really must be going if we are to catch your father."

"To Gare Saint-Lazare!" Thomas proclaimed

"No," Holmes replied. "To the Orpheum Theater." He swung open the door and stepped out.

Thomas clapped shut his dangling jaw and followed. Anna brought up the rear. They descended four flights of switchback stairs, walked down a long hallway, and at last came out on the bustling streets of Paris. Thomas strode up on one side of Holmes, and Anna stepped up along the other, each of them risking an occasional glance his way, waiting for an explanation. . . .

At last, Anna could take it no longer. "How do you know my father will be at the Orpheum Theater?"

"He won't," Holmes replied flatly.

Thomas actually growled. "Then why are we going there?"

"Because they're preparing the French premiere of *A Doll's House* by Henrik Ibsen."

Thomas and Anna chorused together. "So?"

Holmes glanced at each of them and said, "*I'm* Henrik Ibsen." With that, he rounded the street corner and strode up to the front of a grand vaudeville house with a marquee that read, "*La Comédie Française présente Une Maison de Poupée par Henrik Ibsen.*"

Holmes stepped to the front door and pounded solidly on it. An angry shout came from within, muffled but clearly meaning to repel unwanted visitors. Holmes knocked only the louder. More shouts resulted, growing nearer behind the door. Holmes rapped again.

A bolt shot back, and the door of the theater swung open. A little old man stood in the gap, his spectacles magnifying bloodshot eyes and white hairs standing like electric discharges across his pate. "*Au nom de Dieu, pourquoi me réveillez-vous de cette façon?*" Holmes turned to Anna serenely and said with a thick Norwegian accent, "Would you please tell this man that I am Henrik Ibsen, come to inspect the theater where my play will be performed?" He then lifted a picture of himself, cut from *Le Temps* that morning. Trying to hide her smile, Anna translated Holmes's message.

As she spoke, the old man's eyes grew wide with excitement and alarm. He responded in French, and Anna translated for him: "Forgive my foolishness. I didn't recognize Mr. Ibsen without his muttonchops."

Holmes replied, "Facial hair is a friend to bandits and renegades. When a man has a play like *A Doll's House,* though, he must shave so as to be noticed."

After Anna's translation, the proprietor responded in French: "Mr. Ibsen. Forgive me! What an honor. Come in! Come in!"

Holmes nodded with the air of a man utterly deserving of the deference given him.

The proprietor led them through the theater, pointing out

the somewhat frowsy foyer, the auditorium with its curved seats, the boxes and balconies that ringed all. . . .

"The stage, man! The stage!" Holmes cried.

The little man scuttled on, leading the group onto the apron and the proscenium, into the wings, and backstage. Holmes made a show of checking the flies and the lines that secured them before saying, "Thank you, my good man, but I need time to meditate, to explore." Anna translated even as Holmes went on: "Please get back to your other duties so that I may commune with the place."

With a grateful bow, the proprietor backed away.

Once he was gone, Thomas hissed, "What's all this for? Moriarty will be arriving at Gare Saint-Lazare in thirty minutes."

"Thirty-three minutes," Holmes corrected, "and we will be there—but in costume." He led the other two down beneath the stage, finding the wardrobe department and a much-used assortment of face paints, wigs, and prosthetics. "We must work quickly. We have a healthy walk ahead of us."

Anna lifted a ball gown, very ornate, but with a bust that would have left her exposed. "What am I to be?"

"Actually, my dear, the costumes are for Thomas and myself," said Holmes, tossing the dress away. "Your father would recognize you in any costume, so you must go as you are."

Thomas glared. "This is your plan?"

"Anna, you must pose as yourself," Holmes continued smoothly, "but outwardly repentant."

"Repentant?" Anna asked.

"When you see him, break into tears and run to him. Tell him I regained my mind and repudiated you. Tell him even Thomas thinks you're a traitor. Can you do that?"

"Yes."

"No she can't," Thomas said. "He'll see through it. You're putting her in mortal danger."

Holmes shook his head. "Danger, yes, but not mortal danger. As deranged as Moriarty might be, he has never shown the will to kill his own daughter. No, she must go as herself."

"Or stay behind," Thomas said.

"I won't stay behind," Anna said.

Holmes nodded happily. "Then it's settled."

Thomas gathered the ball gown from the floor and held it up to him. "And so, am I to be the lady?"

Holmes tossed a rumpled pair of trousers to him, along with a dirty gray tunic and a worn-out cap. "You'll be a porter."

"Aw, I was hoping to be a scamp."

"It's too close to your true self. Be a hardworking man for a change—but do your best not to get distracted lugging luggage. Instead, watch for Moriarty—and guard Anna."

While Thomas began to change into his costume, Anna turned away and watched Holmes pull a black cassock from the rack of clothes.

"What are you going to be?"

"A priest," he said as he drew the robe over his shoulders. Then he went to the makeup table, lit the lamp, and set to work on his face. He spread spirit gum across his jawline and attached a very ragged beard and mustache. He also set a round-brimmed black hat on his head.

"You don't make a believable saint," Thomas piped, coming up in his ragged work clothes.

"Most priests are not saints," Holmes pointed out, his eyes flashing at Thomas's costume. "And you might actually have to do a little work to be convincing."

"No, I'll be a loafer," Thomas suggested.

"Enough fooling," said Holmes. "Twenty-seven minutes

left." He led them up a back stairway and into a dark alley among rubbish bins. There, he stopped and looked Thomas over. "It'll have to do. If it comes to a fight, let me confront the man."

"Your costume's not that good."

"Perhaps. But this is my fight, not yours. It's a fight that began a year ago on the streets of London and will finish today on the streets of Paris." He walked out of the alley into the morning throng. Thomas and Anna followed.

The three comrades passed a counting house where a clerk swept coal dust from the pavement, a bakery that charged the air with the scent of yeast and fresh bread, a butcher's shop where young lads hauled gutted hogs from a wagon through the front door. . . . The world was going about its daily routine while Thomas, Anna, and their friend Sherlock Holmes marched toward a most desperate confrontation.

"Holmes," Anna said, tugging on his sleeve. "Remember—this is my father."

He glanced her way. Beneath his broad-brimmed hat and above his burly beard, Holmes's eyes were both keen and compassionate. "I have never killed a man, my dear—"

"Never that you remember. . . ."

"Never that Watson reported, either," he replied. "I do not intend to start today." They walked on a few more paces in silence before Holmes hedged. "Of course, your father is a most remarkable opponent, and he is bent on killing me. I will do what I must."

"That's Gare Saint-Lazare, three blocks up," Thomas announced.

"All right," Holmes said. "We'd better split up here and approach in character."

The morning's irritation melted from Thomas's face. He grasped Holmes's arm briefly and said, "Be careful."

The old priest—for that's what he seemed in that moment, smiling and starry-eyed—gave a nod and scuttled
away.

Then Thomas lifted Anna's hand to his lips and kissed the
back of it. "You, especially—be careful."

Next moment, she was anything but careful, pulling him
toward her and kissing him full on the lips.

38

THE MARTYRDOM OF GARE SAINT-LAZARE

The kiss was over before I realized it was happening. Anna drew away from me, and there I stood, a ragged young porter with feet planted on the Parisian pavement and heart pounding and lips tingling. I don't know why she did it—the kiss. I wanted to chase after her and ask, but already her skirts receded in the morning crowd. A moment later, she was lost in the mob that poured down the street.

Shaking out my wobbly legs, I strode toward the Gare Saint-Lazare station. By now, Anna was somewhere inside, and her father was as well—or soon would be. I glanced up at the giant wrought-iron clock that filled one gable of the station—8:48. What had Holmes said? Seventy-one minutes from when? From 7:38? That meant that just now . . .

Ahead of me, in one of the glass-topped aisles of that huge station, a behemoth of metal snorted its way forward. Black smoke belched from its smokestack, and white steam jetted from its pistons and brakes.

"That's it!" I said to myself, hurrying across the street among a herd of businessmen. I dodged past them, beginning to run, and broke from the crowd to descend to the platform.

Already, porters were hanging from the sides of the train, their outstretched legs reaching for the platform as it slowed below them. With a final hiss, the engine rolled to a stop, and coupling after metal coupling clanked as each car nudged the one before. The porters leaped down and unfolded the metal stairs and extended their hands to ladies alighting and men who fumbled for a sou to tip them. These porters were the old ones, with seniority and stiff joints. They had the easy task, while their younger brothers hauled trunks on their backs or dug crates from the undercarriage storage bins.

I stood near the engine, watching as a tide of humanity poured off the coaches. Which man was Moriarty? It was a long train, stretching a quarter mile ahead of me, and I could only be certain of the passengers debarking the first four cars. Beyond that . . .

There was Anna. She'd posted herself near the center of the train and was looking up and down the length of it, wringing a white handkerchief. At first, my heart broke for her—so afraid—but then I realized she was acting, playing her part. Every now and again, she even stood on tiptoes and perched her hand above her brow like some Bo Peep searching for her sheep—or rather for the wolf among them.

And beyond Anna, I caught sight of a priest with a big hat and a bigger beard. Holmes had taken his post at the rear of the train. I felt suddenly better. We three were smart and vigilant. It was just a matter of time before one of us spotted him.

A man grabbed my shoulder and turned me about. His face was craggy like an eroded stone, and he wore the coal-and sweat-soaked tunic of a fireman. *"Toi, paresseux! Bouge-toi! Tu vois toutes ces caisses qu'il faut bouger!"* He wanted to know why I was just standing around when there were so many cases to move.

I smiled fearlessly at him and replied, *"Liberté, Egalité, Fraternité!"*

He snarled and took a swing at my head, but I simply ducked under the blow. My tormenter overbalanced—perhaps a bit tipsy—and staggered on past. With a cocky grin, I watched him go. This new persona of mine—the lazy lout with a loud mouth—felt right.

I walked to a pile of trunks and baggage that had been unloaded by more industrious types, sat down on one crate, leaned against another, and tilted my cap so that I looked asleep.

Ah, the perfect cover. From this vantage, I could see the first four cars clearly, and every person that descended those iron steps. I also could watch Anna in her distressed dance, kerchief coiling like a living thing in her fretful hands. Good acting. Good girl. And with a little roll of my eyes, I could even see Holmes moving among the tide of passengers.

He seemed to look toward me in that moment, and the sunlight suddenly flashed beneath the broad brim of his hat to show wide eyes. The effect was almost comical. Holmes turned toward me and began swimming through the tide of passengers, as if he had just discovered something.

Someone tapped the sole of my boot. It was another railroad official, a tall, thin man with a gray uniform and a cruel face. *"Qu'est-ce que tu fais? Paresseux! Lève-toi et va mériter ton salaire."* He, too, thought I was a lazy lout who didn't earn my keep.

I tried my previous line—*"Liberté, Egalité, Frat-"*—but before I could finish, I recognized that vicious face.

Professor Moriarty plunged a knife into my chest.

I gasped and heard the air rush, bubbling, past the buried blade.

"Thomas, you're the first to go—bait to capture Mr. Holmes," Moriarty whispered as he drew out his knife. "Die knowing that you were killed by the greatest crime lord who ever lived."

39

Confrontation

Anna felt alone. Thomas lounged on a set of crates near the engine, and Holmes poked about among passengers at the caboose. Meanwhile, Anna was stuck in the middle, watching for Father. There was no sign yet.

A burly porter shouldered his way through the crowd, a heavy trunk on his back. With a groan, he swung the trunk around and let it crash down on the planks beside Anna's feet.

She glared at him. *"Regardez ce que vous faites!"*

He looked at her thickly and jabbed a thumb over his shoulder. *"Il m'a dit de le faire."*

"Who told you to—?" Anna began. But then she saw the distant man.

Her father, dressed in the blue suit of a conductor, was leaning menacingly over Thomas.

"Father?" Anna took a step toward him, but someone grabbed her arm and yanked her back. It was Holmes.

"You mustn't," he admonished, pointing. "Look!"

Her father drew back from Thomas, and a bright wedge of steel glinted between them—a knife tipped in a triangle of blood. Withdrawing the knife into his sleeve, Moriarty turned toward Anna and flashed a triumphant grin.

Anna tried to break free from Holmes, but he held on.

"Wait till I've run him off. Then go to Thomas."

With that, Holmes darted away, weaving expertly through the crowd despite cassock and beard.

Anna's father laughed wickedly and dived into a mass of passing travelers. He disappeared among them.

Anna rushed after Holmes, but the crowd closed around her. She shoved her way forward.

"*Pardonnez-moi,*" a woman snarled as Anna pushed her aside.

Others turned at the ruckus, eyes annoyed and lips brimming with reproach, but Anna shouted, "He's been stabbed! *On l'a poignardé!*" A path cleared ahead of her, and she charged down the corridor of bewildered faces to reach Thomas.

He lay on the crates and gasped for breath. One hand clutched his chest, and bright red blood foamed out between his fingers.

"Thomas!" Anna set her hand on his. "Your heart."

"My . . . my lung," he managed, coughing. Blood rimmed his gums as he looked up at her in panic.

"Help! We need help! *Un homme a été poignardé!*"

The mob pressed up around them, but no one offered aid. One young man took a look at Thomas, pivoted, and emptied his stomach on the ground. The lady beside him collapsed in a magnificent faint.

"*Est-ce que quelqu'un peut m'aider?*"

A man in a pinstriped suit muscled through the line of gawkers, his fleshy fingers gripping the handle of a medical bag. "What's it? What's happened?"

Oh, that blessed London accent! thought Anna. "He's been stabbed in the lung!"

The doctor set his bag beside Thomas, wrenched it open, and drew out a scalpel. "Pull his hand away." Anna did, and the doctor sliced the dirty tunic away from his chest.

The wound was a vermilion puncture, two inches wide and very deep, and the skin around it was paper-white.

"Help him!"

Hand shaking slightly, the doctor reached into his bag and drew out a roll of gauze and pressed a wad of it into the wound. Then he held his hand over the spot.

Eyes clenched in agony, Thomas gasped, "I can hardly breathe!" The words rattled in his throat.

"His lung's collapsed. It's filling with blood. We have to get him to hospital." The doctor's eyes fixed on Anna's. "I don't know Paris."

She swallowed. "The cabbies do. Can you lift him?"

The doctor nodded once, gritted his jaw, stooped down, and hoisted Thomas over his shoulder. Anna staggered back in awe. The doctor seemed almost a bear—so brawny and powerful. "Clear the way!"

"*Dégagez le passage! Dégagez le passage!*" Anna pushed back the crowd of gawkers. The good doctor marched out behind her. Two young Parisian lads ran ahead of them, taking up Anna's shout and shoving pedestrians aside.

She broke into a run, heading for the street. A line of cabs waited there, and Anna charged for the first one. "*A l'aide! A l'aide! Nous avons un blessé!*"

The cabby looked at her in terror, cracked the reins, and sent his carriage bolting away. Anna stopped, stunned, and then saw, within the compartment, her father's devilish face leering out at her. The next carriage in line bounded out after it, driven by a priest with cassock and beard.

The doctor trudged up behind Anna. "Quickly now. His life hangs by a thread!"

She ran toward the next cab, fifty yards farther down. "*A l'aide! A l'aide! Nous avons un blessé!*"

This time the cabby, noble soul, drove his coach up onto

the pavement, scattering pigeons and pedestrians and heaving to a stop right in front of Anna. She grabbed the coach door and swung it wide, and the doctor clambered up the steps to dump Thomas on the seat within. Meanwhile, Anna craned up toward the driver. *"A l'hôpital!"*

"Les Invalides!" he replied with a nod.

She squeezed into the carriage beside the doctor and Thomas and slammed the door behind her. The coach lurched into motion, and Thomas nearly tumbled from the seat. He was unconscious now, blood painting his lips.

The doctor said, "Help me bend him over. We've got to get some of this blood out." The doctor pivoted to grab one of Thomas's shoulders, and Anna grabbed the other. "On three," he said. "One, two, three—!"

They thrust Thomas forward, doubling him over. He groaned, and a great gobbet shot from his mouth, followed by a red gush. Thomas coughed explosively, and more of the stuff came out.

"Haven't had many of these, have you?" Anna asked nervously.

"All too many," the doctor replied. "Bayonet wounds—Afghan campaign."

The carriage jolted, and Anna and the doctor braced themselves to keep from pitching onto the floor.

Beyond the window, the streets of Paris flew by, people running from the hansom's path or standing on the pavement and staring openmouthed as they thundered past. There was a tremendous wailing sound like a siren: The driver stood in his seat and shouted the way clear.

"Il y a urgence! Il y a urgence!"

The coach scraped along another cab heading the other way, and the doctor and Anna struggled to hold Thomas in his seat.

"Help me lift him again!"

Gritting her teeth, Anna leaned back and hauled Thomas upright. She and the doctor braced him there. He was breathing again, raggedly, but his face was still slack and unconscious. He looked horrible—blanched except where the blood was.

"Les Invalides!" cried the cabby as the coach bounded up off the road and clattered down a cobblestone approach. His horses whickered as they passed beneath the first great archway and into the inner courtyard.

The doctor craned his neck out the window to shout, "Take us to admitting!"

"Parlez-vous français?"

Anna yelled up through the trap, *"Le bureau des admissions!"*

The coach turned sharply, and the cabby resumed his call of *"Urgences!"*

Next moment, the carriage jolted to a stop before a broad double door.

Anna pushed open the carriage door and climbed out as the good doctor hefted Thomas once again on his shoulder and backed from the cab.

Behind them, the double doors swung wide, and nurses in white scrambled out. One took a look at Thomas and ran back into the building. Next moment, a pair of orderlies appeared with a stretcher slung between them. They rushed to the doctor, who gratefully heaved Thomas onto the stretcher. There was a trail of blood down the doctor's back.

A French doctor bustled out of the doors, his waxed mustache curling above his cheeks. *"Qu'est-ce que c'est?"*

"Urgences!" blurted the cabby, who had leaped down from the carriage to join in the excitement.

"Il ne peut pas respirer. Il a été poignardé en pleine poitrine— une mauvaise blessure," Anna explained.

Apparently the doctor was unimpressed with her French,

for he switched to English. "Hello, mademoiselle. I am Dr. Maison, and I must ask you a few questions. Is this man a veteran?"

"*I* am a veteran," interposed the Londoner, "and a doctor."

"And this man is a veteran, too," Anna lied.

"Where are his papers?" Dr. Maison asked.

"*Urgences!*" the cabby repeated.

"You'll get his papers after you save his life!" Anna said.

Dr. Maison rolled his eyes and gestured to his English counterpart. "We will take him if you come within and sign for him."

The orderlies carried the stretcher with Thomas through the double doors and into a receiving hall. The others followed.

The space was small and book-lined, with the doctor's desk at one end and a fireplace and armchairs at the other end. The orderlies went through the room to another set of doors that opened into an operating theater. Setting the stretcher down on a table, the orderlies moved back while nurses buzzed about with bandages and alcohol and needles and knives.

"*Vous devez attendre à l'extérieur,*" one of them told Anna.

They wanted her to leave, but she lingered at Thomas's side. He was still unconscious. The rattle in his lung was terrible to hear, and he had room only for the smallest of breaths. "They'll save you, Thomas," Anna said, leaning down to kiss his forehead. "They'll save you."

A nurse tugged gently at her elbow, drawing her away. Anna turned and walked numbly out of the operating theater.

In the book-lined room beyond, the doctor from London leaned over the desk and signed a form that was pinned beneath his hand. Then, turning, he went to Anna. "He's in good hands. It's all we can hope for."

"Thanks for all you've done," Anna told him. "I'm afraid

your suit's been ruined. I'm sorry to have dragged you into all of this."

His weathered face twitched with agitation. "Don't apologize to me. It was my desperate errand, not yours. I fear that you and your friend were merely a diversion to throw me off track." His eyes dropped to his hands, stained in blood and ink, and he muttered, "Every minute the trail goes colder. Ruddy henchman!" Looking up again, the doctor managed a smile and said, "I must get back to Gare Saint-Lazare. Goodbye, my dear." He hastily lifted her hand and kissed the back of it. Then he turned and stormed away, calling to the cabby.

"Thank you!" Anna yelled after him as he climbed into the coach. The cabby snapped the reins, and the horses clomped forward in a great curve. The carriage was dwindling in the distance when Anna realized she had never gotten the man's name.

Turning, she retreated to the receiving room and stared down at the form that lay on the desk. The signature read: "Dr. John H. Watson."

Anna staggered back in amazement.

Of course, she thought. Watson had been at Reichenbach when all this had happened. Surely he'd looked for the bodies of Holmes and Moriarty, had spent a week chasing someone—a henchman—and had followed him to the Paris Express. Watson didn't realize he was following Moriarty himself. Father must have hid away from him and then disguised himself as a conductor to be able to make his exit.

Watson was right. Father had stabbed Thomas merely to create a diversion. With one stroke of his knife, he had waylaid Watson, Thomas, and Anna.

At least he hadn't waylaid Sherlock Holmes.

40

Reckoning

Beyond the leaded-glass windows of the receiving area, night drew down. The fire at the grate dwindled to smoldering coals.

Anna sat there listening to the clamor within the operating theater. It was a comforting sound, all that rushing, all those clipped voices, all that effort. It meant that Thomas still lived.

What she did not want to hear now was silence.

"There you are, Anna," said Holmes wearily, pushing through the double doors. Sometime in the past few hours, he had doffed his cassock and hat and beard and resumed the appearance of an English gentleman. But he looked haggard. His face was lined with care, his skin was pale, and his eyes were twin black coals in his head. He trudged into the receiving room, nodded at Anna as if he had known she would be sitting just there, and then fairly collapsed into a wing-back chair beside the fire.

"You found me," Anna said.

"I'm supposed to be Sherlock Holmes," he replied.

She smiled in spite of all that had happened that day. "Then, being Sherlock Holmes, you must have found my father as well."

He replied evasively, "Surely they have brandy about here, somewhere." His eyes swept the bookshelves around them. "This is a hospital, after all—a *French* hospital."

Anna had seen a decanter on a table beside the doctor's desk and had, truthfully, wished for a nip herself. Standing up, she crossed behind the desk and poured the brandy into a pair of snifters. Swirling them in her hands, she felt the cool liquor warm to her touch. She returned to Holmes, extended a snifter to him, and said, "You're alive, which is the good news. You're unnerved, though, which tells me there is bad news—"

"Yes. Bad news. Very bad," Holmes echoed. He watched the faint ripple of his heartbeat spread in circles across the meniscus of brandy. "There's so much bad to tell."

Anna leaned toward him. "Begin at the beginning."

Holmes took a sip of brandy and began his story. "I had glimpsed our quarry—your father—the moment he left the train. He was dressed in the blue uniform of a conductor, you see, but all the other conductors were within the train, clearing the cars—as we ourselves had experienced just yesterday. That incongruity drew my eye to him, and one look at his devilish face confirmed his identity. But what about his eyes? What were those gleaming eyes fixed upon?

"Thomas, of course. Your father had noted his incongruity as well: a porter who sleeps on crates rather than unloading them. I'm sure your father had spotted Thomas even before stepping from the train. It was the perfect chance. By putting the blade into Thomas, he would kill one of us and tie up at least one other. The professor used his criminal calculus to realize that you would go with Thomas to the hospital, and I would continue after him."

"It's worse than that, I'm afraid," Anna interrupted. "There was also a certain doctor aboard that train, one who was following Father, and who thought he was a henchman rather than the crime lord." Anna leaned toward Holmes and said significantly, "Father wasn't waylaying just me and Thomas and you—he was also waylaying Dr. John Watson."

Holmes sat bolt upright in his seat and looked thunder-struck. "Watson!"

Anna nodded solemnly. "He patched Thomas's wound and brought him here. He signed the release!"

Holmes leaned back and grew a slow, contented smile like the grin of a lizard. "Good old Watson. Hale man, and coura-geous. A bit muddleheaded at times. According to that article in the *Journal de Genève,* he thinks Moriarty and I both are dead, so of course he mistook Moriarty for a henchman. I feel for poor Watson should he ever corner his prey."

"He lost his chance by saving Thomas."

"Yes," Holmes responded. "Courageous and compassion-ate, but sometimes Watson needs to be a bit more hard-nosed. There must have been ten other doctors in that crowd."

"Watson saved him," Anna pointed out, but then added sullenly, "if Thomas survives at all."

"There, there. No more talk of it. I suppose I could learn a little compassion from Dr. Watson." He stood, beginning to pace. "It's simply that this chess match is still going on, and I cannot relax my focus for a moment." He looked up at Anna, and his once faraway eyes became razor sharp. "Your father is still out there, still alive, still hunting us. Our situation now is no different than it was in the train station. He's pinned us down. He knows just where we are—that we cannot move from this spot—and he is slowly closing in, calculating each move so that we cannot slip away, so that the white king falls."

Anna demanded, "Tell me what happened!"

Holmes nodded. With one swift gesture, he downed the rest of his brandy, set the snifter on the mantel, and pivoted,

staring out through the dark room. "Your father threatened a
cabby with his life and so rode away at high speed. As luck
would have it, the next cab was vacant, and I am an excellent
driver."

"You stole it!"

"I procured it for the good of the state. The three francs in
fares that man lost were a pittance compared to the gain to
him and all society had I nabbed Moriarty."

"Which you didn't."

Holmes peered down at her. "Do not mock, my dear. I
risked every extremity; a carriage chase down the Champs-
Elysées—he led me that way out of sheer arrogance, I am
sure—and then north toward the Moulin Rouge. Your father
took me on a tour of Paris from the highest to the lowest. At
last, though, I drove my carriage up alongside his, gained the
lead for just a moment, and then backed my wheel within his
own, engaging the axle and forcing him to slow. I dragged
back on the reins, and my team—brave mares—posted their
legs and struggled to halt both coaches. The other team ran
sidelong into them, but these ladies held their own, bless
them, and Moriarty could do nothing but flee his carriage or
be taken." Holmes stepped away from the mantel, pacing
slowly across the room.

"I followed, of course, hat and beard gone on the wind but
cassock still in place—and knife, too."

"Knife?"

"I know you had asked me to remember that he is your father, but I must ask you to remember that he is Moriarty, the
most dangerous man in Europe."

Anna nodded, but still her hands trembled. "What did you
do with the knife?"

"Nothing, at first," Holmes replied. "I chased him to a
dead-end alley, and there he spun on me, holding the knife

he had used on Thomas and was prepared to use on me. Only then did I show him I was similarly armed."

"What happened?"

"We circled each other as if we carried épées, for both of us have been trained in the art of fencing. But a knife is not an épée. It succeeds only in close quarters. The thing would be decided when we came together. We both knew it, and we both charged. Your father drove straight on at me, but I leaped to my left, letting his knife slide harmlessly beneath my right arm. I stabbed, burying my blade in his chest, and then I withdrew the blade and swung my elbow back to knock the knife out of his hand. It was a master stroke . . . except that . . ."

"Except that what?" Anna asked.

"Except that . . . I had stabbed just shy of the mark. It was as if the same whim of fortune that saved Thomas saved your father. The blade missed his heart but found his lung. I know because he clamped his hand on the spot so that he could breathe and speak. He staggered back and fell among the rubbish bins. I rushed up to tend him, but he shouted me back: 'I opened my heart to your knife, and this is the best you could do? Finish it, Holmes! Finish it!'

"Of course, I would not—an unarmed and wounded man. It would have been murder. Instead, I eased him back to lie there on the cobbles and checked his pulse and heard the rattle in his lung. 'I must fetch a doctor.' I rose to go but could not because he gripped my hand—the hand that held the knife.

"He wrenched the knife down toward his chest and said, 'Finish it now, or I will haunt you again!'

"I twisted free, careful not to let the blade cut him or to let him get hold of it. Then I ran to the head of the alley, hiding the blade in my pocket, and called for a doctor. With the blood on my hands and my crude command of French, long moments passed before I could cajole a doctor to follow me down the dark alley. By the time we reached the spot where your father had been, he was gone, leaving only a bloodstain on the ground.

"I'm astonished. How could he do it? How could your father suffer such a wound and scamper away?"

"Because there's something unnatural in him," Anna said.

Holmes stared at her in surprise, but in the darkness of that fire-lit nook, Anna fancied she saw another face staring—her father's manic, leering face, his eyes red as if they were awash in blood.

"Other daughters lose their fathers to drink," she explained, piecing her thoughts together, "or to gambling . . . or to whoring. But I lost my father to something . . . uncanny. From the time he killed Jack the Ripper, there was . . . something inside him. At the best moments, it was simple cruelty or bloodlust. At the worst moments, it was—it was what I could only describe as demonic."

"Demonic!"

"His eyes would be bloodred, and he would speak words that sounded like sorcery—deep and black."

Holmes sat down beside her and shook his head. "I should not have spoken so wildly. My tale and the brandy have put—have put phantasms in our heads."

Anna breathed raggedly. "It's not the brandy, Mr. Holmes. My father has a demon inside of him. I'm sure of it."

"It's a thought I cannot abide."

"But you must, Mr. Holmes," Anna pressed. "I've been reading about you, how you said that after all other possibilities were exhausted, the one remaining, no matter how improbable, must be true."

"I suppose I did say that," Holmes replied, glancing down

out of the corner of his eye. "But there is only one way to test your proposition."

"How?"

"We must lay a trap for your father, capture him, and submit him to the exorcism machine."

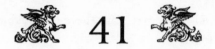

41

THE PENTACLE

The door to the operating theater swung open, and out trudged a weary Dr. Maison. His hands were clean, though his once-white smock bore bloodstains—bright red and dark brown. He looked like a butcher. The doctor strode to Anna and Holmes and stood, staring into the fire. *"Un après-midi des plus difficiles."*

"English, please," said Holmes wearily.

Dr. Maison glared down at him. Then, with clipped pronunciation, he said, "By rights, your friend should be dead. Indeed, he died twice on the table, his lung filling, but twice I pumped out the blood and brought him back. At last, the wound has clotted, and the lung is recovering, but he has lost a great deal of blood. We've taken him to a bed in Ward Four, but he will not be able to be moved from it for at least a week."

Holmes looked gravely at Anna and murmured, "Pinned down."

"Which, of course, is fortunate for you, in that you have no papers to prove that this man is a veteran," Dr. Maison continued, "yes?"

Anna stared at her hands. "We have no papers."

"Indeed, he could hardly be a veteran, this man only just old enough to enlist."

"Yes," Anna said, "hardly."

The doctor gave a perfunctory nod. "Once he is strong enough, he will have to be moved—and you will pay for his care while he is here."

"Of course," Anna replied, though she and Holmes did not have a pound between them.

Dr. Maison smirked. "What a charming liar you are. You should know that I never believed him to be a veteran but, because of your lie, was required to save the man. There is not a doctor in Paris who is my equal at bayonet-style wounds—"

"I can think of one," Anna murmured.

"And this new lie—that you will pay for his treatment here—well, it doesn't fool me, either, though it will satisfy the state." He brushed his hands off. "I've done all I can do."

"You make a most likable hero, Dr. Maison," Homes said wryly, "reluctant, perhaps even petulant. But I should warn you that your heroism has only begun." Slow dismay bloomed across the doctor's face. "This stab wound didn't result from some back-alley brawl. It was a deliberate attempt at murder, and the murderer remains at large, bent on killing this man. As a result, we must remain with him to guard him. Also, I have sent for a gendarme to help us keep watch."

"A gendarme?" the doctor objected.

"I stopped by the Metropolitan Police before coming here, and they are sending a man."

Dr. Maison snorted. "Why would the Paris police guard a vagrant?"

"And why would the surgeon of Les Invalides operate to save one?"

"She claimed he was a veteran! A lie is a lie."

"And a life is a life," Holmes responded pointedly, "whether the life of a vagrant or a grandson of Napoleon."

"Grandson of Napoleon?"

Holmes changed the subject. "But whoever this young man may or may not be, the Paris police want to catch his would-be killer."

"The Metropolitan Police have no equal," said Dr. Maison suspiciously, and he felt compelled to add, "but this is a hospital, not a garrison. We haven't accommodations for you and the lady *and* a gendarme."

"This is a *military* hospital, man," Holmes snapped, standing up in front of the doctor, "a haven for those at war. I cannot imagine four people more at war than that stabbed man, this woman, and I—and the gendarme who will guard us. Besides, we do not need 'accommodations,'" he pronounced the word with a faux French accent, "but merely two chairs, moved alongside the sickbed where our friend lies. In fact, *these* two chairs will do." With that, he hoisted the wingback chair where he had sat and held it before him. "Please show us the way to Ward Four."

"Highly irregular!" the doctor responded, stepping away.

"I should hope so." With a wink at his companion, Holmes turned to follow Dr. Maison. Anna went along. They crossed through a doorway and entered a long room lined on either side with sickbeds. The chamber held perhaps fifty beds, but it had no inmates except for Thomas in the bed nearest the door. Holmes snorted to see the room: "No accommodations!" He set the chair down.

Dr. Maison shrugged. "The empire is at peace. What can I say?"

As the doctor left and Holmes walked out to bring in the other chair, Anna knelt down beside Thomas's bed. He was nearly as pale as his sheets, and his face was drawn and still. She kissed him. His lips were cold, but gentle breath luffed against her cheek. She clasped his hand. "Thomas, you have to survive."

"He will," Holmes assured, setting down the other chair. "He has youth, which is almost the same as having immortality. And he has you. Thomas is not going to vanish from this world . . . unless your father gets at him again."

"We'll stand guard, night and day," Anna said.

"Yes. And the gendarme will help us. It took some doing to convince the police that I was not a lunatic—but at last I did. I expect the gendarme any moment."

"Good," Anna said, standing. "He and I can guard Thomas while you go to the garret and get the exorcism machine."

Holmes paled. "I can't abandon you—"

"You said we had to use that machine on Father. It's our only hope." She grasped Holmes's hand and looked him square in the eye. "I want my father back. This is the only way. If there's no demon in him, he may be unable to attack for a week or more, in which case we're safe. But if I'm right about this demon, Father will attack us by tomorrow, and we'd better have the exorcism machine."

Holmes looked down at Anna's hand on his, and he smiled warmly. "I have never been one to be swayed by the soft touch of a woman. But I have always been persuaded by sound deduction. You're right, Anna. I'll get the machine—once the gendarme arrives—"

As if on cue, a gendarme stepped through the doorway to Ward Four and marched up to Thomas's bed. The officer was a young man with a clean-shaven face and blond hair parted above blue eyes. He seemed all too eager to prove himself.

Holmes was eager to do so as well. He stepped up before the officer and barked, "What do you mean, arriving so late?" Holmes lashed out, slapping the man's cheek—and received a punch to the stomach for his efforts. Holmes collapsed to the floor, clutching his belly in pain even as he laughed. "Very good! Very good!"

"What *is* this?" asked the officer in stilted English.

"A test, simply," Holmes said, groaning, "the slap to tell me whether your face was a mask or real skin, and the punch to tell me whether you have the reflexes for this assignment."

"And . . . the result?" asked the young gendarme, extending a hand to help Holmes to his feet.

Gratefully receiving the assistance, Holmes said, "You passed—with flying colors. . . . Now, how much have you been told about the situation?"

"Everything, I believe."

"You understand that the man who is trying to kill this patient is none other than a criminal mastermind?"

"I understand."

"And that he excels at disguise and deception, so that you must meet everyone who arrives with the same ill treatment you have just now received?"

"Yes."

"And you understand that these two young people are precious to me, and that if any harm befalls them, well—you will have to reckon with me. And the only opponent I can imagine who is more formidable than the murderer is myself. Do you understand?"

The gendarme blinked thoughtfully and bowed his head. "I understand."

Holmes smiled and lightly patted the young man's cheek, which he had so brutally struck only moments before. "Good. I will return." He stepped over to Anna. "See what you can do to wake Thomas. The exorcism machine is utterly worthless unless he knows what to do with it. We'll need Thomas to build this trap—this strange pentacle of his."

"I'll do my best," Anna said.

Holmes gave the gendarme one final look up and down and then headed out of the ward. The gentle clink of glass in the room beyond told them that Holmes had one last gulp of brandy before he stalked out the double doors into the night.

The cold and dark and isolation of the place settled heavily on Anna.

The gendarme was watching her. His eyes were youthful and eager but distrustful of all things adult. Anna averted her gaze, sitting in the chair beside Thomas's bed. "Wake up, Thomas," she said, stroking his hair. "You have to wake up. Holmes said so. *I* said so. I need you, Thomas. Please, wake up."

He didn't stir beneath her trailing fingertips. He barely even breathed.

42

AWAKENINGS

The last thing I remembered seeing was that devil Moriarty leering into my face as he shoved his knife into me. Then everything went black.

The first new thing I saw was the angel Moriarty—Anna Moriarty—stretching her lithe body in the pink light of morning above my hospital bed.

"Where am I?" I asked.

Anna turned, her eyes lighting with surprise and joy. "Thomas!" She came to me and sat down on the bedside. "Good morning."

"Good morning," I replied.

Tears came, but she dashed them away. "You're alive. You're awake. It was more than I'd hoped for."

"I'm fine," I told her, though I felt anything but. My chest was leaden, and every breath was a labor. Still, I tried to laugh away my pain. "It takes more than a shiv to kill a scamp like me."

"It was more than a shiv. It was almost a sword. A few inches nearer to your heart and—" Anna shook her head, mastering herself. "It's just been—such a long night."

"Where's Holmes?"

Anna gestured out vaguely past the windows of the ward. "He caught up to my father—gave him a stab like yours—but . . . Father escaped. . . . Even with such a terrible wound, he could still run." She steeled herself. "It's the demon in him. . . . That's what I told Holmes. . . ."

A chill went through me. "I saw that demon. Those eyes . . ."

"We have to drive it out." Anna turned toward me. "Father's only hope—*our* only hope—is the exorcism machine. Holmes has gone to get it."

The exorcism machine! What a faint hope . . .

"When Holmes gets back," Anna explained, "we need you to use it to build an electric pentacle."

I nodded emptily. Back at Cambridge, I would have leaped at the chance to build such a device, but I would have had books and research facilities. Here, in this hospital, I had only what I could remember from the books at Bern—a crude schematic sketched in my mind. . . . and I had to build a device that would stop a demonic madman. . . . "This is a desperate plan, Anna, likely to end badly."

"What about the plenary worm?"

"Your father is no plenary worm," I snapped. "He's a man—a genius . . . with a demon inside of him."

"So, you won't build it?"

"I didn't say that."

"Then, what are you saying?"

I drew a deep breath. "Listen, Anna. We've shared every danger so far—"

"Every danger," she repeated.

"But this is . . . different."

She scowled at me. "How?"

"It's different because you don't have to be here."

"He's *my* father!"

"He's not your father, Anna. He's a demon."

Anna paused, glancing sidelong at the gendarme who stood silently at the door. "I know. I've known it for years. It's all the more reason I want to stay. I want to be here when the demon is gone and Father is healed. Besides, you need me."

I nodded. "Yes. Until Holmes comes back, until we've set up the pentacle. But then you should go away with the gendarme and leave this to Holmes and me."

"No," she said quietly.

"Why won't you listen?"

She smiled. "Because I love you." She leaned down and kissed me.

The kiss was warm and wonderful; I returned it. But when our lips parted, fear settled on my heart, as if I would never have the chance to kiss her again.

A shout came at the door: "Aha! He's awake!" Holmes swept into the room and held the generator aloft. "Got it, without any trouble. Now, let's see if we can't build this pentacle of yours." Holmes approached the bed and set the generator beside me.

I grimly studied the contraption—the heavy crank, the six black wires and alligator clips. "Well, I first saw the pentacle on you, Holmes, when these clips were attached to your extremities—ears, hands, feet. That's what the pentacle is, a representation of the human body. It's an electric field that drives out the soul."

Holmes nodded. "But we may not have the luxury of hooking your father up the same way. If a knife can't stop him—"

"Instead of hooking the machine up to him, maybe we could . . . we could create a pentacle and lure him onto it. Perhaps we can . . . form the pentacle out of some conducting material."

"What about scalpels, bone saws, clamps, tongs?" Anna asked. "There must be enough metal in the surgical theater to form a pentacle. . . ."

"I doubt we could simply sneak in and carry it off. Besides, it's too obvious. We'd never be able to lure your father onto it. No. We need something subtler. . . ."

"What about a liquid?" Holmes wondered. "We could paint the pentacle on the floor. Simple saltwater would conduct electricity—"

"It would evaporate too quickly, and we'd be left with nothing."

Anna stood and wandered to a tall white cabinet on one wall. She opened the door to find row upon row of bottles. "There's liniments of all kinds in here. Here's alcohol."

"No," I replied. "Evaporates even faster than water—and it might catch fire."

Holmes stepped up beside her. "What else is there?"

Anna said, "Well, let's see. They're alphabetical—alum, bleach, camphor, Epsom salts, ipecac, hydrogen peroxide, iodine, linseed oil, petroleum jelly, quinine—"

"Aha!" Holmes snatched up two bottles. "The jelly will create a substrate, and the quinine is a base that will make the mixture conduct electricity. Any acid or base is a natural conductor." Holmes hunted up a mortar and pestle, a shaving brush, and a few other implements and began mixing his concoction.

Anna said, "I'll be the one who cranks the machine."

I sighed. "Holmes, before you arrived, I was trying to convince Anna that she should leave this confrontation to you and me."

"Nonsense," Anna said, waving her hand to dispel the thought. "Thomas has a collapsed lung, and you—Holmes— you're the bait."

"Help me, Holmes," I pleaded.

"You heard her," he replied, grinding the quinine with mortar and pestle. "You have a collapsed lung, and I'm the bait."

Anna smiled in triumph as she approached my bed. She looked down at the generator. "Let's hide this under a blanket on my lap so Father won't suspect. Then, the moment he steps onto the pentacle, I'll start cranking."

Holmes's face was lit with delight as he came toward us, dabbing the shaving brush in the thick mixture of jelly and quinine. "How large should I make it—the pentacle?"

"The same size as Moriarty—six feet from point to point. Paint it as a single unbroken line. We'll use only two of the generator's cables—concentrating all of the charge—and"—I turned to Anna—"it'll be up to you to keep those clips in contact with the two ends of the pentacle."

She was already arranging the cables and clips, hiding most within the seat but running two down the leg of the chair. Holmes meanwhile worked on hands and knees, meticulously painting the five points of the star. In a matter of minutes, the arrangements were complete, and we three stared down with a certain flushed enthusiasm at our creation.

"Let's give it a try," I said.

Anna sat down, drawing the generator onto her lap and covering it with a blanket. She glanced down to make sure that the clips were sunk into the viscous jelly at one point of the star. Then she began to turn the crank. A spark leaped beneath her feet, and the quinine jelly began to glimmer and zap with power.

Holmes reached his hand above the outer line of the pentacle. "It tingles. There's some sort of field above the lines." He shot an amazed look my way. "This just might work."

"It worked on you," I said. "And make sure you keep your head out of that field, unless you want to lose your mind again. As much as I liked Harold Silence, I like Sherlock Holmes better." I turned to Anna. "All right. That's enough of a test. Give your arm a rest. You'll need all your strength when your father comes."

Anna stopped cranking.

The gendarme at the door poked his head in. "Excuse me," he said with a thick French accent. "May I go? My replacement has arrived."

"Ah!" said Holmes, striding toward the door and winking. "I'd like to give him the customary interview."

The gendarme nodded knowingly as his replacement stepped through the doorway. He was a tall, thin man with black hair, a large nose, and a waxed mustache. Holmes stepped to the man and looked him up and down. "How long have you been with the Metropolitan Police?"

The gendarme shook his head and said, *"Parlez-vous français?"*

Holmes simply smiled. "Well enough." He gestured to the young officer. "You may go." To the replacement, he said, "Luckily for you, we have someone who will translate for me. Anna, could you please tell the man to come in? There are a few remarkable details I must apprise him of."

As Anna spoke these words in French, a terrible dread poured through me.

I recognized this man.

It was Professor James Moriarty.

43

Entertaining the Devil

Ever since my optimistic pronouncement, "Piece by piece, I am becoming Sherlock Holmes," I have had deep doubts. What real man, after all, could live up to the legend of this great detective? Am I great? Am I *still* great? The next moments will be a test case.

I greet my archnemesis at the door to the infirmary. I can tell immediately that it is he. This is a good sign. Moriarty's disguise is impeccable. The false mustache is done up out of real human mustache hair, and the foam appliances at jowls and cheekbones are almost indetectible even at short range. It's not the costume that gives him away but those naked eyes of his. Those demonic eyes. He cannot disguise his hatred of me, and so in those eyes I know his identity.

I have passed the first part of the test. We shall see how well I do with the rest.

If I am Holmes, I will survive this encounter. If not . . .

We shall see. . . .

44

THE END OF ALL THINGS

I felt deep dread, lying there as Moriarty stood at the door, no doubt fingering a knife in his pocket. Anna must have been frightened, too, for she gave a little gasp, and her hand tensed on the hidden crank of the exorcism machine.

Sherlock Holmes, however, showed no sign of fear. His gaze was steady and knowing, and the words that poured out of him seemed to be spoken to a friend, not to a demon. "Officer, you have a daunting task before you." As Holmes spoke, Anna translated his words into French. "The young man you see lying in that bed was stabbed not by some thug in an alley, but by a genius." Holmes was baiting Moriarty with that word, knowing he would be flattered to the core.

"*Genius?*" Moriarty replied, inflecting the word in the French way. For good measure, he added, "*Sacré Coeur!*"

"*Coeur*, yes," Holmes said, "heart. Courage. That's what we need, for the would-be killer is cunning, fearless—a mastermind!" He turned his back on Moriarty and headed toward me. "Come, let me show you the man's handiwork."

Moriarty followed, his hand quivering in his coat pocket and his feverish eyes locked on Holmes's back.

"Come right up to the bedside," Holmes said as he stepped into the pentacle.

Anna watched fiercely, ready for the moment when Holmes would exit the pentacle and her father enter it.

"Let me move aside so that you can see the wound." Holmes stepped from the pentacle.

Moriarty stopped short of it and stared balefully at the quinine jelly that sketched across the floor. "Clever," he said, no longer making any pretense of speaking French. His voice was dreadful and calculating as he went on: "A very clever trap, indeed. But the trap must always be more clever than the quarry."

Holmes spun to see the angry, bulging eyes of his great foe, Professor James Moriarty. The man stood there with an ancient-looking gun raised in his hand. He ripped the false nose and mustache from his face and pulled the wig from his head. "Last time we met, your knife work proved to be a little better than mine, Mr. Sherlock Holmes. And so I acquired a gun. Do you know what kind of gun this is, Detective?"

Holmes stood just beyond the pentacle, his hands at his sides and his eyes fixed on his mortal enemy. "A blunderbuss, I would guess."

"Yes. A very old weapon with a very large iron ball inside it. It's a pirate's gun, a sort of handheld cannon. It's useless at long range, but at short range, as we have here, it kills with a certainty. The one-inch lead ball in this gun will destroy whatever it contacts. Whether head or torso, arm or leg or hand—whatever it hits will be gone, and the rest of the body will bleed out in minutes."

Holmes nodded. "An imprecise and indiscriminant weapon. . . . How far you have fallen, Professor. Once you could take over the whole of London with a single equation. Now, you can't kill one man with anything less than a blunderbuss?"

"I can kill you any way I want," Moriarty growled, "but there is something satisfying in the thought of splitting you in half."

Holmes shook his head and tsked. "When your wife handed you the keys to world domination, they were such subtle things—numbers on a page. But look what your ham-fisted efforts have turned them into! A half-pound lump of lead."

Moriarty stepped past the pentacle, careful to keep his toes from its rim, and approached Holmes. The blunderbuss quivered in his hand. "Do not mention my wife."

"Why not?" Holmes challenged, standing his ground. "Su-sanna was a genius. A true genius."

Moriarty paused as if mesmerized. The vision of his beau-tiful Susanna seemed to fill his eyes.

Holmes continued. "You think you saved her from a life of prostitution. You think you educated her about logic and phi-losophy, that you lifted her out of the gutter and made her into something worth loving. But it is all reversed. She was a creature worth loving before you met her. Susanna was a mir-acle, and she saved you. She elevated you, transfigured you from a little mathematical nebbish into a professor."

I cringed, waiting for Moriarty to explode, but instead, he drank in the words as if they were truth long denied. He held the blunderbuss leveled, but his finger was slack on the trig-ger, and his eyes were slack on Holmes.

"She saved you," Holmes repeated.

"Yes."

"I know I'm talking now to the man James Moriarty, the professor, the mathematical genius, the misunderstood child," Holmes said carefully, "not to the preternatural crea-ture that has taken him over."

Moriarty only nodded vacantly, his once-rapacious eyes gone dark.

"I know I'm talking now to the man who lost his wife, the love of his life, to a killer and who mourned her until he found her spirit again in his daughter Anna, and who loved her and would do nothing to harm her."

Moriarty nodded again blankly, his eyes shifting to Anna. Even so, his gun remained trained on Holmes.

Anna rose from the chair, set the generator beside me, and approached her father. She stepped in front of the blunderbuss, putting her body between the gun and Holmes.

"It's me, Father. It's me. Your Anna. Put down the gun. We'll get this demon out of you."

Moriarty snarled, lifting the blunderbuss to point at his daughter's face.

"You won't shoot me," she said to him, though her voice trembled. "The part of you that's really you, the part of you that's alive and true, won't shoot me. Father, you're stronger than the demon. It can't kill Sherlock Holmes if you won't kill me."

"Move aside, Anna," Moriarty said, his hand shaking.

"You have only one shot, and I'm not going to step aside."

"The ball will go through you both."

Holmes said quietly. "He's right, Anna. You'll only be sacrificing yourself without saving me. Step aside now."

Anna shook her head and smiled. "He won't do it. He won't harm me."

Dread tied my stomach in knots. "Step aside, Anna," I said. "He's not your father."

Moriarty's eyes shifted from his daughter to me. He looked disgusted. "You thought she could love you—you vagrant!"

"I do love him!" Anna shouted, shoving her father toward the pentacle. Moriarty staggered, foot coming down on the quinine gel. He slipped and tried to catch himself. His free hand snagged Anna's shoulder and dragged her down on top of him.

The blunderbuss discharged. The lead ball hit the ceiling

and smashed through lathe and plaster. Anna fell atop her father within the pentacle. He struck his head on the floor and lay there stunned as Anna rolled away to one side.

The moment she was beyond the pentacle, she groaned, "Now, Thomas! Crank the crank!"

But I did not. I could not. I could only gape at the wide red hole blown in her side.

Anna clutched the wound and cried out again, "Now, Thomas!"

I cranked the exorcism machine. The cylinder hummed, and sparks crackled down the wires into the quinine gel. All around Professor Moriarty, the pentacle lit up, and as I cranked faster, fields of energy projected up to the ceiling.

Within those walls of light, the professor convulsed. He shuddered and staggered to his feet and tried to shove his way out of the pentacle, but the mystic fields were too powerful. He hissed and recoiled. Sheets of energy folded down around him and clove to his skin. Moriarty thrashed as electricity swarmed across him. He twitched and spun and whirled and staggered. An inhuman roar erupted from his mouth. He fell to the ground and trembled in a seizure.

Then his eyes turned crimson. I feared for a moment that the man was cooking within his skin, but this crimson color poured out of his eyes and nose and mouth and ears, poured out or was leached out by the energy that surrounded him. The liquid then boiled away into a red cloud in the air.

It was a soul—a demonic soul—and it seeped through the electric field. Rising beyond the pentacle, the demon roiled above us.

"Look out!" I panted, out of breath from cranking. "Look out, Holmes!"

The cloud descended on the great detective and whirled in a cyclone around him. Holmes crouched and swatted at the spirit. It was no good. Whenever his hand struck the crimson vapor, evil sank into his skin. Slap by slap, stroke by stroke, the demon was possessing him. The cloud condensed around Holmes and permeated his every pore.

In mere moments, the last of the wicked spirit had poured out of James Moriarty and into Sherlock Holmes.

I couldn't crank any longer; my lungs were bursting with each breath. I released the handle. A final few sparks zapped out through the quinine gel, but then the pentacle went dark. The electric fields that mantled Moriarty's body fizzled away. Smoke rose from his crumpled, panting form.

"He's all right," I said breathlessly to Anna. "He's alive."

She lay beside her father and wept. "But look at Holmes."

Across the room, Holmes, who had been crouching away from the demon attack, now slowly rose to stand upright. His eyes were wide and red, though in a moment, the crimson color drained away into his pupils. Then he smiled a smile like a set of knives. "How clever you are, Thomas Carnacki— dabbling in the black arts, playing with the ancient pentacle of life." Even his voice had changed, deep and malevolent. "You built your exorcism machine well enough, but all you've done is drive me from one body to the next. I like this one better." The demon in Holmes's body stalked across the room toward Moriarty. "The Shadow of Reichenbach Falls has moved on."

He reached down suddenly to Moriarty's belt, drew a knife, and plunged it into the professor's heart.

"No!" Anna shrieked. "No!"

Her cry was answered by another shout. Dr. Maison stood at the door and gawked at the bloody spectacle and cried, *"Gardes! Gardes! Au meurtre!"*

The demon pulled the bright-red dagger from Moriarty's chest and smiled at me with Holmes's teeth. "I wish I had time to use this on you, but you would try to hold me down until the guards came. Ah, well, *ainsi va la guerre!* Thank you, Thomas, for setting me free. Everyone in Europe is hunting Moriarty, but everyone will be thrilled to see *me* again—to see Sherlock Holmes!" With that, the demon turned and dashed away. He disappeared through the far door.

"Father?" Anna said. She dragged herself to his side. "Father?" She grabbed his blood-soaked shirt and shook him. "Daddy!"

The professor's eyelids fluttered, and he rolled his head to one side. "Oh, Anna . . . it's you."

"Yes," she gasped. "It's me. And it's you, too."

"Where are we, Anna?"

"A hospital."

"Oh, good. I don't feel very well."

Anna gave a weak laugh, though her eyes were burgeoning with tears.

The professor's hand fumbled along the floor and finally found Anna's and squeezed it. "I'm glad you're safe. I hope you didn't—didn't see what happened."

Anna's breath caught. "Father, I was here. It was—"

"Jack the Ripper . . ." Moriarty said.

"Yes, Father. Jack the Ripper."

"He was hiding in our apartment. I knew he would be. That's why I left you with Mrs. Mulroney." He shook his head in chagrin. "I was sure I could defeat him. Typical arrogance."

"But you did defeat him, Father," Anna replied, letting the tears stream now. "You killed him. Jack the Ripper is dead and gone."

"Good. Good. Your mother's avenged, then," Moriarty said. He took a long breath. "Anna, I'm afraid he's killed me, too. I don't think I'll make it."

"Oh, Father."

"And I want you to know, before I go . . . I love you."

She nodded. "I know, Father. I know."

Professor James Moriarty gave his daughter's hand one final squeeze, and then his grip went slack, and he was gone.

I slid down out of the bed and onto the floor. "Anna." My chest wound burned furiously, and my lungs were ripped to rags, but I had to reach her. "Anna."

"Oh, Thomas." She took my hand, and her bloodstained fingers were icy. "This is it, then."

"No! Dr. Maison saved me. He'll save you, too."

"No, Thomas. I'm dying. Dr. Maison can't stop it. Neither can you. . . ."

"You can't die. I love you."

"I know. And I love you. But love . . . can't stop death. . . . This wound of mine . . . oh, Thomas!"

She trembled, and before I could kiss her one last time, her soul had fled away. It was as quick as that. One moment, she lay there beside me. Next moment, it was only a body.

"Anna!" I kissed her all the same. "Anna!" I caressed her cheek, wrung her hand. "Anna!" I clung to her as the door to the ward barked open and two guards and Dr. Maison rushed into the room.

"Where's the killer?" Dr. Maison shouted.

"There." I waved my arm toward the far door. "Out there somewhere."

While the guards rushed off, Dr. Maison knelt to check for pulse and breathing from Professor Moriarty. *"Mort."* Then he shifted to Anna and checked her the same way. *"Morte."*

"She can't be dead!" I said. "She can't be!"

The doctor glared. "She is. And look at you. Your lung is a wet paper bag. I've stitched it together, but all of this—this lunacy—may have ripped it open again. These two are dead, yes, young man, but unless you remain in bed, you could die, too!"

"Yes," I said bleakly. "I could die, too."

WHAT A desolation I felt, lying in my bed beside the bodies. They were covered now, of course. There were plenty of sheets in that empty ward.

I wasn't sure if Dr. Maison had spread the sheets to preserve the dignity of the dead or to preserve the sanity of the living. He'd failed on both counts. There was no dignity in lying crumpled on the floor while fresh linens soaked up your blood. There was no sanity in sitting in a bed and breathing slowly while the woman you loved and the man you hated lay breathless not ten feet away.

I wept.

Tears are strange. Distilled grief. They bite like liquor and they get you drunk and they leave you hungover and headachy . . . and they help you survive what is unsurvivable.

She was gone. She was gone like a footprint under a tide. She was gone like a familiar name spoken in a crowd of strangers. She was gone like a butterfly in the gullet of a crow.

I told myself that I had known her for only two weeks, that my life had been happy before these two weeks and would be happy again. That's what I told myself, but it did no good. It was as if that lead ball had ripped a hole in me.

The shadows of afternoon were lengthening when the police arrived—four officers, ranging from a black-haired rookie to a white-haired veteran. They entered the ward grimly, and when they laid eyes on the blood-soaked sheets draped over the bodies, their faces clenched with dread.

Dr. Maison entered the ward, and the gendarmes surrounded him and quietly badgered him with questions. I understood a few words here and there, but the French was too quick and too quiet for me to catch most of it. Finally, Dr. Maison had had enough and excused himself. Then the officers turned to me.

"*Savez-vous qui sont ces deux personnes?*" asked the silver-haired one.

"Do you know English?" I replied.

The youngest officer stepped forward: "Do you know the victims?"

I nodded and was on the verge of telling them all—of James and Anna, of the demon that had been within Moriarty and now dwelt in Sherlock Holmes—but the whole story seemed ludicrous . . . or outright dangerous. "I knew the girl. I loved her. She was Anna Moriarty, daughter of the crime lord James Moriarty, who died at Reichenbach Falls. As to the man—no, I did not know him. He was part of Moriarty's gang, but I never knew him."

The young gendarme turned to his fellows and translated. Their eyes slowly widened with shock and consternation. One of them wrote down every word on a small tablet. After trading comments with the others, the young gendarme said, "Did you witness the murders?"

I nodded numbly. "The thug, here, killed my Anna."

"Killed her . . . ?"

"Yes, with a blunderbuss. A big pistol—there, on the ground, half beneath my bed. You'll find the ball of the pistol in the ceiling." I pointed up.

While the older three rolled their eyes to the ceiling, the youngest man stooped to drag the blunderbuss from the floor. He studied the device, checked to make sure the gun was not loaded, and sniffed the barrel. When he had been satisfied, the gendarme asked, "Why? Why would someone from Moriarty's gang kill his own daughter?"

I shook my head. "Loose ends."

The gendarme pointed to the bloody bandage on my heart. "And what happened to you?"

"Stabbed. By that man there, two days ago, at Gare Saint-Lazare."

"It was the two of you, then. Lovers. But the henchman loved her, too."

"Yes. I think he did."

"And so, a confrontation," the young officer elaborated, his eyes filling with romantic dreams. "He fought you at Gare Saint-Lazare, but the girl—Anna—saved you. And the henchman was driven mad with jealousy and came here to kill you, but she saved you again . . . at the cost of her own life!"

I nodded miserably. "I think you have the shape of it."

"But who killed the henchman? You?"

"No. I'm in no shape for fighting. Another henchman, a man named Harold Silence, was battling this fellow here for control of Moriarty's criminal empire. Silence killed this man."

"And what did this—Harold Silence—look like?"

"Tall, thin—a hawklike nose, silvery eyes."

"Where can we find this man?"

I released a long sigh. "I don't know. Watch the papers. Watch for outlandish crimes, things that will draw the public eye. That's what he wants."

The young man retreated to the other gendarmes and told them what I had said. They nodded with the solemn silence of strangers staring into an open grave. The gendarmes stood there a while longer, murmuring decorously and glancing down at the linen-covered figures. At length, they started to shift, crouching, lifting sheets, studying faces, letting sheets fall back into place.

What were they looking at? Anna was dead. Her father, too. Three of the gendarmes drifted in a knot toward the door, but the young one approached me and leaned down as if to speak to me. Instead, he drew the exorcism machine from the floor and lifted it.

"What's this?"

Embarrassment lit my face from ear to ear, but I managed to say, "Therapy machine. Swiss therapy." I reached for the device.

The gendarme set the machine on the side of my bed and smiled tightly. *"Thérapie suisse."*

Those were the last words any of them spoke to me. The young gendarme tipped his hat and went to tell Dr. Maison that he could have the bodies removed. Then he joined his comrades at the door. They lingered there a moment more before passing through, leaving me with the dead Moriartys.

Divine Horsemen

This is how a spirit of the dead finds a new host among the living: The divine horseman cries, "Whoa," and steps down from one mount and steps up to straddle another. Then he cries, "Yah!"

New horseflesh always feels good to ride. One wants to take it for a gallop, to see what it can do.

This horseflesh—Sherlock Holmes—can do quite a lot.

46

LE TEMPS

Night was falling beyond the ward windows when Dr. Maison returned with the orderlies. They carried Anna and James away and mopped up the blood and the pentacle. A splash of pine oil, a few more swipes, and nothing remained of the Moriartys. The hospital staff withdrew, leaving only me and a flickering gas lamp and that damned hole in the ceiling.

Sleep came slowly, and when it came, it was haunted . . .

by Anna . . .

by her father . . .

by Jack the Ripper . . .

by the exorcism machine. . . .

I DREAMED that the machine had its clamps on me. I dreamed that electricity pulsed into my head and hands and feet and reached toward my heart. It jolted my spirit free. Protoplasm seeped out of my mouth and nose and ears and eyes and every pore and coalesced in the air.

I hung above my body. The last of my spirit peeled away from my electrocuted flesh, and I rose.

A tunnel of light formed ahead of me, stretching up and away. I entered the tunnel.

"Anna!" I called. She was the light ahead of me. "Anna!"

I wanted to follow the cave of light toward her, but

something laid hold of my legs and drew me down. I sank through the floor of the tunnel, out of the brilliant, loving light and into the shadows.

The shadows cleaved to me. They held me as if I were their own. Possession.

I reeled. I pitched. I bucked until I threw the shadows off and galloped out of the darkness and back into my world, back into my flesh.

I JOLTED awake as the morning edition of *Le Temps* flopped down on my chest.

Above me stood Dr. Maison, scowling. "Here's your handiwork." The doctor pointed to the headline on the front page: *"Bataille des Associés du Seigneur de Crime Chez Les Invalides."*

I sat up, struggling to read the article.

Dr. Maison snatched the paper away and translated:

> The daughter of Professor James Moriarty, the London crime boss slain in Switzerland last week, died in a double murder at Les Invalides yesterday. An unidentified henchman of Moriarty killed the professor's daughter, Anna, while she tended another member of the crime syndicate recuperating at Les Invalides. Afterward, the henchman was himself slain by another Moriarty underling, Harold Silence, in a bid for the throne of the London crime syndicate. Harold Silence apparently remains at large in Paris. One witness referred to Silence as "the Ripper of Paris."

"You sensationalist!" Dr. Maison spat.

"I didn't even speak to reporters!"

"But you spoke to the police. You misled them!"

"I told them the truth!"

"The truth? Just *look* at you—a young Romeo with a weeping wound over his heart and a dead Juliet by his side. They saw a romantic tragedy and gave it to the press."

"I—I—I . . . How is this my fault?"

Dr. Maison sputtered. "Crime lords! Murderers! Reporters! You brought them here—you, who aren't even a veteran!" He was on a rant, and there was no reasoning with him.

Instead I tried to distract him with the article: "What else does it say?"

"A few other things."

"What other things?"

He sighed heavily and read:

> According to Dr. Maison, chief surgeon of Les Invalides, the young witness was another criminal from the London gang. "Mr. Carnacki tried to kill this henchman before but was stabbed," Maison testified. "He would have died from his wound if I had not saved him. I am an expert in bayonet-style wounds."

"*You* spoke to the reporters?" I demanded.

"I am the chief surgeon."

"You told them I was a criminal?"

"A misquotation. The reporters could not write as fast as I spoke, so they put words in my mouth."

"You gave them my *name*?"

Dr. Maison folded the paper and dumped it in my lap. "You'd better get healthy and get out. I cannot shield you from the press any longer."

Suddenly it struck me: I could use *Le Temps* to draw Silence in.

The demon within him desired one thing even more than blood: ink. He was planning to return to the public stage as

Sherlock Holmes, was no doubt already committing the crimes that he would later "solve." Every morning, he would be reading *Le Temps* from masthead to obituaries, would be looking for depictions of his own crimes to see how he was portrayed. I would make sure he got some bad press. A few printed sentences every day could draw him in for a final confrontation.

"There's no need to shield me from the press," I called after Dr. Maison as he walked out. "Let them come."

HE LET them come.

First to arrive was a young, nervous man from *Le Temps*, and then a middle-aged Brit—the Paris correspondent of the London *Times*—and then a succession of men from penny presses. Each reporter said he would feature me if I promised an exclusive. I granted one exclusive after another for the mere price of a subscription to each paper, delivered right to my bed.

Next morning, I awoke feeling markedly improved: a clearer lung, a sharper mind, and a pile of newspapers across my bed. I read all of them with interest. My tale, which had grown tall in the telling, had grown even taller in the writing. *Le Temps* reported it as follows:

THE "VETERAN" TAKES ON THE "RIPPER"

A day after the double murder at Les Invalides, the witness has thrown down a gauntlet for the killer. "Harold Silence is a thug," said Thomas Carnacki. "Paris shouldn't fear this man. He's not a Ripper. He's not even a Cutter. He's more of a Scraper, a Filer—irritating but not really dangerous. He's no Moriarty. He's playing at crime. Moriarty was crime."

Carnacki received treatment at Les Invalides by pretending to be a French veteran. He is in fact an English con man who speaks only pidgin French. "Harold Silence wants to be a big man. He'll stage a few crimes, badly planned, but sure to capture headlines. He'll try to terrorize the city, but Paris shouldn't fear a titmouse. Once I'm well, I'll capture him myself."

I smiled in satisfaction. The reporter had included all my best lines—all that Ripper, Cutter, Scraper, Filer nonsense, the bit about Moriarty being crime, the contention that Silence was a titmouse. That was rhetoric.

The account in the *Times* was less conscientiously written—but more powerful.

GENERALS FIGHT TO SUCCEED EMPEROR OF CRIME

James Moriarty, the Caesar of Crime, lies dead. Now the men who slew him are fighting for his throne. His Brutus, who struck the "most unkindest cut of all," was a onetime underling named Harold Silence. Moriarty's Cassius, the other "honorable man" who struck a blow, was a Cambridge-educated Russian named Thomas Carnacki. Both men now lay claim to Moriarty's empire, and they are turning Paris into their battleground.

From his sickbed in the veteran's hospital in Paris, Carnacki promised "murder and mayhem" once he was well enough to stand. Harold Silence meanwhile has begun what Carnacki considered a crime spree "bent on stealing headlines."

Carnacki believes he is the rightful successor to Moriarty, who was brilliant and relentless. "Silence isn't the right material. He's a stupid post."

I laughed aloud at those lines, even though I hadn't actually spoken any of them. The middle-aged man from the *Times* was apparently a frustrated novelist, compelled to turn facts into literature. Still, he'd done well. It was just this sort of grandstanding that would bring Silence out of the woodwork.

The best piece of sensationalism, though, came from the *Raconteur,* a penny-press paper that twisted my tale by putting it into Silence's mouth:

RIPPER OF PARIS VOWS TERROR
The "Ripper of Paris" sent a postcard to the *RACONTEUR* about his current crime spree. The postcard appears below:

Dear Raconteur:
*   Paris belongs to me. I will take all the money, and the Metropolitan Police cannot stop me. They are too stupid. The one man who could help you is lying near death's door at Les Invalides. I will kick him across the threshold. Once he is gone, I will crown myself emperor of France. Bide my warning!*
                                                  Ripper of Paris

An obvious fabrication: Silence would never admit that I could stop him. In fact, he would be affronted by the notion.

A postcard that sounded much more authentic appeared in another article in *Le Temps:*

METROPOLITAN POLICE WAYLAID BY "BOMB"
The city police department was paralyzed this morning by a postcard signed "Ripper of Paris."

Good morning, men!
*   Hit your beats. Keep the street urchins safe, but let your own brats die. A bomb! A bomb! Call off classes and get the kids out and look under the headmistress's desk.*
                                                  Ripper of Paris

This threat sent the detectives of the Metropolitan Police rushing to the school of Madame Bouvoir, where their children were enrolled. Officers cleared the building and found, beneath the headmistress's desk, a wooden box crudely nailed to the floor. After hours of careful work, they removed the box to discover that the prankster had left not a bomb but a similar postcard, which said simply, "Next time . . . boom!"

This was no joke. Terrorizing children, waylaying law enforcement—Silence was showing Paris how powerful he was and how vulnerable it was. And while Paris focused on this great, empty crime, it nearly missed what Silence truly was up to:

FOILED BREAK-IN AT THE LOUVRE

The palace of the Louvre and its treasure trove of great artwork were the targets of a petty and cowardly criminal last night. In the early morning hours, a night watchman heard a crash and came running to discover a back door hanging ajar. Its wrought-iron knob and lock had been shattered by the blow of a blunt instrument. The guard called for comrades to sweep the museum, but the perpetrator had apparently been scared away. By dawn, the management had sent a locksmith to replace the ruined knob and lock.

This was no foiled break-in. No thief would destroy a wrought-iron lock when the building had a thousand windows. The perpetrator's target could not have been artwork, but rather the lock itself.

Silence must have been the "locksmith" who appeared the next morning. He probably hadn't even been summoned by "the management," but had simply shown up, counting on bureaucracy not to notice. He had then replaced the lock with one to which he held the key, giving himself an open door into the Louvre.

But what was he after? I could only guess that he planned an elaborate heist—to strike at the heart of Paris, steal her most precious artworks, sell them for a fortune on the black market, and then "solve" the crime by handing a patsy over to the police.

Next morning, *Le Temps* reported a story that confirmed it:

RIPPER THREATENS ARTWORKS

The Louvre received the most recent Ripper postcard last night. The card is reprinted with the hope that readers might identify the penmanship.

Dear Louvre—

I'm coming. Your art is mine. No masterpiece is safe. Watch me take Mona from under your eyes. You cannot stop me. No one can, especially not that pretender Thomas Carnacki.

Ripper of Paris

This message was undoubtedly from Silence. I recognized the handwriting, for one, but also, I recognized the demon's opinion of me—disdain bordering on loathing. The postcard had prompted the Louvre to hire two more security guards—and I would have wagered that both of them were in the employ of Silence. He was stacking the deck with men on the inside and a door on the outside. No doubt he was making dozens of other adjustments so that he could walk out with the greatest works of Western art.

Then, of course, "Sherlock Holmes" would arrive on the scene and catch the thief.

My plan had failed. I had not drawn Silence in for a final

confrontation. The only way to stop him was to go to the Louvre. But how could I, weak as I was, alone as I was?

NEXT MORNING, a man appeared at the door, a man with a kindly, mustachioed face and broad shoulders and a long black doctor's bag clutched in one hand. He approached my bedside and said, "Hello, Thomas. You may not remember me, but I helped save your life. I am Dr. John Watson."

Stunned, I stared at him for perhaps ten seconds before I found my tongue. "An honor, sir." I shook his hand.

Dr. Watson lowered himself into the chair where Anna had last sat. "I hope you're doing well."

"No," I said truthfully. "Well, physically, yes—thanks to you, and to Dr. Maison. But in other ways, no."

Watson nodded. "I know. Or at least, I know in part. You've been the speculation of Paris—you and this Harold Silence . . . heirs to a criminal empire." He laughed bleakly. "I have to wonder what sort of man I rescued."

I sat up—the wound in my chest ached to do it, but I wanted to look Watson straight in the eye. "The papers have it wrong. I'm not trying to become a crime lord. I'm trying to stop Silence from becoming one."

Watson blinked thoughtfully. "I'd suspected as much. A good doctor has intuition about his patients—those who are telling the truth and those who are lying. You were unconscious, of course, on the day that I saved you, but the woman—Anna—she was a truth teller, and she loved you, and in her eyes I knew you were a good man." A gentle smile creased his face, but the look dissolved a moment later into sadness. "How is it that you got tangled up with Moriarty—?"

"Well, uh—it was because of Anna. She was his daughter."

Watson clenched his jaw. "Yes, I'd read as much."

How much should I tell him? How much could he absorb

before believing me to be insane? Guardedly, I told him about that first day: "I met her in Meiringen, Switzerland, and fell in love with her. She took me out to the Reichenbach Falls"—Watson stiffened—"and we witnessed a murder."

"The murder of my friend Sherlock Holmes," Watson supplied.

"Yes," I responded, "and the death of her father, too. Anna was traumatized. She hadn't known what her father was planning. I tried to whisk her away, only to get shot in the shoulder." I pulled down the neck of my hospital gown to show him the wound. "It was one of Moriarty's henchmen—the one you read about. To him, Anna and I were just loose ends—Anna because she was Moriarty's heir and I because, well, because I loved her. We escaped him at Reichenbach, but the man caught up to us at the Gare Saint-Lazare station, and, well, you know the rest."

"Yes. I know. I was on that train. I had tracked that man to Bern and followed him onto the train, but I lost him then. He had assumed the disguise of a porter, which I later found out, but not before you were stabbed."

I nodded grimly.

"But why have you been giving all these interviews?" Watson asked, his eyes wide and almost feverish. "Why have you been—filling the papers with all these stories?"

What to tell him? "Are you a religious man, Doctor?"

His hale features flushed. "Not less than any other good Englishman—but not more, either."

"Do you believe that spirits live on after death?"

"I do," he said with a firm nod. Watson seemed to stare beyond Les Invalides, beyond Paris to some dusty battlefield. "I was in Afghanistan, and I saw thousands of men die. Sometimes . . . I could feel the uncanny creep of the spirit up into the air."

"Then I will tell you what I saw a week ago. I saw my Anna die, and I saw the evil soul of her killer rise from his body and take hold of Harold Silence. Do you understand?"

"I do," Watson said, as if in a trance. "I had the most . . . preternatural experience . . ." He turned to me, his eyes lit by an inner flame. "When I was in my stateroom on the Paris Express from Bern, I felt a presence. I felt a mind—*the* mind—the greatest mind of the nineteenth century there with me, prodding at me, almost laughing, telling me not to grieve or fear, telling me that he was still alive. Do *you* understand? I mean the mind of Sherlock Holmes!"

I stared in shock at the good doctor and could not find words.

Watson waved a hand before his own face, and his eyes clouded. "I know! I know! Fantastical tales. Faerie stories. Holmes is dead. I know that. I must accept that." He slowly lifted his face, and the flame had returned to his eyes. "But for a moment on that express train, I knew that he was alive. In some land of the dead, my friend Sherlock Holmes was still alive. And so, Mr. Carnacki, I *very much* understand what you are saying."

"That's . . . that's good. But you had the opposite experience to me," I said. "You felt the soul of a good man return to you from beyond. I saw the soul of an evil man enter Harold Silence and remain here on earth. And I want to stop him, if for no other reason than to avenge Anna."

Watson sat for a long while, considering.

"Silence is planning a heist at the Louvre," I said.

Watson paled. "I'd hoped that postcard was a hoax!"

"I'm afraid not. He plans to steal the greatest works of Western art and fence them on the black market. I want to stop him, but I need your help."

Watson bit his lip but then said, "Why do you need me?"

"You're the partner of Sherlock Holmes—the greatest detective who ever lived!"

"Quite."

"I need your expertise," I said, looking him straight in the eye. "Will you come with me to the Louvre for a final confrontation?"

Watson drew a long, slow breath and said, "Yes."

47

Exorcism

Dr. John Watson felt certain reservations about his new companion—this callow lad who had so readily deceived the press. So proficient a liar as Thomas Carnacki could in fact be lying once again.

But Watson believed Carnacki, for a number of reasons.

First of all, the lad loved Anna, and he was trying to avenge her. He wouldn't lie about something like that.

Secondly, Watson was certain that Carnacki was no crime lord. Thomas was capable of caprice, yes, but not malice. He was a scamp, not a murderer. During the Afghan campaign, Watson had learned to take the quick measure of a man and decide if he was friend or foe. Watson had guessed wrong only once, and it was the reason he took a bullet and was retired from the service. He felt certain he was guessing right about this man.

But perhaps the most compelling justification for Watson's trust was that Carnacki was just the sort of man that Holmes would have trusted. Carnacki could have been a graduate of the Baker Street Irregulars—a bright-eyed, streetwise rogue with hands dirty from hard work and a back strong from heavy lifting. He would have scored well with Holmes, and so he scored well with Watson.

"I trust him," Watson told himself. "But I still want to see him in action."

The first measure of Carnacki's tactical skill would be his escape from Les Invalides. Dr. Maison had decided to bill young Thomas for a great many things: a four-hour surgery, a week of aftercare, personal damages to Dr. Maison's cheek (caused by the slap of a gendarme), property damages to Les Invalides (caused when Harold Silence broke a window to escape), and ethical damages to Paris itself (caused by the rabid reporters and their sensational stories).

Watson could have paid to get him out, but instead he planned to test the young man. Carnacki was the only patient in the entire ward, the ward had no low windows or easy egress, and he could not move very quickly. If he succeeded in this small matter, perhaps Watson would throw in with him in the Louvre operation.

Thomas had a plan, and the first step was to summon the reporters of Paris. Watson arrived to watch the show.

"Gentlemen of the press," Thomas Carnacki said, his voice ragged and his face ashen as he glanced weakly around his sickbed. "Thank you for coming . . . to witness my death . . . my murder!"

That got them. The whole flock of reporters scratched and scribbled furiously.

"Thank you for writing about me. . . . I'd hoped . . . that your words could save me . . . but my enemy was too strong. He has killed me."

"Harold Silence!" hissed one of the reporters, his voice charged with disbelief and anger.

Flash powder went off, casting the scene in stark light and spectral shadows. The dry scratch of lead on paper trailed off, and one or two reporters swallowed.

"Silence has silenced me at last. . . . I was under his thumb. . . . Lived and died by his whim. . . . My only hope was blackmail. Yes. That's what they call it. . . . But it was not blackmail for money. It was for my life."

"What did he do? Why are you dying?" one reporter asked.

"Look at my face," Thomas said, raising his blue-white visage toward them. "Cyanosis. Cyanide!"

That caused a sensation. Reporters wrote down that terrible word and nattered about the horrible crime.

"How could Harold Silence get past Dr. Maison?" asked one reporter.

Thomas fixed the man with a terrible look. "Harold Silence *is* Dr. Maison!"

The room erupted in angry cries. In the welter of emotion, Thomas slumped back gently into his pillow, let out a last long breath, and stared with fixed, dead eyes. The reporters froze. More flash powder went off, and Thomas did not blink.

"*Il est mort,*" one reporter said, "*assassiné par Harold Silence—par le docteur Maison!*"

"*Est-ce que quelqu'un a dit mon nom?*" came a voice from the doorway.

Watson glanced over to see a most unfortunate Dr. Maison standing at the threshold and smiling with curiosity that quickly turned to dread.

The reporters rushed him, yammering, and Dr. Maison fled into the hospital. Waving pencils and notepads, the journalists went for him like hounds after a fox.

When the last one vanished beyond the door, Watson stepped to Thomas's bedside, extended a hand to him, and helped him stand. "I have a carriage waiting."

"Let's go, then."

They could not go quickly, even after Watson took the heavy contraption that Thomas insisted on bringing along. Out the far door of the ward they went, finding their way through the rooms beyond. At last, they reached an exit and passed through it to climb into a waiting hansom.

Watson knocked on the roof of the coach, and the hatch popped open. "Take us to the Louvre, please, driver." The hatch closed, and the carriage lurched into motion. Watson fixed Thomas with a steady stare. "That diversion was deftly done, my boy. You *are* a confidence man. It proves the truth of the old saying, 'Better not make a friend of an actor.'"

Thomas replied with a smile, "I've always heard it the other way: 'Better not make an enemy of one.'" Thomas produced a handkerchief and used it to wipe the blue pigment from his face.

"Your clothes are in the bag there."

He lifted the stack of clothes from the corner, dragged off his hospital gown, and pulled a new shirt over his shoulders.

"So, what's the rest of your plan—the plan for the Louvre?" Watson asked.

"It's simple. I'll be me and you'll be you, and we'll walk through the Louvre and wait for Silence to confront us. He's there; I have no doubt." Thomas pulled up his breeches and fastened them. "If he sees me, he'll try to kill me. If he sees you—the famous Dr. Watson—he'll size you up to decide why you're there. Whoever is approached first should cough twice loudly, thereby signaling the other to give aid."

"Give aid?" Watson asked. "How?"

"Knock him out."

"With what?"

Thomas blinked, looking at his empty hands. "Well, see, I've got a left jab and a right hook. Did you bring either of those?"

"A pugilist, aye? I happen to have a haymaker that's a legend in three counties. Nothing wrong with a good clean fight."

Carnacki nodded. "Guns have turned *fight* into a dirty word." He paused a moment and added hopefully, "You don't happen to have a gun—"

"No such luck," Watson replied, staring out at the Parisian apartments that rolled past. "Once he's knocked out, then what?"

"Then we use this on him." Thomas lifted the strange contraption he had carried beneath his arm. "Give me your bag."

"My bag?" Watson said dully even as he surrendered it. Thomas took the bag, opened it, and dumped the surgical supplies on the seat beside them. "What are you doing?"

"Knives are useless against this man. Only this"—he pushed the contraption down through the mouth of the bag—"only this can stop him."

Watson gingerly plucked his scalpels and clamps off that leather seat where hundreds of hindquarters—French hindquarters—sat daily, and slipped the implements into his coat pocket. "If you don't mind my saying, this plan seems a bit ragged."

Thomas gave a smile and slapped a hand on his comrade's back. "I'm no Sherlock Holmes. My plans are a bit rough and ready."

Beyond the cab windows, the great palace of the Louvre loomed up. Magnificent walls of stone held row on row of enormous windows.

As the hansom pulled to a stop, Watson said, "How will I recognize Harold Silence?"

"Ah, now, there's the roughest part of my plan," Carnacki allowed. "You see, Silence is a master of disguise, so it would be no good telling you what he looks like, because you would then know only the one man *not* to look for."

"Sounds like my old friend Holmes," Watson said offhandedly.

Thomas gave a startled look. He then lifted the medical bag and stepped out the hansom door. "Pay the cabby, would you?"

A graduate of the Baker Street Irregulars, indeed, thought Watson. After counting out the fare, Watson rushed down the pavement to catch up with Thomas at the entrance to the Louvre. He was just in time to pay a shilling and sixpence for each of them to enter.

Just beyond the ticket booth, a map on the wall displayed the layout of the museum.

"There are parallel galleries throughout this place," Thomas said, pointing. "See here. I'll start in Roman sculpture while you wander through Greek. At the end of each gallery, there's a door that connects them. Each time you come to such a doorway, linger nearby until we can make visual contact. Then move on."

"That sounds fine," Watson said, "but let's also pick a meeting spot a few galleries down."

"Look here—this worn spot on the map, here in the middle of the Renaissance paintings . . ."

"What of it?"

"A hundred fingers tap that spot every day. That's where the *Mona Lisa* must be. That's the one painting we know Silence is after."

Watson nodded. "Then let's make our way toward the great lady."

Thomas headed off into a gallery of Roman statuary, while Watson lost himself among the Greeks. It was a haunting feeling to wander among all those ancient figures carved by dead hands—all the while knowing that a killer stalked among them.

Watson reached the end of the first gallery and looked through the doorway but did not see Thomas. Pretending interest in a bust of Agamemnon, Watson waited until Thomas appeared. When he did, the coconspirators nodded ever so slightly to each other before moving along.

In the next gallery, Watson walked among medieval altar

paintings, with their jewel tones and their gold-leaf halos—icons, emblems, codes in the clothing and in the posture. All of it spoke of Christ and his death and his power. At the end of that gallery, there was Thomas standing beyond the door.

Onward, then, through a hall of Renaissance paintings. Watson was mesmerized. Here was art through a different eye, through a modern, scientific eye. Every person in the paintings looked at something within the frame or beyond, and often the most important person looked at the viewer. So staggered was Watson by the masters' works that he lost track of time, and when he arrived at the doorway between the galleries, Thomas was not there.

Perhaps Watson was ahead of him. He settled in beside the Raphael painting *The Virgin in the Meadow*. Mary was on a grassy field, apparently sitting on a hay bale, her red dress and blue robe framing the naked figure of the infant Jesus, who clutched a long thin staff. John the Baptist bowed before him. The composition was centered and balanced, the hues without hint of blackness, and the babe naked and unashamed. Raphael's brushwork was so fine Watson could not make out a single stroke. He stepped up closer.

"Reculez s'il vous plaît," said an old guard, moving up beside him.

Watson did not understand much French but did understand that he had gotten too close. *"Pardonnez-moi."*

The old man smiled at Watson's accent, but his own was just as thick when he switched to English. "Raphael was a genius, yes?"

"Yes," Watson responded, shooting a look through the doorway and still seeing no sign of Thomas. "It all seems so balanced, so perfect."

"Raphael had an eye for composition," the old man said—for old he was, with white hair jutting from beneath his cap and wrinkles around his spectacled eyes and a white mustache and beard around his mouth. He rocked back on his heels, clasped his hands behind his back, and chuckled. "Yes, Raphael achieved the perfect balance in the end, but do you know that he sketched many versions to compose this one painting? He kept at it until he got it just right."

"Thank you," Watson said, not wanting to be rude but beginning to fear what had happened to Thomas. When the old guard frowned, Watson continued, "Really. It's quite remarkable. I have an altogether deeper appreciation for Raphael's work." With a smile and a nod, he stepped onward, crossing through the huge double doorway into the gallery where Thomas should have been.

He was nowhere to be seen, but Watson's eyes did lock on a familiar face—one that he knew better than his own. The *Mona Lisa* hung nearby. It was not a large painting, not given a spot of any particular prominence, but those eyes that had burned their way through Leonardo's mind would not let Watson look away. He wandered across the gallery toward the *Mona Lisa* and stood there before her and let her peer into him. What strange eyes, dipping into shadow at their corners, and what a strange smile, doing the same.

"Magnificent, no?" said a voice, and Watson startled, turning to see the old guard behind him. "The effect is called *sfumato*—hiding details in shadow. Da Vinci knew that whatever expression he might have given to her face would not be as satisfying as the expressions we would have given, so he left the key parts in shadow, left us to project on her what we wish to see—"

"Look, this is all very interesting, and I appreciate it, but I don't have time—"

He quirked his eyebrows. "You're in the Louvre, before the *Mona Lisa*, and you do not have time—?"

"I know. It sounds foolish. But . . . a friend . . . I was supposed to meet a friend here, and he's not here. He's long overdue."

The guard tossed his old, narrow hands in the air and smiled. "Let me help. I can help. I'm a guard." He pointed to the chevron piping on his coat sleeve. "What does your friend look like?"

Watson was not a fool. He knew that the guard may well have been Harold Silence. His friendliness, his chattiness, the way he lingered . . . the disappearance of Thomas—all of these clues told Watson to beware, but he still wasn't certain enough to strike an old man. "He's, uh"—Watson coughed twice loudly—"my friend is, well, young, British, with dark hair, a ratty trench coat."

"Ah," the guard said. "An art student."

"Yes, an art student." Watson pressed his hand into his coat pocket, feeling the scalpel there. At least he wasn't defenseless. If this old man tried anything . . . He coughed twice more. "My friend . . . he liked the *Mona Lisa* most of all. Said he would meet me here—but I don't see him anywhere."

"Wait a moment," the guard said as if in thought, "a young British art student with a thin mustache and goatee?"

"Yes."

"Well"—the guard scratched his head—"you see, there was a young man like that taken to the infirmary. He couldn't breathe—blood on his lips. Blood on his shirt, too, right here." He touched his heart.

What if Thomas truly has collapsed? Watson wondered. *In his condition, it's not only possible, but also likely.* "Where's the infirmary?"

The guard crooked a finger above his shoulder. "Here, let me show you." He turned his back and strode with a bandy-legged step down the middle of the gallery.

Watson followed, letting go of the scalpel. He couldn't cut this man's throat, even if he were Harold Silence. And Watson *had* brought a haymaker, after all. At the first sign . . .

"Through here," the old man said, gesturing toward a door that read INFIRMARY. Nothing suspicious about that. But then he opened the door and stepped back and motioned Watson through. "After you."

Watson shook his head. "You know the way."

Shrugging, the guard stepped through the doorway. He and Watson descended a short flight of stairs, passed through a hallway, and came out into a long, low room. Cots lined one wall, and a doctor stood at a surgical table in the middle. On it lay Thomas, writhing beneath straps. Blood foamed on his lips and spattered his shirt and coat.

"Is that your friend?" the old guard asked.

"Yes." Watson rushed past him to Thomas's sickbed. "Out of the hospital, into the infirmary . . ."

Thomas looked up with imploring eyes and tried to speak, but he could only hack out a gobbet of blood.

Watson shook his head. "He shouldn't be strapped down this way. He can't clear his airway." He grasped the great buckle that ran across Thomas's chest and started to loosen it.

As he did, Thomas gasped a breath and sputtered, "Look out!" A shadow moved across his eyes, the shadow of a man's fist.

Watson saw a flash of white light.

Then everything went dark.

As he crumpled to the floor, he heard a voice say, "Welcome to Paris, Dr. Watson."

Then there was only silence.

48

Repent of Heaven

Here are the things I was banking on:

1. Watson and I would be irresistible bait for Holmes.

2. Either Watson or I could hold Holmes off in a fight until the other arrived.

3. We had the element of surprise, so Holmes would not be able to marshal his guards to swarm over us.

4. Holmes would not risk a public scene that might alert the police to his plans.

5. Holmes would attack with his wits rather than his fists.

I was wrong about every item except the first. I seemed to have forgotten, you see, that Holmes was not Holmes but a demon.

"So far so good," I said as I stood among medieval paintings and spotted Watson in the adjacent gallery. He gave me a circumspect nod, his eyes level and serious. I returned the look and strolled onward

The next hall held Renaissance works. On the far side, patrons clustered around the *Mona Lisa*, though on the near side was an even more impressive masterwork: Michelangelo's sculpture *The Dying Slave*. I approached the towering figure, nude and swooning in anguish, his flesh and muscle all supple and alive in white marble. I thought of the sculptor nearly four hundred years before, and of his model—and of both of them lying now in separate graves, both of them living still in this one figure. So rapt was my attention on the statue that I forgot for a moment about myself.

Something struck my heart.

Pain! I staggered back, groped at my chest, felt for the knife handle that must be jutting there—but no. It had just been a fist, one that knew where the wound was and smashed it and reopened it. Blood rose in my throat. God, the pain!

"Vous allez bien?" shouted a man, very near—too near.

As I collapsed to the floor, the man swooped down over me—a tall, thin man with white hair, mustache, and beard. His eyes glowed briefly red, and he smiled the smile of a barracuda. The demon Holmes spoke in a voice that gushed concern, *"Vous saignez, monsieur."*

Of course I was bleeding, but the demon did not speak these words for my benefit. A museum patron had just then knelt down on the other side of me, and he asked, *"Vous saignez, monsieur?"*

I tried to tell the man what had happened, but I was gagging on blood.

The demon's eyes had gone dark, and his grin had turned to a look of concern. *"Je ne sais pas. Il s'est effondré tout à coup!"*

The man pointed to the blood on my mouth. *"Il saigne de la bouche!"*

Nodding decisively, the demon pointed toward the infirmary door: *"Aidez-moi à l'amener à l'infirmerie!"*

I spat blood and gasped a breath and tried to get up, but Holmes and the other man looped their arms under mine and hoisted me. I tried to protest, but already my throat had filled again, and I hacked it out across my shirt. I kicked to break free. *"Il ne peut pas respirer!"* said the other man.

"Vite! A l'infirmerie!"

Two more men arrived—guards dressed like Holmes—and the knowing look between them told me that these were his accomplices. They were burly, with stubbled chins and missing teeth, thugs that Holmes had somehow charmed into his service.

The demon said to the museum patron, *"Nous prendrons soin de lui."*

The patron backed away, letting the guards take his position as they dragged me down the gallery.

I struggled to get loose, but one of the thugs drove his knee into my side. I coughed more blood. Couldn't Watson hear? The cough was our signal. I tried to cough again, but Holmes seized my throat, choking off the sound. Watson would never hear now. Part of me was glad. I didn't want him to be doomed along with me.

The brutes lugged me to a doorway marked INFIRMARY, and the demon Holmes released my throat so I could hack a breath. He said to his henchmen, "Take him to the infirmary and strap him down. Make sure none of the personnel know. Only our people."

"What then, boss? Kill him?"

"No. I'm going to finish him myself." He lifted Watson's black medical bag, dandled it a moment before my face, and handed it to one of the thugs.

"How long will you be?" the man asked.

"Only as long as it takes me to nab the other one," Holmes replied, flashing his red eyes my way before turning and striding away.

The passage beyond was too small for two men to go abreast with me slung between, so one of the thugs stooped down and hoisted me over his shoulder. Blood shot from my mouth across his back, and I called out, "Help!" My cry was cut short as the man bashed my head against the wall.

The other thug slammed the door behind us. "Shut up, you!"

"Why are you doing this?"

"Boss says."

"Don't you know . . . who he is . . . *what* he is?"

The guard answered with a wicked smile. "He's the boss."

We descended a short set of stairs, passed through a hall, and ducked under a doorway. Beyond lay an infirmary with cots along the walls, medicine cabinets at one end, a human skeleton at the other, and a steel table in the center of it all. The man who carried me dumped me flat on my back on the table. I riled, gasping. The man grabbed my hands and held me down while his partner cinched wide leather bands down over my legs and waist and chest. Once the straps were in place, one man went off to secure the entrances and the other man dragged a doctor's coat onto his shoulders. He stood above me, grinning.

Now the true horror began. Lying on my back, I couldn't get my throat clear. I sputtered and gasped tiny breaths, but they came foaming back up on my lips. I was suffocating. I flipped my head from side to side, spitting out what I could, but it was no use.

And then Watson came walking in. The moment he saw me, he rushed over to the table. "Out of the hospital, into the infirmary . . ."

I tried to scream a warning but could only gurgle.

"He shouldn't be strapped down this way. He can't clear his airway," Watson said, leaning down to undo the strap over my waist.

I hacked, grabbed a breath, and shouted, "Look out!"

It was too late. A fist cracked Watson in the jaw and sent him spilling to the floor.

"Welcome to Paris, Dr. Watson," said the demon Holmes, who had stepped up behind him.

The two criminals stared down at the prostrate form. Holmes nudged Watson with his boot, got no response, and then kicked him in the side. Still, Watson didn't move.

The demon squatted above Watson, rolled him over, and peeled back his eyelids. "He'll be out for hours. Won't remember a thing. Perfect." He smiled up at his comrade. "I'd always known he had a glass jaw—spotted it in the gray vein along the left side of his face—but even I couldn't have hoped for a one-punch knockout." The other thug returned, and Holmes said to them both, "Take him down the hall, far enough that he can't hear the screams. Guard him until I come."

The two thugs stooped down, grasped Watson's wrists and ankles, and hoisted him between them. "What if he wakes up and starts asking about his friend?"

"Put him off. The murder of Thomas Carnacki will be part of our larger case—the *Mona Lisa* Mystery." The demon fondly brushed Watson's bruised jaw. "Sleep well. When you awaken, the Louvre will have lost a million francs' worth of art, and I—your old friend Sherlock Holmes—will be on the case!"

After his henchmen lugged Watson from the room, the demon turned and crossed to the table where I lay. He grasped the tabletop and leaned his manic face over me. "Hello, Thomas. At last, you arrived."

I spat blood into his face.

The demon didn't flinch, didn't wipe it off, but simply let it drip from his fake mustache and beard. "I'm surprised how long it took you. A full week. I'd put every clue in the papers, every scrap of evidence you would need, day after day. I was starting to think you would never arrive. But now, the cha-rade is over." He peeled off the mustache and tugged off the beard and wig, and his face was once again the face of Sher-lock Holmes—except for the blood that spattered his cheeks.

I coughed out another gobbet. "Holmes . . . Listen . . . Drive out the demon . . . Take your body back."

He began to pace, a smile on his lips and a laugh deep in his throat. "Your friend is gone. I'm not Holmes. I'm not Mo-riarty. I'm not Jack the Ripper. I'm the Undying Evil that rides them. I'm a divine horseman."

"You're . . . what—?"

"It's voodoo, Thomas. Voodoo!" He waggled his fingers beside his bloodstained face. "Voodoo mambos call the spir-its of the dead the 'divine horsemen.' They enter people and possess them to live again. They ride people like horsemen ride horses. I've ridden so many.

"I was riding a voodoo mambo in Haiti when a ship's mate named Enoch Jones killed her. I rode him back to London, where a Whitehall hooker named Martha Tabram plied him with rum till he died and then rolled him for his two months' wages. I rode Martha for a long while until another sailor lad—John Harder—took us along George Yard and told me that the other men pushed him into it, said they thought he was homosexual, said he had to prove himself a man by lay-ing a whore. He proved it, all right. Thirty-nine stab wounds proved it. And so I rode John Harder after that, and I made him into Jack the Ripper, and he killed and killed and killed."

The demon glanced down at me, seeing that blood filled my mouth and tears filled my eyes and I was about to lose consciousness. He blinked once and then bent down and pressed his lips to mine and drank the blood out of my mouth. As repelled as I was, I could breathe again.

The demon licked his lips and said, "We love murder. It frees us to enter a new host. Our blood is the key. Sacrificial blood. When someone kills us, we can travel from victim to victor. We trade up. And even if we're caught and it's the noose or the blade, we just skip merrily from the snapped neck or the severed head into the trap man's fingers or the axman's arm."

"You trade up. . . ." I repeated incredulously, only beginning to catch on. "Murder for murder . . . And when Moriarty killed Jack the Ripper—?"

"I rode Moriarty. How grand a ride it was! Genius. Until Holmes brought him down. Until Holmes made him the most wanted man in Europe. Then, where could I ride Moriarty? Where except to prison—? Unless . . ."

Horror overtook me. "You never wanted to kill Holmes—"

"I wanted *him* to kill *Moriarty*!" the demon proclaimed. "I wanted to trade up, from the genius Moriarty to the greater genius—Sherlock Holmes!"

Suddenly, it all made sense. "You planned it all along."

"Yes. I brought a knife to the falls and pulled it on Holmes and slashed at him. At the first chance, though, I let him knock it from my hand, hoping he would snatch it up and bury it in my heart. But no. The fool would not take an unfair advantage. He threw the knife over the cascade. Then we grappled, and I hurled myself backward to shatter my head against stone, but Holmes held on and slowed my fall and lost his balance and plunged over the falls. I watched him go, hoped he would survive, hoped I could fish him from the river and take him to an inn and force him to kill me so that I could enter him—but you and that Moriarty brat changed all my plans. I chased you, tried to catch you so Holmes could kill me—even caught him in an alley and pleaded for him to do so."

I trembled. "But now you have his body. Now you have everything you'd been after."

"He understands at last. My final foe knows the man who will kill him. Oh, it is so much sweeter to kill a man who understands than to kill a fool." The demon lifted the exorcism machine from the black bag and set it on the table beside me. "And sweetest of all to kill a man with his own weapon."

The demon knew everything Holmes knew—understood how the electric pentacle would form around my body, how it would drive my soul out of my flesh and kill me.

"Exorcise, electrocute, execute," the demon said, punctuating the words with clicks of the alligator clips. One by one, he positioned them.

Metal teeth bit down on my toes and fingers and earlobes. I struggled against the straps, but they held firm.

"Do you want to know the truly delicious thing, Thomas Carnacki? Even if you somehow manage to escape and kill me, I will merely take over your body. Though I may die a hundred thousand times, I will live forever." He shrugged. "Of course, you won't manage to escape. You're no match for Sherlock Holmes. And since that's the case, well . . . it's time for you to die."

He cranked the handle of the generator. The rotor hummed, and sparks snapped. Energy poured through the black cables and jolted into my extremities—feet, hands, and head. Toes curled and soles arched, fingers clenched and fingernails cut into palms, jaw clamped tight and teeth clenched together and ground like rocks.

"It's statues. The children's game of statues," the demon opined, cranking all the harder. "Fling a fellow onto the grass and see what crazy contortions he takes and when he freezes in some ridiculous pose, give him a name."

I convulsed, my body arching up beneath the straps. "Anna! Anna!"

"That name's already taken. You need something with Thomas in it. Let's see . . . Not Doubting Thomas, no. Your fault is not doubt," the demon said, cranking faster. "I will call you Believing Thomas!"

My feet and hands and head jangled with electricity. Charges gathered in my extremities and jagged through my torso. The white-hot energy converged on my heart. It struck.

I seized up. I was dying.

IT WAS just like my dream. I had ceased to be flesh anymore— wasn't physical, but an ectoplasmic spirit. I seeped out of every dying cell in my body, gushed forth from every riven pore out into the air. I gathered myself in a cloud and looked down at my poor, electrocuted form.

How much better this was. No more pain. No more sucking wound to the chest. I felt so light. Flesh is heavy, tired, shot through with trouble, but I was done with trouble. I was done with fighting and breathing and heartbeating. How much better it was to drift upward.

Good-bye, then. Good-bye, earth.

A tunnel formed above me, leading up and away, and a light dawned at the end of it. I moved toward the light. I moved toward Anna. I could see her face now. Pain and hope warred on her features. She was not welcoming me.

Go back, Thomas. Go back. You have a body. Use it to fight him. You must go back and kill the Undying One.

"How?" I said. "He'll just take me over, ride me until I'm murdered. . . ."

No he won't. I'll show you how. You must turn around. You must go back.

It's hard to turn around, wherever you are, whatever you are doing. Alcoholics can't turn around . . . opium addicts, prostitutes, crime lords, hit men. . . . Only one in a hundred can turn around, and that action is called repentance. But when a man is in the tunnel of light, heading toward beauty and out of horror, repentance feels like death.

Turn around, Thomas.

I repented of heaven and clawed my way back down that tunnel, away from the warm light and into the cold darkness. For her, I did it. For the one I was leaving.

AND SUDDENLY, I was back in my body, convulsing on the table. What horror! Voltage ripped my nerves. Blood boiled in my throat. Breath steamed in my lungs. What misery it was to be bound down to this table while the demon beside me cranked the engine of my death—

Bound down? But I was not. The belt at my waist had slid loose of the buckle.

It was Anna's work, surely. She had freed my hands, had shown me the way.

I lifted my hands, clips still clinging to fingertips, and seized the demon's wrists. The electric pentacle spread from my flesh to his. Galvanic energy surged up his arms to his shoulders.

The demon shrieked and tried to let go, but the sparking current enervated him. Blue charges danced across his chest and met over his breastbone and poured down his stomach and hips and back. The electric pentacle surrounded us both. It reached his toes and his fingertips and the bristling hair across his scalp.

I held on and kept cranking.

The demon seeped from Holmes's pores, as if blood were being squeezed slowly out of his skin. Red protoplasm gathered in his eyes and sloshed from his mouth and rolled out of his nostrils and ears.

A crimson cloud formed above our heads. It boiled and coiled, eyeing us, wishing that it could dive down into our bodies, but the pentacles kept it at bay. At the edges of the cloud, dark tendrils hissed out into the air, dissipating.

The Undying Evil was dying.

"There's no one here to possess!" I shouted victoriously. "And you can't live in air."

"I can live in anything human!" the spirit cried. It gathered itself and shot out through the air, coalescing around the human skeleton that stood on one end of the infirmary. Red energy mantled the bones and sank to their marrow and vanished.

I let go of Holmes's hands.

He staggered back, eyes bleary, and looked around the room. "Where am I?"

"Let me loose!" I shouted, reaching up to undo the buckle on my chest.

Holmes shook off the funk that possessed him and lurched forward to loosen the buckle on my legs.

Even as he fidgeted with the strap, the skeleton in the corner pulled free of its stand and clacked down on the floor, facing us. Its jaw chattered, its hands rose in bony claws, and it stalked forward.

49

WHAT WOULD HOLMES DO?

I release the open buckle and stare at Thomas and then at the walking skeleton and wonder what Sherlock Holmes—what *I* would do at a time like this.

The answer is elementary: "Get him, Watson!"

50

PHYSICS AND METAPHYSICS

The only thing more incredible than a walking skeleton was Holmes's reaction to it. "Get him, Watson!" Though I was not Watson, I, happily, did know how to "get him." I hefted the generator above my head and hurled it at the skeleton. The machine smashed the skeleton's sternum, and the wires entangled its legs, sending it reeling.

"What are you doing?" Holmes blurted.

"The demon is bound to the physical form until its blood is shed," I said, swinging my legs down off the steel table and standing shakily. "Luckily, this time, it has no blood. It can't get out. We just have to dismantle it."

"With what?" Holmes asked.

"With whatever comes to hand." I pointed. "Chairs—"

Holmes grabbed a chair and brought it smashing down on the skeleton, separating the left ulna from its humorous and cracking all the left-side ribs.

"Belts—" I grasped the leather thongs that had been holding me and scourged the skeleton with them, seeing the buckles crack in the ribs and stick there. "Jars—"

Holmes darted to a nearby cabinet full of medical supplies, and from its innards he hurled jar after jar: cotton balls, swabs, gauze, tongue depressors, alcohol, iodine. . . . Only the last two caused much damage. The jar of alcohol caved three ribs, and the jar of iodine smashed heavily within the pelvis, cracking it in half and causing a leg to fall clean off.

The skeleton teetered and toppled, crashing onto the tile floor. More bones shattered and scattered from the twitching figure.

"What else?" Holmes asked, hands raised, eyes scanning the room for other weapons.

"Shoes," I suggested, stomping on the skull. My foot caved the cranium. I then kicked the remainder of the skull down onto the spine. Bone flexed and shattered, the neck snapped, and ribs cracked away all down the back. The skeleton was in pieces, with just one leg and two arms and no ribs. I took care of the rest of the ribs by jumping up and down on them, like a child stomping autumn leaves.

It was a dance of joy. Every fracture, every hunk of bone, meant that the Undying Evil was trapped in smaller and smaller chunks, for all eternity.

Holmes joined me in my mad dance, and between the two of us, we stomped the faceplate down to fragments and snapped each leg and arm bone thrice over. In the end, the demon lay in a few large chunks, hundreds of shards, and a small pile of bone dust.

"Now, to contain this stuff," I said as we stopped our dance. There was a dustpan and broom in one corner of the infirmary, and I went to get them. "Holmes, did you see any empty jars in that cabinet?"

He crossed to it and came back with two large, empty jars, one labeled "Cotton" and the other labeled "Sheep Stomach." "How about these?"

"Fine, fine," I said as I swept the fragments of the demon onto the dustpan. Holmes set down the jars and prowled around the periphery, hunting up any fragments that had traveled farther afield. It wouldn't do to have the infirmary of the Louvre haunted by an Undying—albeit impotent—Evil. In the end, we had filled both jars to their plugs, and I wrapped them in a bedsheet to keep them from shattering and slid them into Watson's surgical bag.

"Watson!" I exclaimed in sudden dread.

"Watson?" Holmes echoed.

"Damn it. He's in with those two thugs."

"Dr. John Watson? Here?"

"You really don't remember, do you? Yes. Watson's here, captive of those two henchmen you rounded up. We have to rescue him. Where's the mustache and beard?"

Holmes stared blankly at me. "Henchmen?"

I pushed past him and stalked the floor, looking for the fake hairpieces. They were scattered, marked with the tread of our shoes, crinkled up with dried blood. "It's no use. If we had your disguise, you could just tell the thugs to let him go. But if they see you without your disguise—"

"I don't want Watson to see me yet. Not this way." Holmes looked into my eyes, and there was something frightened in his expression. "My mind isn't my own. I don't *trust* it."

I understood. "When Sherlock Holmes doesn't trust his own mind, he's not Sherlock Holmes." I crossed to the door, opened it a crack, and peered out into the hallway. It was empty, but I heard a crash and boom. Flinging the door wide, I stepped into the hall and was greeted by a muffled shout and the thud of someone crashing to the floor. "Watson needs me."

Gritting my teeth, I strode down the hall. I was hardly fit for another fight, but what choice did I have? Halfway down the hall, I realized I still carried the broom. Well . . . I needed some sort of weapon . . . and this was better than nothing.

I reached the door and tried the handle, but it wouldn't budge. A pleading wail came from within. I reared back and kicked the door just beside the handle and was rewarded with a shattered lock and splintered wood and a door flying inward to reveal a scene of complete carnage.

The small room had been a custodial closet, with mops and buckets, brooms and tools and a wide utility sink. Now, every mop and boom was broken, every bucket staved. The tools lay scattered across the floor beside an unconscious figure, and another bruised and bloodied man was stuffed in the utility sink.

In the midst of all this wreckage stood Dr. John Watson, one side of his jaw swollen and his eyes blazing. He held a broken broomstick high overhead, ready to bring it down on me. His hand paused, and he returned my look of amazed shock.

"You're alive!" we said simultaneously.

Watson lowered his broomstick, and I proffered the one that I carried. "Looks like you need to do some cleaning up."

He didn't take the broom or the joke, his eyes still wary. "What about the ringleader? Where'd he get off to?"

"We had a fight of our own," I said. "It turned out in much the same way. I've gotten the mastermind all bottled up, though I'd better get back to check on him—and to summon the police. Can you keep these two . . . subdued—?"

"Of course," Watson said. "The rough work is done."

WE HIT the papers one last time—Watson and I. Holmes ducked out of the whole affair, evading the police and the reporters and avoiding the notice even of his erstwhile partner. Still, Watson and I took our moment to bask in the acclaim of *Le Temps*:

NEW CRIME DUO FOILS LOUVRE ROBBERY

Yesterday, two men from London foiled a plot to steal some of Paris's greatest treasures. The first man, Dr. John Watson, is the one-time companion and chronicler of the deceased

Mr. Sherlock Holmes. Watson joined forces with a Cambridge student named Thomas Carnacki. Carnacki was recently touted as an underling of crime lord James Moriarty, but in fact he is a British agent who was working undercover to clean up the remains of the Moriarty gang. Together, the two men caught a ring of thieves intent on stealing no less than the *Mona Lisa*.

"They had an elaborate plot," Dr. Watson outlined, "replacing the lock on an outside door, gaining positions on the museum guard staff, and using the infirmary and a custodial closet as their base of operations."

The thieves planned to steal the greatest treasures of the museum, including paintings by Titian, da Vinci, Rembrandt, and Caravaggio. Though the plan originally involved only grand larceny, it evolved to include murder.

"They found out about us," Carnacki said in his sickbed. He is recovering from a stab wound to the chest. "They ambushed us on the museum floor in broad daylight. They tried to execute us." When asked why the men hadn't succeeded, Carnacki indicated, "We're better fighters."

Watson and Carnacki handed two of the three thieves to police, though the ringleader escaped. The amateur crime fighters described this third man as tall and lean, with white hair and a white mustache and beard. The Metropolitan Police Force is busy combing the city for the man.

Their search began at a garret apartment near the Gare Saint-Lazare, where Carnacki showed the police a map of Paris on which the gang had pinned all the major crimes of the last two months. Police describe the map as a "godsend," and they anticipate using it to break numerous criminal networks throughout the city.

Though Watson and Carnacki saved priceless artworks and helped police mop up crime in Paris, they deny claims that they will form a new detective partnership. "I'm no Sherlock Holmes," said Thomas Carnacki.

Watson had his own reasons for parting ways. "I have been eternally blessed to have known and worked with Mr. Sherlock Holmes, and his loss is one that I will never recover from—nor will London. Instead of playing about at a business that was most serious to Holmes, I would rather confine myself to helping my patients live long, happy lives."

OF COURSE, for the papers, it was all crooks and detectives, villains and heroes—and I must confess that our adventures had been dramatic if not melodramatic. But only after the flash powder had ceased its lightning and the public had ceased its thunder did I have a moment to realize all I had lost.

SHE LAY within the gray walls of Perè Lachaise cemetery. It was in the days when poor folk still could be buried there, before Oscar Wilde and dozens of others made it a dying ground for the elite. Anna was allowed in, though her notorious father had been denied. He had been cremated, his ashes stored among thousands of other urns in a vault for criminals.

Even though Anna had rated her own plot, it was perhaps the smallest plot in the place. The mound of dirt atop her body was barely two feet wide and six feet long—I know, for I paced it out. I wondered if they had even given her a coffin. And her headstone was small and round, a baby tooth perched temporarily between all those adult monuments. It said simply "Anna Moriarty 1872–1891."

"Anna, I'm sorry."

I told myself that she was in a better place. I'd even seen her there and would have joined her except that she sent me back. Anna lived now in the realm of spirit, while I was stuck in the world of flesh.

I stayed by that spot for hours. I sat on the crypts beside hers, even lay down on one sarcophagus and slept. Of course, the family of the man entombed there might have been offended, but on the other hand, that same family would mourn while standing atop my Anna.

I remembered her bonnet and her blue dress and the basket with bars of cheese shining like gold. I remembered her haunted eyes when she returned to me in the library in Bern, her blond braids hanging down beside her face as she told the story of her father's life. The child of two geniuses— Anna had so much left to do with her life, not the least of which was to love me.

Then I heard in my mind, like the whisper of a pen signing a signature, *I'm not done.*

Her work wasn't finished. After all, it was because of Anna that I lived—and Sherlock Holmes and Dr. Watson, too. It was because of her that the Undying Evil that had created Jack the Ripper and the Napoleon of Crime was trapped forever. Anna had shown me the way, and she would keep guiding me. In little ways and large, she would be with me.

I got up from the sarcophagus, brushed grave dirt off my clothes, and said, "Thank you."

At last I could leave her grave behind. Anna was going with me.

SHERLOCK HOLMES sighed, letting the latest issue of *Le Temps* slump down into his lap. We sat in our small rented rooms on the Left Bank, and below our second-story window, an open-air market rumbled and rattled. It seemed to be giving Holmes a headache. I had wondered whether this location would be too noisy for him as he recovered his mind, but I couldn't resist the bustle of it, the young philosophers and poets and artists roaming the streets at all hours, the partial views of the Seine and of Notre Dame. Besides, it was the only place I could afford, drawing the last money from my university account.

This afternoon, though, the agitation beyond the windows seemed to be getting to Holmes. He rubbed his forehead with fingers stained by newsprint. "It's such a struggle to read French."

I glanced toward him from my perch beside the window and laughed. "You seemed to speak it fluently when you had a demon inside you."

Holmes shot a look of annoyance my way. "It's just that sort of comment that will keep me from ever getting my mind back."

"What sort of comment?"

"'When you had a demon inside you.' That sort of comment. It's nettling enough to have whole sections of my memory blacked out, erased by amnesia, without your turning it into voodoo."

I was shocked. "It *was* voodoo."

"It was amnesia, pure and simple!" he pronounced. "It was a physical reaction—like dropping a perfectly tuned violin and picking it up to find that all the strings must be retempered."

I shook my head. "It wasn't just amnesia. You remember Anna, don't you?"

"Yes, of course. Anna Moriarty. Daughter of James Moriarty."

"You remember our whole adventure with her, from the morning she fished you from the Reichenbach River to the morning we reached Paris, yes?"

"Of course!"

"You had amnesia that whole time. You couldn't remember who you were—Harold Silence and all that. But you were making new memories. That's what amnesia was like. This blackout, though—from the moment when Anna was shot to the moment when you were standing in the Louvre infirmary—that was not amnesia. That was demon possession."

"Bosh," said Holmes, shaking his head violently. "Stuff and nonsense."

"*I* remember what happened, even if you don't. I *saw* the demon inside of you. I tracked you down, and you ambushed me, held me hostage. The exorcism machine saved us both!"

"Ah," Holmes said, lifting a finger to stop me. "There it is, yes? There's the crux of this whole dilemma: that damned machine. It's a generator. That's all. It creates electricity, and electricity has bizarre but perfectly scientific effects on the human mind. The mind is electrical, Thomas. Lightning can derange a man, make him violent and vicious like a beast, but it's a physical effect: the scrambling of brain signals. It's not a metaphysical phenomenon."

I laughed bleakly, realizing that I was destined to have this argument *ad infinitum* with my friend. "You were no brute, Holmes. You were demon-possessed. Your eyes glowed red."

"Red is the color of the retina, and the glow may have been due to electrical overstimulation of the optic nerve."

"What about the skeleton? We fought a walking skeleton!"

"What I remember, and correct me if I am wrong," Holmes said, "was a mad confusion in which we thought a skeleton was attacking us and we shouted things to each other and I hurled jars from a cabinet and we ended up dancing on top of bones. Lunacy! We had both just been electrocuted, Thomas. That episode was not about a walking skeleton but about two men whose electrified brains had been reduced to monkey meat."

"Monkey meat?"

"Yes, monkey meat!"

"No. Voodoo!"

"Monkey meat!"

We stared at each other in utter frustration and both blurted simultaneously: "You're hopeless."

Holmes snapped the paper up in front of his face, and I cast my gaze out the window and across the marketplace. We lapsed into silence. The street noise below gradually rose to fill our ears: laughter from young lovers, quarrels among old scholars, the cry of a middle-aged baker, the music of a hurdy-gurdy man. Life. I simply sat and let those sounds sink into me and wash away the rancor I felt in my heart. A few deep breaths, and I realized just how wonderful the world was.

At length, I ventured a new conversation. "So, when are you going to let Watson know you're alive?"

"When I *am* alive," Holmes growled back behind his newspaper. "When I have my mind again. There aren't even any crimes here worth investigating."

I nodded and stood, crossing to my tattered greatcoat, which hung on a peg by the door. "Of course not. The great crimes aren't in the papers until after they are solved. The great crimes are out there, Holmes."

He lowered the paper and stared toward the windows, where the sky was giving way to evening blue, and lamps one by one sent up their gaslight glow.

I pressed: "You won't get your mind back sitting up here alone. You don't tune a violin by playing it by itself. You have to play it with other instruments. In concert. Come on, Holmes. There's a city full of crime out there, and there's a genius detective in here. You need to get out into the streets if you ever want to get your mind back."

"A new mystery," he said quietly, though his voice was

feverish with hope. "That's the thing. Some great crime that requires the most rigorous deduction." He looked at me and nodded. A small smile played at the corners of his mouth. He stood and strode to the door, taking down his own cloak.

"Now, you'll have to be patient," I admonished. "We may not stumble on the crime of the century in the first few minutes."

"Yes. Yes," Holmes replied. "We'll find it, though. And in the meantime, there are a few smaller things I need to acquire to get back into fighting form."

"And what would those be?"

"A pipe and tobacco," Holmes said, "and a violin."

I smiled. "I think I have enough money for the pipe and tobacco. As for the violin, I don't think I can afford even a cheap one. And this is a small flat. Neither of us could stand the sound of a cheap one."

Holmes nodded. "Then that will be my first goal—to solve a mystery that pays well enough for a good violin."

ABOUT THE AUTHOR

The Shadow of Reichenbach Falls is John R. King's twentieth published novel. He wrote much of it in the woods behind the Saint Charles Cemetery while sitting on a rock and smoking a cigar—actually, hundreds of cigars. He also wrote portions of this novel while sitting in the hallway of the Lakeview Neurological Rehabilitation Center while his son practiced for his role in *Peter Pan*.

Aren't laptops wonderful?

By day, King is the editor in chief at Write Source, a division of Houghton Mifflin that produces writing instructional materials. By night, he stars in productions of such shows as *The Complete Works of William Shakespeare (Abridged)*, *No Way to Treat a Lady*, and *Arsenic and Old Lace*.

King's other hardcover titles include his critically acclaimed Arthurian trilogy: *Mad Merlin*, *Lancelot du Lethe*, and *Le Morte d'Avalon*.